C000213560

"Meewezen's beautiful story-tell
of the Cato Street Conspiracy
Turtle Soup for the King is m
of painstaking visits to archives and ...
beyond, as well as creative immersion in the back-story of a
momentous, but all-too-often overlooked historical moment.

It is an essentially British story, but it is also a local story
with universal significance. We need this kind of fiction to
understand where we come from and, in this case, where we
might be heading - particularly in the light of recent global
events that seek to restrict human rights and frustrate personal
ambition, and in which populations feel increasingly alienated
from those who seek to govern them.

Looking at and reading the completed novel, with its
radiant prose, I am struck by how much I want this story to exist;
I was staring into space, and now I see it all in my mind's eye.

I will recommend the novel to all students studying the
Romantic period, which I teach passionately. This book will
make them understand what those times were all about.

Turtle Soup for the King explores and maps human tragedy
and great emotions against the facts of a misfired conspiracy - a
very human story, that from now on, needs never be forgotten."

– Dr Sibylle Erle, Reader in English Literature,
Bishop Grosseteste University, Lincoln.
William Blake scholar.

"It is exceptionally well researched, and shows a deep
understanding of the circumstances, personal and historical,
that could lead people to imagine that they could assassinate
their own government and set off a popular rebellion. There

are fictional events and characters, but these fit so well with what is known that the dividing line is almost imperceptible, even to the well-informed reader. It pulls off the trick of making the conspiracy seem at the same time both bizarre and understandable. The historical landscape is described in evocative detail, the characterization is compelling, and way the period setting is evoked is almost miraculous. The wives and families of the plotters emerge particularly strongly, giving the whole extraordinary drama humanity and depth. The build-up is tense, and the closing sections genuinely moving. This is one of those rare historical novels which even historical specialists can enjoy. The sections set in Manchester should give it an additional regional audience, building on awareness of Peterloo."

– Robert Poole, Professor of History,
University of Central Lancashire.
Author of *Peterloo. The English Uprising*.
Oxford University Press, 2019

TURTLE SOUP FOR THE KING

THE KING

The Cato Street Chronicles

A historical novel

by

JUDY MEEWEZEN

Adelaide Books
New York / Lisbon
2021

TURTLE SOUP FOR THE KING
The Cato Street Chronicles
A historical novel
By Judy Meewezen

Published by Adelaide Books, New York / Lisbon
adelaidebooks.org

Editor-in-Chief
Stevan V. Nikolic

For any information, please address Adelaide Books
at info@adelaidebooks.org
or write to:
Adelaide Books
244 Fifth Ave. Suite D27
New York, NY, 10001

ISBN: 978-1-954351-35-6

Printed in the United States of America

For my children, Lucy Meewezen Fraser and Carl Meewezen

and in honour of Emma Arthur Abercrombie

kitchen-maid, head cook and the beloved grandma we shared

Contents

Acknowledgments

The patience of anonymous librarians is the eighth wonder of the world. I owe immense gratitude to those who have assisted over the years, especially at the British Library in London (Rare Books and Music), the UK National Archives in Kew, the Westminster City Archives, the London Metropolitan Archives, the Lincolnshire Archives, the Horncastle Library and the Library of the University of Cape Town, Special Collection.

I thank all at Adelaide Press, New York, especially Stevan Nikolic for his faith in the project and Dr Katie Isbester of Claret Press, London for recommending him.

I am indebted to Professor Robert Poole, whose expert eye graced the penultimate draft, for suggesting small factual changes.

Professional guidance and kindness were offered by Dr Sibylle Erle, English Romanticist at Bishop Grossesste University in Lincoln, England and Sue Ogterop, former archivist at the University of Cape Town, South Africa. In Northern Ireland, the late Rosemary Wright, a descendant of the Hampshire butcher, provided insights about the Ings family, who continue to live in Portsmouth. Some years ago, local historian, Pete Harness led me informatively through streets of Horncastle in Lincolnshire that would have been familiar to Arthur Thistlewood.

Judy Meewezen

Final revisions prior to submission were made in accidental exile in Austria during the first COVID lockdown, when, on invitation, Christine Eltayeb, formerly of the English department of Sultan Qaboos University, sent briefings from Oman, a chapter a day, on punctuation and typing errors, while in Austria, Markus Reiner and from London, Jeanette Dear offered technical support.

This book was written while travelling on a shoe-string and would never have happened without the listening ears and quiet writing spaces of old friends, many on several occasions. Foremost are Ross Devenish and Charles Whaley, in whose cottage in South Africa's Western Cape, the first words (including Brunt's much-rehearsed poem) were composed and the Reiner family of Treffen, Austria, who frequently tolerated me with kindness and good humour, as this project developed and then for most of the COVID pandemic, to which we succumbed together. Peter Sinclair was infinitely patient in various locations in Kenya and Europe, while my thanks are also due to Shalan and Hemant Sirur in Pune, India, my sister, Susan Cottrell, niece, Emma Cory and nephews, Ludovic Williams and Ben Cottrell, all near Perth in Western Australia, and to Dr Barbara Karhoff and Wilhelm Lückel of Marburg, Germany.

The Hawkes clan, Dr Charlotte Llewellyn, the late Professor Michael Langford and the late Mrs Violet Hawkes, all of Dry Drayton, Cambridge nurtured me over many years in soul, spirit and digestion, and the Hawkes loaned a weaving shed to write in. The Dear / Babb "Forest Girls" read an early draft aloud in Crockerton, Wiltshire and offered guidance on everything related to rural life. I also acknowledge the support of my friends, Josephine Ward, Carol Parks, John Akomfrah, Helen Lederer, Craig Pinder, Paul Bradley, Jean Hyland, Frances Dockerill, Deborah Yhip, Sewrawit Alazar, Jeremy Conway and

12

Neville Phillips in London, Kay Patrick and Paul and Hilary Williams in Yorkshire, the Gatliffe/Szabo family and Patrick Vittoz in Stockport, Amy Edge Bovair in Newmarket, the Delves in Ilford, Ian Pattison and Karen MacIver in Glasgow, Fabrice Maufrais and George Reid in Edinburgh, my brother Graham Williams, with sons, Laurent and Xavier, our many cousins, especially Jean Audouin and Doreen McCormick, also, in Austria, the Weber Family and Christl Szeppanek in Treffen and Barbara Oberrauter in Klagenfurt and finally, Carine Maurais in Somerset West, South Africa and the Eltayeb family of Muscat and Dubai.

My son's passion for modern politics inspired me to tell this story and my daughter's wisdom and constancy produced the strength to persist to the end. Thank you.

The sound of cannon-fire, off.

Preacher: *They're burying the Commander. This is an historic moment.*

Mother Courage: *An 'istoric moment were them punching my girl in the eye. She were half done-for already. No man will want her now. Damn this war.*

(*Mother Courage and her Children* by Bertolt Brecht)

Principal Characters and their Close Associates

(As they appear in the novel. For a full factual/fictional list, please refer to the appendix.)

ARTHUR THISTLEWOOD b.1773
Apothecary, soldier, swordsman, adventurer, radical and chairman of the Water Lane Group
<u>Tupholme in Lincolnshire</u>
>   Wm. John Thistlewood, b 1716, "Farmer John", land-agent, Arthur's grandfather
>   William Thistlewood, b.1743, Farmer John's disabled son, Arthur's father
>   Annie Burnett Thistlewood, b.1752, Arthur's mother
>   Jane Thistlewood, Farmer John's 2nd wife + Ann and John, Arthur's young siblings

<u>Horncastle in Lincolnshire</u>
>   Dr John Chislett, town apothecary/surgeon, Arthur's master
>   Dr and Mrs Edward Harrison, experimental physician and his wife
>   Mr and Mrs Wilkinson, prosperous butchers, Susan Thistlewood's parents

Gautby in Lincolnshire,
>   The Vyner family, wealthy landowners, the Thistlewoods'
>   landlords and employers
>   Aunt Mary Innett, Farmer John's daughter, Arthur's aunt,
>   widow of Vyners' gardener

Horsham Gaol in Sussex and Lincolns Inn Fields in London
>   Susan Thistlewood, Arthur's wife, née Wilkinson from
>   Horncastle
>   Julian Thistlewood, Arthur's son by another Lincolnshire
>   woman, b.1808

JOHN THOMAS BRUNT b.1781

"Tom." Bootmaker, poet, member of the Water Lane Group

Union Street near Oxford Street in London
>   Walter Brunt, Tom's father, a tailor
>   Mrs Brunt, Tom's mother, née Moreton
>   Harold Moreton, also of St Marylebone, fishmonger and war
>   hero, Tom's grandfather
>   Mr and Mrs Brooke, young Tom's Master and neighbour, and
>   his wife.
>   Fox Court, Holborn in London
>   Molly Brunt, Tom's wife, née Welch, of Derbyshire and
>   London
>   Harry Brunt, their younger son, b.1806, schoolboy and
>   drummer
>   Joe Hale, Tom's apprentice, b.1803

RICHARD TIDD b.1773

"Tiddy." Bootmaker, long-standing radical. Sometimes Acting
Chairman, Water Lane Group

Market Square in Grantham
>   Mr and Mrs Cante, Tidd's employers

Hole-in-the-Wall Passage, Holborn in London
Eliza Tidd, his wife, b.1775, a seamstress
Mary Jane Tidd, b.1793, Eliza's daughter, later Mary Tidd
   Barker
Tidds' twin children: Jeremy & Charlie b1808, Marjorie
   & Francis b.1811

JAMES INGS b.1783
"Jim / Jimmy." Once a prosperous butcher and landlord in Portsea,
Hampshire
Portsea in Hampshire
   Ma and Pa Ings, James's parents
   Aunt Alice and Uncle Percy, James's paternal uncle and wife
   James's three younger brothers, including Freddie
   Cousin Jack, clever son of Alice and Percy
   Aunt Lizzie, (later) widow of Cousin Jack
Portsea in Hampshire(later) and Whitechapel / London
   Celia Stone Ings, James Ings's wife
   Their children: William, "Bill" b.1806, Annie, b.1808,
     Thirza b.1811, Emeline b.1813
Chancery Lane in London
   Mr Pyke, a lawyer
Whitechapel and Spitalfields in London
   Celia's late uncle, Silas Stone + Godbold cutlers
   Fleet Street in London
   Richard Carlile, radical journalist, publisher and coffee-shop
     owner
   Patrick Philbin, war veteran from County Wexford

WILLIAM DAVIDSON, b1786
"Will." Former law student, cabinet maker. Later member of the
Water Lane Group

Kingston in Jamaica
 Will's father, John Davidson, Scottish Attorney General
  of Jamaica
 Will's mother, Phoebe Davidson, wealthy Jamaican woman
 Will's nurse: Tulloch
 Lichfield in Staffordshire
 Miss Salt, Will's sweetheart and her father, Mr Salt, an
  industrialist
 Sandon Hall in Staffordshire, seat of Lord Harrowby
 Ned Jackson, an apprentice and his parents.
Grosvenor Square in London
 Lord Harrowby's butler, John Baker
St Marylebone in London
 Sarah Lane Davidson, Will's wife, Sunday school teacher
  and former milliner
 Sarah's children by the late Mr Lane: Abraham b.1805 and
  three younger boys
 Will and Sarah's children: John b.1815 and Duncan b.1819

GEORGE EDWARDS b.1781
Model-maker, agent provocateur and government spy
Gin Palace, Old Street and Banks Court, Cripplegate in London
 Mrs G, businesswoman, George's mother
 William Edwards, undercover policeman, George's younger
  brother
 Cornelius Thwaite, "Uncle Con," ex sculptor, Mrs G's
  occasional partner
Johnson's Court, Fleet Street in London
 Tilly Buck, entertainer, George's on-off partner
Ranelagh Place, Pimlico in London

HENRY HUNT Orator Hunt" radical reformer, Wiltshire,
London, Manchester

REV JOSEPH HARRISON radical preacher, Essex, London, Stockport

WHITEHALL and **BOW STREET**
> Lord Sidmouth, Home Secretary (former Prime Minister, Henry Addington)
> Henry Hobhouse, Permanent Under Secretary, Home Department
> Lord Castlereagh, Anglo-Irish Foreign Secretary (helped suppress the 1798 Rebellion)
> John Stafford, Chief Clerk at Bow Street, Sidmouth's recruiter of spies
> Bow Street patrole, groups of officers, e.g. Ruthven, Bishop, Lavender and Salmon

WINDSOR
> George III, King since 1760, Regent's father, afflicted by mental illness, d. Jan. 1820
> Regent (from 1811) formerly Prince of Wales and from Jan. 1820, King George IV
> Queen Charlotte, Regent's mother + Princess Charlotte, Regent's daughter d.1817
> Princess Caroline of Brunswick, Regent's wife and from Jan. 1820, Queen d.1821

PART ONE

At the time of writing his testament, James Ings's mind and spirit had strayed into an arena that was desperate and chaotic. Years later, his eldest daughter took it upon herself not only to collate her father's papers, but to correspond with the families of his associates, so that their story might be told truthfully and, in a manner, faithful to its patriotic purpose. In pursuit of that ambition, Miss Ings also visited their enemy's mother, who had applied for parish support and, wishing to be uncoupled from her son's sinful conduct, handed over the confessional writings he had addressed to the priest at St Etheldreda's for posthumous publication.

Annie Ings died before her gargantuan task was complete, and the hoard was discovered early in the twenty-first century by an inquisitive estate agent and passed to a well-wisher.

Monday, 1st May, 1820

St Sepulchre's Church, City of London

It is a strange way for a boy to celebrate a fourteenth birthday, standing alone among strangers on a church roof. The people are excited, they jostle and complain, but the boy does not hear what they say. He watches with intensity because it is his history that is being constructed down there, his future demolished on the street below. Everyone else will play at astonishment and go home afterwards to just another day. He has the best view. His mother is not here. The other families are not here either. They are all somewhere else, distracting themselves with weeping, hiding from the truth and from their own history, which is happening here, now.

The door opens, the lodge at Newgate, and a young man, dressed in black, exits, carrying a sack. He climbs the ladder briskly, without looking at the crowd. The people fall silent. The young man opens his sack and starts casting something, like sprinkling seed for hens. It is saw-dust, the boy supposes, and soon it will darken with blood, the blood of his father, which is his blood and his history. The young man moves to the other side of the scaffold, to the church side, the boy's side, behind the gallows. There are five coffins, all of them open.

Which will be his father's? Does it matter? When he is dead, is that body still his father? When does he stop being his father? Did fatherhood end with last night's hand-shake, or will he still be his father tomorrow? The young man, first assistant to the executioner, throws saw-dust into the coffins. He is careful, respectful, mindful of his duty. The crowd shouts, taunting and trying to provoke him, but he never looks up. What is he thinking, that executioner's assistant?

Dust. From dust we come, and to dust we shall return.

The door of Newgate lodge opens again, and the crowd makes a momentous gasp; then a procession of nobles and gentlemen, followed by a Reverend and four prisoners, but not the boy's father. Not the boy's father. The crowd cheers at Thistlewood, who responds with a weak smile and then looks up, scrutinizing the sky; a farmer's son, measuring the weather in Heaven. Thistlewood is followed by Tidd, Ings and Davidson, taut and solemn as he has never seen them. His father is not there. The irons have been taken from their legs. Their forearms are tied. They seem bewildered by the daylight and by the hushed crowd that pushes against the poles across Giltspur Street, Newgate, Old Bailey and Skinner Street. The prisoners look round, over to the church garden and up at the roof where he stands. Breathless, in awe, the boy waves, but they do not see him.

Where is his pa? The prisoners turn to listen to the sheriff, who places an orange into each right hand. Davidson refuses his and moves to the Reverend's side. Three men suck on oranges; why not his father? Thistlewood is first to climb the ladder, and he does so with dignity. His face is flushed, and once on the scaffold, he eyes the drop anxiously. A woman screams, "God Almighty have mercy!" The crowd murmurs its sympathy.

There are five ropes; five nooses for five necks, but still no sign of his father. Perhaps the fifth is not for pa, but for the man whose name the boy cannot speak, who will appear at any moment, spitting at the crowds. The people will boo like thunder, mount the scaffold and tear the fiend apart. The boy's heart skips a beat as he contemplates clemency. The letter he helped pa compose, the letter about sobriety and loyalty and love for his country. Perhaps after all, the king has seen it, has sat on his golden throne and commanded the immediate release of John Thomas Brunt. Hallelujah!

Here comes Jimmy Ings, dancing up the steps like a bear at a fair. On the scaffold, he lifts his pinioned arms to the crowd. They cheer enthusiastically. When they fall quiet, Ings turns to look in the boy's direction, but not at the church; the master butcher taking one last glance towards Smithfield. He responds to the crowd's cheers with cheers of his own; three times "Hurrah!"; loud, hoarse, delirious. The butcher looks down at the coffins and up at the crowd, who fall silent again. With a savage cry, he shouts out so clear that on his roof, the boy hears him; "Give me Liberty or give me Death!" The people repeat the same words twice, and the boy feels a surge in the crowd behind him. A stranger pulls his coat and him away from the edge. If he falls from this height, will he cause a distraction? Will the people panic; the executions be cancelled?

Still there is no sign of his father, and the boy's hope rises. Richard Tidd is next. The bootmaker grins as he stumbles on the steps, and the crowd laughs nervously with him. Ings continues to babble and seems to enjoy the spectacle. "Enough of that noise!" commands Thistlewood, or some such instruction, and Ings is quiet. Now Will Davidson climbs the steps. The black man is solemn, dignified, head bent. The Reverend follows him up to the scaffold, presses his hand into Davidson's. Their lips move in unison;

As we forgive those who have trespassed against us.

Thistlewood grasps Tidd's hand, wishes him well and repeats the gesture with Ings. Then the door opens again. A second sheriff and a second assistant escort his father to the ladder. His father, who is no longer his father, because he is dead, almost dead. The boy's legs want to give way, but he plants them in the stone or the slate of the roof. His eyes cannot move from him. Pa is calm, composed. He makes that crooked smile that always comes when ma has one of her turns, and he does not know what to say or do. Pa accepts the sheriff's orange and guided by the second assistant, climbs the steps steadily, holding that familiar look. On the scaffold, he acknowledges his fellow-prisoners and then looks out at the crowd. For some glorious reason, his eyes turn towards the church, to the crowds in the garden and up to the roof. The boy waves the kerchief ma gave him. Wildly he waves. "Pa! Pa!" Brunt sees him and laughs and raises his pinioned arms in greeting and is his father again. The executioner summons him away.

The bell of St Sepulchre, the bell of Old Bailey begins to toll; so close and loud it takes possession of the boy's brain, his heart beat and the flow of his blood. He cannot escape that sound; not now, perhaps not ever. This is his history; not the wars his father and grandfathers fought in France and America, Spain and India, not even the events that led to this awful moment, but the moment itself, as it lives and breathes.

The executioner arranges the prisoners, one by one. The rope is round pa's neck, round the necks of four other men he has laughed and played with; uncles, in whose schemes he has partaken. At their command, he has stolen iron, ripped down fences, and helped create objects with deadly purpose. The boy wants to shout out that if his father must die, then so must he, because he is guilty too, but his voice lodges in his throat. At last he screams, "Stop!" but the bell is too loud and the din and push and crush of the crowd. He turns to flee, but the people misunderstand and tell him crossly not to shove and not to spoil their view.

The prisoners' eyes are covered. Their backs are towards him, and he cannot see pa's face. Can his father hear the same crowd that he hears, or have his senses travelled elsewhere? The Reverend is still whispering to Davidson, when the trap falls. First to die is Thistlewood. He struggles for a moment or two, then his body spins on the rope three times and is still. The crowd howls for the loss of a brave man, who longed for nothing more than their good. Tidd and Davidson die quickly too. Ings, who is shorter, struggles and after a couple of minutes, the young assistant and his companion give his legs a tug. The body turns and Jimmy's face is the colour of raw liver.

Nobody out there has noticed that his father is still moving. His head is twisting, his limbs shake. Then the assistants pull at his legs, but Brunt's breath is defiant. They swing on his thighs like the branches of a great oak. Pa is an oak, the boy tells himself; strong, purposeful, English. Perhaps, even now, he will survive. Then Brunt is still. There is no hope, no pretending, and the boy, whose name is Harry, is alone in the world. From the far, far corners of his mind, a dark voice whispers of triumph. He is dead, it says, and you are alive and young. The voice unsettles him; he drives it away.

The people let him through. He is just a boy, they conclude, with no stomach for the final stage, when the barber surgeon will do his work and lift the heads high for the crowd. They do not know, and they cannot see the splintering rage in his heart, as he goes to find and comfort his poor, mad mother.

CHAPTER ONE

Tuesday, 14th July, 1789

THISTLEWOOD

Tupholme, Lincolnshire

At noon on the day a crowd stormed the Bastille, an elderly Lincolnshire farmer stood at the edge of his fields and studied the sky. It was a daily habit, inherited from his father and his father's father. The sun was bright with a dazzling halo that perforated a sheet of lucent cloud. To the west, a band of dappled cloud nuzzled the horizon and then split into spidery fingers, all pointing ominously towards Tupholme. He sighed. Heavy rain would lay waste to the wheat that, as far as the eye could see, stood green, proud and already two feet high. It was urgent, therefore, to check the drainage and move his lambs from the lower pastures. What sins had he committed, he asked himself, that his legs and his back should plague him, when there was so much to do?

Before he could start, he needed to ride out to Gautby, where he was employed by the local land-owner, a wealthy and principled parliamentarian. The labourers were angry that their right to cut firewood had been restricted. There had been brawls between those men who used the privilege honestly and their brothers who, in these hard times, had sold the Squire's timber to feed their families. He had kept the rumours away from the estate office and, for the first time in his life, peppered reports with half-truths, so that no child on the estate would starve. Today, Farmer John, as he was known throughout Lindsey and the Wolds, intended to get the men back to work before the landlord arrived from London and deprived them of their livelihood and their homes.

William John Thistlewood was trusted by the men, just as his father and grandfather were trusted by theirs, and his mission, though challenging, was successful. In the early evening, he arrived back at Tupholme, thankful for a robust heart, but with bones as weary as Methuselah's. The sky was almost clear, and the dark clouds had moved further east to create mischief for the fishing fleet. The drainage could wait another day. Hugh, the red-faced stockman, waiting in the yard for final instructions, tactfully helped the master dismount. He agreed that the lambs would be safe overnight and confessed that a heifer had gone missing.

"I counted at milking," he said, "and she weren't there. Fences and t' gate are aw sound, sir. Unless t' young master took her, I cannot answer for it."

Though Farmer John rarely spoke of his only surviving son, he suspected at once that William was to blame. The stockman would be in a hurry to get home, so he wished him good night and went to search the barns and clamber through the ruins.

There was no sign of the missing heifer or of his son. Farmer John stood in the shell of the old abbey, and as he watched a family of bats, squealing and flitting like bad angels against the slowly fading light, he felt certain that God had some purpose for his present predicament, but he had not the faintest idea what it might be.

He turned sharply and made his way back to the yard, where he checked the poultry and fed the hounds. As he bent to pull off his boots, the body that had dug a thousand ditches, seemed fit to break. He bathed his feet in the bowl of warm water that William's wife had left, and retired to his study till supper.

It always soothed him to enter this small, calm space, away from the mayhem of the estate and the skirmishes between Jane, his second wife, a widow grown sour, and Annie, his pretty daughter-in-law. For a few precious moments, Farmer John could forget his troubles and sit at the wide desk, fashioned from the last of the Tupholme walnuts, salvaged when the grove was cut for gun-stocks in the American War. He found comfort in opening the great pages of his journal, dipping his pen into the glass ink stand, as he formulated his thoughts and composed the day's entry.

Tuesday, 14th July, 1789: Wind west, south west and south. Cloudy forenoon, afternoon fair. Afternoon to Gautby.

No sooner had he recorded the facts in a straight line beneath yesterday's than there was a knock at the door, which he had kept ajar for William's wife.

"Enter in peace!" he called.

As Annie entered, chuckling, he noticed that his old heart began beating faster. She trod cautiously, not to waste a drop of his ale. He frowned at the bruise on her fore-arm, as she placed the great jug on its mat. Annie asked if the kitchen should wait for her husband, who had not yet returned from Horncastle. How soft her arms. She looked no older than nineteen. Or perhaps his aged eyes made her seem so; as Arthur's mother, he knew she was nearer forty. He did not covet her, only appreciated her beauty as he might a helpless lamb.

"Was he driving a heifer?" he asked.

She looked at him, eyes blue as harebells, clear and round as twin moons. How did a wretch like William deserve such a creature?

"Yes, father, the brown 'un. He was going to meet Arthur."

The old man scowled, imagining the profit wasted on liquor, dirty girls and the corruption of his beloved grandson.

"Where did you get that bruise?" he asked.

"Ain't worth the worry," replied Annie.

"I say it is."

"Someone left the peg bag on the laundry step," she said, "and I tripped."

It was a lie, another lie.

"Whoever left it deserves a whipping."

"Don't be sad, father," said Annie with a smile. "I've not wasted my tears. Drink your ale."

Farmer John growled that he had a report to write, but would be along for supper in twenty minutes. Then he put a twinkle in his eye, found a sixpence in his pocket for Annie and said to be sure there were no lumps in his mash.

JOHN THOMAS BRUNT
West End, London

At about two on the afternoon, when all Paris was in ferment, a small boy sat in a heap at the corner where Conduit Street met the broadest part of Swallow Street. He had been knocked down twice, first by a bearded ruffian with long, flailing arms and then by the constable runner in pursuit. The child's torn breeches, the blood oozing from his knee and now the agony of his hand were as nothing, compared to the loss of a dozen pearl buttons. They had spilled on to the road as he fell, to be trampled or lost in a dung-hill. Having rescued two of the items, the boy, whose name was Tom Brunt, had been attempting to reach a third button, when a hoof landed on his wrist. The horse clopped on, and not a soul turned to enquire about the howling child. When he gathered himself sufficiently to look for the buttons, not a single one could be found.

Master Brunt considered his options. If he went home now, there would be a beating. With no buttons, his father would lose his second-to-last-order, while his mother, after a day or two complaining about the empty larder, would send him with a sealed letter to Grandpa Moreton's shop on Maryle-bone Lane.

What if he went straight to grandpa's now? He could explain his situation honestly and without fear. He would borrow two shillings for new buttons and repay them over the summer by cleaning fish and fetching tobacco. He imagined the indulgent smile, as grandpa gutted a pail of mackerel without even looking and told wild tales of the 84th Regiment of Foot. He imagined asking the haberdasher on Mill Street for more pearl buttons, of which, since he had managed to salvage two, only ten were necessary. That left fourpence for his mother's favourite flowers. Were violets in season in July?

Such was the train of young Tom Brunt's thoughts, when he became aware of a gloved hand on his shoulder and a full, twilled cotton skirt that might have been one of pa's. A familiar face was peering down, examining his injuries.

"I've only been robbed!" he heard himself whine, adding with emphasis; "An 'orse stood on me 'and an 'all!"

Mrs Brooke was all for dragging the child straight to the constable runner, but she had a pressing appointment, and the rain was about to come down. She advised Master Brunt to bind his wrist well and his knee, and always play his part in ridding London's streets of crime.

As Mrs Brooke hurried across the road, Brunt pulled himself to his feet. Why, of all people, had he told a fib to the shoemaker's wife? In a spirit of false neighbourliness, she would report the incident at the wash-house tomorrow, if not earlier, and Mrs Quirke was certain to tell his ma. A comforting visit to Grandpa Moreton was out of the question. Perhaps he should pretend it was not the buttons that were stolen, but his father's two bob? But what if the haberdasher, a long-time associate of his Pa, told his parents the buttons were already bought? And anyway, what thief would imagine a ragamuffin like himself to be in possession of pearl buttons? There would be no mercy for a boy foolish enough to have his pocket picked. Oh, the bitter cruelty of life! It began to rain.

Brunt crossed Oxford Street to the market, but nobody had an errand for a drowned rat with a limp, and only asked what breed of mischief had caused all that blood and the damage to his breeches.

Twenty minutes later, as Walter Brunt reached for the strap, he promised that it gave no grain of pleasure to acknowledge his only son as a fool, whose recklessness was as responsible as any blasted Frenchie for depriving the family of income. Thomas would be confined to the outhouse with a candle and a pile of tacking. The time of his exit was dependent on the tidiness of his stitching, and there would be no concession to his poorly hand. Mrs Brunt cleaned the knee and bound his wrist with scraps of muslin. She was not at liberty, she said, as she sent him to the outhouse with no supper, to discuss any disagreement with his father, but advised Thomas not to waste a single inch of thread, to devote extra thought to his prayers tonight and trust in God's mercy.

His wrist ached more than his whipped back stung. He had learnt on such occasions to distract himself. Today he thought about brave men, sailing to faraway lands to fight for justice. He imagined forests and tigers and the rescue of drowning sailors from the high seas. Master Brunt had never seen the sea, but Grandpa Moreton, hero of the Battle of Wandiwash, had often entertained him with tales of the Maharajahs, Nabobs and their golden palaces, of magnificent sunrises, tribes of wild men and the creatures, great and small, of the jungle. He tacked until the light dimmed, the shouting on the streets had stopped, and all he could hear was the gentle rain and the barking of a distant dog.

By the last flutters of his candle, he knelt on the stone floor with his good knee and asked God to bless his parents and grandparents and stop his wrist from hurting so much. He asked for forgiveness for telling Mrs Brooke that he was robbed, when he was not, and for lying about Mrs Brooke to his parents (to which he had confessed at once, for fear of a second beating). He swore that as long as he lived, he would never tell a third lie.

As he scratched and wriggled about on the lumpy mat, Tom Brunt asked the Almighty what His purpose had been in letting the bearded ruffian and the constable runner collide with him so the buttons dropped out of his pocket in the first place. He thought about his father in the cosy cottage with his soup, his snuff and his silent wife, and he wondered how the Almighty chose which men should be more comfortable and well-fed than the rest, and whether there was any connection to the amount of misery they caused. He listened as hard as he could for God's answers, but unless the rain that began hammering on the iron roof was Heaven sent, there came none.

ARTHUR THISTLEWOOD

Horncastle, Lincolnshire

Farmer John's son and his grandson did not, as he imagined, waste that Tuesday at the mercy of the conscienceless girls, who loitered in the notorious Dog Kennel quarter of town. They were visiting a house on West Street, premises of a prosperous experimental physician from Scotland. Dr Edward Harrison's ideas and his innovative practice were debated by the opinionated minority of the county and condemned as quackish by almost everyone else. Arthur Thistlewood, whose master, the town apothecary and surgeon, was a friend of the doctor, had cajoled his father into accepting help by threatening to expose a recent gambling incident, in which William had lost their entire inheritance from the Jamaica uncle.

Ever since a fall in the limewood, William Thistlewood had suffered from daemonic moods, with intense pain in his head and spine. While the local population was of the unyielding opinion that the condition was proper punishment for a life committed to drink and gambling - William had climbed the tree by torchlight as a wager after a night at The Bull - Dr Harrison considered his symptoms no less worthy of treatment than typhus or cholera.

By the third session, the benefits were clear, even to the patient, and there was no need for Arthur to stand guard, as the physician pummelled the muscles and bones in his father's neck and spine. Arthur stayed because Dr Harrison fascinated him, more even than Old Bob Vyner at Gautby Hall or Sir Joseph Banks, whose hand he had shaken when, in his capacity as Lord of Horncastle Manor, the great man visited the Grammar School.

Harrison's medical interest – for which William Thistle-wood was an ideal specimen – focused on connections between malformations of the spine and mental illness. With the support of the same Sir Joseph (in his capacity as President of the Royal Society), Harrison had also embarked on an ambitious social experiment; the establishment of England's first free dispensary, for which the Thistlewoods' brown heifer had been a donation.

The physician found the work in Horncastle rewarding, but it isolated him from verbal discourse with other scientists, and his famous patron was rarely free to visit Lincolnshire. He was intrigued by Chislett's apprentice, who seemed unlike any other Horncastrian and was an exceptionally clever and thoughtful young man. With no more patients expected and the apothecary in Lincoln till Thursday, Harrison suggested, when William fell asleep, that they enjoy a little conversation. He guided Arthur to the parlour, where they sat on a yellow settee with soft, silk cushions.

The doctor's wife approached with a plate of strawberries, a gift, she explained, in her lilting accent, from a patient recently departed from the small hospital in their garden. As his grandfather had taught him, Thistlewood stood up, inclined his head and expressed his gratitude. Planting the plate on the table, and inviting her guest to help himself, Mrs Harrison proceeded to enquire whether he or any member of his family was in need of piano lessons. There was a fortepiano, Thistlewood had noticed, beside the window.

"How kind," he replied, "but we are far too busy with the farm for luxuries such as music."

"And we Scots admire honesty," said Mrs Harrison, the colour rising nevertheless in her cheeks, "do we not, my dear?"

"Aye, Margaret, we do"

"Indeed," continued Mrs Harrison, "my husband and I are devoted to the ambition to stamp out hypocrisy in the medical professions and wherever else we find it!"

"Young Arthur here would sooner lose his tongue than tell a lie," replied Harrison.

"It's true!" said Arthur. "As far as music is concerned, ma'am, "I'm afraid there's no instrument at the farm to practise on."

"A life without music?" asked Mrs Harrison. "How do you bear it?"

"My Horsington grandpa taught me the spoons, ma'am, but that is the limit, and my singing voice is remarkably bad."

"Perhaps you'll attend our next musical evening, Master Thistlewood, with your spoons."

"I couldn't dream of playing in such a fine parlour," replied Thistlewood, "but I should gladly attend in a listening capacity."

When Mrs Harrison returned to her baking and they had enjoyed most of the strawberries, her husband handed the lad a handkerchief and launched his enquiry.

"Tell me Arthur. Why did you decide on a career in medicine?"

"I'm too bookish for farming, sir," replied Thistlewood, clean around the mouth now, but clutching the handkerchief, anxious about social procedure.

"My young brother, a scholar in Yorkshire, is better suited to both the land and estate management. After I finished at the Grammar, the headmaster recommended me to Dr Chislett, whom I had met on occasion previously."

"You did not choose to be an apothecary?"

"I enjoy it well enough, but when the apprenticeship is done, sir, I shall serve in the regiment."

"Of course - and afterwards?"

Thistlewood had never been asked that question before, except frequently by his step-grand-mother, a busy-body in pursuit of mischief. He hesitated, leaning over to place the handkerchief on a side-table.

"You may speak frankly, Arthur."

"Thank you, doctor. The truth is, I'm sure of nothing."

"Nothing at all?"

"Except that I will not, as my forefathers have done, sacrifice my life and soul to the gentry, nor, forgive me, to the thankless fields of Lincolnshire. Neither will my first duty ever be to myself nor to any self-seeking master, but to the people of the country I love. I am a Thistlewood sir, and proud of my county, but above all, I am a patriot. Just as you have identified your destiny and pursued it, so also must I."

Harrison was equally disarmed by the outburst and flattered by the trust it implied.

"I see you have a passion for politics, Master Thistlewood."

"I believe so, though Grandfather says it will never keep body and soul together."

"It's an uncommon interest for a young man of these parts, Master Thistlewood. I'm curious. I believe John Chislett dabbles in politics. Has he persuaded you?"

"When I was bound apprentice, sir, my family set a condition that such matters are not to be discussed."

"Being forbidden, the subject enticed you?"

"No, sir. Sometimes, when I accompany Grandfather to Gautby, we're invited to dinner. Old Mr Vyner talks about the goings-on at Westminster and St James. I listen for hours, sir, long after his family has retired and Grandfather has fallen asleep in the chair."

"And you find yourself in sympathy with Mr Vyner?"

"Quite the reverse," said Thistlewood. "In fact, I should like the King and all the well-fed men of Parliament to visit Horncastle and see the vagrants shuffling barefoot through the streets, begging like dogs for a morsel of food and sleeping in misery and fear under the bridges. How can that be justified, Dr Harrison, when other men may gorge himself to death, if they wish? Mr Vyner is kind to me, but he spends nearly half of his life in London, and instead of looking desperation in the eye, he sends my grandfather to evict farmers and their families, because illness has prevented them from paying rent."

"And poverty from calling a doctor," said Harrison.

"Precisely!" cried Arthur, "when one dinner in Pall Mall would pay for a cure."

Taken aback by the sensitive young man's zeal, Harrison took a moment to consider his response. The pause alarmed Thistlewood, who was aware that many in Lincolnshire would consider his philosophy dangerous. When he asked whether he had inadvertently caused offence, Harrison responded emphatically. As a medical student, he had been just as angry, he reported, with the high-minded doctors of Edinburgh, who imagined that disease only affected the wealthy and seemed content to ignore the city's poorest communities. Harrison had joined the Reform Club and, after reading Jean-Jacques Rousseau, made the journey to Paris, where he found the clubs and coffee houses alive with passion and intent.

"You went to Paris?" cried Arthur, leaping awkwardly from his seat. "I understand that such talk risks consequences," he said as Harrison hesitated, "but if you will tell me more, I swear it will go no further."

Harrison looked at the apprentice, whose hazel eyes were bright and dancing, and could no more refuse than leave a hungry child unfed.

"France is bankrupt, young man, because nobody takes responsibility. The noblemen – far more plentiful than our own – never visit their estates, but live all together, enslaved by fashion, and squeezing every last sous in taxes to pay for their extravagance. The evil-hearted king sucks the life-blood from everyone, living in absolute splendour, while the peasant class barely survives. When the harvest fails, as it failed last year, the monarch snatches bread from starving babies. It's insufferable."

Thistlewood sat quietly for a few moments, connecting this new information with his knowledge of Dr Harrison's practice. Harrison watched him, kindly, seeming to read his thoughts.

"Young man, a solution may be closer than you think," he said. "If you accept my proposal, you can fulfil your dream, while making both your family and your master proud."

"Please tell me how!"

"Come and work at my new Dispensary. It will open before Christmas and you'll begin your professional life at the forefront of medical innovations that will transform the nation. I shall recommend you to my patron in the highest terms. If you're prepared to start at once, Dr Chislett is sure to come to an arrangement for as long you're bound."

Arthur Thistlewood gave thanks and promised to give the idea careful consideration. Privately, he knew that he could never be beholden to a nobleman, not even the philanthropic Joseph Banks. For now, as long as his father slept, he longed to hear more about Dr Harrison's time in France, and wondered where in Horncastle or Lincoln, he might find books about French philosophy.

As the daylight faded, and he watched William Thistlewood riding confidently back to Tupholme, Arthur's heart and his mind were still singing. He had forgotten the assignation with Sally, the wheelwright's daughter, who was waiting at her first-floor window, and showered him with white saxifrage as he passed on the street. The tiny, damp flowers clung to his hat and breeches. He looked up, laughing and Sally hurried down to forgive him. She borrowed her mother's cart and a lantern and drove him to the limewood, where they built a nest and, for an hour or two, enveloped each other in gentle pleasure.

Later that night, while the great city of Paris faced its epiphany, Arthur Thistlewood lay sleepless in his bunk in the apothecary's kitchen, listening to the rain tapping softly at the window. Before the bell at St Mary's struck eleven, he knew, with perfect certainty, what he must do.

That rain fell relentlessly over the county of Lincoln until Sunday morning, when Farmer John recorded in his journal a storm and an unusual display of thunder and lightning. Half his wheat was spared, which, with the surplus in the grain store, would be sufficient for the current year. His clever older grandson, whose secret plan became more resolute every day, divided his apprenticeship between the shop and the new dispensary and helped the apothecary's neighbour, Butcher Wilkinson when the High Street flooded. He listened to Dr Chislett's forbidden, homespun radicalism and learnt about the Newcastle schoolteacher, Thomas Spence. Every spare moment, now and in the months ahead, Arthur Thistlewood devoted to a French primer and a dictionary, borrowed, in exchange for a little chemistry tuition, from the Grammar School.

Sunday, 26th July, 1789

RICHARD TIDD

Grantham, Lincolnshire

In the third week of July, while the starving peasants of Alsace, Brittany and Languedoc staged their protests, rain fell abundantly over the entire County of Lincoln. Fertile fields were transformed into eerie brown lakes, destroying farms and wrecking dreams. On Saturday night, two corpses were found in a barn, floating between a dead calf and a broken wheel. The couple, both in their fifties, had devoted their lives to reclaiming a marsh, built banks with their bare hands, and defended them with equal ferocity against burrowing rodents and malicious legislators. The tempest had rendered the entire sacrifice futile. Scrawled in chalk on the highest beam was an apology that would haunt their family forever.

The nearby market-town of Grantham was spared catastrophe, but by the early hours of Sunday, the sky was splintered by jagged flashes of gold and white, which split and cracked, before erupting in a mighty explosion beside the tall, thin spire of St Wulfram's. In every street, old soldiers woke, reached for their muskets, only to be startled by the softness of their pillows. In her crooked house at the corner of the square, Mrs Cante, the bootmaker's wife abandoned her bed and declared that she must make her peace, because God was taking his revenge.

Mr Cante suggested that his wife could make her peace just as well in the morning, but Mrs Cante was resolute. If Church and town were to be spared, she must act immediately. She knew the correct psalm, but had foolishly left her Prayer Book down by the fireplace. Mr Cante turned towards the wall and groaned, his aching skull a reminder of last evening's excess at the Guild. All hope of slumber was dashed, when the air in the hallway turned blue with curses.

Presuming Mrs Cante's lament to be a sign that St Wulfram's was struck, the boot-maker heaved himself to the edge of the bed. As his plump toes stretched out and sought for boots, he heard a new explosion, which flashed and cracked, illuminating the room and snapping at the window. He brushed the curtain aside. A pane had shattered; yet another unwelcome expense! All at once, the heavenly spectacle subsided, and there, through the broken glass, stood church and steeple, as erect and magnificent as ever. When he turned, Mrs Cante was at the bedroom door, her face crumpled in despair.

"No need for tears, my cherry-bun," he said. "St Wulfram's is saved!"

Mrs Cante would not be pacified.

"Did I not tell you he was no bloody good?" she cried. "Did I not say so, the moment I saw him, that lazy eye was a sign of the devil?"

Mr Cante's confusion was short-lived. His apprentice had vanished, had illegally abandoned his indenture. As Mrs Cante submitted to her confusion, Mr Cante took his candle and inspected Master Tidd's room in the attic. Finding no sign of the young man or his property, the bootmaker forgot his headache and hurried down to the workshop to count his tools.

The truth is that Richard Tidd had been happy enough with his master, who was jovial and undemanding and taught him all he needed to know about making boots to a high specification (and smoking a pipe beside), but the young man had fallen into a desperate situation that he was ill-equipped to manage. Mrs Cante had been paying him the kind of attention that no woman of forty-one ought to bestow on a boy of seventeen, no matter how lonely and neglected she feels, nor how lack-lustre her husband's attentions.

Last Tuesday, she had dosed Mr Cante's beer with her special remedy, and when he was safely snoring, had crept out of their room and up the squeaky stairs to Tidd's attic. Though startled and embarrassed, the apprentice, being in equal measure reluctant virgin and obedient servant, succumbed without audible protest, and the pair made love till dawn. The ritual was repeated on Wednesday and Thursday. On Friday, Mrs Cante sent her husband for a sack of flour before whispering words of romance and teasing the apprentice's ear with her tongue, as he sharpened his awl.

"Oh, Richard," she murmured. "With your graceful limbs, strong arms and curly brown hair, you are the answer to a woman's prayers."

Even with his lazy eye and lack of worldly experience, she said, she would prefer the remainder of her life to consist of one week with Richard Tidd than thirty years tied to dull George Henry Cante. When, despite the storm within, the lad said nothing and continued filing, his mistress kissed his curly brown head and suggested Monday for their elopement to Leicester, where there was work for bootmakers and she had a sympathetic sister.

The impending catastrophe and the conviction that the fault was entirely his own demolished Tidd's ability either to think in sequences or even stitch in a straight line. His master's especially cheerful mood was almost more than Tidd could bear, especially when Mr Cante explained confidentially that his wife was so especially buoyant lately that he anticipated the miracle for which they had prayed nightly for nineteen years.

On Friday afternoon, Tidd confronted Mrs Cante with a messy sentence about the confusion into which their adultery had plunged his conscience. His mistress dropped the sock she was darning, pressed his right hand firmly to her bosom and murmured that Richard's delicacy made him even more appealing. She had every necessary desire to ravage him, right here in the parlour, even if Mr Cante should find them and bludgeon them both to death with a poker. When she saw the fear in the young man's eyes, Mrs Cante said her words was only a bit of fun, and there would be plenty more of that when they got to Leicester.

When Mr Cante retired to his beer on the Saturday afternoon, Tidd visited his uncle, landlord at the Grantham coaching inn. Uncle Charlie was wary, but on condition that his nephew's unexpected departure was honourable, he was, for the sake of his sister, Richard's mother, prepared to offer a solution. He had a parcel which must be delivered by the early morning coach in Nottingham, where he had a friend with contacts in the shoe-making trades.

So it was, that on the evening of the great storm in Grantham, while the Cantes were making merry at the Guild, and while France was convulsed by peasants' revolts, Richard Tidd packed his few belongings into a sack and slipped away to an uncertain future.

June, 1794

JAMES INGS
Portsea, Hampshire

In his twelfth year on earth, when Master Ings, heir to the Ings butchery, allegedly had a will of his own, the parson blessed him and pushed him by the shoulders, under the cold, salty water. The holy words were almost indiscernible against the crashes of the foaming sea, but the Baptist congregation, pressed hard against the harbour wall and, protected from the breeze by woollen shawls, cheered as one, when James Ings emerged, a gasping, soaking, shivering, fully-fledged member of the family of Christ.

When the date was subsequently described as the Glorious First of June, Ma Ings said it was because her first born was baptised that day. A more plausible explanation was produced on the 26th of the same month, when the family gathered to mark another special occasion. The King and Queen would be driving through Portsea on their way to Spithead to inspect the flag-ship of the battle in the Atlantic that had taken place on the very day of James's baptism.

"Both sides claimed victory," explained pa, as ma poured tea into the china cups. "Damned Frenchies because they got their grain through, and the British because the French lost seven ships and we lost none, which left Admiral Howe free to start the blockade!"

"Hip, hurrah for the Admiral!" cried Uncle Percy, raising a tiny tea cup with his thick, butcher's fingers.

"Hurrah!" cried everyone else at table, except Cousin Jack. A year younger than Jim, and bound for Portsmouth Grammar, Jack waited for the cheer to fade and then proclaimed that the first of June was anything but Glorious for the five thousand sailors, sent to their deaths without any leave to choose who they'd fight and who they wouldn't. The room fell quiet. Amused by his cousin's audacity, Ings looked round the table, to see how it had been received. Everyone was staring into their cups or looking away, except for Jack, who caught Jimmy's eye, steady and determined.

"Here's sixpence for union flags," announced Aunt Alice, producing a coin from her skirt pocket, "so the lads can wave properly at their Majesties, when the royal carriage drives past."

She aimed a competitive smile at Ma Ings. In such fine weather, the laundry could wait, but someone would have to stay and bake pies.

"Jimmy!" commanded Aunt Alice. "Toss that sixpence!"

"Tails; I go!" cried Ma Ings, and tails it was. Aunt Alice, who had talked of nothing else for days, shrugged and said they'd be lucky to see so much as the royal pigtail.

After tea, Ings was summoned for a private word with pa.

"As the oldest lad," pa said, "you are responsible for the family. If you see or hear any hint of fighting, Jimmy, ask no damn-fool questions, just alert ma, grab the boys' hands and fly home, quick as a flash. If Cousin Jack refuses, tell him he must answer to me."

"There won't be no trouble, pa," said Ings, "not with all Portsmouth so proud and happy to see the king."

Pa Ings shook his head.

"Don't be fooled. There are men at large, son, who look like common fellows, but who believe we should have no king nor Parliament neither, or at least no Parliament made up of noblemen and such. One of them, wrote a wicked book and ran away to France. Tom Paine, his name is, curse him, and now he's going to court.

"That's why there might be trouble?" asked Ings, mightily puzzled.

"No." replied pa. "It's because the lawyer representing him is the Member of Parliament for Portsmouth.

"Why would a Member of Parliament help a person who wanted to get rid of that Parliament?"

Pa Ings replied that he'd heard enough clever questions for one day, especially with his mind on the venison just come in, and Percy too busy in the stockyard to help out.

"Just steer clear of trouble," he said, "and watch our Jack, with his wayward style of thinking, or you'll both get locked up. Ma would never stop weeping, and then where would we be?"

As the three boys and Ma Ings purchased their flags and joined the waiting throng, Ings was as excited as everyone else, but inwardly, since his father's warning, it was if he possessed some higher knowledge that separated him from the crowd. He was suspicious of everybody. That fellow in blue beside ma, with no hat and long black oily hair; was there a missile, hiding in his pocket? The military gent in front, with a wooden leg; was he secretly embittered after a battle that went wrong? Could he have a dagger under his coat, ready to murder the King?

Ings was distracted by a tug at his pocket. Freddie protested that he was too small to see anything, and the King would never see his flag. Ma complained that she couldn't breathe because the crowd was squashing all the puff out of her. Ings lifted Freddie on to his shoulders and shouted, "Make Way! Make Way!" As the family squeezed and jostled forward, all complaint was drowned by a melody that approached from the left, like a great wave.

This was the charter, the charter of the land,
And guardian angels sang this strain:
"Rule, Britannia! Britannia, rule the waves:
Britons never will be slaves."

Flags waved frantically amid the lusty cheers, whistles and shouts of "God Save the King! God Save the King!" When they heard a bugle and the trot of horses, the Ings boys jumped and squealed and so, without shame or restraint, did their mother. That is when little Freddie Ings let go of his brother's ears, released his legs and slithered to the ground before charging, with all the might of a determined four-year-old, towards the royal party. His family watched with alarm, as he ran into the street, tripped and fell in front of the first carriage of the royal procession. Drivers shouted, shiny, black horses whinnied and reared up, and the royal carriage stumbled to a halt. Ings and cousin Jack hauled Freddie to his feet, and the humiliated infant ran, wailing into his ma's skirts. In front of them, the carriage door opened. Its cheers reduced to an anxious murmur, the crowd gasped, as a uniformed officer, tall and proud, leapt out, brandishing a sword.

"Please, sir," called Ings, feeling a thousand eyes upon him. The officer glared, his frown emphasising the raw scar on his cheek.

"Please, sir," said Ings again. "This ain't no person of danger, but little Frederick Ings, carried away by enthusiasm. He is four years old, sir and wouldn't harm a soul, even a fly, sir, nor any of God's creatures, saving a hog or a sheep in the slaughterhouse, and he was obliged to."

A few nervous chuckles sounded in the crowd, but the haughty officer ignored them, sneering as he turned his sword this way and that, surveying the hushed crowd for potential assassins. Ings was wondering how soon they would be arrested, when the carriage door opened again, and the prettiest girl in the world stepped down. She wore a white and pink dress, as soft and full as a summer cloud. The officer snapped at her to return to her seat, but the girl ignored him. She looked at Freddie and then fixed her clear blue eyes on James Ings.

"The poor child's knee is bleeding," she said.

"It's my baby brother, miss, as only wants to see the King," replied Ings.

The girl put a finger to her lips and whispered into Jimmy Ings's ear. "I'm afraid he shall be disappointed."

Ings forgot the crowd. He forgot his brother, his cousin and his ma, who all stood there, like startled deer. He knew his face was burning, but he could see and hear nothing but the girl in the white dress.

"Promise you will tell no-one," she whispered. "Do you swear?"

"I do," said Ings, "I swear". It was more of a croak than a whisper.

"The King is not here."

"Because of Mr Paine?" Ings heard himself ask, but the girl seemed not to know the name.

"Mama is here, but papa is not quite well today" she confided, lowering her voice even further. "Nobody but the officers must know."

She smiled, seeming to invite a response, but James could only stare.

"What is your name?" she asked.

"Ings, miss," he said, "James, oldest son and heir of Ings the butchers in Portsea, at your service."

"Well, James; I am your friend, Amelia."

And Princess Amelia presented her hand, which was covered in a glove, white and soft as the crest of a wave.

"Jimmy! You've to kiss it," hissed ma, but James had frozen.

The tall officer grasped the girl's arm and urged her to stop the nonsense and return to the carriage. Ignoring him, the princess took a handkerchief from her sleeve and pressed it into James Ings's collar. It was to nurse little Frederick's knee, she said, and James must keep it as a memento of their secret. She smiled like an angel and was gone.

When Ma Ings had recovered from the shock and the attentions of the crowd, she bound little Freddie's knee with a kerchief of her own and took charge of the royal item. At home, Uncle Percy said the officer was likely Prince Ernest, and the scar came from Flanders. The newspaper had reported he was wounded there, leading a charge, and would attend Spithead with his parents today.

After Ings's close encounter with two royal personages, everyone around him, the customers, the congregation and all the citizens of Portsea, even his parents, treated him with a kind of reverence that he felt he did not deserve. The story grew, as stories often do, gathering dimensions with little connection to the truth. Most were forgotten, eventually, but with this brief incident, with the visit that the king was not fit to make, Ings became aware of a larger world and of behaviours he had never encountered in Portsea.

Long after his allegiance to the aristocracy collapsed, James Ings held Princess Amelia's image and her whispers in his heart. His tears were hardly less bitter than the mad old King's at her premature death, and he would tell no-one the cause of his sorrow. He kept her secret until, in the weeks before his death, he composed his testament. Never soiled by the blood of an Ings, the royal handkerchief was carried in 1816, with Freddie's luggage, on a ship bound for Nova Scotia.

CHAPTER TWO

1790-93

Nottingham

TIDD

During his employment at Nottingham, bootmaker Richard Tidd's interest in politics was inflamed by a radical school-teacher from Newcastle, who came to speak at the Guild one evening. Thomas Spence promoted the fair distribution of land and the reestablishment of parts of the Saxon constitution. After the lecture, which also referred to the Magna Carta, Tidd became an enthusiastic Spencean and began seeking out radical literature. His commitment to the cause was confirmed by an incident soon after his promotion to journeyman.

Tidd and his master had begun copying a new design for water-resistant footwear, popular with regiments bound for the monsoons. When a young army captain tried to leave town without settling his bill, Tidd pursued him with a dagger and demanded payment. Their combined swordsmanship would not have alarmed Napoleon, but the captain suffered a bloody nose, and his mendacious account was accepted by the magistrate, an associate of his parents. Tidd found himself slammed up in the infamous dungeons of Nottingham County Gaol.

Following his release three year later, Tidd took revenge by signing for several regiments under different names, each time absconding and sending two thirds of his bounty to the Spencean Fund in London. After the final donation, with three regiments and two widows in pursuit, Tidd fled to the capital, where there was rumoured to be plenty of work, and where he could lose himself in the crowd and partake more actively in the struggle.

Monday 28ᵗʰ July, 1794

Little Turnstile, Holborn, London

Now secretary of the London Spenceans, Tidd retreated temporarily from politics during his courtship of the seamstress, Mary Eliza Parry, so that no rumours of his secret life could spoil his chances. Today, his room-mates had gone to work, and since the bootmaker's shop was closed on Mondays, he was free to rehearse his marriage proposal in private. He intended to deliver it this evening, having missed the opportunity after chapel, where Eliza, in the blue embroidered dress and ribbons had been the cause of such inner tumult that he found it impossible to recite his catechism. Instead of waiting at the gate to walk with her and find some secluded place in which to fall upon his knees, Tidd had hurried away to recover himself in private, leaving his sweetheart bewildered. Early this morning, he had delivered a sealed note to the upholsterer's shop where she worked, asking if she would meet him, when the shop closed.

Evidence of a rival had made it essential to elicit a promise now, even if they must wait for the wedding. Eliza's parents had been taken by the dysentery two years ago, and there would be no dowry, but also no guardian to disapprove of him. He would assure his sweetheart that far from afflicting his vision or his capacity to work, the minor impairment to his eye made him even more determined to succeed. They would marry as soon as there were sufficient savings to lease a small shop and adjacent accommodation. With Eliza at his side, with shared commitment to hard work and thrift, Richard Tidd's boots would soon be the finest in London. In short, he was offering a joyful path to a contented and prosperous family life. How could she refuse?

Tidd cleared his throat to practise the speech, in which he would not forget to emphasize his sound bodily health, a product of his childhood in the pure air of Lincolnshire. And, of course, he would stress his undying devotion to Eliza. The rehearsal was interrupted before it started by vigorous hammering at the door. In the hallway stood an agitated young man, his friend and neighbour, Willie Spence, son of the radical philosopher.

"Hush and come inside," said Tidd, pulling Willie through the door. "I suppose you've had no breakfast?" He indicated the box of sweetmeats Eliza gave him last Thursday.

"Nor dinner, neither" said Will, snatching a sweet and scoffing it in the same breath.

"Is your father well?" asked Tidd, a little guilty that he had not kept abreast of developments.

"Oh, he sits calmly at his window at Newgate, with nothing to do but read," said Willie, "while the rest of us never stop toiling on his behalf."

"Still no word of a trial?" asked Tidd.

"No," said Willie, scooping another sweet.

"Hell-fire!" replied Tidd. "I'm sorry for him."

"Father's better off than any of us," continued Willie. "His disciples queue at the gates with food, which he distributes fair and square to his cell-mates. I swear he'd stay at Newgate forever, if he could."

As Willie Spence sat forlornly on the chair, with his torn cap and weary expression, Tidd understood that his friend would rather be a baker or a candle-stick maker or almost anything else but the son of a philanthropist. Tidd resolved always to keep his own domestic and political affairs separate, no matter what the cost to his conscience.

"Where have you been these last weeks?" asked Willie.

"Busy," replied Tidd.

Every man was entitled to his secrets, and Willie Spence said no more.

"If that's all you wanted to know, why hammer so loud at 't door?" asked Tidd.

"I almost forgot!" said Willie. "History is in the making, Tiddy, and you and I will divert it!"

Master Spence had been woken before daybreak by a messenger. A friend in France reported that the disgraced Robespierre, having been captured and detained at an hotel in Paris, was on the run. He was believed to be heading for the coast, and there were rumours that he would seek refuge in London. Willie took the news straight to Newgate, where his father became exceptionally agitated. Robespierre's presence in England would push an already terrified government towards desperate measures, he said, and just as the reform movement most needed unity, it would split the radicals in two. The Spencean policy of non- violence was opposed by other, more gullible radical groups, who would quickly align themselves with the charismatic, highly dangerous Robespierre.

"Tom Spence expects us to stop Robespierre crossing 't channel?" asked Tidd with a caustic grunt.

"I've no doubt Richard Tidd could do that, if he wished!" replied Willie.

"Let the Parliamentarians do 't work!"

"Father insists that only Spenceans can prevent a blood bath."

The sentiment confirmed Tidd's creeping concern that too long as a celebrity prisoner had inflated Tom Spence's opinion of the movement. Still, he was the founder and his wishes must be fulfilled.

"What does he suggest we do?"

"Spread the news across London before those damn fools at Westminster hear of it and use Robespierre's exile to split the movement."

Tidd confessed that while he was disturbed by the potential risk, he had urgent private business today, and suggested Willie ask for help at the imminent meeting at The Ship. Willie looked crestfallen.

"Nobody persuades the men as well as you, Tiddy, nor has so much experience of action."

Tidd pictured Eliza at her needlework, longing for the end of her shift, when he would be waiting. Would she peer through the window and look for him? Would she ever talk to him again, if he failed her a second time? Richard Tidd could outrun most men, but what would Eliza do, if today, he tripped up and was arrested; if he ended up in a cell at Bow Street, instead of outside the upholsterer's window? Would she accept that fool apprentice, who hung around her all day with his lumpy nose and soft, besotted eyes?

"Three hours after the meeting, that's all we need!" Willie begged. "Just think what a difference those hours could make to history. We need you, Tiddy. My father needs you. England needs you!"

The Spences' shop, The Hive of Liberty, stood almost opposite Tidd's lodgings on Little Turnstile. It traded a conglomeration of old and new coins, books and pamphlets, including

Tom Spence's own socio-political works and his dictionary of revised spelling. The chaotic establishment was managed by the philosopher's second wife, a fiery dame and competent deterrent to any officer, who came snooping in the hope of an easy arrest. Grace Spence, who had met and married her new husband within a day, brought to the business a side line of dried herbs. The aromas of lavender, sage and thyme almost stifled the musty smell of books and, when the window was open, hovered in the alley, transporting, for a moment, anyone passing through to the Ship Tavern or Lincoln's Inn Field beyond.

The shop's bell jangled its cheery alarm, Willie shouted their names, and they squeezed between the bookshelves into the hidden cavity, where Mrs Spence was busy with two mighty volumes. The centre section of each had been cut out, and she was filling the empty space with handbills, which she had printed in the basement. Four copies of Bunyan's *The Pilgrim's Progress*, had been donated by a benevolent librarian. Two had been cut for the handbills, and two remained unspoiled. If approached by a figure of authority, the carrier would present his intact version, with an innocent smile and a Christian sentiment, and offer it for sale at an absurdly high price. Straight as a pencil, good Thomas Spence would never have sanctioned such subterfuge. His wife and his weary son believed that if every Spencean was honest on every occasion, the gaols would fill up in a flash, and there would be no-one to do the work.

GEORGE EDWARDS
Old Street, London

On the day of Robespierre's escape from the Hotel de Ville, reports arrived at Mrs G's Gin Palace that Admiral Nelson had lost an eye. The tragedy, which had occurred seventeen days previously on the island of Corsica, provided Mrs G's ten-year-old son, George Edwards with one of his big ideas, perhaps the greatest yet. He considered whether to reveal it to ma's friend, Cornelius Thwaite, but decided to wait for the outcome of another plan before suggesting anything new.

Uncle Con claimed to be an artist of high renown, but Mrs G claimed that anyone capable of consuming so much spirit in one day was incapable of holding a brush, let alone creating a work of genius. In that, as in so many of her opinions, Edwards's mother was quite wrong. Until his downfall, Cornelius Thwaite had enjoyed a glittering career as a sculptor. He recognised in the young George Edwards an unusual mind, a kindred spirit, while the boy found in Uncle Con a more intriguing case than his ma's other customers. Master Edwards became a regular visitor at the lowly studio on Golden Lane, where in exchange for certain personal services, an arrangement silently condoned by Mrs G, Thwaite began training his sweet Georgie in the skills he had learnt as a modeller with Josiah Wedgewood. In this way, George Edwards discovered his talent for creating life-like figures in plaster. Occasionally, he pleased one of his ma's customers with a flattering likeness and earned a few pennies for it.

That Sunday, after beating the boy soundly with the leather belt, instead of the usual requirements, Thwaite came over all philosophical and confided the circumstances of his decline.

The subject of his particular grief was a Phrygian shepherdess, who represented the goddess, Venus in disguise on Mount Ida. Using a new kind of artificial stone, Thwaite had created the life-size figure in his premises in Lambeth, which he shared with an unscrupulous businesswoman named Eleanora North. When they argued, Miss North has dismissed him amid an explosion of fallacious publicity. As if that humiliation were not enough, the same dragon continued, after their acrimonious parting, to profit from Cornelius Thwaite's moulds. There were rumoured to be twenty-eight Phrygian shepherdesses, adorning grand houses and gardens in England, from which the creator had received not a penny in commission. A twenty-ninth was said to be en route to Hanover for a relation of the royal family, rendering future sales even more lucrative.

To George Edwards, the story was as fascinating as anything from *The Arabian Nights*. Obviously, Uncle Con had been a fool to trust a business partner, but if someone so mediocre in spirit could create work that was desired by the wealthiest in the land, then so, too, could George Edwards.

Upstairs in his bed that night, as his little brother slept tight and his ma frolicked with customers downstairs, the idea occurred to George Edwards. By Monday morning, he had devised a plan. As soon as his patron was likely to be awake, he made his way to Longacre, snatching as he walked by, a loaf from a baker's cart.

Uncle Con thanked him for the bread and said he would listen with interest to sweet Georgie's plan. Before disclosing any details, the boy requested one third of any profit, should he succeed in rescuing the mould. Thwaite laughed until, with remarkable composure for a ten-year-old, Edwards responded that he might continue without Uncle Con's participation, in which case, the entire profit would be his alone.

Cornelius Thwaite's eyes flashed, first in the direction of the leather belt that hung from a hook on the blue door, and then at his protégé. The boy's hint at defiance would normally have sufficed for a beating, but the artist wanted that mould. He gritted his teeth and signed the contract that George had already written out on paper torn from Mrs G's ledger.

Since the warehouse overlooked the river, young Edwards explained, removal of the shepherdess would be easy, and since transport could be arranged with the help of ma's customers, discretion was assured and expenses would be low. He would require information about the warehouse, including the owner's character, the precise location of the mould store, and an address to which his associate could deliver the item, when the deed was done.

Thwaite was amused by the idea, not least by the prospect of revenge on Miss North. When he asked for details, Edwards replied that the less Uncle Cornelius knew, the more genuine his outrage, when an officer of the law came to question him about the mysterious disappearance of his shepherdess.

TIDD

The Ship Tavern, Little Turnstile, Holborn

Each of the Spenceans who made their way into The Ship dropped a penny into the collection box in anticipation of a talk, entitled "New Ploughs and Ploughing". When the numbers were complete and Willie had bolted the door, Richard Tidd rang the nautical bell, suspended above the bar. Thee room fell silent, but for some smart fellow, who wanted to know who or what Tiddy had been hiding from these last weeks.

"None o' your bloody business!" came a helpful reply from the rear.

"Thank you, my friends," said Tidd. "Whatever my reasons, I am pleased to be back amongst you. However, it is my solemn duty to divert this meeting and bring, from a reliable source, news of grave danger. Monsieur Robespierre is quite possibly on his way to London."

A roar of fury filled the room, obliging Tidd to ring the great bell again. When silence fell, he offered his apologies to the learned speaker, who had travelled from St Albans, and asked for a show of hands to postpone the lecture in favour of immediate action.

The result was unanimous, and Tidd reported that a message, dictated this morning by Mr Spence at Newgate, must be distributed to every corner of London. There was nothing in the message, that might ordinarily lead to arrest, but with the government as jumpy as fleas, Their leader had requested the highest level of precaution. Handbills should be dropped discreetly in the most sensitive areas, and also in some districts south-east of town, through which the Incorruptible was most likely to pass from Dover, and where, by good fortune, Mrs Spence's herbal business was well-known. Everywhere else would be divided between the membership, who would begin whispering campaigns at every corner of London. The message was short, and it must be memorized by every man present.

Grave risk to Britain's unity and security! Robespierre has escaped capture and seeks refuge in London. The population must beware false rhetoric. Any stranger who approaches, speaking in French, should be arrested and taken at once to a magistrate.

Armed each with two copies of *The Pilgrims' Progress*, bootmaker Tidd and Willie Spence dropped handbills furtively around Bow Street, Westminster and St James. While the wider membership streamed into other parts of the capital, Grace Spence took a ferry across the river and visited her regulars in Southwark with a sack of home-made remedies, in which she had hidden a few dozen hand-bills. The new doorman at a tannery, who had replaced an old customer, considered the prospect of Robespierre's dash to England absurd and, for the sake of his own security, preferred not to be found with any such leaflet in his possession, no matter how harmless. Nor, being in the rudest health, was he at all interested in the produce of her witchcraft. A porter at Borough Market thought Grace had finally lost her senses, but hoped the Incorruptible's boat would sink and promised to disperse a few bills in exchange for the tansy infusion that helped his aching joints. Dorothy Bakewell bought the potion particular to her employment and promised that her girls would warn their customers of Monsieur Robespierre's intentions. The curate at St Saviour's agreed to enlist his congregation and accepted the donation of Mrs Spence's nettle tincture; a certain cure for baldness.

By four o'clock, the membership, including Tidd, had reconvened at The Ship, tired, but modestly confident of success. As they enjoyed their ale or listened to Mrs Spence's account of the day's conquests. When the landlord struck the nautical bell three times, signifying half past five, Tidd leapt up. Ignoring his friends' high-spirited curiosity, he hurried away; if he sprinted, he might reach the upholsterer's premises before his sweetheart finished work.

On reflection, Tidd thought that if he arrived a little late, she was more likely to be angry than despondent. That is what excited Tidd most about her character. Eliza never whimpered, like the widows of Nottingham, nor entreated, like Mrs Cante in Grantham. Eliza was spirited, and when she blazed, she blazed gloriously, her eyes shining like diamonds, her mouth pursed tightly and impossible to kiss. How he loved to win Eliza round when she blazed! But not today, please not today, or he would lose his nerve.

A few yards from the shop, Tidd stopped to catch his breath. There, exiting the door, was his own Eliza in the company of the upholsterer's lumpy-nosed apprentice. And they were laughing! Obviously, she preferred to leave with that rogue than wait a few moments for the man she professed to love. Subduing the urge to cut the fellow down with the dagger he kept hidden in his breeches, Tidd decided instead to follow them and discover how true Eliza was to her word.

The apprentice wore grubby boots that were far too long for his feet, but he was not the fool that Eliza had suggested. Tidd could see from the pattern of their walking that the joke continued, and that Eliza was enjoying the wretch's company. What favours would she grant, when they reached their destination?

Suddenly, and with a jaunty wave, the young man shouted "Good Night, Eliza!" and slunk off into some god-forsaken alley. The relief was greater than any since Tidd walked out of Nottingham Gaol. He resisted the temptation to run after her, which would suggest a suspicious nature, and continued his pursuit.

As she continued alone, Eliza's gait indicated an untroubled mind. How could that be? Was it of no consequence that her sweetheart neglected her? Just then, she turned, not as Tidd expected, right, into Grays Inn Field, where she had lodgings, but left, towards a row of low, brick-built houses with front gardens.

It was never simple for a longshank like Tidd to find a hiding place, but today, fortune provided an old oak on the corner of the street. It was a poor specimen with nothing green about it, even in the height of summer, but the trunk was as wide as any in Sherwood. Thanking Providence that the tree had never been cut down for the navy, Tidd took up his position. He watched as Eliza approached the third house on the row. The door was opened by a stern-looking woman in a grey dress and red apron. Eliza followed her indoors.

As he watched and waited, Tidd was startled by an old man with thin, straggly hair, who poked at him with a stick and demanded to know what mischief the scallywag was up to, lurking by the tree like that.

"I ain't afraid of nothing nor no-one," he growled. "These eyes seen sights would curdle thy mother's milk!"

Perceiving that the fellow was a veteran of the wars, Tidd responded that he honoured all heroes, and meant no harm. He was waiting to surprise his sweetheart.

"A learned fellow, art thou?" asked the stranger, poking his stick at the book under Tidd's arm,

Without noticing it, Tidd had carried a copy of *The Pilgrim's Progress* all the way from the Ship. It was one of the intact volumes.

"Not especially sir," said Tidd, praying that Willie had taken the other three books away. "I had a few years' schooling, and if it would give you pleasure, I shall read a section aloud."

"Indeed, it would!" said the old soldier, adding, with a wink, "I'll keep an eye out for lasses. If a pretty one passes, chances are it'll be thine, and I'll gi' thee a nudge."

Tidd had read little more than the title, when a few urchins approached and asked if they might listen too. The reading party been sitting at the base of the oak for about fifteen minutes, when he felt the old man's stick on nudging his neck. He looked up to see his own Eliza approaching, her expression proud and smiling. Tidd's heart sang. He finished his paragraph, closed the book, and, on a whim born of happy expectation, invited the little audience to return next Monday for more.

As Tidd's audience dispersed, Eliza took his hand and confessed that because he never disclosed his opinions, and she had no parents to quiz him, she had often wondered what filled his heart and spirit. Now she had proof that Richard Tidd was a clever, god-fearing man, who loved old folk and children and commanded their respect. She could hope for nothing more, except that she might be present, when he read the book again. Eliza had never had the chance for learning, and said she would be obliged if he would read out his note to her, because she had not dared show it to anyone else, in case the contents were private.

His rehearsed speech quite forgotten, Richard Tidd bent to kiss Eliza's tender mouth, and beside that bare oak tree, asked if one day she would become his wife. Instead of beaming with joy and kissing him back, as his heart yearned, Eliza sighed.

"I should like it very much," she said," but when the truth is out, Richard Tidd, I fear that you will not."

"What truth?" asked Tidd, anxious that Eliza had accepted the apprentice, after all.

"Follow me," she said, and led him back to the row of brick houses.

The woman in grey was surprised to see Eliza again and nodded courteously when Tidd was introduced. They followed her into the back kitchen, where half a dozen listless infants sat on the floor. At the sound of adult voices, their faces turned in mournful unison, perhaps hoping that rescue was at hand.

"Her name is Mary," whispered Eliza, "for my own poor mama."

Her voice was warm, and her gaze moved over the infants to the corner, beside the fireplace, where a child of about ten months was standing unsteadily, gripping the sides of its cot. Her cheeks were scarlet, and she was chewing on the arm of a rag doll. When she saw her mother, Mary laughed, her round face glistening in the heat of the fire. Her eyes were cut from the same diamonds as Eliza's. She had a pert nose and thick, wavy black hair. She dropped her doll, raised plump little arms and smiled brightly at Tidd, who was entirely unused to babies.

"Ain't I too rough for 't bairn?" he asked.

As he bent to lift her, the child's thick peal of laughter was his answer.

"Her pa was a midshipman," whispered Eliza, "lost at sea before we could wed. He never knew his Mary, and Mary never knew him."

Overjoyed, Richard Tidd kissed the child's soft, crumpled wrist and said to Eliza,

"I'd say it's time 't lass found herself a new pa, wouldn't tha?"

On the second day of Tidd's betrothal, news reached London that the "Incorruptible" had been recaptured in Paris. After a botched attempt to shoot himself, he had lost his head in the usual French manner. Tidd and Willie Spence agreed that their efforts were not wasted. The exercise had confirmed that they had sympathisers all over London, who could quickly be informed and animated even in these challenging times.

Monday, 11th August, 1794

EDWARDS

Old Street, London

Early one morning, while Nelson's men were still celebrating victory in Corsica, George Edwards stood in his ma's kitchen, scrubbing his brother William's face, neck and hands. After a final rehearsal of the routine, he marched the little fellow down to the river and over the bridge to Lambeth.

A diminutive lady with a sharp face and dressed from crown to toe in black lace, Miss North, the factory owner looked, William Edwards would later recall, like a huge, startled bird, as she caught sight of the two waifs, who followed the secretary into her domain. Young Master Henry Ward and his brother had a private petition, Master Bench explained, which they would disclose only to Miss North. The lady intended to eject the boys at once, but they smiled at her with anxious and beseeching charm, and she relented.

"You find me uncommon busy, Master Ward," she said. "I give you two minutes! Speak!"

As Miss North glared at her clock, Edwards explained, as fast as the words would come, that he and his brother were the smallest and uppermost members of Walter Ward's Human Pyramid, which had been engaged, until very recently, at Astley's Amphitheatre. Their parents had left for an assignment in the Prairies, and until they returned, the brothers had pledged to care for their sisters. For that reason, they wished to contribute to Miss North's magnificent sculptures and architectural features by cleaning her kilns and chimneys. Exceptionally nimble and experienced climbers, they were unafraid of hard or dirty work and considered themselves perfect candidates.

A spinster without experience of the duplicities of children, Miss North, whom the speedily delivered story had distracted from her clock-watching, regretted the boys' predicament, but could offer no hope of employment. However, she would not deny such well-presented youngsters a tour of her factory. With the flutter of a lacy hand, she summoned the secretary and commanded him to be their guide. Master Bench's smile simpered, and he had tufted black eyebrows that met in a kind of pyramid, as if he were in a state of perpetual enquiry. It would be as easy, young George Edwards thought, as eating pie.

Master Bench was glad of a break from his dull routine and agreed to conduct the brothers to the warehouse first. They came to a corridor, crammed full on one side with white lions and unicorns, eagles, griffins and cherubs, and on the other, with an impertinent jumble of the deities of Greece and Rome. On another occasion, Edwards would have studied the handiwork closely. Today, he was far too anxious about the tide and his boat-man's patience.

"Did I hear that Miss North owns a particularly splendid Phrygian shepherdess?" he asked, casually.

"Indeed, Master Ward, she does!" replied the secretary, delighted with the little fellow's enthusiasm. "Follow me!"

At George's nudge, William clasped the secretary's hand with a fierce grip.

When they stood before the life-sized shepherdess, George Edwards was taken aback. How perfectly formed she was; her nose and mouth, the curves of her chest and the folds of the ribbons on her dress at the hips were all as real. He almost expected her to breathe. What sublime beauty and dignity were contained there and how different from ma's poxy upstairs girls. What a great artist Uncle Con was, and perhaps would be again, when his plan succeeded!

The reverie collapsed, when Edwards observed that the shepherdess was all front and no back. Where was the profit in half a statue? His mission was lost! Misinterpreting the alarm, the secretary explained that the shepherdess knew no pain, since she was not real. Moulds were generally made in two sections, and the shepherdess's back stood right behind them.

George Edwards turned, his mind racing. Uncle Con had not informed him there were two moulds. He must adapt the plan. When he caught his brother's eye, William read the look as a signal for action and began wailing like a banshee. Too soon! He needed time to recalculate. He tried a furtive kick, which the six-year old took as a sign of encouragement and proceeded to groan that he had come over all peculiar and must empty his bottom at once.

With an air of irritation, Edwards explained that his brother had a tendency to fuss, but was perfectly capable of managing his own ablutions. He would like to admire the work a little longer, if Master Bench would kindly lead the child to a suitable location. Trained to obedience, the secretary hurried away with William in pursuit of a pot.

The moulds were not heavy, but they were cumbersome and, being constructed of a kind of ceramic, more fragile than Edwards had anticipated. Of more immediate concern were the warehouse windows. The proportions were suitable, but on tiptoe, even with his arms stretched, the ten-year old could only touch the ledge with his finger-tips. The urgency began to clamour. What if William was unable to sustain his lie or forgot his name was Ward? If anyone put a stick to him, the brat would crumple, and all would be lost.

He was in a long corridor, parallel to the river. At the far end, he saw a cupboard, tall enough to hold a ladder. He ran to it, but it was bolted. He turned a corner into the next corridor and saw, stacked in an alcove, half a dozen chairs. Pulling one loose, he checked in both directions for snoopers and carried it quickly to the window nearest the shepherdess. He tore off a boot, which must be his hammer, and clambered on to the chair. As he covered his eyes and smashed the window, success seemed, at last, attainable, and Edwards sensed a kind of delirium.

Even from three floors up, the river was noisy, its stench overpowering. The hired tug was moored near the factory entrance, as agreed. The boat-man, who was busy with ropes, had been commissioned to lasso a large, unidentified object that would land beneath the warehouse window. He was not prepared for two items, and unless Edwards signalled the change correctly, the fellow was likely to row off in possession of only one.

The burning question was which mould to dispatch first. Despite the alluring hat, the twirls of hair and the detail of the skirt, the shepherdess's rear would be less valuable than the front. If he could be certain that the boat-man would wait, it might act as a practice run. But if the boat-man rowed off with a single load, it had to be the more profitable front, with its perfect face, graceful neck and breasts, so real and tender that despite his dilemma, the boy felt strangely flustered.

He stood at the open window, waved his kerchief and whistled, as agreed, but in the excitement, the sound was less robust than usual and would never be heard above the traffic. When, on the third attempt, the boat-man raised his right arm, Edwards responded with a frantic signal. The fellow shrugged, uncomprehending. Edwards could waste no time. He jumped down and lifted a mould on to the chair. Shutting his eyes tight and, with as much traction as his thin body could raise, he propelled the rear half Uncle Con's creation through the window. When he dared to open his eyes and look out, the tug had not moved. The boat-man's arms were open in bewilderment. Following the fellow's gaze, Edwards was dismayed to see the shepherdess collide with the stern of a sailing vessel and shatter, the dainty heels of her embroidered shoes slipping into the murky Thames.

The boat-man looked up at the window. He seemed irritated. Edwards made a vigorous gesture and jumped down to fetch the second mould. Please, please, he begged, as if the pretty mould might somehow order the boat-man wait. One, two, three, a much heftier push and she was launched. Edwards gasped as the shepherdess landed with a bump at the water's edge and watched in horror as she was swept away by a side current, bosom up and surrounded by filth and detritus.

Edwards cursed the boat-man and Cornelius Thwaite for their incompetence, and then, with his right boot under his arm, hobbled to his escape; a hoist and a rope at the back window. At least Uncle Con was right about that.

Waiting, as instructed, by Westminster Bridge, William knew from his brother's stony expression that the mission had failed.

"It's all your fault!" said Edwards, as he pulled on his boot and tied the laces. "You howled too soon.

"There ain't gonna be no river trip, neither?" asked William.

"Stop snivelling," replied Edwards, "or I'll throw you under a cart."

In silence, they trudged back to the gin palace, where Cornelius Thwaite was enjoying a drink with ma. On hearing that one half of his shepherdess lay on the river-bed and the other had probably arrived in Greenwich by now, Uncle Con drank a toast to all the fish who pecked at her arse and all the sailors who ravished her bosom. Mrs G said she would second that.

The loss of an object of beauty, and his own part in its destruction were more of a blow to George Edwards than the absence of reward. Although his contempt for Cornelius Thwaite was complete, the fool had served a purpose. Half an hour's unpleasantness now and then had been a fair price for the training that would soon transform his life.

In the subsequent days, Edwards blackmailed several of his ma's more pliable customers and acquired enough cash and materials to begin executing his new idea. He talked his way into galleries containing portraits of the rich and powerful. He visited bookshops and libraries and made copies of the Viscount's likeness until, at last, he was ready to create the mould for a figurine, about twelve inches high, of a proud Horatio Nelson with an eye-patch.

Nelson's misfortune enabled George Edwards to move away from his ma's Gin Palace and away from the perfidious Uncle Con. He rented a large cupboard and half a bed on Wych Street, and he promised to fetch William as soon as he was able, when they would celebrate their reunion with a ride up-river.

Meanwhile the Nelson statuette became a modest success. It was also the start of George Edwards's long acquaintance with Fleet Street, where at the age of ten and a half, he could be seen at the corner with Fetter Lane, flogging his one-eyed Nelsons. He had enough to eat, and before the frost set in, purchased warm clothes and big-enough boots, returning the old ones, by messenger, for William.

After Nelson's triumphant return aboard HMS Agamemnon, it was revealed that while the Admiral had lost his sight on one side, the eye itself was intact, and there would be no patch. The collapse in sales was not a special disappointment to Edwards, who had received requests for another famous figure. Marie-Antoinette would be his first, but certainly not his last association with royalty. He had never seen Her Majesty's likeness, but neither had his public. The inspiration would be a shepherdess, whose watery demise was, in the artist's secret heart, no less tragic than the poor Queen of France at her scaffold.

1817-1818

INGS

Portsea, Hampshire

James Ings, the butcher would often wonder how different their fate might be if Hercules Cookson had never broken his leg. If that well-cover had been securely fastened, instead of lying there, on the path, Hercules would never have tripped over. He would have carried on being the night-watchman, and would not have been forced to sell his capricious mare. If Hercules had not been forced to sell the mare, Cousin Jack would never have bought it. Jack would never have lost control of the mare, the mare would not have bolted and thrown him into the Creek, and Jack would still be with them today. Who was it forgot to replace the cover on that well?

Hercules claimed a wind had blown up and knocked his lamp out, and that's why he had not seen the well-cover on the path. Ings's wife, Celia thought Hercules had drunk too much liquor, as a consequence of his brother's return to Portsmouth barracks, and that's why he failed to see the cover. If that brother's ship had been delayed by misadventure or the tide, or if the moon had shone more significantly on that Thursday, instead of being clouded over, it would not have mattered about the lamp blowing out. But the ship was not delayed, the moon did not shine bright, and now Cousin Jack was dead and the fortunes of the Ings family had changed forever.

James and his Cousin Jack owned the butcher's shop in Portsea founded by their grandfather in the first year of His Majesty's reign. Old Ma Ings and Celia made the sausages, puddings and pies, while Jack's wife, Lizzie took care of the laundry and the children; five girls altogether and James's lad, William, known as Bill. There were eleven mouths to feed, all without Jack's cleverness to guide them. How different their future would look now, if it were not for that moon and that lamp and that capricious mare!

Cousin Jack, who had attended the Grammar School, understood mathematics, had a good head for business and owned a healthy herd of pigs besides. Jack was of the firm opinion that it was a mistake to combine English stock with foreign breeds. It was a fashion, he always said, that would fade, just like the fashion in ladies' hats, and he never let any of those new-fangled boars from Naples or China anywhere near his sows. Jack had a point, because James Ings made first-rate bacon off his cousin's pure Hampshire hogs, and customers came all the way from Winchester for Celia's puddings and pies.

In a way, the family's success contributed to the sorry changes ahead. Portsea was growing fast, and there had been talk of a canal. When Cousin Jack suggested expanding into the property business, they had leased a pocket of land from Thomas Croxton and built a row of houses. They called it Tin Street. At first, the rent came in regular as clockwork. Nobody, not even Jack reckoned with the government breaking its promise to stop the emergency taxes, which were supposed to have paid for the wars with France and America. Instead, the tyrants found more and more ways to rob the people. Celia said it was all Napoleon's fault. If Boney had not insisted on a war with Britain, she said, the government would not be in such a pickle. If the government were not in such a pickle, it would not impose impossible tolls and taxes. James reckoned they could argue politics till the cows come trotting home, it would never help their predicament.

Back then, Ings did not understand politics. His strength was in telling what animals produced the tastiest meat, and no man in Hampshire could take a knife to a carcass with half the skill and precision. If a customer came in for a sheep's head or thruppence worth of brisket, Ings knew exactly where to cut, so that not a farthing was wasted. But when people started asking for tuppence worth and then a penny ha'penny, there was less and less money to pay the stockyard. The beasts he bought for slaughter grew scrawnier every week. Without Jack's hogs, the family would never have survived.

One day, Bill, Ings's son and heir had the bright idea of running hogs into Wiltshire. The soil in that county being more suited to sheep and grain, quality pork would raise top prices there. Bill knew enough back paths to avoid the toll demanded at the county border. The first three attempts were successful, but he grew careless, or he was betrayed, because the watchman got wind of it and jumped out of a hedge one day to surprise him. The hogs were confiscated, and Bill was only kept from arrest by one of his ma's figgy puddings.

Soon, none of the tenants on Tin Street could afford the rent, and the Ings accepted their time and labour instead. Celia saved what food she could for the hogs, just to keep the bacon trade going. On Tuesdays and Fridays, she would drink a jug of stout instead of her meal and sing silly songs to make the children forget their hunger. The puddings and pies on those days were higgledy-piggledy affairs, but people bought them just the same. Celia always had a magic touch with flavours, and drink or no drink, she could turn half a pound of gristly shank into pies for ten hearty men.

One day, Jack made a secret visit to Mr Croxton and asked for a loan against the properties on Tin Street. Croxton agreed, but because his own business was suffering with the duties on property, demanded an extortionate rate of interest. Jack must have accepted, because when it all came out, there was his signature, loud and clear on the land-owner's ledger. No doubt he had conceived a plan to make the family prosper again. They never discovered what the plan was, nor even where Jack had deposited the money because two days later, the capricious mare threw him into the Creek with his secrets, and he drowned.

The first the Ings knew about the loan was when Croxton's thugs repossessed the houses on Tin Street and threw all the tenants out. Croxton blamed Cousin Jack, insinuating that he had squandered the money on some disastrous enterprise and fell into Portsbridge Creek on purpose. When Ings heard the allegations, he ground his best knife and prepared to put an end to the land-owner's life. He would have done so there and then, had his beloved Celia not positioned herself between her husband and the shop-door, begged dear Jimmy not to worsen their plight by becoming a murderer, closed her eyes and whispered her twenty-third psalm.

"Oh, Celia!" Ings would murmur in time to come, "where was your twenty-third psalm on the twenty-third of February last?"

CHAPTER THREE

Friday, 23rd April, 1819.

ST. GEORGE'S DAY

Lewes Assizes, Sussex

The defendant clutched the bar with thick, yellow fingers; a private, whose name has been forgotten, accused of killing his captain. His black hair was short and stiff as a brush above a crumpled, sallow forehead. The only discernible movement was in his eyes, which were dark and sparkled with defiant bemusement, as if he had tumbled into an assembly of lunatics. When asked to defend himself, the private delivered a remarkable speech. Without raising his voice, or shifting the tone for emphasis, he described the intense provocation of a sneering bully, who found entertainment in physical and mental torment. Where a reasonable officer would inspire his men with pride and patriotism, this tyrant flogged them without mercy, deprived them of food, sleep and all other essentials of human dignity, while he grew fat on their rations and satisfied his desires with the abuse of their bodies. With one clean shot, a monster's life had ended, and a regiment of men could sleep easily, eat decently and become more efficient servants of His Majesty's Infantry.

When the speech was over, the judge asked whether the defendant, who was allegedly illiterate, with no means to pay an advocate, had composed the speech himself.

"In part, sir, though I was helped by an acquaintance," said the private.

"Which learned fellow is that?" asked the judge.

"It were Mr Thistlewood taught me, sir."

The judge took a sharp breath and banged his fist on his desk, causing the pages of his Bible to flutter. The dry old clerks arched their eyebrows and exchanged eloquent glances, while a murmur swept, low and growling, through the court. As the sound swelled to a hubbub and a crescendo, the sparkle in the defendant's eyes flickered and flipped into panic. He gripped the bar more tightly, and as order was restored in court, he knew exactly what would follow.

Had that poor, brave private given almost any name but Thistlewood, he might have ended his days in the Cape of Good Hope or in New South Wales instead of at the Horsham scaffold. It would be the first hanging in Sussex for ten years.

INGS

Portsea, Hampshire

Gripping the knife tight, Bill made a deft movement and lifted the kidney out, cautious in his triumph. Ings peered into the carcass.

"Well done, my boy!" he said. "Not a single speck of blood."

It was the last of Cousin Jack's hogs. The rest had been slaughtered in the expectation of an almighty profit at the St George's Day fair in Gosport.

"Sun's coming up," said Celia, arriving at the cold-house door.

She had kept Annie up all night in the kitchen, and they had two hundred and twenty pies and four stone of sausage to show for it.

"We've packed the crates," she continued. "We need help loading. At the gallop!"

Bill was excited by the prospect of an outing. They would drive across the island like last year, and be ferried across the water, listening to the wherryman's stories of pirates and press-gangs. His mother would shudder, and the fellow would wink at him over her shoulder and tell an even taller tale, as they rowed into harbour. The selling would be over in an hour, and they could enjoy the pleasures of the fair until the tide was right. Bill would buy treats for the little 'uns with the pennies he had earnt, sweeping and carrying at The Anchor and Hope.

The girls clamoured as their father and brother loaded the cart.

"If I'm big enough for the kitchen, I'm big enough for the fair!" chanted Annie, already a champion of her rights.

"After the night we've had, madam," retorted Celia, as she tightened Gulliver's harness. "You're fit for nothing but your cot! I'd give every hair on my head for the day of idleness coming your way!"

As Gulliver, the dappled pony led the cart in a westerly direction across the island, there was a light breeze. Yellow as the finest butter, the gorse danced and glinted in the early sunlight, stretching out as far as the sea. Celia closed her eyes for the pleasure of the air, so fresh against her cheeks after the heat of the kitchen and the odour of flesh in the shop and slaughterhouse.

The wherryman accepted a pork-pie as payment and stood by, in an advisory capacity, while Ings and Billy stacked the crates on to his boat. When all was done, Ings chivvied the pony and hurried back to the shop, confident that tomorrow, he would pay the stockyard.

TURTLE SOUP FOR THE KING

The wherryman was a member of the same Baptist congregation, and although Celia was aware of a good many rumours concerning his private life, it was her fixed opinion that only God may judge her fellow creatures. Besides, she did not want Billy's curiosity aroused.

"Mr Dart," she began, "how bonny your little girl looked in chapel the other day, with her pretty Easter bonnet!"

"Yes, Mrs Ings," replied the wherryman, "after her mother sat up all night, stitching it."

"What a fine needlewoman she is indeed!" said Celia, unable to suppress a blush at the reference to poor Mrs Dart.

The wherryman was about to launch into a story to distract Mrs Ings from her customary preoccupation with his personal affairs, when the conversation was interrupted.

"Ma! Quick!" yelped Bill. "Mr Dart! Chuck us the bucket!"

Then Celia saw the water, seeping through the bottom of the boat. It had trickled on to their boots and was creeping up the sides of the precious crates. Celia and Bill bailed water as fast as they could, praying for divine intervention, while the wherryman slackened the rope and threw the end to his mate, who sat chatting as he mended nets on the jetty and failed to hear the shouting. The vital rope fell short and slithered into the sea, and a brief moment later, the little vessel sank. They were not far enough out to endanger life, but they were submerged to their ankles in mud and to their knees in cold, dark water. The pies were ruined for certain, and when Billy proposed salvaging everything else, Celia said that it was the pies made the proper money, and if the sludge had infected her sausages, they would end their days in van Diemen's Land.

As they waded to the harbour steps, the wherryman said he was proper sorry for Mrs Ings and her dilemma, but there was no hope of compensation. He would never have allowed so many crates on his boat, he said, had he been told the proper weight. When Celia protested, Mr Dart hinted at a charge against the Ings for knowingly overloading a vessel that had been tested for sea-worthiness only a week ago.

With their sodden, mucky clothes clinging to their skin, Celia and Billy Ings trudged back across the island. Clouds veiled the sun, and the gorse seemed hostile now; dark, thorny hideouts for demons or robbers. Celia said they had nothing worth the stealing, but the chill could be the death of them.

At home, Lizzie hurried them to the kitchen fireside. She produced cloths and bowls of hot water and went to fetch Ings, who was mincing offal at the back.

"There are city merchants lose far more," he said, by way of comfort, "when their ships go down in the Bay of Biscay. We should be thankful it were just a few pies, and not one of us that got drowned."

"Just a few pies, husband?" protested Celia. "You dare say that to me, what was on her feet all night, preparing them, and has no picture in her head of what we shall eat when the last carcass is gone? Them pies was our salvation, Jimmy Ings, unless you can name another?"

Ings wiped his hands on his apron and approached to comfort his wife, but Celia was in no mood for embrace. Then he remembered.

"Annie took charge of a letter, while you was out," he said.

"How did she pay for delivery?" snapped Celia.

"With my blessing and a hand of sausages," replied Ings.

"Is it good news or bad?"

"That's for you to discover, my sweet," said Ings. "The envelope is addressed to Mrs James Ings.

Celia was perplexed. "Who is there'd be writing a letter to me?" she asked.

They hurried through to the parlour, where Annie had left the envelope unopened on the mantel. It was the colour of pure cream, and it was sealed. Celia's heart was beating too fast, and she said her husband must read the message aloud to her. The correspondent was Mr Ignatius Pyke, a lawyer from London, who wrote that her guardian, Silas Stone had died of a fever, and that Celia Stone Ings was his sole heir.

Mrs Ings did not know whether she ought to mourn the loss of Uncle Stone or make merry, because in his death, the brute had saved them. Her husband ripped off his bloody apron, and they clutched each other and whooped and danced around the parlour till they fell, laughing into their chairs. With all that noise, the girls came clattering down the stairs, and Lizzie and Bill arrived from the kitchen. When the news of their salvation settled in Ings's mind, and for the first time since Nelson departed aboard HMS Victory, he felt the spill of tears.

They pawned Pa Ings's silver spoon for the coach tickets and borrowed, from friends in the parish, clothing that might be pertinent to a lawyer's office in London. A week later, on the penultimate day of April, 1819, there was a sad, but hopeful farewell to the children, the old folks and Lizzie. Bill must be temporary head of the family, his father said, as he kissed the sad little faces of the girls, promising to convey their best wishes to the old King for his recovery and to return with presents for everyone.

The only money the couple possessed at that time was the coin Celia had stitched into her bodice for emergencies. Neither dared contemplate the fact that half a crown was insufficient for a return journey for two.

Thursday, 29th April, 1819

THISTLEWOOD

Horsham Gaol, Sussex

Horsham was the most unpleasant, but it was certainly not the first – nor the last - prison to accommodate Arthur Thistlewood. Following the collapse of a previous trial, he had demanded the return of personal items taken during his illegal arrest, including his grandfather's glass ink stand, his son's paints, and his wife's silk umbrella. When the Home Secretary failed to oblige, Thistlewood challenged him to a duel. Lord Sidmouth ignored the invitation, and Thistlewood responded by publishing their correspondence in pamphlets that were read aloud in taverns and coffee-shops, drawing rooms and parlours all over the capital.

The streets, alleys and courtyards of London echoed with laughter, at least in the mind of Lord Sidmouth. Thistlewood's re-arrest and subsequent committal to Horsham failed to dampen His Lordship's humiliation, which transformed itself quietly into something darker.

Among the Home Secretary's frequent dining companions was the judge who had presided at the Sussex Assizes on St George's Day. When, immediately after the controversial judgment, the same judge challenged the Horsham Gaoler about the free association between weak-minded prisoners and a notorious radical, the Gaoler admitted that he had been forced to act after intercepting Thistlewood's latest letter to the Home Secretary. It complained of unrest at Horsham because cells of only seven foot by ten were occupied by three men each instead of one.

Although the letter never left Horsham, the Gaoler could not ignore it. He had summoned Thistlewood, whose imposing presence exuded, even in the sordid surroundings of a gaol, charm and authority. Thistlewood protested about the filthy, congested accommodation. At least in The Tower, he had been given a daily allowance and every now and then, an orange to suck. The Horsham Gaoler chortled and promised to produce an orange a week if Thistlewood could keep the prisoners calm. Thistlewood retorted that if it was peace the Gaoler wanted, there was an easy solution. Until humane accommodation was available for all, inmates must be permitted to spend at least four hours a day in communal areas. The Gaoler considered for a moment. New cells could not be built overnight, and if he agreed to Thistlewood's terms, feeble-minded prisoners would be exposed to dangerous ideologies. On the other hand, if the Gaoler agreed, he was less likely to be assassinated by a mob tomorrow. The deal was done.

As they dined that Thursday afternoon, the judge, who had misgivings about the recent death sentence, informed the Gaoler that he had been a fool to allow Thistlewood access to simple-minded fellows like the condemned private. If any trouble resulted from the execution, the responsibility must be the Gaoler's alone.

Friday, 30ᵗʰ April, 1819

BRUNT

Fox Court, Holborn, London

On the last day of April 1819, Molly Brunt, the bootmaker's wife suffered a tragedy. At seven in the morning, her canary was sitting on the rim of her plate, pecking at her porridge. At twelve, he trilled a pretty jig to accompany lunch, but when his mistress returned from the market at four, Ringo was lying on his pretty yellow back, his feet stretched out like one-inch tacks. After a moment of dull horror, Mrs Brunt hurried to the pantry and pinched out a morsel of the seed cake she had baked for tomorrow. Tremulously, she opened the cage door and lifted the bird out, but she found not the tiniest hint of appetite.

Mrs Brunt was still holding the dead canary and weeping, when Joe Hale, the apprentice arrived with a request for small beer for himself and the master.

"I know a body'd give you fourpence for the cage," he said.

Molly Brunt, whose older son was apprenticed at Derby, thought that lads never know what to say on sentimental occasions.

"What plans do you have tomorrow?" she asked.

"Helping Mr Brunt finish the order."

Mrs Brunt was taken aback. Her husband never worked on a Saturday, not even when they were making profits worthy of a Lord. Mr Brunt always divided Saturdays equally between his family and his poetry.

"Which order?" she asked.

"A big one," said Hale.

"Has my husband quite forgot the date?" asked Mrs Brunt, with a sharpened tone.

Joe Hale looked away. His ma had warned him never to get drawn into domestic matters, but since moving into his master's premises in the cramped courtyard off Grays Inn Lane, there was scarcely a word between the Brunts that he had not heard.

"It must be very important," continued Mrs Brunt.

"Shall I ask the master to come for his beer?" asked the apprentice.

"You do that, Joe."

Tomorrow would be May Day, but it was also their son's birthday. Mrs Brunt had encouraged Harry to take his drum to the sweeps' parade. Brunt had brought the instrument home one day and, in exchange for polishing veterans' boots, Harry had taken lessons at the Military Training School on Grays Inn Lane. On May Day, Molly Brunt planned to follow her son down the Strand with a garland in her hair (she had bound it before lunch, when Ringo still breathed), while her husband distributed name cards. The occasion would be merry, and it would be good for business.

"Small beer's waiting, and the canary's dead," said Joe in the workshop. Brunt was closing an upper, and his mouth was full of pins. He twisted and jerked his chin upwards, from which Joe understood to bring the dish and a hammer.

"I know where to get you thruppence for the cage," said Joe.

The master spat the pins into the dish and pushed and pulled the awl through the layers of red Moroccan leather, to make the final hole, before drawing the bristle and the thread through. As Joe stood there, with the hammer and the dish, he said in a low voice,

"Mrs Brunt's made a fine garland for tomorrow; primroses and all sorts."

Brunt was hammering out seams and appeared not to hear him.

"Have you noticed anything?" asked Mrs Brunt, when her husband held out his pot for a refill.

"I notice my wife has money for primroses when I'm due at the tanner's on Wednesday," said Brunt, indicating the garland on the shelf.

"You said you had a decent order."

"Not if I waste my Saturday in pleasure," replied Brunt. "They're for delivery on Monday, and must be worn in."

"Can't you finish them tonight?"

"I'm due at a meeting."

"I see," said Molly with a tone.

"The editor of *Sherwin's Weekly* will be there, and I shall read the new poem out."

Brunt hoped for a compliment, but his wife offered only silence.

"Molly," he said at last. "You take Harry to the parade tomorrow with my blessing and as many primroses as you like. I shall go out tonight, and I shall work tomorrow, and so will Joe. Maybe Sunday too. When I'm paid, I'll take the bird for stuffing. How does that sound?"

Before Molly could summon a reply, they heard footsteps on the stairs outside. It was Harry, arriving from school. Mrs Brunt thought it wise to open the cake tin and celebrate his birthday now.

Harry Brunt was saddened, of course, by Ringo's passing, but supposed it would be easy to find a younger, prettier, even more musical canary on Leather Lane any day.

"A bird has no soul", he informed his mother, when the men returned to work, "and should not, therefore, be mourned."

Later, when Brunt had gone to his meeting and the apprentice visited his mother in St Giles, Molly Brunt told her son to leave his school work and fetch a stool to sit on. A thirteenth birthday was, she had concluded, the proper time to enlighten him about the connection between the late canary and the Brunt family history.

"Harold Moreton Brunt", she began, "you are practically a grown man."

"Yes, ma."

"You understand that grown men make mistakes?"

"Is pa in trouble? What did he do?"

"It ain't pa I'm talking of. It were the writer of a most hateful letter."

"What letter?" asked Harry.

"A long time ago, mi'duck," said Mrs Brunt, "during the occupation, when your pa and your brother was in France. I had a letter, claiming they was stealing from the quartermaster."

"Pa would rather drown than steal or tell a lie!" retorted Harry.

"I know that, and so would your brother, but them villains said they took a dead sheep!"

"It's not true!" cried Harry.

"There's worse," continued Molly Brunt. "The letter claimed they'd been tried and condemned to the firing squad! Harry, I truly believed your pa and your brother was dead. Even though I knew, if they took a sheep, it was for a generous purpose; to feed battle-weary friends, who lived on dry biscuits, while the officers feasted on beef and port wine."

The masters at school had advised Harry to respect facts, not speculation.

"I'm truly sorry, ma," he said, "but pa is here now, and my brother's in Derby. What has any of it to do with me or the canary?"

"Everything!" cried Molly. "When the parish couldn't help us, and Mrs Rogers demanded the rent, I went straight to the Bootmakers' Guild. Pa's friends agreed that Thomas Brunt would never lie nor steal, not even if his life depended on it. They helped me write a letter asking the Colonel for an explanation."

"What did the Colonel say, Ma?"

"Well!" exclaimed Molly, quite flustered by the memory. "I got to the barracks, and the sentry told me he had heard of the case, and my husband and son was both dead, without a doubt. I slapped his face and said they was certainly alive, and what's more, descended from Harry Moreton, hero of Wandiwash, and they deserved proper respect."

"Well done, ma! I bet that changed his tune."

"It did, my son. He gave me a kick and told me to scarper, before I got charged with assault."

"What did you do?"

"I ran and I ran, Harry, till I got to the river. I wanted to die, but only dropped to my knees in muck. A pair of clergymen rescued me. They tipped me into a cart and delivered me to St. Luke's."

"The asylum, ma?"

"Yes, Harry. The asylum"

There. Molly Brunt had confessed, and there would be no more dreading that her son would hear it from some gossip in the market. Harry nodded sagely, as if someone had explained trigonometry.

"The landlady was Mrs Rogers, without the gin in them days, and she sent for my sister at Derby, who took you in. Imagine poor pa's shock, when he and your brother arrived from France and found strangers, where a welcoming family should be. Of course, the minute Mrs Rogers explained, pa marched all the way to St. Luke's. When the attendant said my husband had come for me, I spat at him and said my darling was dead. But the attendant was a good Christian, Harry, and he took my arm, gave me a clean gown and helped me brush my hair. And there he was; your own dear pa, almost as dazed as myself. He said we had both grown thinner and paler because of the bloody war, but he loved me just the same as when we were married, and whatever the hospital made of it, he had come to fetch me home."

Harry began to understand why his ma's temper got so bad, when his shoelaces were left undone, and why she wept when his elbow made a hole in his coat. He said how brave she'd been, and must be again, now that Ringo was gone.

"Ah, Ringo!" said Molly with a sentimental smile. "We was walking home from St Luke's, when he flew out a window, right by the corner of Grays Inn Lane. He were that frightened, he flew round and round our heads, till he couldn't fly no more, and he fell right into my pocket. That's when I laughed for the first time, Harry. Pa said we would call the bird Ringo for all the circles he flew. We agreed it were an omen, and the family would have good luck as long as that canary lived."

EDWARDS

Cripplegate, London

On the last day of April 1819, George Edwards, the model-maker rode from Windsor to London. He was more than usually savage with his whip, not through any particular haste, but because he was in a fury of humiliation. His petition to make a bust of the Regent had failed. The note from His Royal Highness's secretary was pure condescension, as if Edwards were some Nobody from Nowhere. Had the man not read the recommendations of satisfied clients or the letter from his friend and associate, Sir Herbert Taylor, private secretary to the King? Was he ignorant of the exquisite figurines Edwards had created of the Regent's late, lamented daughter, and of the old King himself in happier times, both of which adorned drawing rooms all over Britain and America? Was the Regent ungrateful for the goodwill created by George Edwards's work for a family that had all but forfeited public respect? Or was the son so bitter towards the father that anyone who served His Majesty must automatically be excluded from the custom of the Prince?

In his haste, Edwards had accepted a long-standing, but derisory offer for his work-shop on Eton High Street. The profit left enough to pay off the noisiest debts and survive until his prosperity was restored by a new idea. To entertain any hope of success, he knew he must learn to manage his temper. Sentiment was for fools, and emotion, in any extremity, the enemy of ambition.

Nevertheless, Edwards's pride demanded he respond to Prinny's rejection, as well as compose a careful letter to Sir Herbert, explaining his departure from Berkshire, conveying best wishes for His Majesty's continued recovery, and the hope that their association might continue in some other form. He rehearsed the contents of both in his mind as he rode into Smithfield in search of mutton and to Moorgate for stationery.

At last, he arrived in Cripplegate, with the distinctive medley in the air of brewer's malt, stale fish and piss. When he rode into the livery on Chiswell Street, the manager, a small, sneery fellow, gave Edwards's mount a cursory glance and walked off, barking at the stable hands to sweep faster or get their pay docked. Undeterred, Edwards followed the manager and boasted that although his horse was fourteen years old, it had been bred and schooled at the royal stables.

"Yes, but is she harness broke?" asked the manager. "Ain't no market in London for mounts. If she can't drive, that nag's less use to me than a hedgehog. I'd have to train her before there's a penny profit."

Eventually, the manager offered five shillings and a discount on any cabs the gentleman might hire in future. Edwards grinned, accepted six shillings and a stable hand to carry his bags.

The maze of alleys was thick with the smell from the vinegar works on Old Street. He had forgotten it; the stink that had filled Cornelius Thwaite's studio on sordid afternoons. He stopped and wretched.

"Alright, mister?" enquired the stable hand, hoping the customer wouldn't cop it, before he parted with a tip.

Having abandoned her gin palace during the war, Mrs G lived in a tall wooden house among six identical premises in an alley with no air that was known as Banks Court. There was no welcome for the prodigal son, whose saddlebags contained his mother's favourite gin and a packet of chops. His brother, William snoozed on the rocker by a dead fire in the parlour and groaned when he was nudged. Ma was probably down the Crown and Sceptre, he yawned, whipping up custom. If George wanted, William would run and fetch her back. George said he had eaten nothing since breakfast, and nobody cooked a mutton chop like ma. Obedient as a lamb, William hurried away.

Edwards took a swig of the gin and sat at the table to begin his correspondence. The letter to the King's secretary was straightforward, but as he planned his second, to the Regent, he wondered if he should bother. Even if he persuaded Prinny to pose for sketches, who, beyond a handful of sycophants and royal mistresses would buy the figurines? The people hate the Regent, he thought; they hate his extravagance, his maltreatment of his wife, his hypocrisy and above all, his failure to inspire a population that had been dragged to its knees. Why bother with a royal libertine, when his customers needed inspiration on their mantelpieces, champions of a brighter future?

His ma and William were at the door. Without a greeting, Mrs G looked her first-born over, fingered the mutton and sent his brother off again for taters. When they were alone, she told George to pour some gin into her cup.

"I knew you'd be back," she said. "You always are. This time, get yourself a proper occupation."

"Did you have something in mind?" George Edwards's sarcasm was not veiled.

"Don't use that tone with me, my boy. With all the plotting and sedition in the streets, what London needs is more constables. William's making a success of it, and your brain's double the size. There ain't much pay in it, but the work's steady. And as far as I can see, there are perks."

"I'll think about it."

"You got to pull your head out of them clouds, George. Even if no wife will have you, there's me to think about, not getting no younger."

"No man keeping you warm at night, then?"

Mrs G scowled. "Don't think you can stay here forever without a job," she said, "exploiting your poor ma, what's hardly got two farthings to rub together."

Although his mother never discussed her financial arrangements, Edwards knew that she had plenty of farthings to rub together, and guineas, too. He did not know that like most Londoners at the time, Mrs G was feeling the pinch. Her business, which operated on the outskirts of the law, was in decline, not because of the recession, but because she was being blackmailed and could not pay the men who occasionally served as bodyguards. In other words, Mrs G's sons had become a convenient deterrent to anyone intent on visiting at night to strangle her. Two constable sons would solve all her problems, present and future.

George and William Edwards agreed that after supper, a visit to town was preferable to the tales of sacrifice and woe that would dominate an evening with ma. William had a professional commitment, which might provide an entertaining prelude to their night of pleasure, he said, and demonstrate the surprising rewards of life as a London constable.

CHAPTER FOUR

Friday, 30th April, 1819
(continued)

THISTLEWOOD

Horsham Gaol

The private was executed on the last day of April, 1819 by a hang-man so inexperienced that the event lasted over an hour. When reports of the botched execution circulated in Horsham Gaol, Arthur Thistlewood wept.

Some hours later, unable to settle his mind to sleep, he began to compose a complaint to Sidmouth, a seething protest at the agonising death of a faithful citizen, who, had he defended his comrades as selflessly on the battlefield, would have been proclaimed a hero. As he sought for the phrases most likely to shift the Home Secretary's opinion, Thistlewood found his thinking paralysed. Why waste this last sheet of paper, when there was no hope that his words would even leave the gaol?

He took refuge in thoughts of his wife. The recall of Susan's tender voice, her crooked little smile and soft, submitting body was probably all that stood between Arthur Thistlewood and an episode of insanity. He dipped his pen and began:

"My Dearest Susan, with each day, I love and long for you more than ever."

As he attempted to continue, words swarmed from all directions, forming a maze of disconnected vocabulary. Usually Thistlewood controlled language with ease. Tonight, he felt dazed, as an army general might if his soldiers were suddenly replaced by a herd of elephants. He put down his pen, and as he closed his eyes to summon calm, there came a vivid memory.

May, 1817

Thames Embankment, London

They were standing at a jetty on the south bank of the river. The storm that had broken the long drought made the ground slippery beneath their feet. It was night, and beneath the gas light, raindrops lingered like diamonds on the lamppost. Susan's eyes shone brighter still. They shone that way because of the new life she was about to beginning with Arthur and his young son, Julian. When Arthur was released without charge following a riot at Spa Field, Susan's parents, prosperous butchers in Horncastle, had made a proposal. If Arthur promised to renounce politics and accept apothecary work in Boston, they would donate three tickets at forty pounds apiece, to cross the Atlantic. The little family had said goodbye to the few friends they could trust in London, and now Arthur, Susan and Julian Thistlewood waited to be ferried to the ship that would sail them to the land of hope and opportunity. All the family's possessions were packed into the great black trunk that Julian and Arthur lifted when they heard the watery strokes of the ferryman. As they carried the trunk down the steps, and the ferry burst through the shimmering reflection of the gaslight, they heard a shout, harsh and alarming, behind them. Julian begged his father to jump into the river and swim to the safety of the ship. But the men who wanted Arthur Thistlewood carried daggers. Their knuckles were at his neck, and he was arrested on a charge of High Treason.

Susan ran after them, begging them to leave Arthur alone; he was a devoted husband and father, a talented apothecary, heading for a new life overseas. She would give them her silver cross and chain, if only they would pretend they had never seen him. It was pointless. Two ruffians dragged him by the collar and pulled along the quay, another hauled the great black trunk up the steps and away. Thistlewood shouted into the air, begging Susan to forget him, leave him now, and take Julian to the new life they could lead in America. Susan ran alongside him, refusing ever to abandon the man she loved more than daylight. Thistlewood insisted he would be hanged in a month, and the ship's passage, her opportunity for a new life, would be lost forever if she failed to climb into the ferry. When Susan refused, Thistlewood pulled himself free, turned on her, ordering her to stop whining and stop being a sentimental fool. She had promised to obey him, and now he was telling her to take herself and his son to America. They were neither wanted here, nor necessary.

His captors tied Thistlewood with chain, and as they dragged him away to the Tower, young Julian was left to comfort his stepmother, who stood on the riverside, stiff and silent as a stone. Eventually the ferryman shouted up. While he was truly sorry for their misfortune, he had other passengers to fetch and would they please make up their mind. Julian waved him away.

Friday, 30th April, 1819
(continued)

Horsham Gaol

As he thought about that arrest, the subsequent court case and its collapse on a technicality, Thistlewood considered the price his wife and child had paid for his ideals. It would be better for them if he had been hanged. Susan was still a beauty and could easily remarry; a prosperous merchant perhaps, or a lawyer, and here he was, two years later, imprisoned again, at Lord Sidmouth's pleasure, and apparently, his wife loved him still.

He wanted to find words to comfort her, but he also longed for a reply, for the assurance that his family was not suffering as he feared they might without his protection, especially that Julian was continuing his lessons and had not been forced into some deadening occupation. Even if he could find the right phrases, and even if Susan received them and replied, how would he identify what was true in her letter, and what was intended to ease his mind?

Eventually, those few first words of love seemed adequate, and he added simply,

"Always your faithful husband, Arthur Thistlewood."

INGS

Chancery Lane, London

Their joyful anticipation crumbled, when the coach that carried the Hampshire butcher and his wife left the green fields behind and proceeded through the streets of Southwark. The enormous scale of the capital, the hustle, bustle, noise and stench of it silenced them, until they crossed London Bridge and Celia ventured that her home town had doubled in size and filth since she was a girl. The King himself could not procure her removal here. Ings replied that having come so far, they must stay long enough to hear the lawyer out.

When they had found Mr Pyke's premises in a court off Chancery Lane, and began mounting the stairs, Mrs Ings's opinion began to shift. The steps and walls were of the best oak, fresh polished, and she was welcomed on the second floor by a friendly, furry-chinned clerk, not much older than their very own Bill, who gave them hot tea in china cups and asked for patience, while the master finished with another client.

Ings explained to his wife that no matter how generous the terms of her uncle's will, she must not expect to sink into such a fine piece of furniture every day of her life. Celia pulled a defiant face, but being overcome by the surroundings, made no reply. When the office door opened and they were summoned by the lawyer in person, her hand reached out to grip her husband's, which was as clammy as raw liver.

Mr Pyke was a smiling fellow, round as an egg, with a head to match and not a whisker in sight. He welcomed the Hampshire couple as if they were gentry, instead of modest traders, who had travelled for hours in ill-fitting clothes. Ings commented that the lawyer's physique demonstrated his appreciation of good beef. Mr Pyke conveyed his gratitude to first-class butchers, such as Mr Ings and their late uncle, Silas Stone.

In moments, Celia was transformed; chattering as if she and Mr Pyke had known each other for years. He had taken the liberty of booking a room for them at Cooper's Hotel on Bouverie Street and said it would be an honour if they might dine together at The Black Lion, which was connected, though the entrance was separate, on the next street along. From the way she rose, beaming, from her chair, Ings knew that his wife felt exactly as hopeful as he did.

TIDD

The Mitre Tavern, Fleet Street

Richard Tidd, Acting Chairman of the Water Lane Group arrived at the Mitre early. Secretary, William Edwards, had offered to stand him a drink. While William was a carefree bachelor, the bootmaker was a family man with almost no work and could rarely afford tavern ale. He waited in a corner where, in the early evening throng, the landlord would not trouble him.

Time had served Tidd well, though his long back had curved from perpetual bending, and, dependent on his mood and the circumstances, the lazy eye produced an air of either mischief, mystery or menace.

Today, it erred towards menacing because Tidd was irritated by a pair of articled lawyers on the other side of the bar. The high and mighty diction of the young men, the presumption of superiority and easy access to privilege were, to Tidd, equally fascinating and repulsive. The lies of just such a fellow had dispatched him to three years in a hellish dungeon. The self-control he had learnt there, his close association with the late Thomas Spence and passion for universal suffrage all contributed to Tidd's appointment as Thistlewood's deputy. He was not entirely comfortable in the role, which, in the chairman's absence obliged a man of action to supervise endless debates and stop the men from fighting among themselves.

It was precisely that conflict that interested William Edwards's secret paymaster at Bow Street. Since arriving in London, Tidd had never discussed his history, nor been questioned about it, but the authorities knew him as a volatile character who, apart from the assault charges in Nottingham, had escaped conviction for his role in a plot to murder the king and had twice been charged with fraudulent voting at Parliamentary elections. There would be a decent bonus for Constable Edwards, if he produced enough information to put Tidd back behind bars.

Tidd never doubted that William Edwards was a lamp-lighter by trade and was pleased to meet his older brother, returned only today to London. Before he would take the beer with which they had filled his pot at the bar, Tidd produced his size-stick and offered to measure their feet. Accepting that neither brother was in need of new boots just now, Tidd returned the stick to his rucksack and downed the beer without stopping for air.

"I needed that!" he said.

A ruckus had arisen on the other side of the bar. Edwards indicated the same young men, whose arrogance had irritated Tidd. A newcomer was bragging about cheating his tailor by refusing to pay for repairs until the man produced a sovereign that had allegedly been left in a pocket. As the youth described the bewilderment of the poor, duped tailor, his companions laughed in high-pitched guffaws.

"Parasites!" growled Tidd.

"Don't you feel like smashing their heads in?" asked William.

"Certainly, I do" said Tidd, "them and all their kind!"

"There's three of them and three of us," said Edwards, always quick to read his brother's intentions. "They're half our size and strength. Let's give them each a good punch for their crime against an innocent tradesman!"

"Which one's yours, Tiddy?" asked William, enjoying the larks and smelling his bonus.

Richard Tidd was not so easily roused.

"There's not one of 'em worth it," he said.

"You're not frightened of a few school-boys?" asked George Edwards. "I saw plenty of their type in my shop at Eton, purchasing caricatures of the Headmaster."

"What good will it do?" asked Tidd. "For that small-fry, we spend 't night, or longer, behind bars? Ignore them!"

"Shouldn't they be taught a lesson?" asked William, "stopped from swindling decent, hard-working tradesmen?"

"I say no!" replied Tidd firmly. "Whatever we do can't help that tailor now, and I won't chair no meeting with blood on my face. We have an influential guest."

"We do?" asked Edwards, his tone suddenly earnest.

"Richard Carlile," said Tidd.

Edwards was impressed. A controversial journalist and editor, Carlile had made the judiciary whirr like dervishes in their efforts to convict him of blasphemy and sedition.

"If you're sympathetic to reform, Mr Edwards," continued Tidd, "you must attend 't meeting. Mr Carlile might welcome a contribution to 't *Sherwin's Weekly* about your experiences in Eton."

"Alas, my friend, I'm not a writer, but an artist and a model-maker," replied Edwards, "though it's true, I'd welcome fresh opportunities."

"Perhaps Mr Carlile needs illustrations," offered Tidd.

Beneath his grateful smile, Edwards sensed the beginnings of an idea.

"I'll attend your meeting with pleasure," he said, "unless you have concerns about security –"

"Certainly, we do!" interjected Tidd. "Ever since Sidmouth went to 't Home Office, London's been stuffed with spies. We take every precaution."

"My brother has the highest credentials," said William, though his concentration was distracted by the continued whooping of the young fops, whose number was increasing.

"Being our secretary's brother is enough, Mr Edwards," said Tidd. "It will be an honour to count you in our number."

"Thank you, Tiddy, said William, "and since I'm unable to attend this evening, perhaps George may take my place at the door."

"You're not coming?" asked Tidd, aghast. "What am I to say to Mr Carlile?"

Quick as gunfire, George Edwards produced an explanation.

"One of the lamplighters fell under a horse," he said. "He'll recover soon enough, but William has offered to work two shifts tonight."

"George may not know the men's names," said William, "but he'll stand for no nonsense and he has an uncommon head for figures."

"With your consent, of course, Richard," said Edwards with a degree of caution.

As Tidd agreed with a smile, Edwards felt an odd sense of victory, He made silent thanks to His Majesty's private secretary, for the lesson that a man's face does not need to reflect the activity of his spirit.

As Tidd and his brother left the Mitre to head along Fleet Street, William Edwards thought that perhaps George had a nose for the job after all. He would nail Tidd another day. Tonight, he would mingle with the clerks, discover the names of their fathers and employers and indulge in some private blackmail.

Fully appraised of Tidd's duties as deputy, as Edwards followed Tidd through the arch at Water Lane, he had another burning question.

"What good reason" he asked, "explains your chairman's absence from a meeting attended by Richard Carlile?"

"What a soul of discretion your brother is!" remarked Tidd. "Our chairman is held at Horsham Gaol. His name is Arthur Thistlewood."

An enthusiastic reader of newspapers, Edwards experienced a rush of excitement, as Tidd led him into the yard of the Black Lion Tavern.

BRUNT

Holborn

Tom Brunt dodged the Friday evening traffic of Holborn and hurried down Fetter Lane. The new poem, folded inside his vest pocket was a boot-making metaphor, entitled "Ninety-Seven or Three." It explored the theme, much discussed in radical circles that for every three men of wealth, ninety-seven lived in poverty. The topic had dominated last week's meeting at which Brunt found himself unable to articulate his opinion in plain language. While he accepted without question that in every one hundred men, the poorest ninety-seven were the most productive members of society, he rejected Mr Tidd's suggestion that the remaining three were inevitably disciples of the devil.

When the vote came, and Brunt abstained, there had been hurtful remarks by Richard Tidd, including the threat of boxed ears. Brunt had responded that some of his most loyal customers belonged to that smaller number, and he had seen no evidence of an alliance with Satan. Some were even kind enough to order boots they did not need, simply to secure employment for himself and his apprentice. The laughter that followed his outburst had echoed in Brunt's mind as he walked back to Holborn, scarlet with indignation and for once oblivious to the beggars who lined his route.

On the Saturday after his humiliation, Brunt had asked his wife and son to enjoy their garden outing without him, because he had urgent business at his desk. As he replenished the ink-well, he speculated that since Mr Carlile's father had been in the shoe trade, the editor might appreciate a metaphor in which Great Britain represented a boot. The boot would consist of three pieces of leather (representing the rich) and ninety-seven stitches (representing the poor). If one of those stitches came loose, they would all come undone, the leather would collapse and the boot become unfit for purpose.

The composition was challenging, but when, at last, he read the poem aloud to his family, his studious son considered it a masterpiece of political writing, and Mrs Brunt said that if it did not appear in the next edition of *Sherwin's*, she would eat her hat, or at least stand shameless at the gates of the Courts of Justice and declare Mr Carlile a nincompoop.

Now, on this final evening of April 1819, as Tom Brunt turned on to Fleet Street, with the much-revised poem tight against his heart, he acknowledged a few misgivings. Perhaps last week's argument had been forgotten by all but his injured self. Perhaps some new and urgent matter would dominate the agenda, and by insisting on a recital, he would seem foolish. Deciding that in all events, he faced an opportunity to meet a famous editor, Brunt took a deep breath and turned down Water Lane.

THE GROUP / CARLILE
Black Lion Hall, Water Lane, London

The men who crowded into the yard and jostled at the door had eaten little or nothing all day, but each found the price of a cauliflower for his subscription. The cash was collected at the door by George Edwards, who checked every name and address against a ledger. As Tidd marshalled the men into the hall, everyone strained to catch a glimpse of the guest of honour. A former tinsmith with origins as humble as their own, Richard Carlile had become a highly successful journalist, who mocked the establishment with his wit and insights, while his nimble manoeuvres had kept him, so far, out of gaol.

The huddle of Irishmen, who strolled down every Friday from Gee's Court for an afternoon at the Boar's Head and an evening at Water Lane, claimed that their usual corner had been stolen by the printers, who wanted the best view of Mr Carlile. Fists were drawn, and Tidd was summoned to moderate. Rules about fighting and bad language had relaxed under his management, but occasionally, the deputy was forced to remind the membership that a man without self-control weakened the Group, creating division where unity was paramount.

Somewhat uncomfortably enthroned on the platform in an upholstered chair borrowed from the Black Lion, Richard Carlile decided against observing the clamour too obviously. His attention would only prolong the event, and unless it started promptly, he would miss his deadline, and he was concerned. Important information had not arrived from Liverpool for his editorial on the Orange Order. The Water Lane Group might make an alternative subject, he supposed, given the reformers' increased dependency on tavern radicals. Without a quote from Arthur Thistlewood, the article might lack bite; still, from the mouths of simple men come nuggets of gold, and there is little an editor fears more than an empty space where words belong.

First on the agenda was the continued theme of inequality. Thomas Brunt raised his hand. At a nod from Tidd, he took the poem from his pocket and leapt, bold as a gladiator, on to the platform. As the membership cheered and jeered, Brunt's secret heart thumped like a drum. Tidd advised him to speak slowly and not mumble, and had to ring his bell for silence. When the recital was over, Brunt looked nervously into his audience, who neither clapped nor scorned, but waited for someone else to express the first opinion.

Eventually, the deputy responded that as a fellow tradesman, he appreciated the allusions in the poem and the comparison of Great Britain to a well-made piece of footwear. But Richard Tidd could never be content to compare himself with an insignificant stitch, while the rogues occupying the minority, could lay claim to the all-important leather. Was Brunt suggesting that the substance of the boot; the very pith and strength of Britain, was the aristocracy? At the word "aristocracy", the hall filled with a cacophony of barks, hisses and growls.

Richard Carlile, who understood a poet's anguish better than most, raised his hand. At once, the commotion subsided, as members strained to hear him. Though a firebrand in print, Carlile spoke with a soft, stuttering, west country voice. With a little editing, he said, the piece might be suitable for publication. Should the author arrange to visit his shop, he would be glad to discuss the matter in private. Grinning uncontrollably, Brunt shook Carlile's hand and, in joyful triumph, raised his arms to face his audience. Accompanied by shouts and whistles, the proud poet returned to the floor, even telling Tidd, as he passed, that he was a very good man.

When, with help of his bell and a litany of threats, Tidd had restored order, he invited another guest to the platform and introduced the Secretary's brother, who had made himself familiar while collecting the subscriptions.

George Edwards presented himself as a model-maker, who had returned to London in the hope of changing society for the better. He was as worried, he said, as any decent Englishman by the inequalities that were tearing society apart, and he was honoured to be considered by the most highly-respected radical group in London. In the first instance, he would be seeking work and accommodation locally, and while he appreciated that many members were in a similar position, he would welcome advice.

Carlile listened with faint surprise. He knew Edwards's face and form, but not, until now, his name. Until a couple of years ago, the model-maker had been shadowy presence around Fleet Street, who shunned company; the kind of fellow who would step over an injured man sooner than offer help. There had been no indication then of political engagement. Perhaps time and Berkshire had civilized him.

When a show of hands confirmed his membership, George Edwards promised to be a loyal participant, who would undertake any act of rebellion required, no matter what the risk to his person. The Irish stamped their feet and cheered until Tidd was obliged to ring his bell for peace to hear Mr Carlile, who had raised a hand in query.

In the same gentle tones, Carlile asked whether George Edwards had found different ways of thinking in the Thames Valley. In London, the reform movement was unified in its acknowledgement – following bloodshed in America, France and Ireland - that the only way to achieve change was to reject violence in favour of debate and persuasion. As the great orator, Henry Hunt had often demonstrated, violence was counter-productive and un-British. Furthermore, Mr Carlile had understood the Water Lane Group to be an arena for education and debate, not a breeding ground for insurrection.

James Fairlea, bookseller's assistant of Johnson's Court cried "Aye, aye!" while Tom Dwyer, bricklayer of Gee's Court waved his cap and shouted that Mr fancy-dancy Carlile might be the son of a bootmaker, but sure it was plain that just like Squire Hunt, he had never told his children there was nought in the pantry but bare shelves and empty pots.

The hall erupted in a mighty roar. Torn between embarrassment before their guest and commitment to democracy, Tidd allowed the men to shout for a minute before ringing the bell and announcing that another outburst would bring the meeting to an early end.

Richard Carlile could stomach no more. The momentum for reform would never be served by reporting the antics of such an uninformed rabble. Annoyed to have wasted an hour, he declined refreshment, informed Tidd of his urgent deadline, advised him to focus more on discipline and made his escape. George Edwards hurried after him, pressed him into a corner and asked for a business appointment. Carlile, who never allowed personal distaste to obstruct a story, thought that having lived within reach of Windsor, Edwards – if he could be trusted - might have a juicy royal tale to tell. The appointment was granted, and Carlile fled. By the time he turned on to Fleet Street, he had redirected his thoughts to the Orange Order, and cursed that he had not thought to question a couple of the impassioned Irishmen.

In the hush of disappointment that followed Carlile's departure, Tidd announced that the debate would commence as soon as beer was supped. He would need to make some urgent clarifications to Edwards, but first, Tidd beckoned Tom Brunt and congratulated him on the fluency of his recital.

"Richard Tidd is a man of boots and of action," he said, "but not of letters - which means that unlike Mr Carlile, he is incapable of telling good verse from bad. Will you accept my apology, Citizen Brunt, for doubting you?"

His heart alive with the prospect of publication, Brunt replied that he never took literary criticism personally, and none was taken. Then, remarking that they were virtually neighbours at Brook's Market, he asked whether Mr Tidd might be available tomorrow to help with an order for boots. Tidd, whose greatest fear was not gaol, but the division of his family in a workhouse, replied that yes, he was very available indeed.

INGS

Black Lion Tavern, Water Lane

In all their lives, neither Mr nor Mrs Ings had never once visited an eating house, and in honour of the occasion, they ordered a rack of spring lamb, a seasonal speciality of The Black Lion. Ings was satisfied with the cutting and tying of the meat, but he saw at once that his wife considered the cauliflower over-boiled and the taters inadequately mashed. As Mr Pyke described the many benefits of living in Whitechapel, Celia glanced frequently at another table, where the company had ordered pies. She was contemplating the competition, Ings deduced; a sign that removal might, after all, be imminent.

Mr Pyke provided no information about their inheritance but chatted amiably about the excellent schools in Whitechapel and knew of the General Baptist Church there. The lawyer, who had an appetite to match his stature, ordered another steak and a second bottle of claret, long after his clients had exceeded their appetite and longed for bed.

Eventually, when neither Mr nor Mrs Ings could stifle another yawn, Mr Pyke laid down his napkin, and apologized for keeping them from their slumbers. They thanked him for his kindness, to which the lawyer responded that it was all part of a day's work, and Mr Ings could examine the bill in detail when it appeared on the account. Celia could not hide her surprise, but brightened when Mr Pyke assured her that the bill was a drop in the ocean of her inheritance. She took her husband's arm and, proud as two Punches, the couple walked out of The Black Lion, leaving their companion to polish off his blancmange.

"A drop in the ocean. You hear that Jimmy?" asked Celia. "Uncle Stone has left us a proper fortune!"

Instead of taking the corridor that led directly to Cooper's Hotel, the Ings sauntered down the lane to Fleet Street, hoping that a cool night breeze might rekindle their senses. They looked up at the sky to thank the Lord for his goodness, as they always did in Portsea, even at the worst of times. On that, the Ings's first night in London, not a single star showed itself. The air smelt foul, and they scanned the firmament, hoping that at least the North Star would pierce the clouds above. All of a sudden, Ings felt a sharp pain at the back of his head.

Celia screamed; for God's sake, not to hurt them; they had no money, no, not a penny in the world! They heard the laugh of neither man nor boy, but something in between, and footsteps, running off. Then, Ings felt his wife kissing every inch of his face. His grandfather's watch was gone, she said, but it was half-broke anyway, and it mattered not a jot, as long as her dear Jimmy was breathing. Celia wanted to go back to the tavern and fetch Mr Pyke but was fearful of leaving her husband alone in the street.

That is when they met him for the first time; the man who would play such a prodigious role in their future. Celia had not seen him approach from any direction and in the moment of crisis, supposed he had dropped, like a guardian angel, from the sky. His arrival had scared the thief away and may even have prevented murder.

The stranger said he would gladly stand the injured party a restorative brandy, but he possessed not a single penny, having himself been tricked a few moments ago, perhaps by the same rascal, out of everything he owned. Celia promised a reward, if the gentleman would kindly help her husband to his bed on Bouverie Street, which she believed to be just around the corner.

If only that rascal had chosen another night for his attack. If only they had not lingered at the Black Lion but summoned the confidence to tell Mr Pyke that they had eaten enough and travelled enough and longed to rest. If only they had gone straight to their room by the corridor, instead of taking the night air. But they had not, and now they were guided by that servant of the devil to the front of their hotel, where he explained the circumstances to the door-man and guided poor James Ings upstairs, into his bed.

When the stranger lingered at the door, Celia, who anticipated riches tomorrow, unstitched the little pocket in her bodice and gave him their last half-crown. Edwards whispered a touching good-night and asked how he might be sure of the couple's continued well-being. Since they had no other address in London, Celia suggested their lawyer's office, and promised to help kind Mr Edwards again soon.

Next morning, Ings felt right as rain, but as they feasted on fresh rolls, bacon and smoked herring, Celia worried about the bill and confessed to giving away the last of their money. Ings replied that Mr Pyke had surely made an arrangement with the landlord. What was the loss of a half-crown, he asked, compared with making their first true friend in London?

EDWARDS
Off Fleet Street

What he needed most after the meeting was gin, and the country couple's distress had provided the means. He could not, for the moment, imagine what other purpose the witless pair might serve, but life, Edwards had observed, threw up the most unlikely symmetries. There was no need to sacrifice the payment for his mare, he had an address in his pocket and half a crown to spend at a gin palace near Drury Lane, where he knew a brunette, who might lift her petticoats for him.

At a quarter to midnight he was making his way along the Strand. The song he was singing was Shakespearean; the chorus of *Lo, Here the Gentle Lark*. He had learnt the verse from Tilly, who had learnt it from a singer of comic opera (though the impertinent dance that accompanied the song was certainly her own). Tilly had taken half his money, and the rest, apart from the thruppence in his pocket, had been spent on liquor and a beef supper.

He was still singing to the gentle lark and cursing the damned Regent, when all the clocks of London struck twelve times, and the last day of April became the first of May. He wondered how on earth he had arrived at the St Martin's end of the Strand, when he ought to be at St Clement's. He was leaning against the window of a clock-maker's shop, waiting for all the chimes to end so that he could start his song again, when he became aware of a cluster of men, eyeing him.

He wagered the strangers did not know a word of Shakespeare, and said that for a penny, he would teach them all a sonnet, and for tuppence lead them to the best little strumpet in town. When they responded with menacing glares, Edwards told them life was too short for troubles, and they should try cheering up. One of the men gave him a shove, and Edwards found himself pissing in his breeches. The ungrateful strangers said they were Constables Ruthven, Lavender, Bishop and Salmon of the Bow Street patrole, that the gentleman was drunk and was being taken for questioning.

"If you're the bastard patrole, I'm the Duke of Cumberland," replied Edwards.

"In that case, you'll know exactly what to do with this!" retorted one of the officers, pulling a pistol from his belt.

Edwards lunged. There was a tussle, a blast and then the splintering of glass.

At half past midnight, Edwards walked into Bow Street police station, where he gave the name Henry Ward. A series of charges were recited by the chief clerk, a stout, balding man in his early fifties named John Stafford.

"What do you say for yourself?" he asked.

"I am a friend of Sir Herbert Taylor," replied Edwards.

Stafford seemed to invite explanation.

"Private secretary to the king," continued Edwards.

"I know who the major general is, Mr Ward," replied Stafford. "Do you believe that such a friendship, if it exists, makes you less guilty?"

"Give me paper, sir, and a pen and I shall write to Windsor, asking for his recommendation, and quite possibly His Majesty's too," replied Edwards.

Nothing infuriated John Stafford more than a clever prisoner. He slammed his fist on the desk.

"I'm warning you, Ward!" he said, "Wipe that cocky face off!"

Edwards looked straight into the narrow eyes of the Bow Street clerk and said, "You are mistaken, my man, if you believe you can hold me here!"

Stafford blew his whistle, and two brutes grabbed Edwards by the collar, wrenching his arms half out of their sockets.

"There will be times, Mr Henry Ward" said Stafford, "when you will wish that bullet had went through your skull instead of a clockmaker's window."

George Edwards felt a crack on his cheek bone.

When he awoke, his head throbbed, and his thoughts were sticky and slow. One of his wrists was chained and his boots were gone. It was pitch dark, and the air was thick with shit and piss. He was lying on a board and covered by a filthy rag, too thin to be named a blanket. There was wheezing and weeping all about, and in the middle distance the haunting wail of a woman, perhaps two. Where in God's name was he, and how had he come here? Pale light streamed from above. There was a window with iron bars.

He began to remember the girl. Had the tart betrayed him? If so, with what purpose, since she had already taken his money? Tilly, who swore she had missed him every night he was in Berkshire! Next time, he would squeeze her skinny little neck. Suddenly, a man on the board beside him, thin as a skeleton, sat bolt upright and began to howl; piercing, visceral screams as if he were being eaten alive.

Desperate to escape the present, Edwards closed his eyes and recalled the distant past, reclaiming torments so vivid that they could out-scream the present nightmare. The memories came in intense, jagged sequences. Aged eight and barefoot, carrying William on his shoulders all the way to Bristol, because Mr Gordon had left, and ma could no longer feed them; William's helpless tears, the banging of his brother's tiny heels against George's chest, when he was fit to drop. The carter, who offered them a lift at Reading, until his wife could not endure the stink of filthy boys and threw them on to the road again; the blisters on his feet, the pain of empty bellies, the rage in his young, still sentient heart. Their father, with his bent back, busy with a laughing new family on his grandfather's kitchen garden, the unfamiliar work in the field, and the whipping for treading, by mistake, on corn, still growing. Then came the scowl on ma's face when they returned a year later with even bigger mouths to feed. That's when they first met Cornelius Thwaite, and George refused to call him father. He saw again the icy gleam in the sculptor's eyes, as he tugged at little Georgie's breeches for the first time, the freckled hands, as he twisted the brown leather belt tightly round his fist, the spittle and the stained, crooked teeth, as he raised the weapon. WHACK!

Edwards flinched and found himself back amid the feral screams of his neighbour and the stench of excrement. He stomach surged, his heart raced, and his body trembled, but then, on the verge of vacuum, he heard a small voice, the echo, perhaps of his youthful defiance, insisting that George Edwards would never be destroyed. As if in homage to that lost child, he swore that no matter what the cost to himself or any other mortal, he would never be forced to relive the past again and never, ever to spend another night in such an inferno.

CHAPTER FIVE

Saturday, 1ˢᵗ May, 1819

THISTLEWOOD

Stanhope Street, Lincoln's Inn Field

On Saturday evening, as she moved the buttons on her stepson's shirt half an inch to the left, Susan Thistlewood considered the impact of a letter she had been writing to her parents in Horncastle, asking if they might send new clothes for the boy. Mrs Wilkinson would plead that like any other child, Julian was growing fast. He was blameless, a sensitive lad, who missed his father and did not deserve the further constraint of poverty. Mr Wilkinson would remind his wife that Julian was not their blood-relation and that by continuing to support Susan and the child, they gave their son-in-law no incentive to relinquish politics and seek proper employment. Mrs Wilkinson would ask her husband, a prosperous butcher and prominent resident of the Horncastle, to remember his principles again, on the day their daughter died of starvation.

Picturing her mother's tears and her father's exasperation, Susan wondered if it might be wiser to throw her letter into the fire and cut down Arthur's second shirt instead. She sighed, and was picking out the very last stitch, when there were two brusque knocks at the apartment door. She stood sharply, and the little Dorset button rolled from her lap to oblivion beneath the yellow settee.

It was a young messenger, thin as a rod, with a blue woollen cap and a practised smile. He wondered, while Susan fetched his tuppence, what tragedy had fetched a fine lady to such a bleak corner of town. When the lad had taken his money and run, she saw that the message was not, as she had supposed, from one of Arthur's supporters, but from officials at Horsham Gaol. She was gripped by panic. Had Sidmouth, after all, contrived a death sentence?

Julian stood sleepily at the bottom of the stairs, woken by the visitor and inquisitive. He said nothing, but sat beside Susan on the settee, as she gathered her breath and broke the seal. Three times she read the message without altering her expression. At last, she turned.

"He's coming home, Julian! Papa is coming home!"

Sunday, 2nd May, 1819

Horsham Gaol

Arthur Thistlewood was given no reason for his early release. The Gaoler conceded that the Home Secretary had granted the reprieve unexpectedly but would neither confirm nor deny that His Lordship's aim was to avoid the humiliation of another acquittal.

As he rode out of Horsham at nine o'clock on Sunday, Lord Sidmouth and all he represented did not enter his mind. Three words encapsulated Thistlewood's aspirations: Susan, Julian and America.

INGS

Baker's Row Whitechapel, London

On Sunday, they made themselves known at the Baptist Church and completed arrangements for Uncle Stone's grave, which Celia had found disappointingly plain. The congregation as more reticent than they had hoped. When the pastor heard about the family's connection to the area, the parishioners hovering around him raised disapproving eyebrows and turned away. A seed was set in James Ings's mind that Uncle Stone was not much admired in the district. There would be time, soon enough, for the Ings family to create its independent reputation, and those first few days in the new property were spent almost entirely on their knees. There was no point fetching the children, Celia opined, let alone filling the place with raw meat, until every square inch was scrubbed.

"In all my years," she proclaimed, as they hauled buckets from the well on the corner, "I ain't never seen such a forest of flies as in my uncle's slaughterhouse. Fetch me a fisherman, Jimmy, and we shall profit from the weight of maggots on them walls."

"The odds of finding a fisherman in Whitechapel," replied Ings, "are smaller than finding a spot of dust in my wife's household!"

Celia chuckled. She wasted no time cleaning the pair of striped aprons she found, stuffed under the counter, but shook them out and handed one to her husband. As they worked, Mrs Ings revealed her plan. Until the shop was re-established, Annie would continue helping in the kitchen. As soon as they could manage it, the girls would concentrate on their education and aspire to marriages, if not into the gentry, then to lawyers or even city merchants. Bill would complete his training, and if he proved diligent, they might surprise him on his fifteenth birthday with a new sign; James Ings and Son.

Ings responded that while he admired his wife, as always, for her positive thinking, it was unwise to make detailed plans until they knew the size of their fortune.

By two o'clock on Monday, Celia was satisfied with the state of the premises, and they made their way to Chancery Lane, where late in the afternoon, their hands, raw and swollen, shook Mr Pyke's, which was as soft and plump, Celia would recall later, as a silk pin-cushion. They accepted a sufficient advance for Mrs Ings to collect the children from Portsea, and for Mr Ings to begin setting up their business.

Monday, 3rd May, 1819

EDWARDS / MRS G
Banks Court, Cripplegate

When he did not come home that Friday night, his mother and brother presumed that George had spent the night down cock alley, and when he appeared on Saturday morning, they blamed his grey features on the wrong kind of gin, all of which was partly true. Edwards informed them at once that while he admired William's choice of occupation, he had no intention of joining the Constabulary himself. Within a few days, he would set up his business and be gone. Mrs G knew better than to interrogate her first-born, but she did wonder about the heavy box he carried upstairs on Monday morning, and with that in mind, put an ear to his door.

Mrs G's curiosity did not last long because she had a business to run. A lottery known as Mercy's Go, was conducted in close secrecy in a room, where the gullible might offer family treasures or "borrowed" goods in exchange for the chance to win a fortune in a draw. Such transactions led more frequently to suicide than success, and Mrs. G's prosperity had been built on the shifting sands of deception and misery. If Mrs. G gave any thought to the consequences of her trade, it was to blame victims for the consequences of their foolish greed. Although business so far in 1819 had been sluggish, there were small signs of improvement; two customers already today, and so far, no hint of intimidation.

The third person to arrive wanted a price for a damask table-cloth that had belonged to the Duke of York. The King's favourite son had been in the news lately for breaking his arm shortly after the announcement that Parliament had granted him a salary of ten thousand a year to care for his sick father. Being both royal and topical, the customer contested, the item was worth three times an ordinary tablecloth. Mrs G was still bargaining, when her peace was shattered by an explosion. Convinced that her enemies were upon her, she dived into the pantry. Hearing a second, even louder explosion Mrs G, who was a Roman Catholic, confessed her sins and prepared to die. Then she heard a shout of triumph in the room above, unmistakably the voice of her older son. When, in fury, she emerged from her pantry, the customer had vanished and so had the royal tablecloth and a locket that had lain careless on the mantel.

Tuesday, 4ᵗʰ May, 1819

INGS

Baker's Row Whitechapel, London

When, on Tuesday morning, they kissed one another's cheeks, and his wife climbed into the Portsmouth coach, Ings tried not to look pleased at the parting, which was almost the first – and certainly the longest - of their marriage. As he waited for Celia's fellow passengers to settle and the baggage to be laden, he allowed himself a degree of excitement. He had never imagined himself at the most famous market in all England. How his Hampshire colleagues would smart with envy, when he told them! And how he longed for Cousin Jack and Pa Ings to share the adventure! When at last, the coach vanished around the corner, and he stopped waving, Ings found his confidence wilting. All his life, he had attended markets, but in Hampshire, every man in the trade was as family. At Smithfield, he would have to prepare himself for customs that may seem peculiar to Hampshire ways of thinking. And it would be clear, every time Ings opened his mouth and spoke, that he was an outsider, which might be detrimental to his prospects. Being an ineffective mimic, there was little he could do to improve his dialect, and besides; why should he disguise his proud Hampshire roots? The people of London would have to take James Ings as he was, or do without.

When he saw, on the other side of the lane, a small barber shop, Ings decided that a change to his rustic appearance might enhance his authority. While Celia would consider the purchase of new clothes premature, a fashionable set of whiskers could be claimed a useful investment. Before he could be plagued by doubt, Ing crossed the road. The barber promised a style appropriate to an aspiring London tradesman. He cut Ings's hair close to his neck, shaved off the moustache and trimmed the wilful whiskers into elegant, perfectly matching sideburns.

Thus transformed, Ings strode off in a south-westerly direction towards Chancery Lane, where their lawyer had invited him to sign some documents. Mr Pyke made no comment about his changed appearance but advised that no man of business should be without a pocket watch and directed Mr Ings to a pawn shop at the corner of Fetter Lane. The item cost more than Ings expected, but the broker said it was Swiss, and the gentleman was in London now, where customers and business partners take more note of a fellow in possession of a fine timepiece.

Ings made his way eastwards along Fleet Street, and was about to cross to Ludgate Circus, when he caught site, on the other side of the street, of his only friend in London. Mr Edwards complimented Ings on the hair-cut and the new watch, remarking that he had never seen such an exquisite mechanism. He advised keeping the purchase out of sight, the city being thick, as Mr Ings knew too well, with thieves and vagabonds. Ings promised that he would, and enquired whether Mr Edwards had better news

"I do, indeed!" replied Edwards. "My circumstances are transformed, Mr Ings, and I should like to discuss a business arrangement. No doubt, you have a pressing appointment, and I shan't hold you back for long. Please join me for a celebratory drink, and I shall stand you the best suet pudding in London.

Ings found himself unable to refuse such an invitation, but as Edwards guided him down a little alley at St Bride's, he decided on a forthright response to the business enquiry. He chose his words carefully, so that he should not appear lofty, nor give a friend false hopes with an evasive reply.

"I don't want you taking no offence, Mr Edwards", he said, "but I ain't in search of opportunities at the moment. My wife and I have high hopes for the butchery, which, by agreement with our son and heir, is entirely a family concern. When we're properly settled at Whitechapel, perhaps we shall find some common enterprise, then."

George Edwards led Ings into The Old Bell, an ancient tavern, where, he said, Sir Christopher Wren had enjoyed the suet puddings, which were still acknowledged as the finest, possibly in all England. When Ings wagered that his wife, Celia's were tastier, Edwards replied that he would welcome a chance to sample them and took a note of the address in Whitechapel. When the landlord, Mr Harding heard about the Hampshire pies, he invited Ings, as soon as his business was up and running, to bring a specimen to The Old Bell, and an opportunity might arise. When Mrs Harding called her husband to settle a kerfuffle at the bar about prices, Ings sighed contentedly and remarked that he was beginning to feel at home in London. Edwards lifted his pot of gin, repeated his offer of a golden opportunity, and when it was again declined, smiled and wished Ings the best of British luck with his shop.

Smithfield was vast, but unlike Portsmouth market, which bustled every day of the week, there was not a single cow, sheep nor hog in sight, and hardly a stall was occupied. When Ings noticed a groom with less muscle than a spider, struggling to pitch hay on to his cart, he went to lend a hand. The young man explained that Mondays and Fridays were the days for carcasses or live beasts, but Tuesdays were only good for horses. Ings, who had given no thought yet to a mount, gave the lad a penny for a treat, and went to investigate. As a consequence, instead of walking back up the hill to Whitechapel, Ings rode his new four-year-old, with a cart-load of hay behind. The colour of a late acorn with two white ankles, Jupiter was strong, with an evidently gentle nature. He would make a grand surprise for the children.

Ings spent that Tuesday evening making the stable comfortable for the horse, and sanding down Uncle Stone's cart, ready for the sign-painter. When his eyelids began to droop, he carried the candle upstairs to the apartment. As he rested his head on the pillow, his thoughts turned to Celia, and to everyone fussing round her, all the children, Lizzie, Aunt Alice and his parents. In the moments before sleep took command of it, his mind filled with unexpected melancholy and then with dismay that he was giving up everything he knew to live far-away, among strangers. Refusing to submit to negative thinking, Ings dismissed his agitation as homesickness, which would be remedied as soon as his family arrived, and their new life of prosperity commenced.

Wednesday, 5ᵗʰ May, 1819

THISTLEWOOD / SUSAN
Stanhope Street, Lincoln Fields

In the morning, Mrs Thistlewood found her husband asleep at his desk and the basket overflowing with paper that ought not to be wasted. In the three nights since his return, Arthur had spent barely an hour in her bed and evidently used the time to write and rewrite a resignation speech. Five thousand copies would pay their fares to America, he had said, and until the speech was delivered, the emigration plan must be kept secret. All callers were to be turned away with the argument that Arthur Thistlewood was collecting his strength.

In eleven years of marriage, he had always attended du-tifully to his correspondence, but the little mountain on the sideboard remained untouched. The neglect began to concern Susan Thistlewood, but her husband was not approachable, and the pile was growing. As Arthur walked with Julian to school, she embarked on a rare rebellion.

She opened a letter and read it, and then another and another. They were simple messages of joy and gratitude at Thistlewood's early release, some poorly written, all heartfelt. An old soldier in Kent predicted that under his guidance, Britain would become great again, fair and decent, a fit home for its heroes. An apprentice wheelwright in Suffolk blessed the day, when he and his unborn sons would vote in parliamentary elections, thanks to the sacrifice of Arthur Thistlewood and his allies.

Susan was spell-bound. Next, she removed the string on a cylindrical parcel, which had arrived yesterday from Manchester. She remembered it because she gave the messenger biscuits for his children. The letter came attached to four pages of signatures and marks of the illiterate. Every name was a woman's. The accompanying message seemed, to Susan Thistlewood's gentle heart, barely credible. Thousands of mothers in the north of England sent their children to factories, to work thirteen hours a day so that their families would not starve. Nimble little fingers were needed in the spinning rooms to tie knots in broken thread or replace full bobbins quickly with empty ones. Their bodies were small enough to crawl under machines to pick up cotton flue. Heat and dust filled their lungs and made them ill, often fatally, because no-one could afford a doctor. At eight o'clock, the children were allowed a short break for breakfast, while the machines were cleaned and at one o'clock, more briefly, for lunch. Bad time-keepers of all ages were beaten, regardless of their health. Slackers were beaten too, no matter how exhausted. The final paragraph called for united action by every wife and mother in England. They must convince the law-makers that no man, woman or child should work more than ten hours on week-days or five on Saturdays. On a separate page, there was a request for Mr Thistlewood or his representative to deliver the enclosed petition to Downing Street. Hot tears burnt Susan Thistlewood's cheeks. It had never occurred to her that women could be involved in politics. If her husband was not prepared to leave his desk and take the parcel to Westminster, she would walk there herself.

Beyond complaining about a dour sermon or a poorly conceived novel, Mrs Thistlewood had never thought to nurture opinions on matters outside the home. Her father and husband, in rare compliance, considered newspapers unsuitable for Susan's sensibility. Her childhood in a prosperous market town had been sheltered. At eighteen, she had become Arthur's second wife, and after eleven years, knew little about his activities except that he risked life and liberty to promote justice, and sometimes went to prison for it. At her husband's request, she had never attended his trials. Arthur had always required their home to be a peaceful refuge, where his son could enjoy domestic harmony and a good education. When once she pressed to be allowed to support him in his public life, Arthur explained that the less his wife knew, the safer for them all, and she need never worry about deceiving her parents.

Now, anger bore down on her with an interrogation that was frightening, unfamiliar, confusing. Had she had been deceived all her life, deliberately kept ignorant and passive, to better service the needs of others? Or should she blame herself for complying too easily? Had she been lazy? Content to allow herself the luxury of delusion? And lately, by insisting on emigration, had she condemned the man she loved to a half-life on the far side of the world? Rather than fulfilling the family's dreams, would such a move destroy her husband? What hope would there be then, for Julian, or any children they might yet conceive together?

When Thistlewood arrived home, instead of a welcoming kiss, he was greeted by a wife as pale and stiff as wax. She confessed her trespass and said there would be no America, unless Arthur and Julian chose to sail without her. There would be no more secrets, and she would no longer be excluded from the substance of her husband's life. If he refused, Arthur must prepare himself for her return to Lincolnshire, as soon as the petition was delivered. She would enlist her able-bodied friends and cousins, and together, they would establish a society of eastern English women, new and powerful participants in the fight for reform.

For the longest moment, Arthur looked at his wife, as if she were some undiscovered flower from the desserts of Arabia. Then he drew her to the yellow settee, held her close and began his testament.

Monday, 18th November, 1791

Tupholme, Lincolnshire

On the day after the authorities stood by, while an angry mob burned dissenters' homes in Birmingham, Arthur Thistlewood's grandfather walked out with his hounds. It was an hour since his daughter-in-law took her last breath, and he needed to be rid of the suffocation, to stand beneath the sky again, to feel the earth beneath his boots and a fresh wind on his skin.

As he crossed the yard toward the gate, Farmer John heard the snoring of his intoxicated son in the hay-barn. He ordered the hounds to wait outside. Controlling an urge to beat the wretch, he rested his trusty oak walking stick beside a beam. But then his gnarled thumbs were pressing down on William's neck, which stretched out wantonly on the hay, the chin to one side, the mouth distorted in an infantile smile. A great pain welled high in the old man's chest, forcing him to kneel back and catch his breath. He peered at his son's carefree expression, the straight nose, long eyelashes, soft black hair and high forehead, so like Lydia's, so innocent and so smooth, but for the jagged scar, the wound that had destroyed his only surviving son and ripped their lives apart.

The chest pain surged again, as if the entire burden of his life – and all the Thistlewoods' lives – were trapped there, hammering against his ribs. He knew that if he died today, with his beloved Arthur, away studying in France, and the younger boy still at school, there would be nobody to manage the estate or work the farm. He knelt back and opened his mouth wide. At first, there came no sound, but then, rising from his deepest viscera, as if every trouble he had ever known conspired in devilish unison, Farmer John howled wild, unearthly cries, not heard in the county of Lincoln since the time of the wolves. When at last he was quiet, he heard his hounds whimpering in the yard, while Arthur Thistlewood's murderous father turned in his sleep, sighing, still smiling, dreaming, perhaps, of paradise.

With the unfamiliar warmth of tears on his face, the old man cried out; how had he offended the Heavens that his beloved wife should die so young, and now sweet Annie Burnett, too? That his oldest son and heir should drown in Jamaica, leaving William as his heir, and now Arthur's devoted mother, dead in her prime, with three orphans? The land, to which Farmer John and his father and grandfathers had committed their lives, and which in these desperate times, could only be spared by skilful management, must it all be abandoned?

That evening, as he pulled off his boots, Farmer John told his second wife to stop her false weeping and rejoice that her rival was gone. He would not attend supper, but a bowl of warm water for his feet, a plate of bread and cheese and a mug of ale should be carried to his study, where the fire must be built up sturdy and the bucket filled with logs.

He sat, as usual at the walnut writing desk and wrote in his journal.

Monday, 18th November, 1791. Wind high and cold, cloudy and dry. (Ann, the wife of my son William died this day about 1pm.) Afternoon stormy and very cold.

He composed a letter to his grandson in Paris, providing the barest facts of the death of Annie Burnett Thistlewood. Arthur's younger siblings, little Ann and John were being cared for by the Horsington grandparents, and there was no need to hurry home on their account.

Farmer John wrote nothing of his decision to have Arthur's father committed to the Leeds asylum. In a lucid moment, William Thistlewood had begged to be sent instead to Dr Harrison's private hospital in Horncastle, but the old farmer wanted his son removed from Lincolnshire, out of sight, to where there could be no possibility of a plausible confession, no scandal, no Thistlewood accused in a court of murder. The letter informed Arthur that instead of returning to boarding school after the interment, his brother, John would learn to work the farm. An option to manage the Vyners' Estate would remain open to Arthur until the day after his twenty first birthday. Farmer John enclosed a note that might be redeemed at the British Embassy in Paris, or another suitable authority, promising a further fifty pounds for his grandson's studies.

Arras, France.

On the morning when his mother collapsed with a ruptured spleen, Arthur Thistlewood sat in a smoky first floor café in northern France. Only a few feet away, Maximilien de Robespierre was listening with a fixed smile to a farm labourer, who sat awkwardly at the edge of his chair, gesticulating as he spoke. The peasant, who had no shoes, no teeth and hardly a rag to cover his body, was evidently consumed by his belief in a new and just order. The man's dialect was almost impenetrable to Thistlewood, who sipped his coffee and waited for an opportunity to distract the great man with a pertinent aphorism. As the labourer paused to cough, somebody tapped Thistlewood's shoulder. He turned, and there stood a man of about his own height, with a cool, inviting smile. The man's fingers twitched at his hip, and Thistlewood saw the gleaming, silvery hilt of a rapier.

At this time, he supported himself by his sword, and it was common for strangers to seek out Monsieur Tiesel-voud in the hope of winning a few sous for a meal. One such fellow had drawn blood from the Englishman's chin and paid for it with his life. Thistlewood had not expected his reputation to follow him to Arras.

Just as he noticed the rings on the man's fat fingers – a sure sign that the challenge had nothing to do with hunger - the fellow lifted his rapier and denounced Arthur as a foreigner and a spy, sent by Robespierre's enemies to discover what plots he was preparing. By the second half of the sentence, Arthur was on his feet. The tip of his sword teased his opponent's neck, their eyes were locked. Across the room, chairs and tables crashed, as on-lookers fled. Only Robespierre and two of his brutes remained.

"Come, young sir," said Robespierre. "Lay down your sword. Monsieur Jacques is harmless. None of these men will hurt you without my order, and no man in France is less partial to violence than Robespierre."

"Please tell me on what grounds I'm accused," demanded Thistlewood, his sword still resting on the challenger's neck. Monsieur Jacques's eyes were closed, and he was whispering a prayer to the Virgin Mother.

"That is of less relevance, young man," Robespierre responded, "than your reason for being here, since you are clearly not French. I feel certain that I've seen you in Paris."

Arthur was incredulous. Robespierre had noticed and remembered him! He withdrew his sword and Monsieur Jacques muttered that his intention had only been to support Robespierre, whose former friends had risen against him. With his ringed fingers, Monsieur Jacques fled, deaf to the mockery of Robespierre's guards, his lips mouthing apologies, as he clattered down the stairs, thanking Our Lady that he lived to breathe the cold November air.

The same evening, Arthur Thistlewood dined on garlic soup at a meeting of the Association of the Lawyers of Artois. The gentlemen were discussing matters of constitutional law in a jargon that far exceeded his comprehension. As brandy was distributed, Robespierre invited the young English radical to make an address about his work at home. Thistlewood gave thanks for the honour, and in the best opportunity he could have imagined, forgot his rehearsed aphorism, and explained clumsily that his mastery of French was insufficient to address so distinguished an assembly on a technical matter. One lawyer asked in languid terms what plans were afoot to amend the British constitution. Thistlewood replied that his humble origins allowed him no access to Parliament, but that his ambition was to abolish the British legal system and re-instate the Saxon constitution. Without requesting further clarification, the lawyers, applauded graciously and returned to the subject of France.

When the meeting was over and Thistlewood approached to offer thanks, Robespierre said that he would be returning to Paris as Public Prosecutor. He offered to lend Thistlewood a horse, and said that should they meet again, he would like to hear more about the citizens of Britain and their partic-ular suffering. He congratulated Thistlewood on outstanding swordsmanship, wished him well with his intention to trans-form his country and was confident of his commitment and ability to do so.

Thistlewood was glad of the compliments and the horse, but he was no fool. He had wasted his opportunity. It had been naïve to approach the great man prematurely and with half-formed ideas. Unlike the learned lawyers of Artois, This-tlewood had no elite profession, no private wealth and no ex-pertise beyond the rudiments of chemistry and - thanks to his grandfather - weather prediction, neither of which was of any consequence to a career in politics. At least his reputation with the sword ensured that he would replace his worn-out boots and breeches before the weather turned.

Arthur Thistlewood would enjoy no second conversation with Robespierre. He wept at the news of his mother, took his grandfather's money and wrote that his studies were advancing well, and he would soon join a regiment. Before that time came, Thistlewood attended political rallies in Paris, mounting platforms, moments after the leaders of the Revolution had left. The young Englishmen and his friends spoke with commitment and even passion, but in their broken French, struggled to keep the attention of excited crowds. As Robespierre's power and paranoia grew, and Thistlewood heard with his own ears the Incorruptible's call for violence, he wept with disappointment.

When he saw a woman struck down in an angry crowd, he held the stranger tenderly as she bled, called her his precious maman, and reminded her that she was beautiful and had been loved, deeply. Drenched in the dead woman's blood, Thistlewood vowed that come his own Revolution, no innocent woman or child would suffer.

CHAPTER SIX

Wednesday 5th May, 1819
(continued)

BRUNT

Fox Court, Holborn

On Saturday and Sunday, with his wife and son occupied by
the sweeps' parade and the services at chapel, Tom Brunt completed the order for several pairs of shoes for a society wedding.
Hale, the apprentice resented the intrusion by another bootmaker and protested that he was just as capable of closing and
stitching as cross-eyed Richard Tidd. Brunt clipped the lad's
ear for insolence and ordered him to be content with shaving,
polishing and wearing in.

On Monday evening the footwear was delivered to Cavendish Square, and when Brunt arrived at midday on Tuesday,
every piece was accepted without need of alteration. The family
was in a chaos of preparation, but the butler promised that
payment would be delivered to Fox Court later that day. By
nine o'clock, when still no messenger had visited, Brunt grew
anxious. He was expected on Wednesday morning in Southwark to collect an order of dressed leather. He also needed to
pay Richard Tidd, who had a wife and five children and was
on the cusp of destitution. There was also the tender issue of

Molly's canary, whose corpse had been kept as cool as possible since Friday but had embarked on its decay.

The family on Cavendish Square had never failed Brunt before, nor his master, Mr Brooke, who had made all their boots and shoes before him. On Wednesday, he rose before Molly woke, and at eight o'clock, presented himself at the house. The butler was away, and the housekeeper was sorry to hear that Mr Brunt's assistant had so many mouths to feed, and that Mr Brunt needed to buy a side of leather before he could make any more shoes, but with the family on its way to Derbyshire for a wedding, she was not authorized for more than a temporary payment of three shillings from petty cash.

At ten thirty, Brunt called at Tidd's apartment in Hole in the Wall Passage, not far away, on other side of Brooke's Market. He gave his colleague a shilling in down-payment and the explanation, which, according to Tidd, more than justified his opinion that all aristocrats were disciples of the devil. Brunt, who had no time for debate, went home for his porridge, gave Molly the second shilling, and set off, with the revised poem in his pocket and the dead canary in a nail box in his rucksack, for Southwark.

Molly Brunt's cousin, Sam Welch was one of the few tanners in London who could dress leather himself and thus sell direct to customers. Unfortunately, Sam was not at liberty to give anything away without proper payment, not even for a family member. For Molly's sake, he was prepared to keep the order for seven more days. In the meantime, he would part with a small pig's belly for sixpence down and the rest by the end of the month.

In his disappointment, Brunt might have forgotten about Ringo, had Sam not enquired about the family. Of course, he remembered his cousin's canary! Mrs Welch had often fed Ringo with morsels of cake during their visits, and would be sorry to hear the news. Sam would cut and preserve the little pet with pleasure, he said, while as a competent stitch-man, Thomas could complete the stuffing and sewing himself. Brunt paid his sixpence, wrapped the pig's belly in brown paper and left the box containing Ringo on Sam Welch's counter.

As he crossed Blackfriars Bridge, Brunt thought that after all the walking and humility, half a pint of ale would be in order, before he visited Richard Carlile on the literary matter. As he turned on to Fleet Street, he recognized a man on St Bride's corner. It was George Edwards, the lamplighter's brother, whose aggressive talk had unsettled the membership last Friday. Not in a mood for either niceties or debate, Brunt turned to cross the street, but it was too late. Edwards came after him, clutched his hand, congratulated him on his success with the poem and offered to stand him a beer. Edwards was so convivial, that Brunt wondered if his judgement had been prematurely harsh. But talking hurt neither man nor beast, and a free beer was a free beer.

They sat in the same quiet corner of the Old Bell, where Edwards had recently met Ings. Edwards regretted that he was unable to agree with all the sentiments in Mr Brunt's poem, but he recognised the artistry. Artists, he proclaimed, must always stick together.

"How do you mean?" asked Brunt.

"By pooling our creative ideas, Mr Brunt. The reform movement needs men like us. Two minds always work better than one."

"I see," replied Brunt, although he did not.

Edwards continued that beside being a model-maker, he had another career as a military inventor. Only today, he whispered, he had created a device using nothing but a tin can, brimstone and pitched rope. If the device were thrown, for instance, into a carriage containing a person of substance, it would explode in less than a minute.

"Theoretically speaking?" asked Brunt.

"This morning it destroyed a cushion," revealed Edwards, "but it could just as easily have killed My Lord Castlereagh."

Brunt rose to his feet.

"It is clear you mistake me for somebody else, Mr Edwards," he said. "You may not know that I am descended from Harald Moreton, the hero of Wandiwash, and that I would never conspire to murder."

Edwards grabbed his arm.

"Were you not listening on Friday, Mr Brunt?" he asked. "Was it not clear to you that every man in that hall would prefer certain politicians to be dead?"

"I grant you the Irish have special reasons to be angry," replied Brunt, "but even if they killed them all tomorrow, by next week, even viler creatures would take their places. The enemy breeds, Mr Edwards, like vermin, and murder won't help our cause."

"Mr Tidd agrees with me," said Edwards. "The only thing that men in power understand is fear."

"I repeat, sir," growled Brunt. "Murder will only harm the cause of reform. Don't you read Richard Carlile? Don't you listen to Orator Hunt? These days, even Arthur Thistlewood believes we shall only change society by argument, persuasion and good humour."

"You're a naïve fellow indeed, Mr Brunt! There's not a man in Parliament understands any of that. We have to think as they do or perish objecting."

"Mr Edwards" said Brunt. "I thank you for the beer, but I cannot accept your argument or your devices. Now please excuse me. I have an appointment with my editor. Good day, sir."

Left alone with his beer, Edwards thought that if the boot-maker repeated their conversation, his own denials would be more readily believed. Still, two rejections in a row taught Edwards that not all gruff exteriors re malleable and that wherever this new path was to lead him, he must proceed with greater caution.

EDWARDS

Fleet Street

Considering all the bankruptcies of late, Edwards expected to be out of his mother's place within hours. All he needed was two good-sized rooms with storage capacity, north-facing light and proximity to Fleet Street. The search was proving difficult until, by glorious coincidence, he learnt that his former studio had been purchased by Richard Carlile, who, as a consequence of accelerating success, had left Mr Sherwin's own premises and established an independent print shop further along Fleet Street, at number 55. Carlile had purchased the premises from Edwards's former landlord, a struggling cheese-monger, once resident at number 55½, a property that now, fortuitously, stood empty, except for two bill-boards; one advertising fine cheeses, with the maker's new address, and another detailing the publications for sale next door.

Despite his distrust of the model-maker's person, Richard Carlile admired the figurine of the late Princess Charlotte in a posture of repose, which Edwards offered as a sample. The great journalist and editor was not to be persuaded that Arthur Thistlewood or even Henry Hunt were appropriate models at the present time, but he would consider a bust of Thomas Paine for his shop window.

"Mr Paine is a great author, and I shall be honoured to accept," replied Edwards. "I'll start the sketches at once."

"Good," said Carlile, anxious to return to work, and uneasy when Edwards hovered.

"Is there anything else?" he asked.

"A guinea in advance, sir, would be welcome," replied Edwards, "if I'm to start promptly. I was cheated at Eton, you see, and lack materials. Also, I've learnt never to start a commission without security."

"A guinea, you say?" said Carlile with a chuckle. "I'll see the sketches first; then we'll discuss a deposit."

Edwards stood there, a little awkwardly.

"You disagree?" asked Carlile.

"I accept your terms on the grounds that I must rebuild my reputation in London. But there is another matter. In short, Mr Carlile, I'll need a studio and an apartment and would be a most reliable tenant for the premises next door."

"Ah!" said Carlile, understanding why the fellow loomed so.

"Frankly, Edwards," he replied, "I've been too busy to think beyond a coffee shop, for selling pamphlets and the like. Nothing else will do; certainly not a modeller. The walls are thin, and I won't have dust, contaminating my machines! I look forward to the sketches of Tom Paine. Good day."

With that, Carlile activated his press, so that no further conversation was possible.

Outside, Edwards cursed. How dare the arrogant toad brush him off! Who, in these times, did Mr Carlile imagine would open yet another coffee shop on Fleet Street?

As he burned with indignation, Edwards remembered the example set by Sir Herbert at Windsor. He must restore his composure before the other visit he intended to make today. Until then, he would continue his enquiries about accommodation.

A few local residents remembered the artist from his previous occupancy, but despite his professed royal connections, not one could recall any available premises.

INGS

Whitechapel, London

He decided not to wait until Bill was fifteen, but to include him in the business from the start. The legend, "Ings and Son" would inspire the lad to work hard and learn responsibility. The sign-painter offered a discount for an extra board, to be erected beside the Whitechapel Road, with a steaming meat-pie to entice extra custom and an arrow, indicating the shop's location. When Ings enquired about Celia's uncle, the painter said he had never done business with Old Silas, but he knew a cutler who had; Godbold of Brick Lane.

It must have been some months since Uncle Stone visited his cutler. Celia had found the knives all higgledy-piggledy in a drawer and, although well-forged, with bone handles, most were shamefully blunt. Ings possessed better knives himself, and a sharpening stone would arrive from Hampshire soon with his family. While he had no need of a regular cutler, Ings supposed that any associate of Uncle Stone might be useful for business. He wrapped the neglected knives in an apron, pushed them into his saddlebag and set off in a westerly direction towards Spitalfields, where he tethered Jupiter by a trough on Church Street, in sight of the cutler's premises on the corner of Brick Lane.

The proprietress was a sturdy, expressionless woman of about forty, in a blue, tucked dress with nothing to cover her shiny black hair, which she had tied in a bun at her neck. She had difficulty understanding good Hampshire English, but after Ings had explained his mission four times, replied that the master was indisposed. The customer should leave his items with a down-payment and return for them on Friday. When Ings provided his business address and explained that he was the heir of their former customer, Mr Stone, the woman seemed to freeze, before directing Mr Ings to wait, while she had a word with Mr Godbold upstairs.

The premises were spotless and not unlike any small shop in Portsea, except for the foreign newspaper, tied by string to a nail in the wall. Ings was examining the unfamiliar words, which he supposed must be French, when he heard sharp voices above. Speculating that he had encroached upon a domestic situation, Ings decided to leave at once and return another time. He was opening the shop-door, and the bell was tinkling, when there were hasty footsteps on the stairs. The proprietress grabbed his arm, as if he were a thief in flight. Her face flush and angry, she commanded Mr Ings to take the knives up to her father, whose health was frail, and who, on no account, should be distressed. Had Ings been a different kind of man, he might have been indignant at the woman's rudeness and run off, but he was reminded of Jack's widow, Lizzie, and how grief had altered her behaviour. Who knew what suffering the poor woman had endured in the war?

The staircase was extremely steep and there were two doors at the top, one of which was ajar. Ings knocked.

"Entrez!" called a voice. Pushing the door open, Ings saw, dwarfed by his arm-chair, an elderly man in night-gown and cap. A woollen blanket covering his legs. Mr Godbold, as Ings supposed he must be, made no attempt to greet his visitor. Next to his chair was a narrow bed and beyond that, a bench with tools, machinery and sharpening stones. The window shutters were open to the clop and whirl of traffic and the guttural shouts of the hawkers, offering the best cabbages, taters and fresh cream.

In an accent as clear as he could muster, Ings gave his name and wished Mr Godbold good morning. The cutler responded with a scornful grunt.

Despite the haughty introduction, Ings laid his knives on the cutler's tray and apologized for the neglect they had suffered during his uncle's illness.

Suddenly and with no warning, Godbold reached under his blanket and pulled out a curved dagger, which seemed larger and great deal fiercer than the man himself. Ings leapt back, as the tiny, crumpled man brandished his weapon, snarling that he had transported this petite chérie all the way from India, where she had separated two Englishmen and four Hindus from their heads, each with a single strike.

"The shop-door is locked, pa," announced the proprietress, who had appeared at the door. "Do what you will to the traitor! We can store him in the cellar after."

Ings bristled.

"You may call me many names, madam, but 'traitor' James Ings ain't never been, nor never shall be; neither to his family, his king nor his country! I am a patriot sir, and you will release me, or I shall be obliged to be rough with you and fetch the patrole!"

Mr Godbold laughed with a low dry cackle.

"Who'd have thought it?" he said. "Old Silas's nephew has fire in his belly! What do you make of him, daughter? Perhaps he's in need of a wife; let's hear what he says. Well, Monsieur Eengs, will you have her?"

"I thank you, Monsieur," replied Ings, "for your restraint and your kind offer, which, alas, comes too late. Your daughter is charming, but I am married to Celia Stone and intend to remain so. Plainly put; there is no vacancy."

Godbold laughed and his daughter left the room, unleashing peals of laughter, as she descended again to the shop.

"Monsieur Eengs," said Godbold. "I see you are a decent man, and you have spirit. Alors, our game is over. Be seated on this bed, if you please, and I shall tell you a story about your uncle."

THISTLEWOOD

Stanhope Street, Lincoln's Inn Field

By one o'clock on Wednesday, Thistlewood had explained his engagements in France, America and the West Indies, the journeys which, for Julian's entertainment, he had often spun into disconnected adventures in soldiering and swordsmanship. Susan listened carefully, asked a few pertinent questions and when they were answered, confessed to a secret of her own.

In May, 1817, when her father read in *The Times* that far from sailing the Atlantic to a new life away from politics, Arthur Thistlewood had been arrested and faced charges of High Treason, Mr Wilkinson had ridden at once to London, determined to take his daughter and her stepson to the safety of her family in Horncastle. Susan had refused to leave, insisting that Arthur would need his wife and son as soon as the folly of his arrest became clear. Her father had called her a blind fool, and repeated certain anecdotes, which Susan had denied, but which had troubled her ever since.

She needed to know, before Julian returned from school, exactly why her husband had been arrested on the day of their planned departure for America, why he had been unexpectedly acquitted and the exact circumstances of his later detainment at Horsham. Susan wanted only the truth. She understood her marriage vows, and unless murder was involved, would never judge her husband adversely. Thistlewood agreed without complaint; and invited his wife to outline the rumours that had troubled her.

Susan knew that the mistaken charge of High Treason was connected to the riot at Spa Field a few months before the arrest at the jetty. She understood that Arthur had been betrayed, but was it true that he had led a crowd of five thousand from Islington to the city? That he had fired stolen guns into the air and presented himself at the Tower of London, surrounded by drunken sailors carrying the tricolour? Had Arthur demanded that the guards surrender the Tower of London? And only been stopped by the arrival of the armed cavalry?

Thistlewood admitted that it was difficult to recall the details of that turbulent day. As he collected himself to respond, there was a knock at the door. Thistlewood was inclined to ignore it, but his wife was on her feet.

She smiled at the stranger on the stairwell, who removed his hat and greeted her with a slight bow of the head. No taller than herself, he looked ordinary, with light brown hair and a prominent nose and chin. But for the slightly sad expression of enquiry in his grey eyes, there was something of Mr Punch about him. For some indefinable reason, Mrs Thistlewood was not inclined to send him away.

A Londoner with a slow, deliberate voice, the man apologized for the disturbance and explained that during Mr Thistlewood's absence, he had become a member of the Water Lane Group and hoped to introduce himself to the chairman. Susan asked for his name and trade. As the stranger looked at Mrs Thistlewood, her pale, slender face, the graceful neck at which her fine, fair hair was tied in a knot, and the double crescent of shadows beneath steady sea-green eyes, he thought she was the loveliest, most divine creature he had ever seen.

"Come and sit by the fire!" said Susan with a smile like a thunderbolt.

"Arthur!" she called. "We have a visitor. Mr Edwards, radical and model-maker, late of Eton."

INGS

Spitalfields, London

The eiderdown upon which he had been directed to sit was well-worn, made of exquisite yellow silk, with flowers, embroidered in red, orange and gold. The Godbolds had seen better times, Ings thought; perhaps a fall from grace, or the war in India had driven the old man mad. Alternatively, Uncle Stone was more of a bad egg than he and Celia had suspected.

"Écoutez-vous, Monsieur!" said Godbold quite suddenly, bolting Ings from his conjecture "Écoutez-vous bien, and you will comprehend the nature of my fury."

The cutler's account confirmed the very worst of Ings's forebodings. Uncle Stone had boasted of owning vast tea plantations in China. He had promised the Goldbolds a half-share of the annual profits in return for a quantity of jewellery, which Mr Godbold's mother had brought from Paris in the eighties.

"Those plantations never existed," explained Mr Godbold. "Your relation made of me a fool, Monsieur Eengs, and by stealing my inheritance, has destroyed my family's future!"

"I see," said Ings, whose heart knew the melody of truth. Looking at Godbold now, he saw a pitiful victim, who had defended himself in the only way he knew.

"If you will lend me the receipts," he continued, "I shall take them to my lawyer on Chancery Lane. Perhaps he can trace your jewellery."

"Hélas, Old Silas was too cunning for receipts," replied Godbold. "But we also are cunning. The jeweller, who valued them and witnessed the transaction, has promised to swear an oath before God. Tell that to your lawyer on Chancery Lane!"

"Mr Godbold," replied Ings, "I am a Christian, a dissenter, who has always conducted his affairs honestly. Should any crime be proven, my wife and I shall make full and proper recompense."

Ings gathered his knives from the tray and began to fold them in the apron.

"Mais non!" protested the cutler. "The old fool is dead, n'est-ce-pas, and business is business. I will sharpen the knives tomorrow, you can be sure, as fine as needles."

What else was Ings to do, but give thanks, promise to return soon with news and stretch out his hand in farewell? Godbold clenched it with all the vigour of a boxer.

Ings would have no memory of how he left that shop, but as he emerged, dazed, on to Brick Lane, relief that Celia had been spared untimely widowhood mingled with a new turmoil. Without knowing either the value of Mr Godbold's jewellery or the sum of Silas Stone's estate, how could he reassess his family's prospects? As the implications began to unfold, such was the weight on Ings's heart and mind that he forgot where, in these unfamiliar streets, he had tethered his horse. After searching for twenty minutes, he found Jupiter on Church Street, swishing his tail in careless abandon. With a heavy heart, Ings mounted and cantered back to Whitechapel to ask the sign-painter for a postponement. Then he set off, once more, for Chancery Lane.

Mr Pyke kept him waiting for seventy-four minutes and then claimed to know nothing about investments in cocoa on the Ivory Coast, cloves in Zanzibar or rum in the West

Indies. All of these, as far as the lawyer's investigator could establish, were fake.

Ings was confounded. If Mr Pyke had nurtured such suspicions and employed an investigator, no doubt paid for by the estate, why had he said nothing? Why had he advanced so much money, booked a hotel and eating house and encouraged Ings to purchase a valuable watch, re-establish the business and send for the children, all in the knowledge that Celia's inheritance was in peril?

Pyke replied that Mr Silas Stone had been a first-rate client, who was as entitled as any man to be presumed innocent before proven guilty. Mindful that his family might arrive to find him in gaol, Ings suppressed the urge to punch the lawyer's nose. Only one question remained, and it needed every ounce of self-control to ask it calmly. When all the payment and all the debts had been paid, how much would be left? Mr Pyke put his elbows on the table and rested his round, pink face between his fingers.

"You must brace yourself, Mr Ings," he said.

At least the lawyer had the decency to look sorry. Regret could not rescue them from their predicament, Ings concluded, as he drifted through the chilly streets, but evidence of humanity, no matter how small, was always acceptable.

NINETY-SEVEN AND THREE

That elegant boot on your foot, my Lord
Is of finest Moroccan brown leather.
Did you ever for a moment consider, my Lord
How a beautiful shoe fits together?

When the heel and the toe and the sole are cut
You might think that's all there is to it,
And many a man would agree with you, but
It's the awl and the stitches that do it.

On a foot as distinguished as yours, you see
Be it from Kent or Scotland or Devon
The parts of your shoe come to only three
While the stitches make ninety-seven.

If one of those stitches comes loose, good sir,
The others will follow that way.
No matter how expertly cut they were
The leathers will soon fall astray.

It's exactly the same in this country of ours,
Where each man depends on the others.
Each town will survive through snow, drought and showers
If we all put our trust in our brothers.

If you are the leather, good sir, on your boot,
Then we are the stitches that make it.
Our families' hunger is very acute
We have strength, but no power to break it.

We toil, pay taxes, fight wars, my Lord
For King and for Parliament.
If our voices and pain are ignored, my Lord
You shall know our furious dissent.
John Thomas Brunt, bootmaker.
Fox Court, Holborn, May 1819

Wednesday, 5ᵗʰ May, 1819
(continued)

BRUNT

Fleet Street, London

Richard Carlile's principal objections to the poem were two-fold. As a man of practical training, he wondered whether Mr Brunt had considered the impact on his profession of the admission that expert stitches might easily come undone. Further; while, of course, admiring the sentiment contained in the verses – especially the implied connection between wealth and suffrage - as an editor, Mr Carlile wondered whether *Sherwin's Weekly* was the ideal publication in which to place them. He would be pleased to furnish Mr Brunt with the address of his competitor at *The Black Dwarf*, although that periodical was equally oversubscribed, and he could offer no expectation of success.

It was not the response for which the poet had prepared himself. His mind was in a tangle, no words came to his rescue, and as he struggled to restore his composure, the editor's eyes wandered to a different sheet of paper, and the fingers of his left hand tapped the desk impatiently. The gesture infuriated Brunt. How could the man unleash an assault, more grievous than anything he had suffered in France, and appear so indifferent to the impact?

When Carlile looked up and perceived from Brunt's crimson colour and trembling lips that he had inadvertently upset him, the editor indicated a low stool beside the printing press. Brunt preferred the dignity of an upright position.

"Don't be dismayed, Mr Brunt!" said Carlile. "We writers all face disappointment, now and then. It's part of the trade, I assure you, and nothing to be concerned about. With a few revisions, your poem might be placed with the Bootmaker's Guild, whose quarterly newsletter I have the honour to print, here in this shop. I'd be happy to recommend your piece for the next issue. Would that satisfy you?"

Carlile's tone and his suggestion inflamed Brunt even further.

"Mr Carlile!" he replied. "I thank you for your opinion, and I trust that, in return, you will listen to mine."

"Proceed," said the editor, the glint of impatience in his eyes.

"I'm grateful for this meeting, Mr Carlile" said Brunt. "But see, if I'd arrived, wearing a fashionable waistcoat, and had boasted of my time with Mr Keats at Cambridge or Mr Shelley at Oxford, I have no doubt that my work would appear in the next issue of *Sherwin's*."

Carlile sighed; he had been clumsy. There was an editorial to write, and no time to soothe a thwarted amateur.

"Citizen," he said, "you mistake this for a personal matter. There is no intention on my part to cause offence. The guidelines are fixed by the owner, Mr Sherwin, and it is beyond my editorial power to defy them. If you wish, Mr Brunt, we can publish your entire collection of poetry as an independent concern, but that would require financial investment."

The poet, whose entire fortune were the eight-pence in his pocket and the pig's belly in his rucksack, laughed aloud.

"It's clear whose side you're on, Mr la-de-dah Carlile", he said. "As the son of a bootmaker, you're even more worthy of contempt than the aristocracy you pretend to despise. You've become rich, sir, at the expense of the gullible majority, and you're a traitor to all makers of footwear, including your father, and our entire class!"

Abandoning the editor to his perplexity and his machines, Brunt marched out of the shop. In urgent need of steadying himself and his temper, he headed for The Mitre, where the landlord guided the unhappy fellow to the tap room and accepted his thruppence for a pinch of snuff, a pint of stale porter and a taper. Thus fortified, Brunt held his composition above the grate and set it alight. As he watched the page curl, and as the orange flame licked his creation away to ash and vapour, something hardened in the bootmaker's heart. Just two tuppences and penny rattled in his pocket, as he made his way up Chancery Lane, planning a pair of Turkish slippers with the belly, and collecting words that might satisfy Tiddy and rhyme with "devil."

CHAPTER SEVEN

Wednesday, 5th May, 1819
(continued)

THISTLEWOOD / EDWARDS

Stanhope Street, Lincoln's Inn Field

George Edwards was sitting on the yellow settee beside Susan Thistlewood, and he was eating her lemon biscuits.

"You'll understand, Mr Edwards," said Thistlewood, "that I've become unaccustomed to social conversation. It's a dull existence for my wife, especially when Julian's at school."

Thistlewood was teasing the coal on the fire with the poker he had claimed from Tupholme.

"Oh, not at all" said Mrs Thistlewood. "I could imagine nothing worse than a husband who fills every minute with vacuous conversation. I'm an enthusiastic reader."

"And a first-class baker, if I may say," replied Edwards.

"The lemons came from Jeremy Bentham," said Thistlewood, replacing the poker and wiping his hands on the cloth. "He had them from a friend who has a nephew at Kew."

"You are personally acquainted with Dr Bentham?" asked Edwards.

"With his philanthropic theories, of course," said Thistlewood, "and he has, more than once, expressed sympathy with our cause."

"I dare say he heard of my husband's release, and sent us the hamper," said Susan.

She urged Edwards to take another biscuit from the trolley. The pastry was as soft as snow. Thistlewood sat in the chair beside the yellow settee.

"So you see we are a dull couple indeed," he said. "Perhaps you would distract us with an account of your own life in politics."

"There's little to say," said George Edwards, "except that you see here a radical, an artist, seeking to settle back in London, and a bachelor, the brother of your secretary, sir."

"Edwards, the lamplighter?" asked Thistlewood, with a sudden smile.

Now that he was closer, Edwards observed the scar beside the fellow's jaw and wondered how it came there.

"I'm William's older brother," he replied, "and equally committed to the cause."

"Then, you are most welcome, citizen," said Thistlewood.

"Since you are a radical, Mr Edwards," enquired Mrs Thistlewood, "perhaps you attended Orator Hunt's rallies at Spa Field."

"Unfortunately, not, Ma'am" replied Edwards. "My medium is model-making. On the first occasion, I was busy with the late Princess Charlotte in her wedding gown– and on the second, with Dora Jordan in the role of Perdita."

Mrs Thistlewood's sea-green eyes sparkled.

"Poor Mrs Jordan!" she said. "Such a loss to the drama when she moved to Paris. Mr Edwards, or so I heard. I expect you sold thousands?"

"That life is tiresome to me now, Mrs Thistlewood." replied Edwards. "I'm not here to speak about myself, but in the hope of discovering your husband's vision for the future."

"Then you must be disappointed," replied Thistlewood.

"Arthur never reveals anything that he has not first discussed with the committee," explained his wife. "He's been busy composing his first speech since leaving Horsham."

"Then I must apologize for the intrusion" said Edwards, moving slightly, as if to leave.

"Oh, please don't run off!" said Mrs Thistlewood. "My husband was telling me about the rallies at Spa Field. Perhaps it would interest you to hear him out? Unless your brother has already described them?

"William was too young," replied Edwards, "and I have often longed to hear a first-hand account".

"You have no objection, Arthur?" asked Susan Thistlewood.

"Au contraire," replied Thistlewood, directing steady gaze at Edwards, "These matters can stir a man's feelings. My wife has persuaded me to be more transparent on political matters. Your presence, citizen, as an informed outsider, will encourage detachment. Though frankly, my conscience isn't entirely clear. Memory is a fickle master, is it not, Mr Edwards?"

"Perhaps" said Edwards. "I believe the first meeting at Spa Field was a success."

"Indeed, from Orator Hunt's point of view", said Thistlewood, "it was. But there were repercussions."

Edwards melted against the cushions of the yellow settee, only inches from the divine Susan Thistlewood, and congratulated himself on being, yet again, in the right place, at exactly the right time. Thistlewood moved restlessly about the room as he talked, and Susan closed her lovely eyes to better concentrate on his words. Her skin, Edwards observed, was no less silky and translucent than a white butterfly's wing.

Friday, 15th November, 1816

THE GROUP
The Black Lion, Water Lane

After the successful first Spa Field meeting, Orator Hunt invited a few wealthy gentlemen reformers, to a fish and chip supper at the Black Lion. Since Thistlewood and his associate, old Dr Watson had organized the rally and secured the Orator's participation, they exhorted him to include their hard-working committee. Though his evening's pleasure would undoubtedly be strained by the company of half a dozen unwashed, badly dressed fellows, Hunt had little choice.

Unfortunately, one of Thistlewood's men, a rough northerner by the name of John Castles, took advantage of the free liquor and as soon as his plate was empty, began shouting obscenities. When Thistlewood ordered him either to control his temper or leave the tavern, Castles became more belligerent, drowning the gentlemen's conversation. Henry Hunt chose to ignore the rumpus until the fellow threw a salt-pot, which struck the great man's ear and fell, with a crash to the floor. Everyone fell silent, except the waiter who asked to be excused to fetch a broom. Clutching a bloodied kerchief to his ear, Hunt turned calmly to the waiter and promised that Mr Cooper would be compensated, both for the lost pot and the salt. Thistlewood expected the worse, but there was no explosion of rage, no expulsion, yet, of his unfortunate men. He began to see that there was no occasion Hunt enjoyed more than the smell of drama combined with a challenging audience.

"Gentlemen, citizens," began Hunt in a measured voice. "Our movement needs men of passion and action. Indeed, without them, there can be no reform. However, this is England, not the suburbs of Paris. We shall only succeed; that is, the lives of the great British majority will only improve, if each of us conducts himself in a manner that is rational and civilized."

Permitting his guests a moment to express their approval, the Orator addressed John Castles, who was sucking the last of his meal from his fingers and had to be nudged by Watson.

"Citizen! I believe you to be unaccustomed to dining out," said Hunt, "and I shall therefore overlook your behaviour today. But I should like to know your grievance. Let's hear it!"

Castles rose shakily to his feet. The liquor had muddled his mind and his vision, but he was aware of about twenty heads, staring at him in expectant silence.

"Are enjoying your supper, citizen?" asked the Orator.

"Aye, sir, thank you, sir," mumbled Castles.

"This is your opportunity, man" continued Hunt. "Seize it! Start with your name.

"Castles, your Honour. John Castles from Yorkshire, white-smith."

"Well, Castles. what, pray, is the nature of your protest? Clearly now, so that every man may hear it."

Castles took a document from his pocket.

"Everything I want to say is wrote in this letter."

Amid the gentlemen's scarcely muffled laughter, Thistlewood and Watson looked at each other in alarm. Castles had never spent a single day in education. How could he possibly have written a letter? What was its purpose, why had he never mentioned it, and what could they do to prevent embarrassment?

"Very well," said the Orator. "Will you read it out?"

"'T letter ain't for you," replied Castles. "It's for 't Regent; an appeal sir, and I'd be obliged if you'd take it round to His

Noble Highness, who I believe you have 't honour to know in person."

Castles pushed aside his chair, marched to the end of the table and placed the document in front of Henry Hunt.

"This document is sealed," said Hunt. "How can I agree to deliver a letter without first knowing its contents?"

The room fell silent and Thistlewood and Watson watched powerlessly, as the Orator opened the letter. His eyes widened, and after a few moments, he looked up, his features set in furious resolve.

Mr Thistlewood, Dr Watson; if I needed evidence that collaboration would be misguided, it is contained in this vulgar and seditious. document. The language, which I must assume you have approved, confirms my colleagues' advice that your committee possesses not an ounce of insight or decency and can perform no useful service for the purposes of reform in Great Britain. To all followers of Thistlewood and Watson, I say this; regardless of any assurances given before today, you will henceforth consider any prospect of cooperation null and void. Now go from my table and leave the gentlemen in peace."

As Thistlewood led his men away, he was not entirely disheartened. Hunt was a hot-headed fellow, whose pride had been damaged, but who could be won over again. Castles claimed, when questioned, to be as surprised as everyone else. Since he could not read, he pleaded, how was he to know what was written down? A professional clerk had taken down his words and must have altered them for his own corrupt purpose.

Worse was to follow. The next morning, the same text appeared widely in the popular press, where it was credited as the Orator's speech at Spa Field. A good portion of the gullible public believed it, and Lord Liverpool and his Cabinet danced for joy, predicting the end of Orator Hunt's career, and with it, quite possibly, the entire reform movement. Beyond livid, Henry Hunt published strenuous denials and accused John Castles of being a government agent.

Wednesday, 5ᵗʰ May 1819

THISTLEWOOD / EDWARDS
Stanhope Street, Lincoln's Inn Field

"Since the second rally at Spa Field followed a few weeks later," said Edwards, "may I presume that your foresight proved correct, and Mr Hunt's good opinion was restored?"

"Henry Hunt cannot succeed without us, and he knows it," replied Thistlewood. "Mr Edwards, ordinary men like us understand working people; how they think and feel, how they live from day to day. Thanks to the lessons of the late Thomas Spence, we also possess the insights and the language to explain to working men and women that the law and politics do not exist for the benefit of the rich and privileged. The Magna Carta belongs to us all. In short, Mr Edwards, my committee - and others like us - can harness popular support in ways that are impossible for a gentlemen farmer like Henry Hunt. That is our strength, sir, and without out cooperation, he will never win the mass following he needs for success."

"Well spoken, my dear!" said Mrs Thistlewood.

"Indeed!" added Edwards. "But tell me, Thistlewood; this man, Castles, was he present at the second rally in Spa Field?"

"I regret very much to say that he was."

Monday 2ⁿᵈ December, 1816

THE GROUP
Spa Field, Islington, London

John Castles, whose explanation was eventually, if grudgingly accepted by Hunt, proposed that Thistlewood and Watson arrive at Spa Field two hours ahead of the Orator and deliver speeches of their own. He claimed to have persuaded hundreds of local workers to leave their factories and flock to Spa Field to hear Arthur Thistlewood and old Dr Watson. When the day of the second rally came, Watson, Thistlewood's closest ally at the time, had been sent to gaol again for debt. In his place, sent his son, an inexperienced young buck with a greed for liquor. When they arrived at Spa Field, Castles produced tri-colour flags and a cart, from which he expected Thistlewood to address the crowd. Young Watson taunted Thistlewood and his caution, until he acknowledged that they had nothing to lose from trying.

In the excitement, it did not occur to Thistlewood to question why he had not been consulted about the new arrangement, or where Castles had found the flags or the cart. Instead of the overworked factory folk Castles had promised, the crowd consisted mostly of freshly demobbed and sunburnt sailors, blood-thirsty, it emerged, from watching executions at the Old Bailey, where Castles had rounded them up. Anyone who would follow him to Spa Field was promised money and rum. Almost certainly, Castles had also tinkered with the committee's ale, because both Thistlewood and Young Watson were fired up like bulls. The lad was keen to make a name for himself. He climbed on to the cart, raised the tri-colour and declared that just as the citizens of Paris had stormed the Bastille, the men of London would today take control of the Tower. The crowd was delirious.

Wednesday 5th May, 1819
(continued)

THISTLEWOOD / EDWARDS

Stanhope Street, Lincoln's Inn Field

"You did nothing to stop them?" asked Mrs Thistlewood.

"It would have taken a regiment!" said Thistlewood. "Of course, I knew nothing at the time about Castles's treachery or the sailors or the rum. Nor that he was mingling with the crowd, urging them to plunder gunsmiths, seize property and capture any aristocrats who crossed their path."

"You marched with them, Arthur! Was that necessary?"

"Was I to run away or stay and try to prevent catastrophe? All I remember, Susan, is wild confusion.

"The crowd had grown to several thousand, and still, there was no sign of Henry Hunt. I discovered later that he had been deliberately waylaid. Castles or his paymaster, had planned everything! Once we left Spa Field, I presumed that the Orator, Young Watson and Castles were in the throng ahead of me or behind. Yes, as we all moved forward, I became infected by the excitement, intoxicated with hope that we could succeed. Who, in similar circumstances, would not? When we arrived at the Tower, the crowd was vast. We waved our flags and began the triumphant speeches. That's when the cavalry arrived.

"When I heard the people chanting; 'Run, Arthur, run!' I turned, and there, right in front of me, was Sidmouth's weasel, Stafford from Bow Street, with alarm in his eyes. He raised an arm to take me, but I span round and sped away, engulfed by the crowd."

"Was anybody injured?" asked Susan.

"A few people fainted. A gunsmith's apprentice was shot when he tried to capture Watson at Snow Hill."

"A young man died for this nonsense?"

"Hit in the groin; he survived, Susan."

As Mrs Thistlewood sat quietly, absorbing the information, beside her, Edwards's mind was racing. He smelt profit in Thistlewood's revelations and the challenge was delicious. Thistlewood's hazel eyes were upon him.

"You escaped arrest, then?" he asked.

"I hid in a safe house at Finchley" replied Thistlewood. "As a close associate, Castles knew that, and his testimony led to my arrest. I was released a few days later, but, only so that he could continue spying on us. Susan, I'm afraid John Castles was one of the few people who knew of our plan to emigrate."

"Castles is the reason we're not in Boston?" asked Susan, aghast.

Thistlewood looked at her in sad acknowledgment. Startled by an unfamiliar surge of rage, Susan stood and turned away.

"You never once doubted the fellow?" asked Edwards.

"I doubted him!" said Susan, sharply. "Twice he's been here. I felt at once that he was vulgar and untrustworthy. Arthur is too kind sometimes."

"Not so," said Thistlewood. "Should a man be rejected and treated with suspicion, because he never learnt manners, or because he was born with so many disadvantages? Nobody should be excluded from society because he can't read or write and has never been taught the art of argument. John Castles has as much right as any man to an opinion and a life of dignity."

"Because he was poor and unfortunate, you supposed him incapable of deceit?" asked Susan.

"Powerful men took advantage of John Castles and manipulated him," said Thistlewood. "I failed him, because I did not protect him from the consequences of his own weakness and ignorance."

"You are not angry with him, even now?" asked Susan.

"How can I be?" said Thistlewood. "Of course, his deceptions were wrong; but which man can say he has never made a mistake, he has never done wrong when his survival and his family's were at stake? And what are the consequences? I was in gaol for a time, but it was neither for the first time nor will it be the last. Am I not free, Susan, and is my country not ripe for change?"

"What happened to Castles?" asked Edwards.

"Our brief found a string of convictions for fraud and robbery," said Thistlewood. "He was discredited, and that's why they could not convict us."

"Did they convict the traitor?" asked Edwards.

"I heard they sent him to Ontario," said Thistlewood with a shrug. "At any rate, he disappeared, and he can't hurt us now."

"What came of Young Watson?" asked Susan.

"Sailed to America," replied Thistlewood.

Susan Thistlewood gasped, disbelieving.

"You're saying that John Castles and that foolish boy were given new lives," she said, "while a hero like his father is goaled indefinitely, and you pick up the mess?"

Thistlewood sighed; there was no constructive answer.

"The devil looks after his own!" said Edwards.

"You may be right, Mr Edwards!" said Thistlewood. "And when this work is done, my family and I shall leave for Boston."

Thistlewood took his wife's hand, "If you will?"

When Susan's green eyes looked into her husband's, Edwards thought that it was time to leave. He thanked Arthur Thistlewood for his frankness and invited him to dine at The Black Lion after the next Water Lane meeting. Thistlewood was pleased to have made acquaintance with an intelligent, like-minded fellow, who might bring new blood to the committee.

"I apologize, Mr Edwards, if I have been too open for a first acquaintance," said Thistlewood at the apartment door.

"Please call me George."

"As you see, I am out of practice with social intercourse, but I sense, George that you are a man of discretion."

"Your secrets are safe, Arthur. My thanks to Mrs Thistlewood for the biscuits."

And he was gone.

When Julian arrived home from school, instead of engaging his parents in a discussion about Julius Caesar or a quiz about the world's great rivers, he joined Susan on a brisk walk. Thistlewood, who had asked to be left alone with his thoughts, took the waste basket to the fire-place and burnt every remnant of his resignation. There would be a different speech, spicy enough to sell, without putting his liberty at risk too soon. He had no idea where to begin, and when he returned to his desk to try, his eyes drifted to the glass ink-well.

In his mind, he saw again the strong, reliable fist of Farmer John, with his hand-cut quill, as he sat at the same walnut desk, dipped into the same well and composed his reports for the Vyners, wrote letters to his brother, Thomas in Jamaica or recorded local weather patterns. Looking back, the old man's life seemed as measured and straightforward as his writing. There had been struggles, no doubt, with human nature, not least with William's. But the complexity of Castles's double deceit and the depth of desperation at its core were unknown, even amongst the poorest residents of the Lincolnshire Wold.

Not one word of the new speech had been written, when his family returned in high spirits from Whitehall. Susan reported that a charming officer on Downing Street had offered to hand the women's petition to the Prime Minister in person. Thistlewood responded with a hollow laugh that they might have more success, sending it down My Lord Liverpool's chimney. Those families needed a committed chorus in Parliament, and until that was achieved, no petitions or any other evidence would shift the status quo.

Unsettled by his father's low mood and unable to shift it, Julian was reluctant to go up to his bed. When eventually he did, Thistlewood asked Susan to fetch the casket, hidden under his bed. He was glad to have unburdened his conscience, and he was glad to have met Edwards, but no matter how deep a man's mercy, there are some memories that are best banished, some betrayals so deep that no man should face them twice. Apart from death itself, he knew of only one sure way to forget. Susan implored him to consider the consequences, the impact on her and his son of the dark time that would follow. A solid night's sleep was surely the better solution. Arthur insisted; he had compiled the tincture himself, and there would be no unpleasant effects. Experience had taught her otherwise, but she would not press her husband further. After all, Susan told herself, it was she, who had encouraged him to relive the ordeal, she, who had pushed him to this unfathomable depth, and she had no right to judge his method of retrieving equilibrium.

Thursday, 6th May, 1819

EDWARDS

Cripplegate, London

Early on Thursday morning, long before Mrs G had emerged from her bed, her first-born hurried down to Chiswell Street to hire a cab. Today, even the foul air failed to subdue his mood. Edwards's association with Thistlewood had begun more promisingly than he could have dreamed, and the subsequent visit to Bow Street had transformed his financial prospects. Not only that; he had sat by the most beautiful woman in the world, so close he could see the tiny, transparent hairs on her face, the sweetest tint on her cheeks at moments of agitation and the pallor of her silent fury; a creature of passion and intelligence such as he had never encountered before.

Edwards had a mission, and he had a purpose. His heart was aflame. He would damn Carlile but lease his premises and create the most influential coffee shop in London. The tavern ragamuffins would flock to him like sheep to slaughter, and in the blessed silence that followed, George Edwards would prosper, and when the time came, who could say that he had not done the world a most marvellous favour?

CHAPTER EIGHT

Monday 17ᵗʰ May, 1819

TIDD / BRUNT

Brooke's Market, Holborn

More than two weeks had passed, and Eliza Tidd supposed that the shilling her husband had so far received from Mr Brunt for his labour on May Day weekend was better than nothing. The purchase each week of a few marrow bones, taters and onions had provided, with the last sack of oats, a few wholesome meals for her family. Mrs Tidd had been obliged, on several occasions, to smack the younger twins' legs when she caught them on tip toe, dangling spoons into the pan. Did the family not have enough sorrows, she snapped, without Francis and Marjorie being scalded to death for the sin of greed? When the pan was almost empty, Mrs Tidd exchanged the scrapings with a neighbour for an ounce of yeast and a jar of flour that she could mix and take down the bake house, once Marjorie had squeezed all the weevils out.

When her husband arrived home that Monday evening after another long and hopeless search for work, Eliza cajoled the children into silence. They sat cross-legged on the floor, as usual, while Mary read aloud, having, in better days, spent five years at school. A wedding gift from her husband, The *Pilgrims' Progress* was the only book Eliza Tidd possessed, not counting her father's gold encrusted, Illustrated Bible which lived high on top of the cupboard to be dusted four times a year and fetched down at Christmas, and Easter.

An extract of John Bunyan's book had been read aloud in their home every night since her marriage. It was a thrilling tale of bravery, morality and adventure, and Mrs Tidd was of the firm opinion that by listening to it nightly, her children would be infused by its values and become, inevitably, first class citizens of the world.

Eliza Tidd held many firm opinions and took every opportunity to remind her family of them. Some were connected to matters of the soul, others to tasks her husband had not yet completed or the superior ability of her dear, late father in all matters practical and spiritual. She referred frequently to failings in Richard's habits and appearance, not all of which could be blamed on his lazy eye. There was scarcely a moment of Richard Tidd's home life that was not filled with the wailing of children or the manifold reminders of his inadequacies.

He was grateful to John Bunyan for an uninterrupted smoke of his pipe every night, but since he could no longer afford the baccy, even that pleasure had been absent in recent months. Still, the peace was welcome, and Mary's voice was as clear as an angel, her face just as sweet. His step-daughter would easily find employment in the theatre, if her mother were not so set against it. Eliza would rather die of starvation than offer a child to the iniquitous domain of public entertainment.

When the reading was done, red-haired Marjorie clambered on to her father's lap and demanded attention. Tidd tossed the younger twins, one by one into the air. They clamoured for more, and then Jeremy and Charlie wanted to play too, but Tidd said there was no time, because he was off to see Mr Brunt. Hopeful of payment, Eliza rewarded him with a smile.

It was raining hard as Tidd hurried across the market to Brook Street and into Fox Court, the congested alley, where the Brunts lived. Their first-floor apartment was accessed, exactly like Tidd's, by iron steps leading to an outside corridor, which the Brunts shared with their landlady, Mrs Rogers. Opening his door by three inches, Brunt whispered, for the sake of domestic harmony, that he was glad to see Mr Tidd, and there was a sensitive matter he wished to discuss.

"Sensitive matters are unlikely to provide a meal for my family," replied Tidd, hotly. "All I want is my rightful wage."

"Then we are in agreement," replied Brunt, "if you will spare a moment, I shall tell you my plan."

"Not while I'm out here, getting drenched, you won't!" said Tidd.

"Nor where my family might overhear us," replied Brunt. "Come; I've enough to stand you a beer."

Praying that he would not have to endure another poem, Tidd waited while Brunt fetched his hat and two pots. They made a dash for their local, the White Hart, where Mrs Hobbs enquired cheerily after Molly and Eliza and wondered if the presence of two bootmakers suggested an upsurge in trade. Brunt replied that they always lived in hope, paid for the jug of small beer and asked for their jackets to be left by the fire a while to dry out.

"Well?" asked Tidd, when they were out of hearing. "Where's your plan?"

"Mr Tidd," began Brunt in sombre tones. "As far as the pursuit of reform is concerned, you and I have always occupied opposite sides of the bench."

"Aye," said Tidd, his scepticism unabated.

"For reasons I'm not at liberty to disclose, and after a period of self-examination, I am converted. Mr Tidd; I have made my decision. I am no longer the mild person you knew before. From this day forth, we should consider ourselves to be wearing the same pair of boots. Where you are the toe, I am the heel."

"Very poetic!" cried Tidd, the sarcasm quite lost on a companion absorbed in bearing his soul.

"Give me Liberty or give me Death," continued Brunt, quoting American and French sources.

"I'd rather have my money," cried Tidd, though his political heart rejoiced at the sentiment.

"Quietly!" said Brunt, fearful that even the White Hart was peopled by spies. "I have a solution, but first, I'd like your opinion of George Edwards."

"Fishy, since you ask," replied Tidd.

"Agreed," said Brunt. "Slippery as a herring."

"Why do you want to know?"

"Has he mentioned any explosive devices?"

"What explosive devices?"

"George Edwards has been blowing up cushions." said Brunt. "He told me so himself."

Tidd scoffed. "That'll put a speedy end to My Lord Sidmouth!"

The bootmakers laughed, looked each other in the eye and knew they were friends.

"We're agreed, then?" asked Brunt. "Given due provocation, we do not automatically condemn acts of violence. We treat the model-maker with caution, and we refuse to have any truck with his explosions."

"We certainly do!" said Tidd, raising his pot to meet Brunt's and clinch the deal. "Now then, where's 't plan?"

"While we sit here with rattling bellies," whispered Brunt, "there are folks in Derbyshire, dancing minuets and quadrilles in shoes that you and I have made, for which neither the leather nor the labour has been paid. How do they suppose we'll feed our families or pay the tanner for our next order?"

"'T devils never consider it," said Tidd, pleased to hear himself included in a future commission. "You suggest we march up to Derbyshire and demand payment?"

"No need," replied Brunt. "We shall go together to their house on Cavendish Square. If the occupants refuse to pay the debt, we'll take charge of property that can be sold to the same value. We spare the bailiffs the effort, and who would deny us that right?"

"Bravo, Thomas!" replied Tidd. "There's fighting talk!"

"From this day on, Tiddy" said Brunt, "Where you are the heel, I am the toe!"

"Hurrah!" said Tidd, his mood transformed by solidarity.

INGS

Baker's Row, Whitechapel

When Celia returned from Portsea and heard about her lost fortune, she cried for an hour before opining that city-folk lack the purity of the air they breathe in Portsea and must therefore be prone to misshapen thinking. Ings wondered whether the London air was distorting his own thoughts, because ever since the business with the Godbolds, he had experienced a crisis of faith. Why would a loving God permit the destruction of his family's dreams? Why would He condone the suffering of so many Britons? When Ings stopped going out at night to offer thanks and admire the skies, Celia did not protest, except to ask,

"What use is star-gazing in a place with no stars?"

Early on his third Monday in Whitechapel, Ings tethered his horse for grooming. He picked the mud and stones from the hooves, combed the mane and tail and tugged out the last of the winter coat, which, in Hampshire, Jupiter would have rolled away in the field. He taught his son to make wisps from damp hay, and together, they kneaded and pummelled Jupiter's coat, till he shone like polished copper.

The girls came to admire their pet and bid him good-bye. Annie hoped that Jupiter's new owner would be as kind as pa, and not beat him, as some men do.

"Brush off your tears, madam" was Celia's advice. "There's work to be done, bundling that hay for sale."

Bill's instruction was to cart up the dung and take it to the garden of the Baptist Church, where the congregation might benefit from their misfortune with flowers next year.

At Smithfield, nobody wanted a horse at anywhere near the price Ings had paid two weeks earlier. He met the spidery groom again, who recommended a livery near the high end of Fleet Market, and hoped for another penny treat, but was disappointed. The only livery Ings could find on Fleet Market was empty, and the lads playing ball in the yard said it had closed a year ago, Mister.

Lost for a plan, but not yet dejected, Ings led his mount away. He was standing at the corner of Fleet Street, wondering which way to go, when who should approach, bright and breezy as a corn-field in June, but George Edwards.

"How marvellous to see you again," said Edwards, shaking the country fellow's hand in that feeble way of his and noting Ings's sorrowful expression. "I trust, dear friend, that no cloud has descended upon your fortunes?"

"I fear, sir, that it has," said Ings. "I find myself before a temporary downfall."

"Then I must stand you a treat!" said Edwards. "Perhaps we shall find reason to celebrate."

As he tethered Jupiter to a tree in the Mitre's yard, Ings could not have known that his life was about to change again, a consequence of the proposition George Edwards would make, when his belly was stuffed with liver and bacon, and his head spinning with gin.

If his head had not spun, Ings might have gone back to Smithfield another time, made a fair sale of the horse and returned with his family to whatever shame awaited them in Hampshire. But his head did spin, and he accepted Edwards's proposal to install him as manager of his new coffee shop on Fleet Street.

To Ings's enquiry - whether there might be a market in the shop for good Hampshire baking - Edwards replied gravely that Mr Ings underestimated his new role. He would not be selling pies and cakes with his coffee, but a new vision for Britain! Edwards had rented the premises from a famous radical, who insisted that the new manager sympathized with the philosophies of reform. Such businesses thrived, Mr Edwards explained, in all the great cities of the world, and Mr Ings was fortunate to be thrust into the heart of the reform movement. An apartment was available for his family, and there would be no objection, should Mrs Ings choose to bake there, so long as there was no adverse impact on trade downstairs.

When they had shaken hands and parted, Ing patted Jupiter's head, whispering joyfully, as he mounted, that they were saved, and in a spirit of inflamed optimism, rode back to Whitechapel. Bill was out with his last barrow of dung, but the girls cheered and clapped to see their father returning with the old familiar smile, and Jupiter still theirs.

At the table, helping Thirza and Emeline with their alphabet, Celia saw the ale in her husband's eyes and the silly grin, which grew wider as she pursed her lips in disapproval.

"Put away your worries, wife!" said Ings, taking his seat at table. "The Lord has heard our prayers!"

"Mr Pyke has restored my fortune?" asked Celia, as Ings teased and tickled his daughters.

"Not exactly," replied Ings.

"But Jupiter is saved?" she asked, having heard her husband's approach in the yard.

"Run along, children," said Ings abandoning hope of an easy conversation.

Celia was furious that her husband had failed to sell the horse, and she was firmly set against moving into the sinful heart of London. They had worked hard to restore the premises at Baker's Row, she said, and they should stay here, as agreed, and develop the property as a pie shop and lodging house. Ings explained that all such desirable plans must be delayed while they remove the mountain of debt. Their only hope was to sell everything and hope that the outstanding amount might be paid in instalments. When Celia protested, Ings reminded her that it was only through Mr Pyke's endeavours and Mr Edwards's generosity that he was not in the debtors' gaol already.

As she played with the ingredients and flavours of her broth, the smells transported Celia to the kitchen in Portsea, and peace descended upon her. When it was simmering nicely, she squeezed Jimmy's hand and said she was sorry for her temper, and they would conquer their mountain of woe together. Ings folded his arms around her and said he loved his wife every second of every day and night, but most of all, when she was warm like this, with her cheeks as red as apples.

Celia giggled and told him to get away, but then she kissed him and said she had been thinking about a story Lizzie told, one rainy day in the kitchen. It was tragic, but it might help their situation until his first wage came in.

After Cousin Jack died, when Lizzie wasn't in the laundry, her nose was always in a book. That day, she was talking about French soldiers in the Russian Campaign. Boney never expected the war to take very long, and his army was not prepared for the bitter frosts of winter, that could take off a man's ears. Thousands of soldiers froze to death or were murdered for their uniforms by Russian peasants. The men who survived did so by roasting their horses, which tasted, Lizzie reported, like a sweeter version of beef. Although Whitechapel was not to be compared with the Russian steppe, Celia opined, the French might, for once, teach them a lesson.

There were some trembling lips, but the girls did their best not to make a fuss when they heard that Jupiter would be leaving again, and that their new boots and petticoats would have to be sold. At two o'clock, in defiance of the dark clouds above, they helped Celia to push the cart to market, where they would sell any clothes the family no longer needed, and invest in flour, eggs, salt and a quantity of cooking fat.

Ings and his son went to the stable. Despite the mess it meant for the butchering, they fed Jupiter a final meal of nuts and hay. Ings fetched some chalk and marked the spot, just above and between his eyes, where the kill would be quickest. He told Bill to take the reins and then, by way of practice, aimed Uncle Stone's pistol at an old barrel. Jupiter whinnied at the blast and skipped nervously. Bill steadied him and patted his head reassuringly. The lad's eyes locked grimly on the dark liquid oozing from the shot barrel. His father knew that look.

"There's no shame, son" said Ings, "if you ain't got the stomach for it."

"I shan't be crying for Jupiter, pa." said Bill, "when what matters is our livelihood."

"Spoke like a true butcher!" said Ings.

"He might lunge towards me, when it's done," he continued, taking a position in front of the horse. "So I'll have to move fast. There'll be a second shot between his ears, so's he don't twitch after. Steady, now?"

Bill was steady alright, and quickly, expertly, Ings blew the brains out of Jupiter. The horse shuddered and dropped, without lunging, to the ground.

"Good work, pa", said Bill and offered to take the pistol for the second shot.

When it was done, Bill stood there, calm as a summer pond, while his insides rattled like a shoal of netted fish.

"William Stone Ings," said his pa. "At Jupiter's last breath, my son has become a man. I ain't never known a prouder moment!"

Ings produced the medicinal flask he had secreted in the depths of his apron pocket, and they drank a toast of thanks to Jupiter for his service and his sacrifice. Then they severed the head and the legs, hoisted the carcass on to a hook for bleeding out and scrubbed the yard, so the girls would have no doubt that their pet had gone to a nice home in the country.

In a short time, while Ings and Bill salted away some of Jupiter for the future, the Ings's eldest daughter, Annie, mercifully unaware what flesh she handled, helped Celia to bake seventy-two mouth-watering pies.

TIDD / BRUNT
The streets of London

Ignoring the gathering storm, Brunt and Tidd began the walk from Brooke's Market to Cavendish Square. They made an odd couple. Brunt, with his full head of dark hair and stocky build, was a good nine inches shorter than Tidd. His face was pock-marked and restless, always ready to expose his mood, sometimes before Brunt knew it himself.

As they turned on to Grays Inn Lane towards Holborn, Tidd remarked that a little baccy for his pipe would help his condition no end, and he hoped, by the end of the day, to have some. Brunt said he would settle for a beef pie. When the rain came down, they agreed to avoid the wider thoroughfares. Where a driver might reduce his speed for a gentleman in a tall hat with a lady on his arm, who on earth cared about the comfort or the clothing of a pair of ragamuffins?

The side streets were cloaked in mud. Rubbish lay in damp, foul-smelling piles and streamed in sodden lumps along the gullies. On Bloomsbury Square, they watched a drenched dog bark at a pair of rats that squeaked and picked at peelings dropped on a window sill. Outside the British Museum, a small boy struggling to carry a baby wrapped in a grubby shawl, begged for a penny to feed his little sister, or even a spare farthing would do, or a slice of bread or cabbage.

They marched on, ignoring the relentless rain, Tidd suggested they plan their speech, while Brunt considered it wiser to see the colour of the enemy's eyes and trust to instinct. The discussion lasted all the way to Bedford Square, where they compromised with a choice of three different scenarios. As they stood still to shake hands on it, they became aware of the rain, dripping from their hats into their ears and whiskers. It drizzled down their chins and throats and through the matted hair on their chests. It seeped into their eyes and slithered through Molly Brunt's darning on her husband's sleeve, soaking his right arm. Wet London clay oozed between the seams of their weary old boots, squelched beneath the soles of their feet and trickled between their toes. They carried on.

They negotiated the traffic on Tottenham Court Road without much ado, until they turned the corner into Goodge Street, when a small pig trotted frantically out of a courtyard, as if making an escape. Dismayed by the crash and rumble of traffic, the delinquent panicked, and as it scampered, squealing, across the road, unnerved a pony. The cart swerved, and as the driver tried to avoid a collision, one of the wheels charged through a deep puddle. A great wall of mud rose and landed with a great smack on to Tidd and Brunt. The pig disappeared, and the trap drove on, but the boot makers were stopped in their tracks. They turned to look at each other, and Tidd began to laugh. He stood there, like a six-foot scarecrow, aching with hunger and worry, but hooting and whooping at the absurdity of his sodden friend and his sodden self and their sodden situation. Brunt began to laugh too. They both threw back their heads and laughed. They clapped their hands and hugged each other and howled with laughter, because they could not, and they would not weep. Anyone riding along Goodge Street that Tuesday, who gave the pair a second look would presume two lunatics had taken flight from an asylum.

When they recovered, the rain had softened. Despite their condition, Brunt proposed a sentimental detour to the place where he was born, and had been apprenticed to the kindly Mr Brooke, next door. Brooke fell silent as he looked at the cottages on Union Street, with the park behind and the washhouse on the corner. How small and harmless the buildings looked now, how insignificant his father, the cruel and incompetent Walter Brunt, who always blamed the French and his son for his woes, turned to dust. He recalled the grief at the death of his beloved Grandpa Moreton, and his mother's despair, when the hero's bed was rented to strangers less than a month later, because the tailor took ill and could no longer cut a straight line. As Brunt took one last, sad look at the old cottage, Tidd was sharp enough to ask no questions where questions did not belong.

Arriving at last at Cavendish Square, they knocked boldly at His Lordship's front door, having conspired, in the first instance, to ask gently for their money. The housekeeper looked frightened by the two desperadoes, and asked boldly how they dared to call at the front door like this. Then she knew Brunt's face beneath the mud and amid a peal of generous laughter, asked how Mr Brunt and his friend came to look so like highwaymen.

Brunt and Tidd were silenced. It was not a response for which their plans had prepared them.

"If it's your money you're after," she continued warmly, "I have a note for you to take to Coutts Bank, authorising full payment with a bonus to express His Lordship's pleasure in the workmanship and his apology for the delay."

Brunt turned to Tidd. "Who's a disciple of the devil now?" he asked.

Disregarding the strange remark, the housekeeper said they looked like death warmed up, and she was sorry she laughed. She would hate to deprive the world of Mr Brunt's excellent foot-wear and they might both avoid pneumonia with a tub of hot water and a hearty meal. If they would go to the cellar door and remove their boots, she would see what help could be raised before the idle coachman returned them to their families.

Mrs Brunt and Mrs Tidd were flabbergasted when their husbands arrived home at eight o'clock, clean as plucked chickens, dressed in footmen's livery and armed with a feast of left-over food. They kissed the men robustly for the news of payment tomorrow. The Tidd twins jumped and squealed for joy, all four of them, and Harry Brunt asked when his school-books and his drum would be fetched from pawn.

Tidd had informed Brunt, during their grand journey home, that his philosophical position had not changed. The kindness had come from members of their own class, he argued, whose aristocratic employers were only paying their dues and ensuring a future with decent boots. Still, when Eliza slept soundly at his side, Tidd found himself wondering whether housekeeping might be a suitable occupation for his daughters. Then he remembered that come the Revolution, such grandeur would be extinct.

Thursday, 20ᵗʰ May, 1819

INGS

Bride Lane / Fleet Street, London

Sidney Harding, landlord of the Old Bell remembered Mr Ings and was delighted to meet his wife at last and taste one of her famous pies. Celia's pride flipped to disappointment, when both Mr and Mrs Harding judged the pastry and the sauce superbly flavoured, but the content too rough on the jaw for their discriminating customers. Ings advised his wife not to be disheartened. With so few teeth between them, the proprietors of the Old Bell were not the ideal judges of her baking, which was still the best in Hampshire.

Annie stayed in the lane, guarding the cart and the produce, while her parents took four pies up to Fleet Street, where the tiny Boar's Head was packed, as usual, with Irishmen. The landlord bought three pies without a tasting, and as the Ings squeezed their way to the exit, they heard the rogue calling out double the price he had paid.

Out on the street, Ings remarked that once a person knew how to operate in London, it was easy to turn a profit without lifting a finger. Celia was responding that the secret was in knowing how, when they heard a girlish scream. It came from the corner of Bride Lane and it was, undoubtedly, from Annie.

"Stop, thief!" they heard her cry.

Breathless, but unhurt, Annie pointed towards St Bride's churchyard, and Ings raced off in pursuit. He caught the villain, cowering behind the Temple Church, panting as he stuffed the stolen pie into his mouth. Careless of the holy location, Ings grabbed the fellow by the ear and said that his next destination, after Newgate Gaol, would be New South Wales.

"Have mercy, good sir," said the wretch. "My name is Patrick Philbin, and I mean no harm. I lost this hand in Salamanca, and sure there's nobody will give me work."

When Ings introduced his new friend, who was Irish and a veteran, Celia suggested that instead of thieving and giving their daughter a mortal fright, Mr Philbin might have asked first, but he was welcome to another pie for tomorrow. Ings provided thruppence from their takings and advised Mr Philbin to invest in a broom. There was money to be made, he said, by sweeping the maze of courts and alleys around Fleet Street. Philbin promised to follow the advice and would forever be grateful to such good Samaritans for not dispatching to the other side of the world. If any opportunity arose to repay their kindness, Patrick Philbin could generally be found in the vicinity of the Boar's Head.

After showing his wife and daughter the exterior of their new home at 55½, Fleet Street, Ings led the way into Mitre Court, where Celia suggested that her husband should watch the cart, while she and Annie sold the pies, for which, given the number of lawyers in the district, they could easily ask a penny more. Celia's strategy worked because they sold four pies at the Mitre, and another three at The Old Cock. At the White Lion on Wych Street they sold five pies, while at The Crown and Anchor, Mr Otley wanted none that day, but would welcome their return next week. The Black Dog on Clements Lane took two, and by the time they started on the Strand, only forty-four pies were left and by Charing Cross, twenty-six. With nineteen pies sold, seven gone as tasters and two to the needy Irishman, Mr and Mrs Ings were feeling buoyant.

They followed a winding passage to The Scotch Arms, where the attempted sale resulted in an offence against the virtue of Ings's wife and daughter. Celia reminded her husband of the iniquity of London. The fish in the Thames, she said, were more deserving of her handiwork than any item of London's vulgar population, and she proposed throwing the remaining produce into the river. Ings forbade such waste, and the cart was finally emptied on the south side of Covent Garden, where they forgot their woes and sang a west-country song about Widdecombe Fair until the last pie was sold. Minus the thruppence they had given away, the Ings had made thirteen shillings and eight pence. All things considered, it seemed a fair profit.

As they walked back up to Whitechapel, Mr and Mrs Ings agreed to keep the Swiss watch for emergencies and the butchery tools in case their fortunes improved. Everything else would be divided between two piles – one for the essentials for life and the other for market. Leaving his wife and daughter to make the selection, Tidd took the cart to the cold store, filled it with Jupiter's hide, head, hair and bones and set off for the knacker in Spitalfields.

Another two shillings richer, he headed for Brick Lane. Godbold's shop was closed, but when his daughter looked up from her newspaper, and saw who was knocking at the window, she opened the door and, without a word or any other indication of her mood, inclined her head to the staircase.

"Merci bien," said the old cutler, when he had counted Ings's money and pushed it into a drawer. There was no sign of an Indian dagger, and he looked at Ings with eyes as brown and wily as a weasel.

"Monsieur Eengs," he said. "No lawyer should profit from an argument between fellow Christians, who never meant each other harm. What do you say to transferring your business premises in Whitechapel to my name?" he said. "The bone-handled knives will stay here as a reminder, but I never wish to speak nor hear the putrid name of Silas Stone again. May his soul rot in purgatory!"

Faint with relief that no more would be demanded, Ings hurried away before Mr Godbold could change his mind. At Chancery Lane, Mr Pyke could not hide his regret at the loss of a costly court battle, but agreed to act promptly for the transfer of the property at Baker's Row. He took his client's last shilling against his account and said, quite amicably, that he was continuing to do his best to keep Mr Ings out of gaol.

As he walked eastward again to Whitechapel, James Ings speculated that he might simply have ignored the eccentric cutler and his threats. Cousin Jack might even say that the whole story was a concoction, dreamed up by Pyke and Godbold for personal profit. But Jack was not always right, and what value was there in a life defined by guilt and fear? Ings looked up at the darkening sky, which was streaked with red and purple lines and acknowledged that his conscience was clear and that once again, things were looking up.

EDWARDS
The streets of London

With Mrs G hollering after him that he better not expect no bloody bed tonight, nor dinner neither, Edwards sauntered down to Chiswell Street, where he had an account with the livery manager, who had snubbed his mare. There was no need for his mother or William to know about his habit of hiring cabs, but the new prosperity would provoke curiosity among his associates about the new boots, breeches and shirts, the regular dining out and so on. He needed to hint at a plausible explanation, and the inspiration came, as he rode into town that Thursday.

He was chuckling to himself about his new tenants, the country couple, who had lost their fortune in less than a month, when it occurred to George Edwards that he might have an inheritance. too. He would invent a relation of his paternal grandmother; a Count or Prince, perhaps, who had been robbed of his territories by the Vienna Convention and died tragically young, leaving Cousin George a fortune. He decided upon Bavaria, and as he chuckled at his own brilliance, the driver asked what he had seen that was so funny, because he could do with a laugh too.

A solution to George Edwards's housing problem was more elusive. The apartment above the coffee shop was suitable for a rustic rabble, but far too cramped for an artist of distinction. He decided to visit Brown's Coffee shop in Mitre Court in the hope of finding a helpful associate, who had lodged there in the old days. Publisher of the conservative daily, *The New Times*, John Alcock was an amiable rogue, who profited from his readers' fears by demonizing any person or organization that, in his or his editor's mind, dared to criticize the established Church. So successful was his strategy and his newspaper, that Alcock owned a portfolio of houses and taverns in London and Berkshire. It would do no harm to rekindle the association, and Alcock might know of empty premises nearby.

Standing almost exactly opposite the Courts of Justice, Browns was loud with the chatter of lawyers and thick with the odours of coffee and tobacco smoke. And yes, at the same table as ever, there sat Mr Alcock, a little thinner, but with the familiar thick, white hair and whiskers and tiny, sparkly blue eyes that were constantly on the move. Alcock saw Edwards, summoned him and introduced his editor, John Stoddart. Their work was done, Alcock said, but he would order more coffee in the hope of some royal revelations. Hinting that he had grown weary of Windsor, Edwards revealed that he was back in London and had bigger fish to fry.

"Bigger than Prinny?" asked Stoddart with a sceptical grin.

Edwards smiled back. "Of greater interest, to your readers and your competitors," he said, "than that gluttonous, self-absorbed wastrel."

"You've lost none of your talent for tact, Mr Edwards," said Alcock, who was a sycophant when it came to royalty. "Spit it out, man, and I'll see what we can do."

"Very well," said Edwards. "I'm going into business with Mr Richard Carlile."

"Carlile the journalist?" asked Alcock, a stickler for checking his facts.

"You heard me," replied Edwards.

The two practised newspapermen absorbed the information and gave nothing away until Stoddart said,

"Have you spoken to any other newspaper about this?"

The advance would allow Edwards to complete the purchase of vital equipment, but he was no further in the search for accommodation. On the grounds that ostentation would inhibit his unfolding plans, he decided not to take a room at Brown's and estimated a few tiresome more nights at ma's. After checking the renovation works at his coffee shop, he walked to Fleet Market in search of gin and mutton. He was about to argue about the high proportion of fat in the shoulder he was buying, when he heard a familiar voice at his side.

"Hello Georgie! Where've you been? Don't fancy another dance, do you?"

So much had happened since he last saw her, that Edwards needed a moment to recall Tilly or her special entertainment. He was surprised that such a talented girl offered her services so blatantly, but then thought that times were hard, and Tilly wasn't seventeen any more. He said if she would give him a minute to pay up, he would be all hers.

"Why didn't you say you needed a roof over your head?" she asked, when Edwards explained his predicament.

"I'm starting out in business," he replied, "and in no position to enjoy your company on a nightly basis, Tilly. Not yet anyway."

"I thought it was a roof you wanted, not a doodle-sack to play on!"

Twenty minutes later, Edwards was following Tilly Buck's shapely back-side up two flights of stairs above the bookshop in Johnson's Court, of which, by very good fortune, the Fleet Street entrance was precisely opposite his coffee shop. It was her own apartment, Tilly boasted, a gift from an Admiral. George could have the room at the back for a fair rent, extras negotiable, and the top floor, which had a large window and plenty of north-facing light, for his studio.

When Tilly said if he would light the fire and put that mutton in the pan, she might sing the lark song later, Edwards decided he had the luck of the devil.

CHAPTER NINE

Friday, 9th July, 1819

BRUNT / TIDD / EDWARDS

After the bruising experience with Mr Carlile in May, Tom Brunt had been less inclined to poetic composition, and spent his Saturdays playing cards with Tidd or devising ways to earn a few pennies here and there without stealing work from an honest man or offending the wives' delicate morality. While Molly and Eliza struggled with near-empty pantries, each managing discontent and family cares according to her own resources, their husbands gathered strength in facing storms together, each respecting, for the most part, the fixed ideas of the other.

When Tidd opined that the new deputy had turned Thistlewood into custard, Brunt advised him, instead of resenting the unencumbered rise of Edwards, to be proud of his own achievements. For nearly two years, while Thistlewood was locked up, Tiddy had run the group alone, even fulfilling secretarial duties that had rightly belonged to the hapless William Edwards. Unlike the lamplighter, Tidd had made his contribution alongside the demands of a large family and the grinding search for work. By employing a deputy with no such distractions, Thistlewood was rewarding Tidd with a well-deserved break.

It was an almost inevitable consequence of their new alignment that Brunt and Tidd should also form a working partnership. By moving the workshop to Fox Court, Tidd suggested, they would release space in his apartment, urgently needed for Mary, who was becoming too womanly to sleep on the ledge above the twins. When the Brunt family visited the Tidds to discuss the proposal, Molly Brunt set against it. If Mr Tidd's tools and equipment were transported to her husband's workshop, there would be nowhere for their own child or the apprentice to sleep. Mrs Tidd was of the opinion that the two lads should move into the Brunts' private accommodation, a suggestion crossly opposed by Mrs Brunt, who was not about to sacrifice her privacy or her bed to help a man who had given no thought to restraint or family planning during his youth and must now live with the consequences.

Insulted by Molly and indignant at her husband's failure to defend her honour, Eliza Tidd refused to quarrel in company, and sat staring at her needlework. The stalemate was resolved when Harry Brunt piped up. Mr Brunt and Mr Tidd could share the workshop at Fox Court, he said. Mary Tidd should move into the Tidds' present workshop at Hole in the Wall Passage. Joe Hale would sleep on the ledge above the twins, and Harry would muck in with his parents at Fox Court. They would save money by pooling the equipment, with duplicates sold for profit, which could be shared between the two households.

Molly Brunt's pride in her son silenced all protest, until Eliza Tidd mentioned her joy at the prospect of no more hammering. When Molly observed that there would therefore be twice the noise at Fox Court, Eliza opined that double was better than no hammering at all. As for herself, Mrs Tidd could not expect to feed another man's apprentice, especially one as tall and hungry as Joe Hale.

Brunt and Tidd busied themselves with an inventory and, when they made their way, as usual on Friday afternoons, to the coffee shop at 55½, Fleet Street, they left Harry and the apprentice to measure, count and combine all the tacks and nails, needles, twine and leather. The matter of who, in these difficult times, might wish to buy their spare equipment proved thorny until they mentioned it to George Edwards over coffee (free to committee members). He reminded them of young upstarts, confident of competing with old dogs, but unable to afford new equipment, and suggested Mercy's Go in Cripplegate, where the proprietor was a spirited businesswoman, who paid fair prices. A portion of her profit contributed to a lottery, and they might even win a prize. As the bootmakers considered the idea, Edwards called to his manager to stop wiping tables and bring more coffee. Mr Ings, who naturally had overheard the conversation and, for once, was smiling, suggested that if the citizens were in need of transport, they were welcome to borrow his cart in exchange for a donation, later, in the box on the counter, marked "For the Deserving Poor of Hampshire."

With the transaction agreed and coffee poured, Ings turned to greet a new customer who requested a very strong coffee and the latest copy of Sherwin's.

Edwards drew the bootmakers close and spoke to them in hushed tones. "Political expedience," he began, "is a moon that waxes and wanes, as you know of old, Mr Tidd."

"Indeed, I do," replied Tidd, a little nervous of Edward's conspiratorial tone.

"Very poetical, citizen," replied Brunt, "but where's the meaning?"

"As Thistlewood's deputy," said Edwards, "I can confidentially reveal that the Group's adherence to the principles of Henry Hunt will be short-lived. In the light of new information about the government's plans, it is essential we begin gathering arms."

"Does Mr Thistlewood know about this?" asked Brunt, who had not quite abandoned his caution regarding the exploding cushions.

"In principle, of course he does," replied Edwards, "although at this busy time and with Squire Hunt sniffing around, I'm reluctant to trouble him with details."

"You're not suggesting aggression towards any innocent party?" asked Brunt.

"No!" replied Edwards emphatically. "These measures are purely precautionary."

The bootmakers looked at each other uncertainly, until Brunt said in a whisper,

"If Tiddy will, so shall I."

So that Edwards would know he still had a mind of his own, Tidd responded in equally hushed tones, that he required more information. Drawing the bootmakers closer, Edwards explained that a great many weapons were held at the East India Company's depot off the City Road. He intended to remove them to a warehouse in Pentonville. The weapons would be used when – and only when – the citizens of London were forced to defend themselves. A team of supporters was in place, and he had Tidd and Brunt in mind for a managerial role.

The bootmakers were flattered by the token of esteem, and Tidd replied that, as a close-knit team, they would discuss the matter and give their response at the meeting. Edwards urged them, whatever the outcome, to say nothing to anyone else. Membership had swollen in advance of the rally. The government was as nervous as a cat in a wolf-pack, and there were spies everywhere.

As they set off for Water Lane, Brunt and Tidd contemplated their managerial roles, and concluded that as a purely precautionary step, there could be no harm in taking weapons from the rich to help the poor. Tidd added that while he respected Brunt's commitment to unvarnished truth, it might be wise to say nothing to the wives. Having suffered weeks of cross looks since the canary's little corpse was ruined by the tanner, Tom Brunt said that he could not agree more.

THISTLEWOOD / THE GROUP
Black Lion Hall, Water Lane, off Fleet Street

Since Thistlewood's return from Horsham, a new, constructive mood had emerged at Water Lane. To mark the thirtieth anniversary of the French Revolution, a great rally was planned in Smithfield Square, at which several important radicals would take the hustings. Henry Hunt had agreed to speak, on condition that it reflected the peaceful intent of his successful assemblies in Birmingham, Derby and Nottingham. Thistlewood had agreed, apparently without terms.

Tonight, the wooden hall behind the Black Lion was crammed full, the air thick with sweat and anticipation. Turners and carpenters had turned out, joiners and glaziers, brick-layers and tobacconists, roofers, saddle-makers, domestic servants, milliners, hosiers, tailors, bootmakers, tanners, wheelwrights, road-sweepers, lamplighters and many more. Most were dressed in rags, many had not worked for months, and all were impatient to hear Arthur Thistlewood's most important speech since his release.

When the door was closed, George Edwards had rung the bell, Thistlewood mounted the platform, tall and proud in his black coat and characteristic navy-blue pantaloons. He looked round the room, his eyes alight with affection and optimism, and each man believed the chairman's smile was meant for him alone. Thistlewood allowed the cheer to swell before raising his arms for silence. The speech, dictated without hesitation, was written out in his wife's neat hand, but it had come from the heart, and reading was unnecessary.

"The time of desperation," he began, "is almost over. Citizens, I tell you, reform is on the move at last! In halls and taverns all over the land, its power is unstoppable. A new sense of unity is sweeping the country. In every corner of Britain, from the greatest towns to the smallest villages, we have friends and allies, who share a common purpose. Together and united, we shall experience the birth of a new era! Within a week, every guild and every association of working men in the capital will have joined the new London Union. Workers on the outskirts of London have also asked to join us. That's why the London Committee, of which I am a member, has requested a delay. In order to fulfil its proper purpose, the London rally will not take place next Wednesday, 14th July, but a week later on the 21st. We need that time to organise ourselves and ensure that everyone who wishes to join us at Smithfield is fully informed and safe.

"Citizens, if we seize this opportunity, if we seize it well, we shall no longer be the silent victims. Instead of subservience to the hypocritical cant of aristocrats, we shall be the masters of our own fate! Instead of drowning in desperation, we shall, at last, know the true meaning of hope."

The men stamped, hooted and whistled until Thistlewood hushed them. His voice became sombre.

"My friends we must learn from the atrocities in America, France and Ireland, where too many working men and women died senselessly in the name of reform. We may be angry with our so-called government, and we have sound reason, but our first duty is not vengeance. It is to protect our people and to advance prosperity for every single inhabitant of these islands. Let us confound our enemy! Let us advance, not with violence and hatred in our hearts, but in resolute confidence. The people of Great Britain, with our proud Saxon heritage, are the most civilized in the world. It is the firm belief of your own committee, as well as the London Committee and Orator Hunt, that those aims have the greatest chance of success if we proceed peacefully. Do we agree?"

"Aye!" roared the assembly.

"Any abstentions?" asked Thistlewood.

At the centre of the room, one bold hand was raised. Thomas Brunt, bootmaker of Fox Court said that while he was a man of peace, he had an important question. If, after the rally at Smithfield, no reform was forthcoming, would acts of violence then become acceptable?"

"Good man," whispered Tidd, who understood the source of the question.

Thistlewood replied curtly that the enquiry was premature. All hearts and minds must focus on success.

"Aye, Thistlewood, and in that, I am your true friend and disciple," said Brunt, his face redder than raspberries. "My question was hypothetical."

"Understood," said Thistlewood and continued.

"My friends, our action will proceed in two phases. The first will be the rallies - our own at Smithfield Square on 21st July and, two weeks later, in Manchester. Both occasions will demonstrate the nationwide desire for peaceful change. Then we shall proceed to the second phase; a process of reasoned negotiation with a government that can no longer ignore our voice."

A shout came from the Irish corner, and Thistlewood invited Pat Dolan, roof tiler from Gees Court to speak.

"I want to know whether My Lord Castlereagh understands words like 'reason' and 'negotiation'?

Thistlewood responded that Castlereagh's crimes against the Irish must never be forgotten, but His Lordship's sphere of influence had changed. His present role as Foreign Secretary had no direct bearing on matters of concern to the meeting.

"He's a member of the Cabinet, to be sure, with voting powers," replied Dolan.

"Indeed, Paddy," said Thistlewood, "and Castlereagh will be dealt with in due course. At this time, for our efforts to succeed, there's only one Minister whose opinion must be shaken –"

Someone cried, "Sidmouth!" and the room was soon filled with a chant and the stamping of boots.

"Sidmouth! Sidmouth! Sidmouth!"

"You have it!" called Thistlewood with a broad smile. "The man who has taken possession of my wife's silk umbrella, my little boy's paints, my grandfather's glass ink-stand, my own best waistcoat and pantaloons! And refuses to return them. Has he none of his own?"

The chant turned to laughter, which Thistlewood enjoyed for a moment before raising his arm again for quiet.

"Listen! Listen! And thank you, Pat Dolan. Every one of us must put his private bitterness aside and remember that our aim is to achieve progress. We, who are forced to pay taxes to fund their extravagance, to sacrifice our sons and brothers in wars about which our opinions are never sought. We, the population at large, wish to take up our rightful place in government. Our greatest chance of success is to demonstrate that the British working man is calm, reasonable and resolute. My friends, Mr Henry Hunt and the London Committee have requested that no single act of violence or provocation occurs at Smithfield on the 2ist July. To proceed in a spirit of calm is not to appear weak before the enemy. It is to astonish him, to prove that the British people are confident and capable of responsible government."

Tom Dwyer, brick-layer, also of Gee's Court had another question. As soon as the government heard about the rallies, in London and Manchester, would they not pass a law, forbidding them? Thistlewood thanked Dwyer for his insight and explained that since Parliament would be in recess, only a foreign invasion or the death of the old King would convince Members of Parliament to abandon their gambling or their country fornications for a mere matter of state.

The contempt in Thistlewood's voice was echoed in angry shouts until he raised both arms and asked for quiet for his deputy to outline the principal resolutions to be proposed by Henry Hunt at Smithfield. George Edwards climbed on to the platform, shook Thistlewood's hand and took out the sheet on which his angel had written a precis of the Orator's proposals, and which it pleased him, beyond measure, to recite to the foolish assembly.

"First; from New Year's Day 1820, no man shall be required to pay tax, unless he is properly represented in the government. Second; every parish in the country will be invited to open their books and produce the names of all male residents of sound mind, who have reached majority, and should therefore be entitled to partake in parliamentary elections."

As the recitation continued, William Edwards, standing at the back of the hall, watched his brother with cool, knowing pride. A few feet away, Tom Brunt still smarted with embarrassment, while at his side, Richard Tidd clung to his secret conviction that the men who governed this land were a hotbed of greed and hypocrisy, whose systems would never be toppled by wishful rhetoric, no matter how seductive.

INGS

55½, Fleet Street.

Ings resisted Edwards's attempts to involve him in the reform movement. It was true that meetings occurred in his free time, but especially since Edwards had forbidden either Bill or Annie to help in the shop, Ings preferred to spend his evenings in the bosom of his family. He applied appropriate vocabulary when serving customers and always recommended *Sherwin's Weekly*, edited by the owner, above the rival *Black Dwarf*. With the ready excuse of a busy shop, Ings avoided any situation that might display his ignorance about political theory, which, in better times, had always been Cousin Jack's strength.

As he closed up that Friday, Ings anticipated the stew, of which the fragrance had wafted through the ceiling all afternoon. Rather to his surprise, Celia was waiting at the top of the stairs with the smile she usually reserved for funerals.

"Dinner's ready," she said, "but you must eat it alone. The Portsmouth coach leaves Fetter Lane at seven, and I'm taking the children home. The Swiss watch has paid for the fares."

Ings stood there, half way up the stairs, silent and clenched, as if a boxer had punched his stomach. He looked at his wife in dumb alarm.

"I am sorry to leave you at the mercy of an unfeeling master," continued Celia, "but I must think of the children, and you must make the best of things, Jimmy. Send money as much and as often as you can, and we'll be together again, before you know it."

Ings understood that his wife had been miserable in the dark, tiny flat without a baking oven, and that the children were miserable because she had forbidden them to go out without an escort, even when Bill and Annie wanted to help their predicament by finding employment. He had heard their quarrels through the ceiling, while he worked, and he had begged his wife to keep the children quiet with study, or even walk with them to Hyde Park, but she did not, or she could not, and on Friday morning, George Edwards had marched up the stairs and complained in words so vulgar that Celia dared not repeat them, that her noisy brats were wrecking his business. The sympathetic friend had become a monster.

At easier times, Ings would have explained all the reasons for his family to stay with him, but the London experience had so weakened his spirit, that he accepted Celia's decision without contest. He took his son aside and explained that he must look after the family, until they were reunited. Bill Ings gave his oath, and said he looked forward to his cousins and Aunt Lizzie, the fresh air and stepping into the sea again, now that summer was here.

EDWARDS / THISTLEWOOD
The Black Lion, Water Lane

On the streets of London, Arthur Thistlewood's distinctive appearance and infamous history were so well-known, that every man thought it his right to stop him on the street and exchange a few opinions. For such occasions, Thistlewood had developed a public personality, a parody, perhaps, of his real self. Only with his wife or close friends, could he relax enough to liberate the anarchic elements of his personality. Friday nights at the Black Lion with George had quickly evolved into a weekly highlight. Ostensibly arranged to discuss matters arising at Water

Lane, the extended suppers, funded by Edwards's Bavarian relation, were conducted with an almost sinister irreverence that was forgotten, at least by Thistlewood, as soon as they felt the night air.

Tonight, Thistlewood was in a dark, excitable mood, a combined consequence of the successful meeting and the glass of absinthe he sipped as they waited for the customary table. The green elixir reminded him of Paris and those spirited times, when wine was disdained as the fuel of the aristocracy. Absinthe, he had once told Edwards, opened the mind to extraordinary ideas, ideas that could change art and literature or even the structure of societies. Edwards had subsequently acquired a quantity for the Black Lion, to be reserved, he instructed Mr Cooper, for their Friday suppers.

"Hunt thinks we changed the date because the fourteenth of July is too provocative," Thistlewood revealed, when Mr Cooper had guided them to the table in the corner.

Edwards chuckled. "The squire likes to play it safe!"

"I've seen too much bloodshed already in the name of revolution," replied Thistlewood. "Whatever we think of him privately, Hunt's methods are effective."

"What other reason did the London Committee give for the delay?" asked Edwards.

"Simple," replied Thistlewood. "Without another week's subscriptions, we'd struggle to pay for the speakers' transport and expenses."

"I could have provided the money," said Edwards.

"Thank you," replied Thistlewood, "but we need the extra time, and you're generous enough with the printing press"

When Carlile stopped printing for the tavern radicals, Edwards had purchased a small press, which, for a gratuity, Brunt and Tidd had heaved up to his attic workshop. His first project had been to reissue Thistlewood's letters to the Home Secretary and Henry Hobhouse's replies on Sidmouth's behalf. The new edition sold widely, not only entertaining the public and inflaming the Lord Sidmouth, but producing a fine profit, shared equally between Thistlewood, Edwards and the rally fund.

"Do you think Brunt's question about violence was fair?" asked Edwards cautiously, when Cooper had served the soup.

"Possibly," said Thistlewood, "but premature. Some of the men need no provocation."

"But Arthur," said Edwards, "wouldn't it be wise to be prepared, at least in theory?"

"You've concocted another plan, George?" asked Thistlewood.

Edwards made suggestions sometimes that seemed to Thistlewood nothing more than fantasy or the indulgence of a free, creative spirit.

"Nobody would suspect a man carrying a pile of books into parliament," said Edwards, with a grin. "What if the pages were cut out and the gaps filled with gunpowder?"

"Tell me Tiddy's been entertaining your customers with stories of Gracie Spence!" said Thistlewood. "I hope you said nothing about gunpowder."

"Of course not," said Edwards. "This is just our game."

"In that case, I recommend you wait with your explosive books until after the recess," said Thistlewood, "when significant men will be in the House."

"Think how many brutes we could eliminate in a single operation!" said Edwards.

"And how many innocents we would slaughter!"

"Who, in the Palace of Westminster, is innocent?" asked Edwards.

"Clerks, maids, porters -" began Thistlewood.

"Chimneysweeps?" suggested Edwards with a slightly mocking tone.

"Enough!" snapped Thistlewood.

"Not so fierce, Arthur. It's only make-believe!"

"George!" said Thistlewood, lowering his voice. "Reform is within sight. Can you not smell it? We must stand by Hunt and not talk about alternatives yet, not even in jest. Do you understand?"

Edwards sipped at his cold, clear gin. He knew he must push the mercurial Arthur Thistlewood no further today.

"Alright, Arthur," he said. "No more jokes, no more experiments."

"If you must have a pastime, why not go back to modelling," suggested Thistlewood. "A figure of Henry Hunt will help the cause and turn a decent profit."

"Now, there's a good idea!" replied Edwards.

Though defeated in some points, Edwards was gratified by his better understanding of the contradictions that governed Arthur Thistlewood. They said no more and enjoyed the Black Lion's special pea and ham soup. Then Edwards raised his glass and proposed a toast to success, and as Mr Cooper approached with their steaks, Thistlewood lifted his glass too and accepted the truce.

Saturday, 17ᵗʰ July, 1819

TIDD / BRUNT

Fox Court, Holborn

As the bootmakers played cards that Saturday afternoon, two flames danced in the heart of Richard Tidd, and he needed to choose between them. With all his philosophical being, he wanted to join Brunt on the expedition to liberate the East India Company of its supply of arms. With his pragmatic being, and for the sake of his hungry family, he wanted to answer the call for day-constables at Smithfield. He would be paid, and the registration session had been fixed for 8pm on Tuesday 20th July, precisely the time at which the East India Company's gate-keeper was expected to drop the arms-store keys and take a walk.

Tom Brunt's conscience was busy with a battle of its own, namely how to explain to his family that he could not attend the candle-lit parade down Grays Inn Lane next Tuesday, at which Harry would play his drum. Harry had been obliged to leave school during the present crisis and was especially keen to join his friends and to have both parents in attendance. But Brunt had given his word to Tidd and Edwards that he would go to the City Road on a mission. He asked what reason Tidd had given for his absence on Tuesday.

"'T Pimlico aunt," said Tidd, "but in truth I expect to register as a constable for 't rally."

"Ha-ha" laughed Brunt, "that's a good one!"

"Aye and there's a shilling in it," replied Tidd.

Brunt was flabbergasted. How could Tidd be employed as a constable at their own rally? Was he prepared to join the complacent and the uncaring, the Orange-men and desperadoes, and, for the sake of a shilling, betray everything they stood for?

Tidd retorted that since Thistlewood's spirit had turned to blancmange and there would be no action at Smithfield, the constables would have nothing to do. Why not take a shilling for standing in a good position to hear the speeches?

"What about the East India job?" asked Brunt.

Tidd's brow ruffled. Despite their enjoyment of his coffee and the excitement at the prospect of managerial roles, neither he nor Brunt could summon much faith in George Edwards.

Since the miserable experience with the shoe-making equipment, they were less inclined to trust him unconditionally.

They had tugged Ings's cart, heavily laden, all the way to Cripplegate in the hope of enough profit to feed their families for a few weeks. When they arrived at Banks Court, Mrs G had laughed at the prospect of any sane person parting with cash for a bunch of worn out tools. Brunt protested that they'd travelled far to bring her these rare commodities, and that she had been specially recommended by a gentleman of distinction. When she heard her admirer's name, Mrs G shrieked and said she knew George Edwards better than anyone, and she would never buy a dozen eggs from him, because they would all be rotten. After the disappointing outcome, Brunt and Tidd pulled their cargo to Fleet Market, where Brunt knew a marine store that dealt in all kinds of oddments, and where, at last, their load was exchanged for some soap, two sacks of flour and a kettle without a spout.

"How can we be sure 't East India job ain't just as pointless?" asked Tidd.

"True, Tiddy, but how can we disappoint a man," asked Brunt, "who treats us to coffee every week, listens respectfully to our views and entrusts us with management positions?"

"A few cups of coffee and a dollop of flattery ain't no good reason to risk our lives or our freedom!" said Tidd.

"Indeed!" said Brunt. "You and I are family men, Tiddy, and can't be taking foolish risks!"

Tidd and Brunt agreed that even the shadow of a doubt was worth considering, and bearing everything in mind, they would inform George Edwards that transporting arms from City Road to Pentonville was too precarious for men with responsibilities. They were sorry to disappoint, but their executive advice would be for Mr Edwards to rent a warehouse closer to the ammunition store, and they would reconsider his proposals after the Smithfield rally.

Since such sentiments could not be safely sent by post, the bootmakers set off for Johnson's Court. When they arrived at George Edwards's door, there was such a din of machinery from above, that no amount of knocking would produce a response. They hurried down to the book shop, where Mr Fairlea of the Water Lane Group, provided note paper and a pencil. As the more literary partner, Brunt composed a coded message, which was approved by Tidd, who ran up all the stairs again and pushed it beneath George Edwards's door.

INGS

55½, Fleet Street.

It was about a week after the onset of his loneliness, and Ings was closing up, that he noticed his Irish friend sweeping an entrance on the other side of the street. He called across and invited Philbin to leave his broom in the safety of the coffee shop and take a relaxing stroll by the Thames.

Philbin didn't mind if he did, and they walked down to the embankment and watched the river traffic, carrying people and cargo, the chaotic life-blood of London, dodging and hooting into the hazy evening light.

"All them people, in all them vessels," said Ings, "each and every man and woman's got his own bag of problems, some a lot worse than yours and mine."

"Sure, I ain't doing too badly," said Philbin.

"You'd be better off, coming into my coffee shop every day, instead of wasting yourself at the Boars Head," said Ings, rather more quickly than he meant to.

"That place ain't for the likes of me," growled Philbin, as they negotiated the stony shore.

"You're wrong, my friend," said Ings. "The likes of you is exactly who it's for."

"I don't go in for books," said Philbin, firmly.

"But your spirit, I sense, is gladiatorial," replied Ings.

"Do ye' now?" asked Philbin, with a comical smile. "Well, I can't be doing with all them stuck up fellas I see through yer window."

"They're mostly humble folk like us" said Ings, "except Mr Carlile, who's a good man and the cleverest you ever met. It's only Edwards I can't abide."

"What did he do to ye'?" asked Philbin, stopping to shake his leg and liberate a pebble from his boot.

"Sent my family packing, for a start," said Ings, "and he supposes, a country butcher who never spouts Tom Paine, ain't got a history from which to draw his own conclusions!"

"An do ye'?" asked Philbin.

"I was spared the war," said Ings, "but if you count sacrificing twelve friends and five cousins in His Majesty's service, and Uncle Percy, losing his chopping arm in America. If you count paying my tolls and taxes, without which our island nation would lose its freedom, then I have a proud history, yes."

"Freedom and history are complicated items," said Philbin, gravely.

"They are, too," replied Ings. "What of you, Mr Philbin?"

Philbin was not a man of words, but as they sat, for a moment, on an abandoned jetty, he reported that he was a native of County Wexford. He never had a chance of school, but he fought the Peninsular War, survived the Forlorn Hope at the siege of Cuidad Rodrigo and lost his hand six months later at Salamanca.

"And for all that, you end up begging on the streets of London!" said Ings.

"Not since ye' gave me the broom!" said Philbin. "She's my best friend, so she is."

As they walked on, an idea began to form in Ings's mind. It required a decision, and once spoken, he could not unspeak it. The longer than usual pause puzzled Philbin, who had gauged Ings a chatterbox.

"Are ye' sure you're quite well there?" he asked.

"There could be a vacancy in my home for a lodger," said Ings.

"The likes of Pat Philbin can't be affording rent!" said Philbin.

"Perhaps not," said Ings, "but don't all the taverns and inns of court have kitchens? And don't you and your broom see the backs of them every day? Could you not take your pick of the feasts they throw out?"

Philbin scratched his head and looked at his companion, as if he had explained the movement of the earth around the sun.

"I'll provide the lodgings," said Ings, as if to clarify, "and you bring the dinners and our daily bread. What do you say?"

"Sounds grand," said Philbin. "Call me Patrick."

"Well, Patrick" said Ings, "I'm Jimmy, and I'm very partial to pies."

Edwards's only proviso to the new living arrangement was that any occupant of the apartment must be informed about the reform movement and encourage political conversation in the shop. Philbin said nothing about his own history, and Edwards proceeded to fill perceived gaps in the Irishman's understanding with whispered schemes of brutality against a malignant government. Philbin listened obediently and, when asked for an opinion, replied that he couldn't be bothered with any of it, though he would happily fire a canon into any carriage occupied by that traitor to the Stewart name, Lord Castlereagh.

Where George Edwards failed to make progress, Ings's private philosophy continued its shift. The God he once worshipped had separated him from his family. With the collapse of his wife's inheritance, he had learnt that miracles were only for the privileged. He had even begun to doubt the Resurrection and the existence of the Holy Spirit. Philbin, whose Catholic faith had been mortally wounded on the battlefields of Spain, suggested that Ings mention his doubts at Mr Carlile's next appearance in the shop.

The advice had a dramatic impact. Instead of criticising Ings for his doubts, or dispatching him to a minister of the church, Richard Carlile talked about *The Philosophy of Jesus of Nazareth*. Compiled by the American politician, Thomas Jefferson, it was a version of *The New Testament*, in which all references to the supernatural had been removed. The new philosophy was called Deism, and its followers, who included Carlile himself, believed that God had created the world, but that the world and its organization were not the responsibility of some invisible, divine force, but of mankind himself. According to Deists, officers of the organized church existed only to promote fakery and exploit those gullible enough to accept it.

When his listeners responded with incredulous enthusiasm, Carlile lent them a book about the subject, which Ings read aloud to Philbin in the evenings.

One night, as they tucked into the remains of a gooseberry pie, Ings said he doubted Tom Jefferson would give a fig for George Edwards or his combustibles, and neither, from this moment on, would James Ings.

"Nor Pat Philbin, neither!"

"Just think!" said Ings. "Humble fellows like us think no different from a famous journalist and a Founding Father of America!"

Philbin proposed a toast to Liberty. He had found a flask on Mitre Court, with a trace of gin in it, and he shared it between them.

"What say you, Patrick?" said Ings, as he raised his cup. "Shall our new motto be that great American proverb, Give Me Liberty or Give Me Death?"

"Sure, Jimmy, that's an Irish saying," replied Philbin, and he raised his cup, his eyes twinkling as Ings had not seen them before.

CHAPTER TEN

Saturday, 17ᵗʰ July, 1819

SUSAN THISTLEWOOD / EDWARDS

Stanhope Street, Lincoln's Inn Field

Mrs Thistlewood agreed to remove the shawl and let her hair fall loose over her shoulders. She was reading her new library book, Scott's novel about the first Jacobite Uprising, and she was sitting for Julian's art lesson while Arthur was in town, addressing the Coachbuilder's Guild. Edwards asked Julian to observe and then draw the oval shape of the model's face and to mark the point, about half way down, where the eyes belonged. Susan's eyes were pale sea-green, and the irises, Edwards remarked, contained tiny hazel specks, which were slightly different in the left and the right and which, even in a monochrome drawing, could be used to reflect the subject's character.

Julian enjoyed the attentions of his teacher, who had more patience and more time for him than his father these days. As he sketched, Julian asked whether Mr Edwards received as many applications from the poor as pa.

"The people have no reason to know me," replied Edwards. "A deputy's duty is to support and as chairman, your father prefers to deal with his correspondence privately."

"We often wish there were not so many letters, don't we, mama?" asked Julian.

To Edwards's surprise, although the hue of Susan's cheeks deepened a little, she did not contradict the boy. Did this miniscule betrayal suggest discord between Thistlewood and his wife? Could the lovely Susan Thistlewood be lonely? In need, perhaps, of comfort?

"I also read the letters," said Susan, "and they inspire Arthur more than any political argument. But how can we respond to every desperate plea for help with more than a few kind words? How can my husband help anybody, if he's possessed by their pain?"

"If Arthur had no such feelings," replied Edwards, "he would not risk his life for reform."

"What a wise friend you are, George," responded Mrs Thistlewood, her fingers resting on her open book. "But does no-one consider the cumulative effect? Do you think even Mr Hunt comprehends it? He might be well educated and a powerful speaker, but I doubt the Orator's ability to align himself with the suffering of ordinary families. How can he understand the impact of those letters on Arthur's well-being and who knows what repercussions?"

Julian's pencil snapped and he yelped. He was aware of Susan's concerns, but the rare outburst had unsettled him. Edwards, with his pupil's concentration lost and his model agitated out of her pose, gave the lad a shilling to fetch new pencils and a few marbles for later. Susan tied back her hair, sat on the yellow settee and invited Edwards to pull up a chair. He sat as close to her as he dared and saw the colour rising in her cheeks, like a dawn sky.

"You understand. George" she said, "that I could never burden Arthur with worries of my own."

"With your parents so far away, and Julian so young -"

"I suppose so, yes," said Susan.

"Perhaps I may help," said Edwards.

"You listen well, George" said Susan. "I've noticed."

"Thank you," said Edwards, "and if you chose to confide in me, I would swear to secrecy, Susan, on the soul of my poor dear mother."

It was the first Mrs Thistlewood had heard of George's mother. She reached out, rested two fingers in the back of his hand and enquired, if it were not too painful, what had happened to her. Edwards paused, his mind in a panic. In failing to control his emotion, he had gone too far, thrown his opportunity to the wind, and the boy would be back any minute. And yet, she was here, and she had touched his hand.

"I'm here to listen to you," he said, "not to increase your burden."

"Tell me about your mother," said Susan, "and then we shall be equal with our burdens!"

"As you wish," replied Edwards, thinking that the more dynamic his contribution, the more Susan might reveal to him. "When my father left, William and I were very young. We went to live on the river-bank, close to the Monument. There was a fire. Mother screamed at my brother and me to run outside. She went upstairs to fetch the baby, but the staircase collapsed behind her. Sometimes, I am plagued by her screams, Susan, and the memory of the little sister I barely knew!"

"Oh, how dreadful for you!" said Susan, softly. "How bravely she died, and thank God, you and William escaped!"

The partial truth in Edwards's story unlocked an unwelcome impulse, from which he wrenched free by basking in Susan's compassion. He gazed at the curls at the nape of her neck and thought, with a melancholy sweetness, that Arthur Thistlewood's fingers and his mouth would settle there tonight.

"Your turn," he said.

Edwards's voice as hoarse, his breathing shallow, but Susan was too lost in her thoughts and too inexperienced with men to wonder why.

"As long as I've known him," she began, "Arthur's conscience has been a battlefield. Julian and I are his rock, his peace of mind, and we are happy together. You know how hard my husband works, how deeply he cares for other people. These days, he can't put his duty aside, even for half an hour. He rarely sleeps, he consumes chemical tinctures, and I fear that one day -"

As she paused, Edwards knew that silence would serve him best, but when he saw Susan's tears, it took all his constraint not to lean forward and take her in his arms.

"In Horncastle," she continued, almost in a whisper, "there were rumours."

"Rumours?" asked Edwards, alert again to his mission.

"The Thistlewoods' farm was outside town, and being so much younger than Arthur, I never knew them."

"What rumours, Susan?"

"Of bad blood, of relatives in Jamaica, of unspeakable crimes, perhaps madness."

She turned away.

"The heat of the tropics can drive any man mad," said Edwards, "not to mention the infected flies! It's not surprising his relatives were affected, but it's a long time since Arthur was in the West Indies, Susan, and he was a military man, not on the plantations."

"Arthur's father never went to Jamaica, and he was so unwell after his wife died that they sent him away. My parents have always been concerned about any child we may have -"

Here, Susan broke off, the subject too tender.

"Your husband is a great man," said Edwards. "We must take care of him together."

"Thank you," said Susan, gathering herself and rising from the sofa. "My faith is with his most trusted colleagues, especially you, dear George. Come; you must be ready for a snack. I've made parkin, and Julian will be back."

Edwards was in no mood for a snack. His mind was bursting, his stomach was heaving and he was trembling, partly from the weight of precious information, partly from the impossible proximity of Susan, but most of all from an invasive memory that threatened to engulf him.

"Are you unwell, George?" she asked, that same damned concern filling her lovely eyes, the colour of the Celtic Sea in spring.

"Forgive me," he stuttered, "I'm late."

George Edwards picked up his hat and his bag, and he fled.

EDWARDS

He bolted out of Stanhope Street and fled into a yard, where a chimney-sweep was chiding two boys for clumsiness. Three silent, black faces stared at the breathless lunatic and then hurried away, their cart whipping up spilt soot and flinging a dark veil across Edwards's face, too, as he bent against the cramps in his stomach. He clenched at the assault of sour black powder on his mouth and eyes, forced himself upright and pressed his head, his buttocks and the palms of his hands hard against the wall. He took deep breaths, in an almighty effort to steady the commotion and channel his thoughts to their proper purpose.

Instead, his mind was ambushed by the urgent bells of St Magnus the Martyr, the stench of rotten fish, the roar of untamed fire and the wanton spits and crackles of burning wood.

He was six years old, standing in the street, with William, a toddler, sobbing at his side, while their mother, skirts aflame, dragged out the chest that held everything they owned. George knocked his brother down, so he could not follow, and went inside to fetch the baby from her cradle. Scornful of the smoke that blistered his eyes, scorched his throat and snatched at his breath, young George Edwards crawled up the staircase, but he was too late. The steps splintered and cracked beneath him, and as he tumbled, pissing and vomiting, to the ground, little Hannah, his mother's only daughter was lost.

George was pulled to safety by a tall black man with powerful hands, a kindly giant, who thumped his back to free his lungs and did not wait to be thanked. His rescuer's face was engraved in his memory; wiry brows above brown eyes, deep as pools, the strong nose and steady smile. As a youth, Edwards had often wondered about his saviour and determined to find him one day and demonstrate how well he had used the life reclaimed.

Now, as history receded and his equilibrium returned, Edwards was possessed by a brand-new idea. By unlocking the memory of that fire by the river, Susan Thistlewood had worked a kind of magic. A few moments later, he knew exactly who would implement the plan, and how they would do it, and George Edwards headed home to change his clothes and scrub the soot from his skin and hair.

Mansion House, City of London

Shortly after seven o'clock, he slipped into a formal banquet at Mansion House. A few words with the senior footman was all it took to approach the top table and distract the Lord Mayor from his succulent duck.

"Cock your ear, Jacko!" he whispered, stopping to reach the appropriate organ.

"Ah! Mr Ward!" sputtered the great man, rising to his feet. "Just the fellow I've been waiting for. Follow me!"

John Atkins was a wealthy merchant, a radical-fearing conservative and, until recently, Member of Parliament for the city ward of Walbrook. He loved nothing better than a properly cooked fowl, and was embarrassed by the intrusion of a fellow in street clothes, especially a person armed with too much information about his private and business affairs. He guided Edwards into a side-room, grumbling that whatever the message, it better be bloody good because his duck was going cold, and his companions would ask questions.

Ten minutes later, the Mayor's scepticism was transformed. Confident that his reputation in Whitehall would be advanced, he congratulated Mr Ward, assured him of the Home Secretary's approval for the plan and suggested cooperation on another matter. Satisfaction would be rewarded by twenty guineas or forty guineas for both. Reaching into a cavity beneath his gowns, the Mayor handed over four guineas for materials and discretion, and walked away, beaming, to continue his dinner and report to his neighbours that his latest shipment of Ottoman textiles had arrived in dock.

Johnson's Court

"Georgie!" called Tilly, arriving home from her assignation. "I know you're up there!"

Edwards unlocked the studio door and went to receive his kiss. Tilly was especially tender today. The combination of sweet jasmine scent and Virginia tobacco suggested the Admiral, who often sent for her when he visited town on a Saturday.

"Who are JTB and RT?" she asked, conscious of the impact of her shapely backside as she turned to reach for glasses from the shelf.

"No idea!" said Edwards.

"They've wrote you a message," she said.

In his haste, Edwards had failed to see the note under the door. Tilly handed it over, and he read it, as she poured the gin.

"It's the bootmakers!" he replied.

"What was you wanting bootmakers to do next Tuesday?" enquired Tilly, offering his gin and settling beside him, in the arm-chair, with her own.

Edwards replied that his pretty little lark should not be reading his private correspondence. It pleased him to surprise her now and then, and wasn't she always happy with a new pair of shoes? Now the scoundrels had spoiled his secret!

Tilly thought it a proper shame, but the news was no disappointment to Edwards. With all the distractions lately, he had forgotten about the East India plan, which was also a product of his association with the Mayor. The new idea was better, and there was less risk attached. He chuckled at the thought of it.

"That's more like it," said Tilly and swallowed her gin. "You're twice the man with a smile on your chops. Come here!"

As Tilly's finger-tips teased his shirt just above the collar-bone. Edwards was roused by the combined scents of jasmine and tobacco, but as he turned to kiss her, he remembered the tiny curls at Susan Thistlewood's neck.

"You're breathing mighty shallow, Georgie," she murmured. "What's all that about?"

Edwards replied that a little hanky-panky might be timely, after which they might try the roast duck at The Mitre, an arrangement that suited Tilly quite well.

Sunday, 18th July, 1819

THISTLEWOOD / BRUNT / HARRISON
St Clement's, The Strand

Men spilled out of the side entrance of the Crown and Anchor into the hotbed of indignation that was gathering on the corner of the Strand and St Clement Danes Church. They had been refused admission to an extraordinary meeting of London's tavern radicals.

Security was apparently tight because of the unprecedented momentum caused by the forthcoming rally at Smithfield, and increased infiltration by government agents. That message was of no comfort to the disappointed men, of whom most belonged to the Water Lane Group. Their secretary, William Edwards had failed to arrive with the necessary passes.

Henry Hunt being unavailable for the occasion, Thistlewood was showing the guest of honour around the ballroom, the only venue in London, he explained, capable of accommodating the anticipated numbers, and where Mr Fox had once famously celebrated a birthday. When a marshal approached and reported that some of his men were threatening to climb through the windows and down the chimney, Thistlewood left the guest with George Edwards and went to investigate.

The person responsible for the omission was Mrs G, who had required her younger son to mend a broken stove before he went off to work. William Edwards arrived, panting, at the Crown and Anchor, just as Thistlewood had cajoled the men into an orderly line at the door. They were all for boxing William's ears or tying him to a lamp-post, until Thistlewood warned that folly would result in banishment and ordered them to proceed in peace.

First to receive his pass was Tom Brunt, who ran after Thistlewood and asked for a private word. Thistlewood had surprised him by approving his and Tidd's decision to attend the rally as special constables, and his good-humoured response, that they would be in an excellent position to notify him of trouble, had encouraged Brunt to further inspiration.

"If you are anticipating the possibility of discord on Wednesday," he said, "I have had a brainwave."

"We're expecting the rally to be peaceful," replied Thistlewood, not in the most emphatic tone that Brunt had heard before.

"Yes, but if you will give us leave," whispered Brunt, "on Tuesday night, after registering as a constable, my friend and I will take the barrels for a ride."

"Tom, this is no time for metaphors," replied Thistlewood, anxious to return to his guest.

"I refer to certain items in the Black Lion yard; covered in tarpaulin."

Now Thistlewood understood the reference to the group's hidden cache of weapons. He looked at Brunt with what Brunt considered a degree of quizzical interest.

He continued. "My friend and I will remove them to a place where they might serve their proper purpose."

"Every street will be swarming with officers," said Thistlewood.

"That's what's so bootiful about it," replied Brunt. "If they catch us, we'll say we're special constables - which will be true - that we captured the items from a young ruffian who was too quick for us – which, of course, would not be true."

"How will you move the items?" asked Thistlewood.

"Simple!" replied Brunt. "We'll disguise ourselves as fish-mongers. We load everything on to a cart, cover it up and drive it to Finsbury Square, to which, if the situation demands, we can easily marshal the people from Smithfield."

"Where would you hide everything?" asked Thistlewood.

"There's a cubby in the wall, left of Lockington's Book-shop," replied Brunt.

Thistlewood was impressed.

"Who else will know of your plan?" he asked.

"Only yourself, citizen, and my friend."

"You understand that I can't give you permission," said Thistlewood.

"But you don't object."

"Whatever action you take on Wednesday, citizen, is your own responsibility."

Arthur Thistlewood was smiling.

"I was in France, sir" replied Brunt, "and on the lives of my wife and sons, I shall never lay hands on any weapon without due provocation."

"Leave the items in the fishmonger's yard next to the foundry on Chiswell Street," said Thistlewood, as they turned to enter The Crown and Anchor. "It's closer to Finsbury Square and it's less conspicuous. Return everything to the tavern before dawn on Thursday. I shall deny all knowledge."

From Thistlewood's point of view, Brunt's plan, whether foolhardy or ingenious, was well-timed, and it was all he had. His opinion on defence had shifted after hearing the experiences of this afternoon's guest of honour, who had travelled clandestinely from the north.

Twenty thousand sympathizers had gathered recently in Stockport and heard the Reverend Joseph Harrison declare that by refusing to keep His Majesty or his Regent informed of the

people's true condition and grievances, Lord Sidmouth had defied the Magna Carta. The Home Secretary was therefore guilty
of Treason against the people and must be held accountable.

Naturally, the speech was considered seditious, and Harrison was arrested, but – not for the first time – his congregation in Stockport had raised bail to keep their minister out
of gaol. News that the rebel parson would speak at Smithfield
was certain, in Thistlewood's mind, to induce some reaction by
Sidmouth. In such circumstances, in Thistlewood's view, innocent participants of the rally must be in a position to defend
themselves. There would be no need, he thought, to distract
Henry Hunt.

In the ballroom of the Crown and Anchor, the tones of
Joe Harrison's native Essex, were more familiar to the membership than the dialects of other northern radicals. A slight man
of forty, the parson combined an air of calm with compelling
gravity. He described The Stockport Union for the Promotion
of Human Happiness and its successful experiments with education and the rights of women. He spoke of solidarity and
self-help, of new ways for British people to live together and
of the determination by ordinary folk to make a better future
in collaboration with each other. Stockport was not alone in
embracing the philosophy, he continued, but its success was
evident on every corner of town. He could not pretend that
every man, woman and child in his congregation was free of
pain and poverty. There was urgent work to be done by brave
and decent men such as today's assembly, who would ensure
good governance for every citizen of Britain, not just the favoured few.

He described the anguish of parents, who drowned their
new-born babies like kittens, or left them to God's mercy in the

woods. He spoke about desperate grandparents, approaching the end of industrious, god-fearing lives, who lived in dread of another harsh winter and gave their last loaf to their family before seeking an unobtrusive way to die.

"Just imagine, my friends!" said Harrison. "Good Christian men and women prefer to commit mortal sins, to face the punishments of Hell than to live - or let their children live - a day longer in the land we have so proudly called Great Britain!"

During the jubilant applause, George Edwards looked sideways at two strangers standing by the ballroom door, whose credentials nobody had checked because he had instructed his brother, William to let them in. As the cheering continued, the strangers unbolted the door and slipped out of the Crown and Anchor. George Edwards followed them out and along the Strand. Although his other contract with the Lord Mayor of London required pressing attention, he would show his clandestine colleagues a good time and open the door to fresh opportunities in the future.

Tuesday, 20ᵗʰ July, 1819

INGS / PHILBIN
55½, Fleet Street

In the days before the rally, the usual flow of pamphlets became a flood and the coffee shop was busier, Ings informed his lodger, than Portsmouth dock with a three-decker in. Edwards was nowhere to be seen, which improved Ings's mood, though he would have welcomed practical assistance. Whatever else he was doing, Ings listened eagerly, when every morning, just before eleven, Richard Carlile arrived for his coffee and read the latest news aloud to Philbin. The new workers' unions were interesting, and the mood of national optimism held promise, but with working all day and their Deist studies by night, Ings had little time to dwell on current affairs.

Usually, Philbin would drink his coffee and listen attentively without comment, but when, on Tuesday, Carlile mentioned that the Irish problem would be among the subjects raised at Smithfield tomorrow, he surprised everyone by jumping up and announcing;

"I know a tailor in Lambeth sir, from Tipperary, fast as lightning. Sure, he can run up ten Father Murphy's flags before ye' can spit out the words!"

With his close interest in the Irish problem, Carlile understood the implication better than most. He looked at Philbin darkly.

"Anyone who carries the words "Liberty or Death" through London this week is either a very brave man or a fool, Mr Philbin," he said. "Tell your countryman he'll make better profit with the tricolour."

"I shall, sir, thank ye' sir!" said Philbin and saluted.

When Philbin returned from Lambeth, with a Father Murphy's flag and a large white cabbage for their supper, Ings asked for his candid opinion on the rally tomorrow.

"One day I shall see Castlereagh's head on a stick," said Philbin, "but otherwise, all ye'r politics and ye'r history can go to hell! Pat Philbin's history is the loss of this hand and the seven years he has suffered without it."

Such uncharacteristic rhetoric surprised Ings, who decided that in celebration of the imminent holiday, the cabbage would accompany the last of the salted remains of Jupiter. Mr Edwards had left a message to mark the rally tomorrow and a bottle of gin, which Ings was happy to share with his lodger over their meal. Philbin ate and drank so much, that he soon fell on to his mat and was fast asleep in no time.

Ings had begun writing an affectionate letter to his family, when his employer came, thumping at the door. Cursing at his lost peace, Ings opened the door to see Edwards looking wild and alarmed.

"Ings!" he shouted. "In the name of God and all those you hold dear, move yourself!"

Edwards began kicking at Philbin's mat. "Wake up, you drunken fool!" he screamed, "before the entire city goes up in flames!"

"What's happened?" asked Ings, not quite steady on his feet and reaching for his sack.

"My brother has uncovered a plot!" said Edwards. "Come quickly and ask no questions! Downstairs, Philbin, fast as you can. Or we'll see an inferno and murder, beside which your Rebellion was a skirmish."

Uncertain whether he lived or dreamed, Philbin lurched to his feet. Ings snatched both haversacks and, as best he could, prevented his friend from tumbling down the stairs. In the shop, Edwards gave each man a bundle of pamphlets, of which one sheet was to be delivered to every residence between St Paul's and Temple Bar. Philbin should take the north side and Ings the south. They should not make a racket or wake the people up, which would cause undue panic, since the fire was not anticipated until eight o'clock.

While Philbin, as best he could, set off in a westerly direction, and he headed east towards St Paul's, Ings, who had been more modest with the gin, wondered, how, in a dire emergency, Edwards had managed to print the pamphlets, and why he had spoken with such urgency, when the fire was not expected until morning. Perhaps men of education act in mysterious ways.

Then it occurred to Ings that his own home and work-place were in danger. He stood by the lamp on the corner of Pilgrim Street to read the pamphlet. 'Fire Alert! Fire!' shrieked the front page. 'Plot uncovered to burn the City of London! Abandon your home and save your lives and your loved ones!' As Ings turned the sheet over, a gust of wind blew up, and the entire bundle fluttered away, into the culvert below.

As the pamphlets floated away, Ings considered racing down to the river to catch them, when they arrived at Blackfriars, but the print would be illegible. As he contemplated how many ghastly deaths would be attributed to an untimely act of nature, Ings spotted a single sheet, tangled in weeds on the culvert wall. If he could only reach it, and discover the full facts, he could raise the alarm in person! He was obliged to lie on his belly and push his right arm and shoulder along the culvert, stretching his fingers towards the paper. His clothes would be ruined, but what did that matter against the saving of human life?

He was thus engaged, when he felt a rude kick against his arse. A deep voice, in an unnecessarily irreverent tone, suggested that he was drunk and ordered him to wriggle out of his current location.

"I've lost my papers, sir, and there's a fearful plot afoot."

"Is there now?" mocked the fellow, tugging at Ings's legs. "Well, I'm the night-watchman, and I shall take you to a place of recuperation!"

"Then you'll surely know William Edwards," said Ings, pulling himself free with a grunt. "The lamplighter, who uncovered the plot. It's wrote on that paper, stuck in the culvert!"

The night-watchman, attached an iron cuff to Ings's wrist. "I know every lamplighter in London," he said, "but not one with the name of Edwards. Now you best keep quiet; one more mention of a plot, and I shall silence you!"

With that, the impudent fellow turned Ings over like a side of beef and sat on his back, while he poked around with his truncheon in the culvert wall to retrieve the paper that would incriminate his prisoner. As the watchman sat there, his dead weight on the butcher's back, cackling like an old witch, Ings thought that, with the exception of Mr Croxton at Portsea, he had never been so close to contemplating murder. When the watchman abandoned his efforts at the culvert, and Ings said he would carry the deaths of a thousand Londoners on his conscience, the fellow tied a filthy rag over his prisoner's mouth.

When Ings arrived, gagged and chained, at Bow Street, Philbin was snoring away on the waiting room floor, his ankle tied to a bench. Ings sat miserably on the same bench, his leg similarly bound, and watched an officer waken his lodger and drag him away. About an hour later, the same officer returned and led Ings to the office of the chief clerk, Mr Stafford. When Stafford ordered the removal of his gag and heard the story of imminent arson, he claimed that no such connivance had reached his all-hearing ears, but at least Ings had spoken the same nonsense as the Irishmen. Philbin had two mitigating factors, said Stafford; the extent of his inebriation and his alleged inability to read his own name, let alone the seditious material in his possession. Ings confirmed that his friend and lodger was illiterate. While not at liberty to name the source of their mission, Ings insisted that they had been motivated only to save innocent lives and requested that their situation be explained to his employers at 55 and 55½ Fleet Street.

Ings and his lodger spent the night manacled together in a dingy cellar at a private address on Bow Street. Philbin snored away as usual, but the Hampshire butcher was restless under the fitful watch of a guard, whose grunts, sniffles and attacks of coughing precluded any hope of sleep.

Wednesday, 21ˢᵗ July, 1819

When, in the morning, Philbin awoke, and Ings explained the circumstances of their arrest, the Irishman shrugged and asked the yawning guard to confirm today's date. Philbin smiled broadly and recalled the same day, seven years ago; the spotless blue sky, the shade beneath the cork trees, and the sweet Spanish wine that he sipped from a leather bottle, before riding like a hero, beneath a scorching sun across the River Tormes for the triumphant attack on Salamanca, the day before a Spanish sword cut through his wrist.

The guard must have been affected by the story, because he was not at all rough, as he led them back to the police station, where their chains were removed. Mr Stafford offered no explanation for their release and said only that their good fortune was owed to the testimony of an anonymous friend.

Edwards had already arrived to help them, and after providing the clerk with an assurance of their future good behaviour, drove them, in a proper cab, back to Fleet Street. In the shop, away from prying ears, Edwards explained that there had been no fire, and no fire was ever intended.

"My brother, William was duped by a rumour, created by a government agent, whose purpose was to discredit Thistlewood and the Orator and prevent today's rally. We must not be responsible for embarrassing my brother or causing him to lose his job as a lamplighter. And I apologize for the inconvenience caused to such fine men as yourselves."

Edwards's tone contained too much honey for Ings's liking, and he guessed that in some shape, his employer, too, was embarrassed by the incident. He replied that the secret was safe because neither he nor his lodger would wish the world to know of their night in a cell. In truth, neither Ings nor Philbin had more than the muddiest recollection of the night before, and when a vague memory came to him of the watchman's claim not to know any lamplighter called Edwards, Ings dismissed it as human error, or possibly a bad dream.

Edwards was not quite ready to leave the matter.

"As a mark of my sincerity," he said, "and on condition that you swear, as long as you both shall live, never to mention the incident to anyone, including myself, I shall reward you each with a guinea."

Ings would break that oath for the very first time when he wrote his testament. Meanwhile, in the new-found appreciation of their liberty, he and Philbin agreed that rather than wasting the holiday in slumber, it would be more amusingly and informatively spent at Mr Hunt's rally. They washed, enjoyed their bread and coffee and set off in high spirits for the great adventure, with Philbin all wrapped up in his Father Murphy flag and Ings in a merry mood, imagining the smile on Celia's face, when she touched that guinea.

CHAPTER ELEVEN

Wednesday, 21ˢᵗ July, 1819
(continued)

TIDD / BRUNT
Hole in the Wall Passage, Holborn

When the older twins complained that the younger twins had finished off the treacle, Mrs Tidd remarked that her husband seemed particularly distracted, and his spoon had not even touched his porridge. Tidd replied that he had duties with his aunt in Pimlico and would return this evening with a surprise. Eliza Tidd was sceptical.

"I heard talk of a rally today," she said with an attempt at nonchalance, "at Smithfield. Will your aunt be attending?"

"I heard gossip of a fire in 't city" said Tidd; "it ain't happened, has it?"

"Where did you hear about a fire?" asked Mrs Tidd, sharp as a tack.

"Did I not measure a gentleman's feet at Lincoln's Inn Field yesterday?" retorted Tidd, "provisionally speaking."

When Eliza's eyes widened at the prospect of payment, Tidd handed the spoon and the treacle jar to Mary and hurried away to meet Tom Brunt.

When they reached the hythe at Billingsgate, everyone had heard of Harry Moreton, and two elderly stallholders remembered the old hero and even young Thomas, who had often accompanied his grandpa from the shop in St Marylebone High Street. Before long, everything Brunt and Tidd needed was at their disposal; herrings, barrels, pony and cart, even a pair of fishmongers' hats and aprons.

Brunt had not foreseen that the archway at Water Lane would be too narrow for the cart, and they were obliged to lift the heavy barrels and roll them down to the Black Lion yard. Then came the messy business of replacing fish with pistols, knives and pikes, and covering each load with a layer of dabs or herrings. They worked fast, although Tidd was unaccustomed to handling fresh fish, and a slippery few escaped on to the cobbles, making them both laugh like naughty boys. As they rode along Fleet Street, nobody was interested in a pair of fishmongers making deliveries on a festive day.

They drove flat out to Finsbury Square and found Chiswell Street deserted. Everything was closed up for the rally. Exactly as agreed with Thistlewood, Brunt and Tidd deposited the barrels and the cart in the fishmonger's yard. They tethered the pony to a trough in the foundry yard, where they washed their hands, but could not entirely remove the odour.

Brunt was delighted with the success of his scheme until Tidd reminded him of its solemn purpose. Who knows how the day would end, he asked, if they were obliged to empty these barrels and distribute the contents for the purposes of civil defence? Brunt advised that they focus, for the moment, on their new roles, to which they must appear entirely committed. Tidd agreed, and they sprinted to Smithfield to collect their sashes and mingle with six thousand other special constables.

The damned reformers, their colleagues told them, were armed and battle-hungry! The Lord Mayor of London had foiled a plot by tavern radicals to set the city of London on fire. As a result, Lord Sidmouth, the Home Secretary had taken the extra precaution of engaging several thousand militia, who would lurk in surrounding streets to be summoned at the first sign of violence. Brunt was about to protest, when he felt Tidd's boot on his shin and decided to keep his clapper shut.

BRUNT
Smithfield Square, London

Brunt spent the afternoon perched between two other Specials, high on a scaffold, borrowed from the Old Bailey. Instead of a truncheon (of which the supply was insufficient), he was armed with a note pad and pencil. The registrar, who was overworked and had accepted without question his description of himself as a non-combatant and in equal parts, poet and bootmaker, had given him the role of noting down the speeches, and indeed any interruptions, focusing on phrases that might be construed as seditious. Brunt's neighbours were school teachers, responsible, on one side, for Henry Hunt and on the other, for the visiting parson. Brunt had been given everybody else, which he might have considered the short straw, had his predicament not been the stuff of poetry. He even laughed when his colleagues made uninformed jokes about Arthur Thistlewood.

Thousands of Londoners had made the journey to Smithfield; some for the politics, some for the excitement and most for a dose of each. Hope was reason enough for celebration, and at the very least, it was a day out, and the sun was shining bright. Beside the men, women and children on the ground, revellers filled almost every balcony and rooftop on the square, leaning out of windows, shouting, singing and waving flags

When the speakers climbed the steps to the hustings, the cheers were so loud that Brunt imagined the burghers of Calais, turning to see what monster approached from England. Thistlewood introduced Henry Hunt, and Hunt asked for three cheers for Joe Harrison, who led upwards of fifty thousand Londoners in the Lord's Prayer;

Deliver us from evil, for thine is the Kingdom, the Power and the Glory.

After the Amen, Hunt thanked the crowd for their attendance and said he was humbled by the great number and by the evident good humour before him. When he introduced the parson from Stockport, there was a rapturous roar. Joe Harrison's rousing speech at the Crown and Anchor had ensured that everybody knew who he was. Just as the Orator asked the crowd for quiet, Brunt observed a clutch of uniformed officers, pushing menacingly through the crowd. His mission was to warn Thistlewood, but without wings to fly, how could he reach the hustings before those officers? Regardless of his neighbours' opinion, Brunt attempted a piercing whistle, but produced only a futile hiss. Cursing himself for lack of foresight, he hoped that Tidd was in a more useful position. In the circumstances, Brunt decided, the best option was to stay where he had a good view. If the situation deteriorated, he would clamber down and proceed with his emergency assignment.

When the officers mounted the hustings and approached Parson Harrison in a manner that was certainly not friendly, Thistlewood tried to reason with them, but they pushed him aside and grabbed the parson by the neck. Hunt remained still, but for a few calming gestures to the crowd. Joe Harrison made no attempt to resist, only raising his arm to subdue the crowd's roar. As the officers chained the parson's wrists, Thistlewood began to chant, and the crowd followed.

"Let Joe go! Let Joe go!"

As the voices grew fierce, and Thistlewood continued to remonstrate with the officers, Henry Hunt called out to the crowd.

"Hold your peace! For God's sake, and the parson's, do not be provoked! We must not fall into the trap! Hush, I say, and allow the constables safe passage! Be silent my friends. At all costs, stay calm!"

The crowd obeyed, as Parson Harrison submitted, stiff and sedate as a church steeple. For three minutes, the only sound was the constables' shouts of "Order! Order!" as the people stepped back to let them pass.

On his perch, mesmerized by the Orator's genius in managing the crowd, Brunt watched the little convoy, followed by a stream of well-wishers, as it headed down Giltspur Street. When they were out of view, Henry Hunt broke the silence.

"My friends," he began, "Parson Harrison's arrest before a multitude is a malicious plan by the government to excite the people to violence and justify a military attack. Well, let the tyrants be disappointed again! There will be no violence today because the people of London know that Justice is on our side! Your self-discipline, my friends, demonstrates a fitness to partake in government and you will be rewarded, sooner than you imagine, by a change in the balance of power. If the government refuses to take note of its people, its people will demand their attention!"

Hunt paused to allow the crowd to agree, and then continued,

"My dear friends! Let me tell you this! We Britons have better means to defeat them than either the sword or the guillotine! A government denied funds will crawl to the bargaining table! I am not the first or only man to propose it, but I repeat it now, as I ask for your approval. We shall stop paying taxes! Are you ready? Let them hear us in St James! Let them hear us in Whitehall and Westminster! Let Parson Harrison hear us, and the infidels who would silence him! No more taxes!"

Fifty thousand voices were raised, and the great wall of sound surged through Smithfield and beyond. It may not have penetrated the walls of Whitehall, but as it grew louder, the chant was heard in Fleet Market and The Old Bailey. Discreetly placed battalions, bored since Waterloo, heard it, and were alert, hoping yet for action. Even the deaf old gardener, hoeing flower beds at St Paul's, was distracted by the roar; "NO MORE TAXES!" and at Brooke's Market, the ironmonger's languid dog cocked an ear. On his march to Bow Street, Parson Harrison heard it and told the officers they would never forget the rally at Smithfield, and their own lives would improve because of it.

Struggling to play the impartial constable, Brunt, on his scaffold, was delighted when the school-teachers joined the chorus, and he could abandon all reserve. He thought that although the herring adventure was probably wasted, his grandfather, whose story of a Saxon monk had inspired the plan, who fought so valiantly in the jungles of Tamil Nadu, had contributed in his own way to a day when the history of their great country was on the move again.

TIDD

Smithfield Square

Special Constable Tidd heard the chanting crowd, but he missed the occasion of Harrison's arrest because he was chasing a fellow down Cock Lane for the alleged theft of a baked potato. The lad proved too fast, even for long-legged Tidd, who gave up and returned to his position at a far corner of the square.

He watched a gathering of Irish youths, frustrated because they could not hear the speeches, and were unable to push forward. When Henry Hunt unfurled a tricolour, they shouted and waved their own vigorously. Turning in their direction, the Orator gestured to the youths and to the wider crowd to sing together;

The minstrel boy to the war is gone, In the ranks of death you'll find him.

His father's sword he has girded on, And his wild harp slung behind him.

When the song was done and the mood still hearty, Hunt asked for quiet, while he read out the demands that he would deliver to the Prince Regent, and which would be published in *Manchester Observer*.

Stimulated by the song, but still unable to hear the speech, the youths, affected also by heat, hunger and frustration, became restless. When an old Irishman on the corner performed a lonesome little jig, waved Father Murphy's flag and shouted that only simple-minded folk believed in the Virgin birth, the youths ordered the eejit to retract. When the "eejit" refused to be ordered about by bastard whippersnappers, they snatched his flag, asked where he got it and whether it was liberty he wanted today or death. When Philbin refused to answer, they formed a circle round him and began to punch.

Tidd piled into the scrum, called the youths cowards, a disgrace to their faith and their country, and said they were all under arrest for assaulting a war hero. The youngsters laughed and dispersed into the crowd, leaving a pair of quaking ten-year-olds at the constable's mercy. Since the boys had done nothing but watch and taunt, Tidd clipped their ears and told them to scarper, fast.

Philbin was a writhing, bleeding mess. His eyes flickered, but there was no response to Tidd's query. He lifted the old soldier up, and thought he weighed less than any of the twins. He carried Philbin like a sack of taters down Cock Lane, through Snow Hill and down Fleet Market. Everywhere was deserted. Even the Boar's Head, where a fellow countryman might have offered comfort to the old soldier, was closed. Tidd walked on to the coffee shop and Carlile's print-works, but both were closed and not a soul to be seen in either. Gently, Tidd unwound the flag and laid Philbin out on the pavement. He put his head against the old man's chest, but there was neither sound nor movement. He gripped his wrist, and there was no beat.

As Tidd draped the green flag over the body, he saw that his own clothes were covered in blood. No doubt there would be a bruise on his cheek, too, where the youths had hit him. If anybody saw him here, who would believe that Richard Tidd, with his history, was innocent of murder? He would never prove that he had not killed the old fellow himself, any more than he could trace the youths who had. Tidd was not afraid to hang for his beliefs, but he would not forsake his family for another man's crime. He pressed two fingers against Philbin's forehead, as if to bless him, and thanked the soldier for his sacrifice. Then Tidd tore off his constable's sash, his coat and his shirt and ran like the wind to the river where he dumped the incriminating clothing and washed away sins he had not committed in water that was deadlier than many a human foe.

TIDD/BRUNT

Streets of London

As dusk began to fall, and they walked in silence towards Finsbury Square, Brunt wondered what had brought Tidd so low, when the day had been triumphant. There had been no battle, and no lives had been lost. The convicted parson would have been arrested sooner or later, and Hunt had defied the tyrants and impressed all London with his historic rhetoric and management of the crowd. Unwilling to mention Philbin's fate, even to his friend and partner, Tidd replied that there was no more to his melancholy than having missed the speeches.

When they arrived at Chiswell Street, no officers waited in hiding to arrest them, but the odour of herring, after a day in hot sun, was pungent. The water trough was empty and the pony restless, but none of the cache had been disturbed. A battalion of flies swarmed round the fish and pursued them all to Water Lane and as they rolled the barrels back into the tavern yard. Bracing themselves as they prized the lids open, Brunt and Tidd plunged their hands into the mess of rotting fish and restless flies. They cleaned, as best they could with only their aprons at hand, the knives and muskets, pikes, blades and pistols, placed them back into the barrel and finally covered the cache with logs and tarpaulin. The only difference since this morning, they remarked, was the odour and the flies, which were certain to disperse soon.

As they dropped down to the river to dispose of the fish and wipe their aprons, Tidd contemplated his earlier visit to the shore; yet another escape from the rope that would one day be slipped over his head. For Brunt, the return to Billingsgate was a reminder of his journeys there with Grandpa Moreton. He had been proud of Tom's ambition to be a poet or a philosopher by the age of thirty, and said he had fought a war, so that humble people might be free to live as they wished. Brunt was thirty-five now, and the poetry had not done too bad. Perhaps there was philosophy in his inventive ideas, he thought, for there was certainly morality, and the two were unquestionably related.

When they had left pony, the cart, the empty barrels and the fishmongers' garb in the agreed locations in Billingsgate, Brunt and Tidd walked back to Holborn. They agreed that the day had ended in hope, but should the herring plan be engaged another time, it must be on a cooler day, with fewer flies about. Brunt opined that when the time came for the full and true testament of John Thomas Brunt and Richard Tidd to be told, it would astound their descendants and fill them with pride. Tidd responded that at least they had a shilling each to treat their families, though his own had been docked because his sash was lost in a scuffle. Brunt offered to pay the difference, and when Tidd refused, promised to fill his pipe with baccy instead.

Brunt's mood changed, when he arrived home to find Molly, ostentatiously polishing her dead canary's cage.

"I may sometimes be weak, Mr Brunt," she said, "but I am never foolish. At that parade you missed, so as to help Tiddy's aunt, Harry's drumming was magnificent."

"Good news," said Brunt, though he feared there was more to come.

"And do you know, Mr Brunt, all the people talked about was Henry Hunt, and whether or not to go to Smithfield today."

Fortunately for Brunt Molly's mood was transformed by the news of his gainful employment, and she found a bowl of porridge for him. Meanwhile, Tidd knew from Eliza's breathing that she was awake, and he knew she would ask no questions. He believed that his wife almost certainly knew the truth, and that although the bruise, which Brunt had admired, would require an explanation, the Pimlico aunt was the glue that kept his marriage and perhaps also his sanity intact.

THISTLEWOOD

Black Lion Tavern, Water Lane

While Hunt, Carlile and Edwards tore into their ham pies with the enthusiasm of heroes, Thistlewood's appetite was subdued by anxiety about the Reverend Harrison. When Hunt asked if he were not pleased with the outcome of the Smithfield Meeting, Thistlewood replied that he regretted the security failure, and suspected infiltration by a local informer. Edwards urged him to stop worrying, and explained that Deputy Constable Birch's campaign to lock up the parson had been running for years, and employed every imaginable resource, including a network of local spies and, quite possibly, collusion by the mayor of London. Efforts had intensified after Harrison made his inflammatory speech in June, and a visit to London was the perfect opportunity to arrest him, far from his protective congregation. Officer Birch had undoubtedly anticipated a bonus for disrupting the meeting at Smithfield, and in that, Edwards added, with unmistakeable relish, he had failed.

Henry Hunt accepted the explanation and urged Thistlewood to take heart. Parson Harrison had understood the risks, had thrown himself at the lions, and his congregation would fight like demons for his release.

"What matters to us," said Hunt, "is that instead of being defeated at Smithfield, as our enemies hoped, the reform movement has taken a giant leap forward. With Manchester only two weeks away, victory is tantalizingly close. Take comfort in that, Arthur, and enjoy your pie, while it's warm."

Thistlewood remained uneasy, and at the same time, his opinion of the Orator continued to shift. Undeniably, Hunt had prevented disorder in a most skilful way. But why had he done nothing to protect a vulnerable guest? Was he jealous of the parson's popularity and success in the north? Had Hunt used the occasion to his own advantage, sacrificing a people's hero to demonstrate his own power?

For the first time, it occurred to Thistlewood that he and Henry Hunt were of the same age, and both descended from generations of gentleman farmers. Their heritage, however, was as different as fish and fowl. Thistlewood's forefathers were tenants, obliged to work as land-agents alongside gruelling labour in the exposed landscapes and wild weather of Lincolnshire, where their fields, reclaimed with blood and sweat, needed constant irrigation. By contrast Henry Hunt had inherited fertile estates in Somerset and Wiltshire and had never handled a spade or a plough in his life, at least, not when it mattered.

Perhaps, Thistlewood surmised, those differences explained why Hunt was so effortlessly self-assured, while he himself pursued his goals with restless enquiry. Public speaking came more easily these days, but Thistlewood's confidence was manufactured, and he knew it. How self-satisfied Squire Hunt looked, he thought, dispensing opinions and plunging his fork into his pickles, as if a good, meaty supper were his daily right! The Orator conducted himself like the most powerful man in England, but he lacked empathy with the ordinary people he purported to represent and had no experience of their daily lives. More dangerously, Henry Hunt seemed to underestimate the men in power at Westminster and the mechanisms that kept them there.

The Orator may have sensed the dissent because although he issued an effusive invitation to Richard Carlile to speak at Manchester, he made no such overture to Thistlewood or his deputy. Thistlewood was unperturbed, relieved to be spared the long journey and the time away from his family. London was where he belonged, and where he was known, and London was where he would continue to concentrate his efforts.

A week later, Edwards reported that Joe Harrison had been escorted back to Stockport, where he was kept at Officer Birch's private residence while Magistrates decided what action to take. Somebody must have informed his congregation, because a crowd gathered outside Birch's house and threatened to pull it down unless their parson was released. During the confrontation, Birch was wounded in the chest, and his life remained in the balance. Harrison's own fate was uncertain, and Thistlewood, who continued to blame himself, sent a coded message of support and asked Edwards to keep him informed.

In the following days, Thistlewood received other news from the north; of more families in despair and more patriots ready to die for liberty and their rights. In Leicester and in Manchester, men gathered to be trained by Volunteers and Waterloo veterans in drilling and the use of pikes. In the moors around Rochdale, where no pikes could be found, men exercised in physical fitness and unarmed combat. Similar accounts were arriving from towns and villages across England. The momentum seemed unstoppable.

CHAPTER TWELVE

Wednesday, 21ˢᵗ July, 1819
(continued)

INGS

55½, Fleet Street

Ings found his friend, his poor, true friend, dead on the pavement outside their home. Somebody had been there already, because Philbin's green flag, his precious reminder of the Irish Rebellion, was laid so neatly across the body, and there was a yellow sash beside it, like a special constable's There were splashes of blood in an easterly direction all along Fleet Street. Presumably his lodger had been attacked for that provocative flag, for nobody could have thought him anything but destitute. Mr Edwards's guinea was still in his breeches pocket, and since Philbin had said all his family was dead, Ings vowed to use it for the funeral celebration, which he would arrange with Philbin's acquaintances at the Boar's Head. He sent for the patrole, who turned up, eventually, and said they had more pressing matters to attend than the death of a drunken Irishman. When the undertaker came, he said he expected more business on a day like today, but one corpse was better than none at all.

Ings had last seen his lodger at Smithfield, by the entrance of St Bartholomew's hospital, with the flag wrapped like a huge green bandage around his middle, its white Christian cross and provocative motto rendered indecipherable. Ings had gone off to find somewhere to piss, and when he came back Philbin was gone. There was no hope of finding such a small person in the swirling mass of humanity at Smithfield, so he stayed there, by the hospital clock, hoping his friend would return. If only he had not needed that piss, or had waited a little while longer, the old soldier might still be alive!

It would be wrong to say that Ings forgot about his lodger during the speeches, but at Smithfield, he experienced what can only be described as a metamorphosis. Cousin Jack had held similar beliefs, and he had listened with interest to Carlile's lessons for Philbin, but until he heard Hunt and Thistlewood at Smithfield, Ings had presumed himself apart, unworthy because of his inadequate education and his lack of concentration and competence in intelligent conversation. On that day, Ings understood for the first time that it was not simply a matter of understanding the facts; he had a right to anger.

Now, he understood how deeply the Hampshire people had suffered at the expense of unfair tolls and taxes! Had the pampered aristocracy or the corrupt ministers ever lived a day without nourishment? Bah! Had they given up their lives, their sons or their sanity on the bloody battlefields of France, America or the West Indies? Not likely! By what right did the government steal from ordinary men's earnings, and yet forbid them from deciding how that money was spent?

In the days that followed Philbin's wake (an occasion never to be forgotten as long as The Boars Head stands), Ings's commitment to the radical cause flourished. Instead of selling Mr Carlile's pamphlets in an unthinking way, he made time to read them carefully, to take notes and even made connections between the structures of Westminster and the contents of his wife's imagined pantry.

Thursday, 29ᵗʰ July, 1819

Richard Carlile came into the shop, while Ings was preparing to open up, and informed him that he had been invited to address Mr Hunt's rally in Manchester.

"Mr Ings," he said. "Great Britain will remember 9ᵗʰ August, 1819 as the day the tide turned in favour of our people's unhappy majority."

"I hope so," replied Ings. "You'll make a beautiful speech, Mr Carlile, and take your proper place in history."

"Thank you, Ings," said Carlile. "You're a loyal and hardworking employee, who deserves a holiday. I shall tell Mr Edwards to release you for a week, and if it would please you to attend the meeting in Manchester, you shall hear all the speeches."

When Mr Carlile left, Ings made a little sideways leap, as Philbin always used to, when something tickled his fancy. For the rest of the day, he was too busy to give the matter any further thought, but that evening, standing alone with the dirty crockery, a chill wind blew across his gratitude. If he were entitled to a week's holiday, should he not take the first coach to Portsea, embrace his children and press Mr Edwards's guinea into his wife's palm? On the other hand, Mr Carlile may have proposed his participation for reasons of his own. Perhaps he wished Britain's capital city to be better represented in Manchester, or he was seeking support for his own speech? Perhaps Mr Carlile believed that the proprietor of a radical coffee shop should demonstrate his full and proper commitment to the cause? Or perhaps he was simply a generous, thoughtful man. He came from Devon, after all, which was not so far from Hampshire.

The dilemma troubled Ings that night when he tried to sleep. With the opportunity in sight, the longing to see his family grew stronger, until it seemed to penetrate his bones. Yet an invitation by a man as influential as Richard Carlile was not to be sniffed at. A refusal might offend him; Ings could lose his livelihood, and he might never have another chance to witness history in the making. But oh, for the embrace of his only son, the apple cheeks and open arms of Celia and his little girls!

Ings began to wish that he had not spent Philbin's inheritance quite so trivially. When his clamouring senses could take no more, he decided that the old King must choose, and he took a penny from his purse. If, when it landed, His Majesty looked up at him, he preferred him to go home and damn the consequence. If the coat of arms fell uppermost, then Ings was destined for Manchester.

Hon y soit qui mal y pense. Alas poor Celia! He emptied Philbin's last bottle and slept like a baby till dawn.

HALE / TIDD / BRUNT
Hole-in-the-Wall Passage, Holborn

Ever since Brunt combined forces with Tidd, his apprentice had protested at the low-grade work he was forced to do. Instead of learning the trade he was employed for, Joe Hale was required to empty slops, fetch water and fulfil all manner of female occupations at the whim of the two wives, who competed in their determination to dominate him. If Mrs Tidd sent him downstairs with a bucket of peelings for the neighbour's pig in anticipation of a trotter or a slice or two of belly, Mrs Brunt would require him to go begging to the grocer for half a pound of lard in exchange for a few clothes pegs.

Sweet Mary Tidd observed Joe's unhappiness and invited him to join the school she had established for her young siblings. She was teaching them to read, a task that had become easier when their pa arrived home last week with three slates and a box of chalks; gifts, he had said, from the Pimlico aunt. Harry, who could read well enough already, was Mary's assistant, and kept all four twins in order. The twins loved Harry like a brother, and when they were well-behaved, he allowed them a special lesson on his drum. Joe Hale was eager to learn and not at all unsettled by the cleverness of thirteen-year-old Harry, who thought it an excellent plan for the apprentice to better himself.

One day, quite suddenly, Joe Hale knew that despite her advanced age (she was at least twenty-two), he adored Mary Tidd and would adore her forever. When he confessed his love, gentle Mary confided that she was already stepping out. If there were ever a vacancy, she would tell him, on condition he did not spoil her present happiness by revealing it to her parents. Two days later, there was a collision on the staircase, which was wet because Mrs Tidd had just washed it down. The closeness to Mary drove Joe beyond reason, and he tried to kiss her. Mary pulled herself away but tripped on the damp steps. Joe forgot his distress and tried to stop her from falling, but as Mary fled, she collided with Molly Brunt, who, in the hope of locating her husband, was approaching with a can of milk for the children.

Jeremy and Charlie Tidd, playing hopscotch in the passage, raced up the wet steps and shouted to their mother that droopy Joe Hale had just kissed Mary, and when she told him not to, he pushed her down the stairs. When Mary told the honest truth, Eliza Tidd accused her of foolishly protecting Joe Hale. Molly Brunt protested that her husband's apprentice was the gentlest young man she ever knew, but like everyone else, a little askew from the lack of a good night's sleep and a decent dinner. If anyone should be blamed, Mrs Brunt opined, it was Mary, who had been especially bonny and smiling lately, enough to provoke any lad of a tender age. At this insult to her daughter's honour, Mrs Tidd seized her broomstick and promised to whack the living daylights out of Joe Hale. If Mrs Brunt tried to stop her, she would risk a beating too.

In the back room, playing cards, Brunt and Tidd heard the commotion and presumed that either the police or the army had arrived. In a flash, Brunt climbed on to the window ledge, while Tidd, who had more experience of legal matters, went to investigate.

A few minutes later, Richard Tidd told his family to make themselves useful at the market, because Joe Hale was going to take the thrashing of his life. As the children scarpered, followed closely by their mothers, they were confronted in the passage below by Tom Brunt, who had sprained his ankle while making his escape. Brunt was relieved to hear that no officers of the law were about, but alarmed that Tidd had taken it upon himself to discipline another man's apprentice. Consequently, as Joe Hale quaked, and Tidd fetched his leather strings, Brunt hobbled into the kitchen and ordered his partner to lay down his arms. If an apprentice deserved a flogging, he said, it was his master's responsibility to discharge it, and nobody else's. These were brave words for a man, who was a whole foot shorter than the guilty party and had never lifted a hand to wife or child, nor a weapon to any man, not even under provocation in France.

With her father's permission, Brunt first summoned Mary to the kitchen for questioning, and concluded that there had been a misunderstanding. Nevertheless, if he failed to punish the apprentice, he risked losing the respect of his business partner and both wives.

While Brunt considered a compromise, Joe Hale asked if he might now leave the room and get on with his work. Construing the lad's nervous tone as contempt, Brunt felt his blood boil. He cracked the whip and ordered the apprentice to lift his shirt and crouch on all fours.

Then Brunt closed his eyes and imagined that the bony, pimpled back belonged to a cossetted aristocrat, (whack!) whose table strained under the weight of glorious food, (whack!) but who believed it his right to cheat the poor (whack!) and take advantage of their wives and daughters (whack! whack!)

Scarcely a whimper came from Joe Hale, but when the whip stopped, Brunt had forfeited every ounce of his apprentice's respect. Mary Tidd was summoned to wash and bind the bloody back, and although Joe Hale's pain was soothed, his humiliation trebled. Mary wept and told him she was sorry. She wanted to be his good friend and would forever be grateful that Joe had not betrayed her secret courtship.

It was agreed that the matter would be forgotten, as long as Joe Hale gave up his ledge at the Tidds' apartment and slept forthwith on a mat in the workshop at Brunt's.

The next day, Brunt spent his constable's wages on an ounce of baccy for Tidd, some snuff for himself, a pencil for Harry and a new canary for his wife.

"Oh, husband!" she cried. "You have made Molly Brunt the happiest woman alive. How clever you are, mi'duck. to find a new shade of yellow, and weren't we right to keep Ringo's cage? I shall name her Lottie after the poor late Princess."

As his wife's euphoria continued, Brunt revealed, as casually as possible, that he and Tidd had an opportunity to advance their business, which might entail a few days' travel to the north. All Molly's joy was dashed. On no account would she contemplate her husband's absence with such a delicate matter in the air. She was not equipped to manage a lad of tender age, and what if they were suddenly swamped with orders and both men away? In any case, how would Mr Brunt manage all that walking, with his ankle the size of a turnip?

Under the weight of argument, Brunt conceded. He went at once to inform Tidd of the change of plan, blaming his injured leg and assuring his friend that he need not travel to Manchester alone. The country butcher, who managed Mr Edwards's coffee shop was so eager to accompany them, that he had committed a whole guinea towards the expense. Richard Tidd knew nothing about James Ings's character, beyond his excellent coffee, his ownership of a useful cart, his friendship with the late Philbin and his preference for Hampshire. Tidd replied that he was sure to feel lonely without Brunt but conceded to the wisdom of keeping at least one qualified man in the workshop, and if Hale could be properly occupied, so much the better.

In truth, Tidd was glad of an opportunity for action without Thistlewood, Edwards or even Brunt to restrain him. And Brunt had a better motive to stay at home than a swollen ankle, an anxious wife, a truculent apprentice or even a barely functioning business. Arthur Thistlewood had confided that Henry Hunt would only repeat in Manchester what everyone in London already knew. Nothing definite was arranged for the capital, but Thistlewood and his deputy were developing plans. Should anything materialize, it would please him to depend on the support of citizen Thomas Brunt.

Friday, 30th July, 1819

THISTLEWOOD

Stanhope Street, Lincolns Inn Fields

Sleepless and bleary, Thistlewood sat, that Friday morning, at his grandfather's walnut desk. He was struggling with the speech he had promised to rehearse for Edwards after tonight's meeting. As, at last, the words seemed to flow, he heard the hiss of his wife's skirts and said sharply that on no account, must he be disturbed. Susan left a letter on the corner of the desk and returned to the yellow settee. She had borrowed Scott's *Lady of the Lake* from the library, a distracting, epic poem of passion and politics in the Scottish Highlands.

About an hour later, when Thistlewood had composed a potential opening paragraph, his eyes strayed to the unmistakeable flourishes of George's writing on a letter his wife must have placed there. Opening the envelope, he found a copy of a brand-new royal proclamation. Thistlewood felt the blood in his veins turn cold. From this day forward, he read, each of His Majesty's subjects was required to report on any activity that might be seditious, whether in writing, public meetings or military style drilling. To enforce the new law, the authorities had been given unprecedented powers of arrest.

Thistlewood rose unsteadily to his feet. Could it be true? He looked at the document again, at the unmistakeable royal signature. His head felt light, a pain surged through his body and he roared. In alarm, Susan dropped her book and Julian arrived from his algebra in the kitchen.

"Papa!" he said. "What happened?"

Susan was reading the proclamation.

"Those eagles of destruction dare to accuse us of whipping up discontent!" he cried. "The population is on its knees, but instead of offering the hand of friendship, the cursed tyrants plan to infect every village with suspicion, pitching neighbour against neighbour, child against parent, priest against his flock, until no man can trust another."

"Why would the Regent agree to this?" asked Susan, replacing the document on the desk.

"Oh, he's not interested!" cried Thistlewood. "It's the work of his puppet masters, quaking in their Moroccan leather boots. Let Sidmouth and his cronies starve us all to death, and see who will fill their purses, then!"

"Calm, Arthur," said Susan, who had placed her arm around Julian. "They're trying to unsettle you, that's all."

"Mama's right," said Julian. "If you get angry, pa, the battle is lost!"

"What do you know?" snapped Thistlewood with ice in his voice. "Nothing! Neither of you."

Susan was tired too, but other worries drained her of strength. There had been no donations since Tuesday, and her pantry was almost empty.

"Go back to your arithmetic," she said softly to Julian.

"No!" said Thistlewood and turned, burning, to his son. "He will fetch my casket."

"Which casket?" asked Julian, his voice cracking in the brave attempt at defiance.

Thistlewood turned his gaze to his grandfather's oak walking stick in its nook beside the hearth. Then he looked at his family with a rage that neither had experienced before.

"Arthur," said Susan, a hand on her husband's arm. "This is not the answer."

Moving sharply from the hand that hoped to comfort him, Thistlewood fixed his eyes on his son, but the words were for Susan.

"It is not your place, madam," he said, "to remind me what the answer is or is not!"

"Julian," he commanded. "The casket under the foot of my bed. Now!"

Julian could do nothing but tighten his grip on the arm Susan had placed around him.

"My dear," said Susan. "Your family is not responsible for the proclamation. Please direct your protest where it properly belongs."

"It is also not your place, Mrs Thistlewood, to contradict my instruction to Julian, who is my son and – you forget – not yours. Now, will one of you fetch that casket or must I take the stick?"

With his wife and son apparently turned to stone, Thistlewood pushed past them and took the stairs two at a time. Susan urged Julian to hurry to Fleet Street and summon the only person in London who might calm his father now.

Edwards arrived smiling and reassuring, with white carnations and a bacon hock for Susan and paper for Julian. He made no observation about Thistlewood's wild appearance, but noted privately how pale and thin Susan had become. How, he wondered, had a dupe like Thistlewood deserved such a prize, and how might he make her just a little plumper?

"Don't you worry about the speech, Arthur," he said cheerfully, once Susan and Julian had taken their gifts to the kitchen. "Words will come naturally enough, once we decide what to do."

Edwards took a flask from his sack, reached for Thistlewood's drinking pot and filled it, promising that the elixir would soon brighten him up.

"Whatever we do now, George," said Thistlewood, "the enemy will find a way to destroy us. We have no power, not against such deep-seated greed and tyranny."

"Rubbish!" said Edwards. "Arthur Thistlewood has a better brain than anyone in Westminster. If we want results, the greatest tyrant we must overcome is not Sidmouth, but our own rage, which inhibits good practice. Our members need us both to stay calm and rethink the campaign."

"Yes, yes, you're right," replied Thistlewood, swallowing the absinthe. "You're always right, George."

"For today, Arthur," said Edwards, "relax and enjoy the bacon with your family. I shall deputize at Water Lane and assure the men that you're making a plan."

"I am?" asked Thistlewood, as Edwards filled his pot again. "What do you suggest?"

"Damn the proclamation" said Edwards, "and don't be led astray by Squire Hunt. We shall organise a series of rallies at which the people come prepared to defend themselves. I'll return tomorrow, Arthur, and take you out for dinner. We can discuss everything then."

Left alone, Thistlewood, exhausted, hungry and now muddled by absinthe, was besieged by a distorted image of Henry Hunt, lofty and proud on the back of his horse. The Orator's methods were doomed, he decided. The Squire himself knew it and had planned the Manchester rally simply to secure a northern seat in Parliament. Then he would abandon his followers, forget the struggle for universal suffrage and merge with all the other Westminster tyrants. Not so Arthur Thistlewood! While Hunt was feathering his northern nest, he would arrange a series of simultaneous protests in London, where the people were not so easily deceived. The government would crumble when confronted with the boundless anger of the population they had weakened and oppressed for too long.

On Saturday morning, Susan Thistlewood again found her husband asleep over an unfinished speech. Waking him gently, she told him there was bacon left in the kitchen. A kindly cowman had visited early with milk for Julian, who had asked that a portion be left for his father.

Mrs Thistlewood brought more important news than that. Unless Arthur was willing to tie them down, she would use her father's promissory note and take his son on the next coach to Lincolnshire. They would spend the rest of the school holidays in

Horncastle, where the boy would profit from the fresh air, while her parents would appreciate help during the horse-fair. Thistlewood shrugged, lifted himself up and went in search of bacon.

Tuesday, 3ʳᵈ August, 1819

EDWARDS
Johnson's Court

George Edwards was in his studio, filing the jaw on the figurine of Susan Thistlewood and waiting for the unassailable idea that would line all his pockets with gold. Success, so far, had been partial. For the humiliating end of the arson plot, he blamed himself; he should never have bribed his subjects with liquor, he should have taken greater care with his wording and never mentioned William. But these were chaotic times, and in future, he must be more selective and focus as intricately on his endeavours as he always had on his figurines. Fortunately, his own, or, more precisely, "Henry Ward's" integrity remained unblemished, while Mayor Atkins, having boasted that the idea was entirely his own, had been ridiculed from one end of Whitehall to the other with regard to the fire and blamed for the insubstantial outcome at Smithfield.

Extensive communications with colleagues in Stockport had not produced the desired effect at Smithfield, where Henry Hunt had proved himself a greater threat to the government than anyone had imagined. Increasingly agitated, Ministers were so determined to stop the Orator making fools of them, that they had embroiled Prinny, persuading him to sign a new Proclamation. While the government focused on Manchester, London must be ripe for action. Thistlewood was in the palm of his hand and all Edwards needed now was inspiration.

In the meantime, Thistlewood's health and safety were a priority. He would serve no purpose in an asylum, despite the compensation if Susan Thistlewood learnt that her husband had been declared insane.

"What have you got to smile at?" asked Tilly. She was standing in the doorway with a plate of cheese. Edwards had forgotten to lock the studio door. He knew from her tone that Tilly had observed the special care with which he carved a form that was certainly female and certainly not her own.

"I thought you was making models of heroes and the like!" she protested.

"So I am," replied Edwards.

"I want to know what kind of hero has such an elegant bosom."

"Joan of Arc." responded Edwards.

"In a frock like that? What do you take me for?" said Tilly, making a grab for the figurine.

Edwards pulled it away. "Come Tilly," he said. "You don't want mess on your pretty blouse!"

"Tell me who she is!"

"What if I were to say it's my ma in her younger days?" he asked.

"I'd say you was a bloody great liar, George Edwards," replied Tilly.

"That chin for a start; ain't nothin' like your ma's. That lady ain't never touched gin in 'er life, when Mrs G ain't seen a day without!"

"No woman wants her flaws on show, Tilly, and it's not finished yet."

"Show me the sketches, or you won't be playing no doo-dle-sack till Christmas!

Edwards stifled the retort that there were other doodle sacks he would far rather play than Tilly's worn out instrument.

Instead, he told her the truth. The model was the mother of one of his pupils and the wife of a friend. The sketches were made during lessons and had been kept by the family. The mother had taken the son to his grandparents for the school holidays. The figurine, when it was finished, would be a comfort to the husband.

"Why did you lie to me then, and tell me it was your ma?"

"It's a secret, that's why,"

Inexplicably, Tilly burst into tears. Edwards placed the figurine on his work bench, wiped his hands and summoned her to his chair.

"You're all chalky," she protested, but threw herself at him still. "Sorry I made a fuss, Georgie."

Her face was swollen, and her nose dribbled like a child's. How pathetic, Edwards thought, how ugly, how far from the girl who sang to him when he arrived back in London three months ago and drove him half-crazy with her lark song and that dance!

Tilly kissed his cheek and sprang her surprise.

"It's on account of the delicate condition I'm in."

"What condition?" asked Edwards, though he knew the answer before the question was out.

It was not the first delicate condition that had plagued Tilly Buck. When she said that the woman who usually helped out had disappeared, Edwards suggested a visit to Mrs G, who had medical connections. Tilly, who had hoped for a different response, replied that his mother was the last person she would turn to in a crisis, their only meeting having concluded with two slapped faces.

"Besides," she said resolutely, "I rather fancy keeping this one."

"That's ridiculous!"

"What's so daft about a girl wanting a baby from the man she loves?"

257

"That would be the Admiral, would it?"

"It would not!" said Tilly. "What's made you so cold, George? Don't you want to be a daddy?"

"If I did, it certainly wouldn't be for you."

"What did you say?"

"You heard!"

"I bet you would for Madam la-de-dah Figurine!"

Tilly picked up the half-made creation and threw it against the wall.

By the time Edwards had exited Johnson's Court with his valise, Tilly knew exactly how to ensure a cosy life for herself and her baby, which, by its first birthday, would be dancing the hornpipe.

For the second time this year, George Edwards found himself walking along Fleet Street, homeless. There were several options, until he found a place of his own. He could almost afford a suite at a hotel, but the extravagance would arouse suspicion. He might ask for a room at Arthur's apartment until his wife and son returned, but there were professional complications, and the scent of Susan would be too distracting. He contemplated removing Ings from his lodgings above the coffee shop, but the rooms were poky, and as grubby as hell since the wife went back to wherever it was.

Edwards was not entirely sure why he made the decision, but half an hour later, he found himself in a cab, armed with a bottle of gin and a packet of mutton chops. It could do no harm, he thought, to keep the old girl ticking over.

PART TWO

CHAPTER THIRTEEN

Wednesday, 22ⁿᵈ July, 1812

WILL DAVIDSON
Lichfield, Staffordshire

On the day of the British defeat at Salamanca, where Patrick Philbin lost his hand, a journeyman cabinet-maker named Will Davidson was lying in his bed in The Talbot Inn at Lichfield, recovering from a self-inflicted injury. His engagement to local heiress, Miss Salt, had come to a wretched end. Will's mother in Jamaica had sent £1,200 to give him an equal start, but when the bride's father heard about the wedding plans, Mr Salt took out his pistols and, in one the most terrifying incidents in Lichfield since the civil war, chased the young man down the street, firing wildly. A bullet lodged in Davidson's hat, and Miss Salt's father was locked up on a charge of attempted murder. Opposition to the marriage vanished when Will Davidson agreed to drop charges and delay the happy day, until his bride was of age. Miss Salt, who was sixteen, could not predict whether she would still love a man so far into the future, and ended the engagement herself.

After a night of torture, the thwarted groom marched to the Lichfield apothecary and bought a jar of poison. He stood by the market cross and sang, in a voice still, steady and deep, a parting song, with the words of Rabbie Burns,

Ae fond kiss, and then we sever;
Ae fareweel, alas, forever!

When the lament was done, Will Davidson begged Almighty God and his parents for mercy and swallowed the contents of the jar. The apothecary, witnessing the tragedy through his shop window, snatched an antidote from the shelf and saved the young man's life.

The matter became a cause célèbre in Lichfield, where sympathy fell soundly on the side of the young man. Exotic and foreign he may be, but his father was a Scot and an Attorney General, and Davidson had displayed dignity in his handling of the Salt family, of which this particular branch was the least popular. His recitations and his musical talent had made an impression in Lichfield, too. There were women who attended St Mary's Chapel twice on Sundays simply for a glimpse of his imposing figure and the sound of Will Davidson's magnificent voice, as it soared above the congregation. He was a popular teacher in the Sunday school, while in the twitching, lacy parlours, as often as in the philosophical corners of Lichfield, Davidson was a desirable diversion, with his reminiscences of an indulged childhood in Spanish Town, Jamaica and spell-binding tales of press gangs and life on the high seas. Even as he recited extracts of the Magna Carta (his party piece), Davidson's lilting tones had something of the rhythm of the waves. Some whispered that his Scotch relations were Jacobins, who encouraged radical tendencies. If they had, in Lichfield at least, apart from his popular recitations, Will Davidson kept his politics to himself.

This Wednesday, while all hell erupted in Spain, Will Davidson had begun to perceive that he was not, after all, at Heaven's gate, but sitting upright in a hotel bed. He opened his eyes and a serving girl encouraged him to take a little cold soup. As soon as she had gone, the housekeeper visited to remind him, that sick men were not the responsibility of the Talbot Inn. She had spoken to Mr Davidson's master, who had made arrangements to deliver his journeyman to Sandon Hall, where the firm had secured a commission to build a staircase.

Thus began Will Davidson's fateful association with the family and property of Dudley Ryder, First Earl of Harrowby, recently appointed Lord President of the Council. When, some months later, His Lordship inspected the new mahogany and ash staircase, he singled out Journeyman Davidson for particular praise, and invited him to restore the kitchen cupboards at the Grosvenor Square house.

Will Davidson left his Lichfield master and moved to London. There followed a few happy years, when he could be proud of his craftsmanship and surround himself with interesting new friends. He found plenty of work at Grosvenor Square and elsewhere, and rarely took advantage of the allowance provided by his mother (of which his distinguished father, now retired, knew nothing).

As he befriended other tradesmen, Davidson tinkered, like many of his colleagues, with radical philosophy. He attended debates, where his arguments, delivered in a deep authoritative voice, were informed by a strong faith, a fragmented study of law and the compassion, learnt from Tulloch, who had been his nurse in Spanish Town. Will Davidson's particular slogan was that all crime had the same origin, namely the suffering of weak individuals in the face of insurmountable anguish, the cause of which was invariably social disadvantage.

He taught in the Sunday School at Walworth Chapel on the Camberwell Road, and he fell in love with a widow from Tiverton called Sarah Lane, who brought him four ready-made sons and stood at his side when Davidson was accused of assaulting girls at the Chapel. When prejudice drove the family out of Walworth, they found new accommodation near Old Lords Cricket Ground. Then, the economy slumped, tolls and taxes multiplied and work became scarce, especially for independent craftsmen, and Davidson was obliged to spend the last of his Jamaican money. Lines appeared on the handsome brow, and for a couple of years at least, he was rarely heard to sing.

Soon after the birth of baby John, Sarah announced that apart from Will's tools, a few books and essential furniture, all they owned in the world was her late father's clock. They pawned it for seventeen shillings and in the following week, Davidson presented his professional credentials and his references at dozens of addresses in the West End. Nobody needed as much a picture frame.

Finally defeating his pride, Davidson visited his former employer's home in Grosvenor Square and offered his services for Lord Harrowby at half the proper rate. He was welcomed by the same old butler, Baker, who explained that there was no work at all in London, but plenty at Sandon Hall, where the journeyman who replaced Davidson had joined the regiment. He would be provided with a room to share with the labourers, but there were no facilities for his family. Davidson considered refusing the offer, until Sarah said that they were better apart temporarily than dead forever, a fate which seemed inevitable with hardly a grain in the larder.

Wednesday, 5th November, 1817

Davidson returned to Sandon Hall on the afternoon of the fifth of November 1817, which was another remarkable date in the history of Great Britain. At her Surrey home, Princess Charlotte, the rebellious and only acknowledged child of the Prince Regent, was in labour. She had lied about her dates, and when difficulties arose, the physicians were too nervous to intervene without her father's permission. No-one at Claremont House knew where to find him. His Royal Highness was eventually discovered in the Hertfordshire gardens of his favourite mistress, Lady Hertford, setting fire to an effigy of Guy Fawkes, while My Lord Hertford proposed a toast to the death of all traitors.

Davidson, who considered such festivities pagan, avoided a similar ceremony at Sandon Hall and strolled, instead, to the far side of the estate, reminding himself how beautiful this place was, even by night, and how fresh and bracing the Staffordshire air in autumn. Under a starlit sky, he gave thanks to the Almighty Lord for rescuing his family from adversity.

While Will Davidson slept soundly in his dormitory, a royal coach raced too late to Surrey. The deaths of the people's princess and her baby son made the Regent wretched for a time and launched a succession crisis for the Hanoverian monarchy. Meanwhile, in London's St Marylebone, Sarah Davidson wept silently into her pillow, asking God what He supposed they would eat if the last farthing went before her husband was paid, and whether life could be any worse at the workhouse.

Thursday, 5th August, 1819

INGS / TIDD

Trent and Mersey Canal

For a third of his guinea, the Hampshire butcher paid the passage for himself and Tidd, the bootmaker, on a barge that carried rubber from Chelsea to Liverpool and sugar all the way back. They were steered by a former sea-captain by the name of Vertue, who said that compared to the Bay of Biscay, English waterways were a game of marbles.

In all his life, Ings had never been as idle as he was on that journey, nor had he ever laughed so much. Tidd was not at all the fellow he seemed at the coffee shop, where he would sit in a huddle with his poetic partner and Mr Edwards. In fact, Ings had always been a little afraid of Mr Tidd, with his unreliable eye, his fixed opinions and the rumours of a wild past. But after two days on the water, Ings knew that a more interesting and dry-witted fellow, he could never hope to meet. When he said they could do with a few craftsmen like Tiddy in Portsea, Tidd promised that when England recovered from its crisis, he would explore the options in Hampshire, which must be an excellent county to have produced a fellow like Jimmy Ings.

The captain spent all his time on deck, steering for seventeen hours a day, only stopping to feed the horses or heave the barge through a lock and make his arrangements with canal officers. His two passengers helped when they were needed, but stayed cautious in their conversation. More experienced with boats than Tidd, Ings was confident at the wheel and occasionally took over from the captain.

"I'm Jim Worthington," he revealed, on one such occasion, as Vertue knelt beside him, mending a rope. Tidd stood at the rail in rare contemplation of nature. The towpath was on the left. On the right, ahead of the horses and on the edge of a recently harvested field stood a heron, so still that Tidd wondered if it were man-made.

"My cousin here is Dick Worthington," continued Ings. "We're emigrating to North America."

"Are you, now?" said the captain without looking up from his rope.

As the horses surged forward, the heron flapped its great wings and with the faintest bounce, propelled itself up and away. Something about the bird's defiant grace and its freedom stirred Tidd, but he was not a man to dwell on puzzles of the spirit, and he turned to join his companions.

"In case you're wondering why two cousins sound so different," said Ings to the captain. "I grew up in Wiltshire and Dick's from up north.

"Scunthorpe," added Tidd.

"I don't care if you're a pair of runaway bishops," said the captain. "Just pay your way and leave me in peace."

At nightfall, they moored by an ale house, where Captain Vertue drank with his cronies, and Tidd taught Ings how to play cards. On their third night afloat, when they had settled in their bunks and switched off the lamp, Ings considered it a shame that the entertainment had finished so early. Tidd said it had not and in the pitch black of their cabin, recited extracts from *The Pilgrim's Progress*. Ings said he must have adapted it, because he could never imagine good Christian pilgrims dancing in the streets of Boulogne or stealing tobacco from the King of Naples. Tidd's stories were marvellous, he said, and he should write them down, to which Tidd responded that life was for living.

That night, Ings's slumber was disturbed by guttural cry, as if some wild beast had strayed on to the tow-path and wished to die outside his porthole. He was wondering whether perhaps an animal had escaped from the circus, when he heard movements that were definitely inside the boat. Had the creature come aboard? Was his companion being murdered by trespasser? Ings opened his shutter, and as he turned, by the light of the almost-full moon, he had his answer. It was Tidd, thrashing about in his bunk, clearly in the midst of a nightmare.

"How, now, Tiddy!" he called. "It's me Jimmy, right here. Ain't no cause for alarm!"

The sentiment did nothing to comfort Richard Tidd, who twisted this way and that, still moaning incoherently.

"No need for all that, my friend," said Ings, climbing out of his bunk to fetch the flask the captain had put aside for medicinal purposes.

"Here's rum for you!" he whispered. "Drink!"

The aroma must have calmed Tidd, because he stopped shaking and opened his eyes sharp.

"Old ticker's firing like a woodpecker," he explained, and tipped the flask at his lips. "Nought to worry about."

"I'm glad Mrs Tidd weren't here to witness it," said Ings, and helped himself to a tot.

"Eliza seen it a thousand times," said Tidd. "Tells me to go back to sleep"

"And do you?" asked Ings.

"Generally, I do."

"What's it all about?" asked Ings, "if it's not too private."

"It's my premonition."

"You have a premonition?"

"Aye, I am in no doubt, Jimmy, but I shall end my mortal life in a noose."

When Ings found no appropriate question, Tidd volunteered that he had lived on borrowed time since the business with Colonel Despard. Astonished to learn of his companion's connection to the plot to murder the old King, Ings replied that he had no truck with the Regent, whose lamented youngest sister he had once met, but he had always taken His Majesty to be a modest fellow, respected for his thrift, his love of his family and grief for the children lost in infancy.

"Hah!" scoffed Tidd, his fire restored. "Any Irishman or American with half a brain can list 't crimes conducted personally by King George III."

"Tell that to my friend, late of Wexford," said Ings, "who lost his hand for the king's sake and never spoke a word against him."

"Aye," said Tidd, "Pat Philbin, who carried 't rebels' flag and was murdered by ungrateful compatriots."

The startling news and Tidd's knowledge of it struck Ings like a kick in the belly. Before he could find words to respond, there was an almighty thud, and the cabin door burst open. There stood the stout figure of Captain Vertue, a candle-stick in one hand and a broad-bladed knife in the other. His eyes blazed beneath his night-cap, as he roared that he had made mincemeat of nine pirates off the coast of Portugal and would not hesitate to cut their throats, neither. He had heard every word of their wicked conversation, and they were his prisoners. Supposing they survived till morning, he would escort them to the authorities, and they should expect to spend the remainder of their very short lives at Stafford Gaol.

Tidd submitted calmly.

"I thank you, sir" he said. "After sixteen years' anticipation, it is a relief to be arrested at last!"

The captain was stunned. Ings saw Tidd's good eye winking at him.

"That's a very fine blade!" said Ings to the captain. "In all my years of butchery, I ain't never seen such a splendid knife!"

Confused and uncertain now whether his ale had been dosed, or if this was all a dream, Captain Vertue played it safe.

"If you think, Mr Worthington," he said, "that flattery will alter your situation, you've got another think coming!"

That's when Tidd pounced. He grasped the captain's right arm, and as Ings wrestled the knife away, pulled the nightcap over the captain's eyes. Then Tidd grabbed the left arm, the candlestick clattered to the floor, and it was dark.

"Spare me!" cried the captain, on his knees. "I'm sixty-two years old, with two hundred pounds for you in Liverpool. I'm a Christian and a grandfather and not to be slaughtered like an old goose!"

Tidd instructed Ings to hold the knife to the prisoner's ear, while he fetched rope. Ings whispered that as long as he remained still and quiet, he need not fear for his life. Jim Worthington of Wiltshire might be a butcher by trade, but he was not a murderer and neither was his cousin, Dick. Captain Vertue would soon understand that he had been deceived by a government that had enslaved its people. All that was about to change, and as long as he did not provoke his captors, Captain Vertue and his family could expect their lives to improve, as soon as next week.

Tidd returned with rope, and as Ings held him fast, the captain whimpered, but did not struggle, even when they gagged him with his night cap and bound him tight. He trembled a little, when Tidd promised a wondrous flame when he set light to the barge and trailer, with the captain and all the rubber inside, and he moaned as Ings covered his eyes and Tidd advised him that the correct response was a vow of silence.

Ten minutes later, Ings and Tidd were scrambling across a fallow field, with their sacks on their backs and Ings still clutching the knife. When the canal was out of sight, they stopped to catch their breath.

"It was a proper shame to terrorize Captain Vertue," said Ings. "He was a decent old fellow, following his conscience."

"Aye," replied Tidd, "but don't you reckon his few moments of fear is better than making two widows of our wives?"

Each taking a swig of the rum that Ings had commandeered, they drank a toast to Mrs Ings, Mrs Tidd and another to Hunt and Carlile, and then they ran on, with no idea how they might reach Manchester in time for the rally, nor exactly where, in all England, they were located.

SUSAN THISTLEWOOD

Horncastle, Lincolnshire.

Although by the summer of 1819, every town in the north and east was in the grip of adversity, life in England was not universally bleak. Once a year, hard-working farmers in Yorkshire, Lancashire, Northumbria and further afield abandoned their wives, their worries and their labours and headed south of the Lincolnshire Wolds to enjoy a riotous fortnight, or a portion of it, in Horncastle. During the horse-fair, the country town, home to three and a half thousand, doubled its population. At all twenty inns and taverns, every room was packed with makeshift beds for the swarm of visitors, intent on eating and drinking to excess and exhausting every opportunity for business or mischief.

Alongside the brisk trade in horses for saddle, cart, coach or hunting, farmers invested in sheep and cattle, while young bloods gambled away fields and fortunes in back rooms, which had been scrubbed and scented for the occasion. Thousands of incoming horses needed stables, water and oats, and after long journeys overladen, hundreds of carts and carriages wanted repair. The annual horse-fair enlivened the economy for months, and every Horncastrian and every villager in the district, even those with no brains and nothing to sell, profited from two weeks' solid employment.

Geoffrey Wilkinson Esquire, butcher of 5, The High Street, Horncastle preferred to pay strangers than accept help from the daughter who had persistently ignored his advice and whose misguided loyalty had brought shame on the family name. This harsh message was issued by her mother, when Susan arrived at the shop-door, clutching a bunch of red carnations and with Julian at her side. Mrs Wilkinson, who had seen the pair approach, blocked the entrance to shield them from her husband, who was busy at the mincer.

Susan looked into the familiar small blue eyes and saw pain and disappointment. When her mother looked away, and Susan pressed for an explanation, Mrs Wilkinson whispered that certain articles from the London Courier had been passed round town, and Mr Wilkinson had received threats. The presence in town of their daughter and her stepchild could provoke a boycott or wilful damage to their property. When Susan retorted that the Courier was a dreadful rag, full of lies and distortion, and no one of any sense in London believed a word of it, Mrs Wilkinson replied that London could think as it wished. What mattered to Susan's father was the opinion of his customers, especially during the fair, when stakes were high and tempers ran short.

Susan was shocked. Her mother's letters had been bland lately, but there had been no hint of disapproval. She had supposed her mother to be preoccupied, or to be losing interest in local activities. Now it appeared that Mrs Wilkinson had abdicated all opinion and feeling of her own and harnessed herself entirely to her husband.

"Is it truly your wish, mama?" she asked.

Without looking at her daughter, Mrs Wilkinson replied that Susan should inform them when Arthur's dangerous ambitions had ceased, or when he was dead. Meanwhile, if they needed help, she might turn to his family. What of his brother, and had his sister not married the Vicar of Bardney? Were there not more relatives in Horsington? Susan replied that Arthur's sister had died in childbirth, his brother was estranged and moved to Leith, and they would never impose on the Horsington side, who were likely to be half-starved already. Mrs Wilkinson responded that at least the family name was not forever linked with Thistlewood's in the person of a grandchild. She glanced at Julian.

"The bairn's grown tall," she said, "and though he's not our own, he's innocent, and for his sake, I'll stand you the night in a hotel, but it must be in Lincoln or Sleaford, not Horncastle, where anybody as knows you will pelt you with eggs."

Susan pressed the flowers into Mrs Wilkinson's spiritless arms, took Julian's hand and turned away. A queue had formed behind her, and as they walked away, customers trampled over the spilt carnations. The Thistlewoods' luggage stood on the pavement, where the coachman had dropped it.

"Don't cry, mama!" said Julian.

"I have no intention of crying," said Susan. "I hate crowds; it's impossible to focus the mind."

A few moments later, carrying the luggage between them, Susan and Julian arrived the far side of St Mary's Church, where, within an unremarkable terrace, they found Dr Edward Harrison's famous Free Dispensary. Arthur had often talked about the Scotsman who had changed the history of medicine, with his experiments on spinal injuries and mental illness. Arthur's father William had been one of his first clients, and it was Dr Harrison who had encouraged Arthur's interest in the working poor.

The waiting room was crowded, and the clerk explained that demand for Dr Harrison's cures was always high during the fair, and the doctor was unavailable to social calls, however pressing. When Susan Thistlewood gave her name and promised to return, as soon as the Dispensary closed, a white-haired gentleman, measuring powders at the desk, turned to greet them. Susan responded joyfully and introduced Julian to her parents' old neighbour, whose ginger cat she had tormented as a child. Dr Chislett was Horncastle's apothecary, and Arthur Thistlewood had been his apprentice.

"Hello Julian!" said Chislett warmly, taking Julian's hand. "Your father was the best apprentice I ever had, and now he's England's great hope - if the newspapers don't crucify him first, with all the nonsense they print, these days!"

Weak with relief, Susan allowed the apothecary to lead them into the bottle store, where he indicated, through the window, a low brick building on the other side of a yard.

"That's the grammar school Arthur attended. The Thistle-woods always had fine mathematical minds, but Arthur had far more besides. A small town like this could never have con-tained him!"

"Why do they hate him now?" asked Julian.

"People here lead narrow lives, lad and lack imagination. You wouldn't credit the names they called Dr Harrison when he first arrived. Now, apart from Joe Banks, he's our most respected resident. One day, Horncastle will be just as proud of Arthur Thistlewood, and you shall live to see it, Julian!"

Dr Chislett was sorry to hear that Butcher Wilkinson was too busy with the fair to accommodate relations and said he knew a person who would give them the warmest welcome. Arthur's aunt, Mary Thistlewood had married John Innett, Head Gardener at Gautby Hall. She was a widow now, and as far as the apothecary knew, lived in the same cottage. If Mrs Thistlewood and Julian decided to visit Aunt Mary, they might convey very special regards from John Chislett.

Gautby, Lincolnshire

Aunt Mary Thistlewood was twenty-three years old, when her older brother was killed in Jamaica while visiting their Uncle Tom Thistlewood, who owned property there. Soon afterwards, their mother, Lydia Thistlewood died too, leaving Farmer John grief-stricken. At that time, Mary was betrothed to Dr Chislett, but as Farmer John's only daughter, she was obliged to stay at Tupholme to look after her father and younger brother, William. Eventually, as his grief softened, Farmer John made two decisions; he took, from Bardney, a second wife, and he encouraged William to marry the mother of the tiny grandson, Arthur, who had become the light of his life, but lived with his ma in Horsington. With a stepmother and a sister-in-law installed at Tupholme Hall, Mary Thistlewood was free to marry. She was thirty, and Dr Chislett had waited seven long years. Despite the previous agreement, her father would not accept the apothecary as a son-in-law. They were difficult times, he argued, and a fellow with radical tendencies offered little hope of prosperity. Instead, Farmer John gave his daughter to the head gardener at the Gautby Estate. Mr Innett, who had a cottage and four small children, was a kind man, and Mary accepted her fate, even though it meant she must part from John Chislett and would never nurse a baby of her own.

Being visited so regular by bad spirits from the Jamaica uncle and the front door so heavy, it burst her to move it, Widow Innett thought she would have another turn, when two strangers arrived at her cottage at dusk. But the shy youth and the care-worn young woman who stood on her path seemed to know her and even to love her, even though she could not identify them nor, being very hard of hearing, decipher their words. She indicated a slate and some chalk, and Julian wrote. "Good Day, Aunt Mary. I am Julian Thistlewood, son of Arthur, with my stepmother Susan."

With a cry of incredulous joy, Mrs Innett threw her arms around her great-nephew and squeezed him as tightly as her ancient arms would allow

"I forget myself," she said, pulling back. "No young man enjoys a fuss. I'm sure you'd prefer a bowl of barley soup!"

Aunt Mary led her visitors to the kitchen, where an ear trumpet eased the conversation, and the barley soup was expertly flavoured with fresh celery, marjoram and chives from the garden.

DAVIDSON / TIDD / INGS
Sandon Hall, Staffordshire

On the eve of his second lonely birthday, Journeyman Davidson was invited to supper by the master's apprentice, who lived with his parents in a corner of the estate beyond the orchards. Mrs Jackson's elderberry brew, which was often in demand at the Hall, looked innocent enough, but possessed the power to loosen tongues.

Ever since a few unguarded comments in the workshop, Davidson had suspected that Ned Jackson nurtured similar political views to his own. He was eager for confirmation but also wary of the consequences of a direct query. When he heard at the dinner table that Ned had worked a winter in the coalfield, he enquired casually what the family made of the reform movement. Mrs Jackson intervened sharply. She and her husband disapproved of political talk, particularly anything that might offend My Lord Harrowby, who had always been a generous employer. She would be more interested in Mr Davidson's history. He seemed very refined for a cabinet-maker, and a foreigner at that.

"Thank you for your interest, Mrs Jackson." relied Davidson. "My parents intended me to be educated in Aberdeen and Edinburgh, but I soon understood that university was wasted on a practical creature like myself."

"Tell them about your childhood in Jamaica," urged Ned, "and your adventures on the high seas!"

"Oh, indeed, Will" said Mrs Jackson. "Mr Jackson and I have never stepped out of Staffordshire, except once for a funeral, and we can hardly imagine a life anywhere else."

With plenty more brew to help the stories along, Davidson talked for an hour about pirates and alligators, albatrosses and shipwrecks. Mr Jackson fetched his whistle, and they all sang merrily, until the clock struck twelve.

The heavens were bright, but Davidson had failed to notice the route to the Jacksons' cottage, and he had not a clue how to find his way back to his dormitory. In the grass at his feet, a single daisy dazzled in the starlight. He crouched to pluck it and wished he were in St Marylebone and could give it to Sarah. She would kiss him tenderly and cherish the little flower for a week. But she could not kiss him, and he could not kiss his baby neither, nor had he done so in the eleven months since he was last summoned to Grosvenor Square. He kissed the little daisy instead, lay flat on the grass and recalled a song by the weaver poet, Rab Tannahill, which he sang to the stars above.

We'll meet beside the dusty glen, on yon burnside
Where the bushes form a cozie den, on yon burnside

As he paused to study the moon and the stars, Davidson became aware of an uncommon sound in the middle distance, like the growling of a large dog. He sat upright and saw two ruffians charging at him. The taller man was almost bald with bent shoulders, while his shorter companion brandished a knife. With almost a pint of elderberry wine in his veins, Will Davidson knew no fear. He turned on to his knees, opened out his arms and welcomed the strangers with words by Rabbie Burns.

Scots, wha hae wi' Wallace bled,
Scots, wham Bruce has aften led;
Welcome to your gory bed,
Or to victory!

Confident that they had come across a harmless drunk, Ings asked whether the stranger had any baccy for his friend.

"The name is Will Davidson, sir, a peaceful Scot, who lives here and would help you with tobacco and in other ways, too, if you will explain honestly your situation."

"What is your place here?" asked Tidd, perplexed by the fellow's articulate response.

"A journeyman cabinet-maker, citizen, who knows the stars, but forgot his way home. If you will help me find it, you shall have accommodation for the night, and good tobacco, too."

"We shall accompany you, Mr Davidson," said Ings, "but I shall not renounce my knife until I am confident."

"Then away! Let us do or die!" cried Will Davidson and leapt, with a whoop, to his feet.

At once, Tidd proposed the path beside the copse, which in one direction led to the canal, and in the other, surely, towards human habitation. In a few more minutes, they found the workshops, where Davidson's dormitory was on the first floor. He gave Tidd and Ings a candle and two blankets and directed them to a store-room, where they could lock the door on the inside, and be safe from discovery.

Friday, 6ᵗʰ August, 1819

On the morning of his birthday, Davidson brought breakfast to his visitors. Ings declared the loaf the freshest he could remember, and the milk as creamy as any in Hampshire. When Ings enquired whether he had sacrificed his own portion for their sakes, Davidson replied that the generosity was entirely the dairy-maids', who never asked questions if he asked for double or even triple his allotted ration. His appetite had been dispatched by a throbbing head and sick stomach, which were God's punishment for the liquor he had consumed last night, against the usual inclination of a Wesleyan.

Ings was curious to know where their host came from and whether he had ever worked as a slave. Davidson's reply was emphatic.

"I am a British patriot, sir, and never have been, nor never shall be any man's slave. I am employed as a cabinet maker by Lord Harrowby, on whose land you have trespassed, but my principal abode is in London, where my dear wife and children live in Marylebone, and I am a member of Robert Wedderburn's Unitarian congregation at Soho."

The information was sufficient for Ings and Tidd to shake Davidson warmly by the hand and inform him of their plan to attend Orator Hunt's meeting in Manchester. When Ings asked for the best route by land, Davidson revealed that he had partaken recently in a rally just a few miles south of Manchester and knew the road well. By good chance, there was no work at Sandon until a timber delivery next Thursday, and he would be free to attend Henry Hunt's meeting. Since it was unsafe for a mulatto to wander the countryside alone, he would part with half a crown, if he possessed such an amount, for the pleasure of accompanying them. Ings and Tidd could think of no reason to refuse and agreed that Davidson should keep the half-crown he did not have. They would accept a few pinches of baccy for Tidd, a loaf or two for the journey, some milk, and, if the dairy-maids were willing, a good slab of cheese.

Ned Jackson was desperate to join the party, but feared, in equal measure the wrath of his parents and the loss of his apprenticeship, which would be the consequences of discovery. He promised to soften the master in exchange for a word-by-word account of the speeches when Davidson returned. He told his parents that he and Will wanted to ride to town and buy glue powder and they would fetch the wool Mrs Jackson had been waiting for, too. Pleased that her son had come under the influence of such an educated fellow, Mrs Jackson donated her late uncle's tobacco supply and asked her cousin at the stable to lend a pony and trap.

The four of them sang all the way to Stafford and arrived just in time to spend another portion of Ings's guinea on three tickets for the coach to Stockport, where Davidson had friends, who might offer them temporary lodgings.

EDWARDS
Banks Court

Beneath the scowling surface of their relationship, George Edwards tolerated his ma's failings because he was born of her, and they were the same. In their ascent to higher social standing, moral conscience was no less a luxury than a Swiss watch or a pot of Souchong tea. Nevertheless, there were boundaries, which had been challenged on Tuesday when George Edwards arrived at Banks Court with the usual gifts and his valise to find that Cornelius Thwaite, the scourge of his life, had moved into his room. He seethed, but true to the example of Sir Herbert at Windsor, Edwards contained his rage, greeting the new lodger like a long-lost uncle.

Mrs G knew that look in her son's eyes and tried to distract him with flattery about his smart new suit and good sense in parting from that no-good strumpet. George could stay at Banks Court as long as he liked, she offered. His brother had earnt enough to move to his own place on Longacre lately, and since the light in William's room was unsuitable for an artist such as Mr Thwaite, George would be welcome to use it. In place of rent, she would appreciate a few supplies every week, and considering that neither she nor Uncle Con was getting any younger, occasional help with the business. Edwards replied that the sole purpose of his visit was to monitor his mother's well-being. He was busy enough with his own affairs, but should circumstances be right, he might consider limited involvement.

Mrs G's new enterprise involved the illegal transport of liquor from Rotterdam to the North Kent coast and by steamboat to Shadwell, where she had rented a small warehouse. The barrels, precise copies of legitimate containers, would be filled at the warehouse and ferried up the Thames for distribution. The first consignment was expected in Shadwell on Thursday, but her partner was not confident about siphoning the liquor, explained Mrs G, without a second pair of hands. Sensing the germ of a good idea, Edwards replied that he might be available on Friday until mid-afternoon.

So it was, that on Friday morning, George Edwards arrived at the Monument to the Great Fire, from which Thwaite would guide him to the warehouse. When the bells of St Magnus rang for ten o'clock, the wretched man had not arrived, and Edwards found himself drawn to the river. The church bells, the rumble of traffic on the bridge, the stench of Billingsgate hythe and the tumult of the market beyond, jolted him into another time, when his feet were bare, his belly ached and his life's crusade began.

The warehouses still looked the same, but the cluster of hovels, where he had lived with ma and his brother on parish charity, was gone. The rows of houses and shops around the corner on New Fish Street, remained, tall, sturdy and imposing. To the six-year-old George Edwards, no king's castle could have looked finer. Most of the buildings had been neglected since the depression, and some still stood empty, their windows boarded up. He peered up at the Monument to the great Fire. When he was young and the magical creatures on its base peered down at George's insignificant figure, he hated them for mocking the vulgarity of his existence, and, at the same time, saw in them an escape to a better life. Once, he stole paper once from the parish clerk, and sketched the monsters into a fantastical landscape of high seas and tropical forests. Mrs G showed the picture to everyone she knew, and swore her first-born was destined to be a great artist and would rescue her from misery. The Monument was still imposing, Edwards thought, although, as its monsters gazed at him now, they seemed bereft of breath and adventure, and he gazed straight back at them with nothing in his heart but contempt.

The reverie was broken by the sound of Cornelius Thwaite, who had arrived at the corner of Thames Street.

"Come along Georgie!" he called, as if summoning his pet pug. The words tugged at Edwards's stomach, and he smelt again the vinegar on Golden Lane.

The sculptor's lips curled into the same old grimace; straight on the left, slanting a little to the right, with his head cocked, like a dog waiting for his master to throw a ball.

"Ready?" he asked, his breath irregular and fouler than sour oysters. "Just think, Georgie! Twenty tubs of gin and forty-five of brandy, and every one to be sampled!"

Edwards had no intention of tasting anything, but he would ensure Thwaite swallowed enough to pickle a whale. When the carcass rolled on to a beach in Kent or Essex, there would be no suspicion of foul-play. He pictured his ma's response to the tragedy. Poor Uncle Con had caught his leg in a coil of rope, he would report, and had tumbled into the torrent. In a desperate attempt to pull him out, George tied the rope about his waist, slipped into the swirling water and snatched at poor Uncle Con's boot. But the boot had come away in his hand, and their dear old pal was carried off by the current. In helpless confusion, George had clung to the jetty, hollering to Uncle Con to fear nothing, and that if all were lost, God would be merciful. Thwaite would wave his arms wildly, his frenzied screams lost in the mayhem. As the beast was sucked into oblivion, Edwards would wear his satisfied smile. Their eyes would meet one last time, and Cornelius Thwaite would know the hell he had created and glimpse another, into which he was now dispatched. It was the just punishment for the murder of an innocent spirit. How much speedier his own advance would have been, Edwards surmised, if they had never met! How free his spirit would become, when the monster was gone.

As they walked along the wharf, Thwaite's mood was as buoyant as the boats that bobbed in the river. He marvelled at the forest of masts and sails ahead and speculated about a journey to Italy as soon as he was rich again. His mood changed abruptly when they arrived at Shadwell to find Mrs G's new warehouse bare, but for a few empty boxes. While Thwaite fumed about cheats and traitors, Edwards visited a chandler, who advised that it was always wise to check the daily paper. Very few consignments had arrived from Kent since a blaze that started in the funnel of a steamboat at Margate. Dozens of vessels and almost certainly their own, were held in dock, awaiting repair. Not to be diverted from his mission, Edwards asked the chandler where they might cheer themselves up with refreshment and good company. The chandler recommended The Roundabout, where a gang of coal-heavers was celebrating pay-day.

Distracted by strong ale and rough, muscular company, Cornelius Thwaite soon forgot his disappointment. Edwards sipped medicinal water and considered bribing one of the coal-heavers to tip his companion into the river, but the risks of both failure and blackmail were high. Instead, when enough fellows had witnessed how well he cherished his dear Uncle Con, Edwards slipped away to listen to a conversation that had started among some earnest fellows in a corner. His reward was a tantalizing item of news.

For reasons that the heavers did not yet know, Henry Hunt's Manchester meeting had been cancelled. Reports were confusing, but the Birmingham reformer, Charles Wolseley had already left Manchester, while the whereabouts of the Orator were unknown.

If true, what an excellent development, Edwards thought, and, given his special appointment this afternoon, how timely! Thistlewood would stage an immediate protest. An inevitable violent confrontation would complete the Group's isolation from Henry Hunt, and Thistlewood would surrender entirely to the control of his deputy, George Edwards.

He took out his watch. There was still time to complete his present mission. Thwaite was merry enough to be foolish, but steady enough to walk unaided. All it took to tempt the donkey away from the Roundabout was a reminder of Mrs G's mutton stew. Thwaite followed him meekly, and at Wapping, they turned towards a small, broken jetty. The river was high, the current strong and there was nobody in sight.

"See, Uncle Con," he began, "how prettily the lantern is reflected in the water!"

Thwaite leaned over. A small tap would be enough, thought Edwards, but what if his boots lodged in the river-bed? Would he have to push the ghastly face under the water with his bare hands, while Thwaite thrashed in the water? Was he strong enough to fight this whale of a man? A dead crab floated past, and Edwards felt his stomach churn.

"I see no reflection!" said Thwaite turning to Edwards, his lips twisted in playful mockery. "You always had a rich imagination, Georgie! Come on! Give us a kiss!"

How easy it would be! One little shove! Edwards stood there, tasting the bile in his mouth, unable to speak, unable to move.

"Come on!" pleaded Thwaite, closing his eyes. "You know you want to. For old time's sake!"

Edwards whacked the proffered mouth, knocking Thwaite to the ground. One kick and it would be over! But Edwards found himself as stiff and unyielding as one of his own figurines. Thwaite pulled himself to his feet.

"Sorry, George," he said, "but what's a poor playmate to think, when the man he adores brings him to such a lonely place? Don't tell your ma, what?"

As he set his companion on the road to Cripplegate, Edwards did not reproach himself for failure. Instead he contemplated a new idea, for which Thwaite's life might usefully be extended a little. The precise nature of the plan depended on the outcome of his imminent appointment. Thanks to his alliance with the Lord Mayor of London, George Edwards had secured, this afternoon at five, a private audience with the Home Secretary, Lord Sidmouth.

CHAPTER FOURTEEN

THISTLEWOOD'S FAMILY
Gautby, Lincolnshire

Affection and good company restored Aunt Mary almost to her former self, while with fresh air, country food and none of the stress of their London lives, her young relations flourished, too. The young Master of Gautby, Henry Vyner, who had inherited the Estate at the age of five, was home from Harrow for the holidays and soon befriended Julian Thistlewood. With only four small, irritating siblings for company, at home, as long as the fellow had spirit, Henry was indifferent to Julian's private circumstances, and as long as he stayed away from the horse-fair and out of trouble, his mother and the nurse were content to see Henry occupied.

Julian took to the saddle as if born to it (which perhaps he was), and every morning, they rode out in search of adventure. In the afternoons, they swam in the lake and - with help from a bored footman - built a tree house in Gautby Park, from which they plagued passers-by, or, if they were very lucky, courting couples, with showers of twigs and green acorns.

Meanwhile, under Aunt Mary's guidance, Susan applied herself to the disarray in the Innetts' cottage. When, after two and a half weeks, the place was as clean as a new box of pins, she suggested they invite Julian's friend for afternoon tea.

"Why ever not?" replied Aunt Mary, "it's about time a Vyner crossed my threshold again."

The Innetts' best table cloth was washed, dried in the sunshine and ironed. Susan baked biscuits, while Aunt Mary picked the best delphiniums and arranged them in chipped vases that her husband had salvaged from the Hall after a shipment of new porcelain arrived from Canton. The Innetts' own Staffordshire china was relieved of its dust, bathed and polished till it sparkled.

Henry Vyner had visited the cottage since early childhood, partly for the decent biscuits, but also to exchange the formalities of the Hall with unconstrained conversation. When tea was served, he begged to ask Widow Innett a question. The widow, who had wiped the boy's bottom and his nose at least a hundred times each, was not inclined to acknowledge his status.

"Well, Henry," she said. "Curiosity killed the cat, but clearly it never hurt you!"

Master Vyner grinned at Julian and allowed the old girl a moment to adjust her ear trumpet.

"Fire ahead," she said, "or must I die waiting?"

"Is it true," Henry asked, "that Julian's ancestors and mine knew each other well?"

"Very true," replied Aunt Mary. "I'm sure you've heard of Farmer John, who managed the estate for your father and grandfather?

"Farmer John is a legend at Gautby, ma'am!"

"Aye," said Aunt Mary, "but did you know he was my father?"

Henry, who never thought hard enough about servants to make the connection, admitted that he did not.

"Farmer John, my father was the tenant of Tupholme Hall," Aunt Mary continued, "and like his father and grandfather, he worked as your family's land-agent. Our William, my brother should have taken over, but he fell out of a tree and broke his crown. And that's why Farmer John worked into old age."

"Grandpa William fell out of a tree?" asked Julian, who knew little of his family history and even less of its shame.

Aunt Mary glanced at Susan, unsure how much she had been told, and whether she approved of disclosure in the present company.

"Do tell us more, Aunt Mary!" said Susan. "Arthur is so reticent about the family, and we long to know more, don't we Julian!"

It had been many years since three pairs of eyes had looked at Widow Innett so appealingly.

"My brother's accident was a shock," she said, "especially with our John, my older brother drowned in Jamaica, visiting Uncle Tom. When William failed to recover, we expected Arthur to take over, but, Julian, your papa had different interests, some of which he learnt at Gautby."

Aunt Mary stopped abruptly and asked Susan to pour another round of tea. Susan said she would brew a fresh pot, and advised Henry and Julian to play outside.

"No need!" said Aunt Mary firmly. "I'm putting my brain in order, that's all. Pin back your ears, boys!"

Although the boys giggled at Aunt Mary's eccentricity, they were spellbound, as their shared history unfolded in that little parlour.

"Farmer John, my father often brought Arthur here to visit me. As he grew older and started learning the business, my nephew became a favourite of Master Henry's grandfather, who was a Member of Parliament. Old Bob, as we liked to call him, would beguile Arthur with tales of Mr Fox's mischief at Whitehall or his antics at Brooke's Club. Westminster was a new world that shone through Old Bob's anecdotes, and its population must have seemed as alive to Arthur as his friends and neighbours in Lincolnshire, and much more exciting. When my nephew announced his intention to become a Member of Parliament, too, and change the world for ordinary people, Old Bob laughed till he cried. He repeated the exchange to my father, who laughed with him, but then took our Arthur to the stable and scolded him for impertinence. I know he did, because Arthur came straight to this very parlour and told me the dunderheads knew nothing about the real world, and he hoped they lived long enough to see him prove it."

"Now, then," said Aunt Mary, beaming. "What do you make of that?"

"How I wish I'd met Old Bob!" said Henry.

"How I wish pa had stayed in Lincolnshire!" cried Julian. "Don't you mama?"

"Your father must follow his dreams," said Susan, warmly.

"As his wife must follow him," said Aunt Mary.

"Indeed," replied Susan, unsure whether she was rebuked or supported.

"If there was no chance of entering Parliament," continued Julian, "whatever persuaded papa to leave this beautiful place?"

"Your pa is best qualified to answer that question, Julian, but since Arthur's not here, with mama's permission, Julian, I shall repeat what my father told me, when he lay dying."

Susan, pouring a fresh round of tea, replied that her only concern was that Aunt Mary should not be distressed by sad memories.

"The old gal ain't ready to shuffle off yet!" retorted Aunt Mary, grinning at the boys and resting the ear trumpet on the little polished table beside her chair.

"Two years after Uncle Tom died in Jamaica," she said, "our Arthur must have been around fourteen, when father was obliged to evict a family he had known all his life. The labourer had broke his leg, see. His sons joined the regiment and never came back, and he hadn't paid rent in six months. Father took Arthur along to demonstrate that an agent must always place duty above sentiment. Forced to watch his old friends pile their belongings on to a cart and the father, limping off, leading his family to goodness knows where, our Arthur were distraught. He begged father to let the family stay at Tupholme Hall, but Farmer John was firm. Our home also belonged to the Vyners, he said, and we couldn't use it as a refuge for folk as couldn't pay up. Arthur demanded to know by what right some families led an opulent life and others lived well enough, but many hard-working folks faced nothing but squalor and uncertainty. When my father told him that such priorities were decided by God alone, our Arthur preferred to sleep in the frozen woods rather than return to Tupholme and accept an opinion he despised."

Aunt Mary sank into her chair, adding in conclusion that Dr Chislett might provide more detailed information. Susan knelt on the floor and stroked the old lady's bad shoulder, until she succumbed to sleep.

Julian and Henry were sitting in the shade of the damson tree, when Susan approached to suggest that the young master might be missed at the Hall. Henry made his thanks, accepted the remaining biscuits for his brothers and sister and arranged to meet Julian tomorrow morning, when they would ride out to Tupholme and explore it together.

As the sun set over the lake at Gautby Park, a message arrived at Widow Innett's cottage. The writer regretted, on behalf of Her Ladyship, that while Master and Mrs Thistlewood may remain at their aunt's cottage, they must make no attempt to visit the Hall or contact the young master, who would leave Gautby at dawn and spend the rest of his holiday in Yorkshire.

Julian understood the reasons at once and protested that children should not be punished for differences between their fathers.

"I shall climb into his window tonight," he said.

"Henry would not want that!" replied Susan.

"But we've sworn eternal brotherhood!" cried Julian.

"Henry's a good boy," said Susan. "I'm sure he's just as hurt as you are by the news, possibly more. He would not want a selfish, pointless act of defiance to put Aunt Mary's security at risk."

Such trains of thought were unfamiliar to a modern boy like Julian Thistlewood, who began to understand that for all his privileges, Henry Vyner was not always free.

"I shall write to him at Harrow!" he said.

Susan folded her arms around Julian for comfort and so that he would not know she had seen his tears.

"That's a mighty serious face for a young man," remarked Aunt Mary that evening, as she handed Julian his milk.

"One more question," he said, with a beseeching look at Susan and Aunt Mary. "What happened to pa that night?"

"Fetch the trumpet, lad, or must we all die waiting?" replied Aunt Mary.

"In the morning," she said, when the question was clear in her mind, "father found him half frozen under the old oak on the Horsington road. At the age of seventy, Farmer John lifted that great lump of a boy on to his horse and brought him back to Tupholme. For a week, we thought we might lose our Arthur. Dr Chislett rode out from Horncastle and saved him."

"As I understand it," said Aunt Mary, lowering her ear trumpet, "that's when your pa became interested in studying medicine."

After a few moments' reflection, Julian looked up, his eyes full of the greatest question of all.

"Your mother?" asked Aunty Mary. "Nobody has told you about your mother?"

"My other mother," said Julian, offering up the hearing device and glancing at Susan, who shook her head kindly, as if to say she knew nothing about it.

"Isabella Grant, her name was," said Aunt Mary, "off a farm at Bardney. Pretty girl with sparkling eyes, and the kindest spirit in all Lincolnshire. You have exactly her look and manner, our Julian, adapted for a boy. Arthur made Isabella promises, I'm certain of it, but she bled to death before you was a day old. After that, like a lot of farmers round about, her folks went to a better life in the North American Prairies. They were desperate to take you, Julian, only Arthur said he would no more let go of his bairn than of his hands or feet!"

Julian took the news quietly.

"Wasn't pa clever to find Miss Wilkinson to take care of me!" he said, at last.

"Do you know?" replied Susan. "I never thought of it that way."

FOUR HENRIES

The Home Department, Whitehall

Henry Addington, ousted as Prime Minister fifteen years ago by his old friend, Pitt and better known now as His Majesty's Home Secretary, Viscount Sidmouth, would rather be spending his sixtieth August relaxing in Richmond or preparing for the shoot in Devon. He had been kept at Whitehall by grave concerns about the country and in particular, a forthcoming rally, a so-called monster meeting in Manchester, organised by a band of reformers lead by the cunning Henry Hunt. Sidmouth had urged the magistrates who controlled England's second largest town - and its most disputatious – to do nothing that might provoke insurrection. Nevertheless, detailed plans had been drawn up involving several regiments, as well as the amateur force of the Manchester and Salford yeomen.

Henry Hobhouse, Permanent Under Secretary in the Home Department was reciting a communication from one of the Manchester magistrates, the Reverend William Hay. Like Sidmouth and, twenty years later, Hobhouse, Hay had studied law at Oxford, and his judgment could therefore be trusted. The precautions in Manchester, he wrote, were sensible, and there was no reason for concern. Indeed, Sir John Byng, army commander, northern district was so confident of a peaceful outcome that he planned to remain in Pontefract.

"Hah!" exclaimed Sidmouth. "Aren't there races soon in York, Henry, and isn't Sir John's prize stallion hotly anticipated?"

"The York races have finished, My Lord," replied Hobhouse.

"What about the significant Saxon; wasn't he visiting York on his tour?"

"Prince Leopold dined with the commander on Thursday," replied Hobhouse, "and moved promptly on to Newcastle. I understand Sir John has other, long-standing commitments and sees no reason to cancel his instructions."

"Instructions to whom, Henry?"

"Lieutenant Colonel L'Estrange of the 15th Hussars, who, My Lord may remember, distinguished himself at Waterloo?"

"So he did," replied Sidmouth. "Let's hope the fellow isn't trying to distinguish himself again. Manchester needs calm heads."

Viscount Sidmouth was not a racing man, but as he dictated his thanks to the Reverend Hay with a request to be kept informed etc. etc., he wished he had time to dine with princes and take his pleasure on weekdays.

"Well, Henry," he said, when he had finished. "You may go home to your sons."

"Not quite, My Lord," said Hobhouse and reminded the Home Secretary gently of an appointment with an agent, involved in a case close to his heart. The Mayor of London had taken a shine to the fellow and was confident that a private audience would be advantageous.

"Smoke Jack, eh?" said Sidmouth, chuckling at a memory of Mayor Atkins's humiliation. "Trying to worm his way into favour again, what? Send the bugger in."

Sidmouth had come across Henry Ward before. The way the fellow slithered into the room reminded him of snakes he had seen in the country. Snakes were all part of God's natural order, he supposed, and dealing with them was one of the perils of office.

Although he was pleased to hear of Mr Ward's progress at first hand, the Home Secretary saw no reason for haste. Arthur Thistlewood had been imprisoned more than once, and on each occasion, had wriggled out of custody. He was not to be arrested again until the ultimate conviction was certain to follow.

"Arthur Thistlewood is a clever man," said Sidmouth, "but he's also sloppy, Mr Ward, and he's emotional. Stop feeding him. Give him enough rope, and he'll hang himself; you'll see!"

Anxious to arrive in Richmond before sunset, the Home Secretary agreed, without argument, to the agent's terms. On no account, he instructed, as he indicated the end of the meeting, should Henry Ward be seen in Whitehall again. Future communications should follow the correct procedure. They must be clearly written in pencil on brown paper, marked for the attention of Henry Hobhouse and left with the clerk at Bow Street.

His heart as light and quick as a sparrow's, George Edwards floated through the corridors of power, out of the great oak doors and on to the bustle of the street. The meeting with Sidmouth had surpassed all expectation. The more successfully he controlled Thistlewood and his men, the more grievous crimes they would commit and the more magnificent his final reward. What exquisite anticipation!

Sidmouth had confirmed that the Manchester meeting was postponed. In other words, Henry Hunt and Richard Carlile were likely to be away from London for at least two more weeks, which left plenty of time to launch an independent plan in the capital. The new campaign would need headquarters, somewhere spacious, but discreet. Edwards knew just the place, and as he hailed a cab at Charing Cross, the streets of London had never seemed so ablaze with light, colour and opportunity.

BRUNT

Streets of London.

News of the postponement in Manchester had been scrawled on the front page of each copy of *The Reformers' Gazette,* which Thistlewood distributed in the gaols at White Cross, Newgate and Marshalsea, where many known sympathisers had been hurriedly imprisoned for imagined, or petty offences. The pamphlet owed a debt to Carlile's daily reports from the north, but Thistlewood had revised the content for men with less education than readers of *Sherwin's Political Register.* The vocabulary was simple, the message straightforward and dynamic, and there were concessions to the Water Lane Group's particular principles. In other words, the information provided had undergone a subtle change of emphasis.

Brunt defied his poorly ankle to distribute *The Reformers' Gazette* at barracks, ships, taverns and anywhere else he might come across ordinary soldiers and sailors. Men, thin and colourless as rats, complained of appalling conditions and either low pay or none. Whether or not they could read the *Gazette*, most dropped a penny or two into Private Brunt's purse. When they enquired at which battle he had been wounded, Brunt confessed that his injury was recent, but he was happy to relate his adventures in the Occupation and to listen, as long as time permitted, to their stories too.

When all but a few pamphlets had gone, Brunt hobbled to Stanhope Street to report his success. He was happy to confirm that should either the army or the navy be commanded to disrupt any public action, the lower ranks would support the Radicals. Glad of good news, and more than a little lonely, Thistlewood invited Brunt to stay and rest his leg, rather than walk all the way back to Holborn. When Brunt said he preferred to return to the bosom of his family, Thistlewood replied that he was a very lucky man and loaned his grandfather's sturdy oak walking stick.

MOLLY BRUNT / ELIZA TIDD

Fox Court, Holborn

As Brunt limped homeward, the bosom of his family was far from intact. Eliza had complained to Molly that while her own husband walked the streets every day of the week in search of work, Mr Brunt did nothing to keep their business alive.

"With his swollen ankle, my husband is in no position to walk the streets," retorted Molly. "At least Mr Brunt prefers to stay with his wife and family, while your husband grabbed the first opportunity to escape!"

"Mr Tidd is determined to find work, wherever it may be!" replied Eliza. "I'd like to see for myself, how well Mr Brunt is nursing his injury, for he's hardly ever home. Most likely he's wasting his last penny on philosophy in some god-forsaken tavern, to which, he's doubtless flown like the flipping canary!"

"How dare you?" cried Molly Brunt, wounded by the odour of truth in Mrs Tidd's words. "Thomas Brunt comes from a line of clever thinkers. Without men like him, where's the hope for England? And if Richard Tidd, with his shady past, is walking the streets all day or visiting his sainted aunt in Pimlico, you can be sure his purpose is not to find work, but to avoid his nagging shrew of a wife!"

Eliza reached for the broomstick and was still shouting and waving it about when Harry Brunt arrived to prevent an assault.

"Come with me, ma" he said, cool as you like. "We got better places to be than this."

"Do we?" asked Molly, in surprise.

Harry came up close and whispered, "Ain't we got relations in Southwark?"

"Indeed, we do, you clever, clever child!" cried Molly. "Put that stick away, Eliza! You're on your own! Harry and I are moving out."

"You can't leave!" cried Mrs Tidd, her broomstick clattering to the ground.

"Just watch me!" cried Mrs Brunt and told Harry to put his boots on and fetch his drum and the canary.

"Take that droopy apprentice with you an 'all!" said Eliza. "I get more use from a pan with no bottom. All he ever does is hanker after grub."

"Joe's my husband's apprentice, not mine!" replied Mrs Brunt.

As Eliza stood there, aghast, Molly almost regretted her cruelty.

"You have a grown daughter to help you." she said. "It's not so bad Eliza."

"Oh, but it is," said Eliza. "I'm sorry I upset you Molly, I didn't mean no harm. I miss Richard, that's all, and I worry how we'll get through. Don't leave us alone!"

Molly sighed and replied that part of her was sorry too, but she had feared for her life today, and could no longer be certain of her own safety or her son's.

"What am I to tell your husband when he comes home?" asked Eliza.

"Tell him what you like, mi'duck!" replied Molly, emboldened by the prospect of a new life across the river. "I shall send for him and his equipment when I'm good and ready!"

It was the second unwelcome shock of Eliza Tidd's day, and she had said nothing of the first to Molly. This morning, at St Andrews, Holborn Hill, her daughter Mary had been wed to Gerald Barker, a clerk. There would be one less mouth for the Tidds to feed, Mary said. It was Gerald's second marriage, and he had wanted no fuss. At least there was no expensive celebration, and, she promised, no new baby to worry about. For Eliza, the shock and shame were less in her daughter's secrecy than in the High Church ceremony. She preferred the bride's father, not Molly Brunt, to be the next person to know.

Late on Friday evening, when Tom Brunt returned to his apartment, the stair case had never seemed so steep and despite the help of Farmer John's walking stick, his throbbing foot was the size of a small pumpkin. Rather than disturb his little family (or face his wife's questions), he decided to sleep in the workshop, where the apprentice was waiting, with a smirk, to deliver the news.

Saturday, 7ᵗʰ August 1819

On Saturday morning, in the absence of their spouses, Brunt proposed to Mrs Tidd a little mutual support, on condition he was not expected to listen to any extracts from *The Pilgrim's Progress*. Mrs Tidd replied that the suggestion was improper, and even if it weren't, it was likely to involve Mr Brunt occupying her husband's chair at meal-times and sitting bone idle for the rest of the day. Brunt retorted that he would make his own domestic arrangements, and Mrs Tidd would soon know what she'd lost. An hour later, Joe Hale could take no more and returned to his mother in St Giles until trade resumed. The final blow came when Mary Tidd Barker revealed that instead of living nearby, she and her new husband were off to spend their honeymoon with his family, who lived by the sea in Kent. And so, Eliza Tidd was left quite alone with her four twins, her opinions and her nosy neighbours.

TIDD / DAVIDSON
Cheshire

On Saturday morning, the coach containing Tidd, Ings and Davidson stopped for refreshment at an inn, some ten miles south of Manchester. After paying for their porridge, Ings said that he preferred to stay in Bullocks Smithy than travel the extra distance to Stockport. Having discovered that his employer, Mr Carlile and Mr Hunt were among the overnight guests, Ings preferred to find a billet nearby and would proceed to Manchester in good time for the meeting. Besides that, he wanted no truck with ministers of the church, even Joe Harrison, no matter how well-intentioned.

As the coach rumbled northward without Ings, Davidson reminded Tidd that the local populace were not the dullards that some Londoners imagined. Every pamphlet that Tiddy could read in London was also available at Stockport Library, which had as many women members as men. Hundreds had attended the great rally in June, where Davidson carried his skull and cross-bone flag, and Parson Harrison made the speech for which he was arrested at Smithfield.

Tidd, who was tired and in no mood for conversation, fell silent and looked out at the north Cheshire landscape, which altered by degrees as they approached Stockport. With its steep slopes, dark, imposing factories and warehouses, the district was very different from the landscapes he knew in eastern and central England. When they stepped off the coach and walked through the hilly town of Stockport, Tidd sensed a difference in the people, too. They seemed poor, but they greeted the strangers kindly and seemed less ready than in London, Lincolnshire or Nottingham to look at him and judge him badly.

Will Davidson planned to surprise a friend who lived further along the Manchester road. A weaver with eight children, William Beard would be busy at his loom until evening. In the meantime, Davidson proposed calling on another acquaintance, a Stockport shoemaker, who would be pleased to meet a colleague from London and had space for a billet.

John Boulton was a gaunt fellow of sixty with a mop of curly hair and a shining smile that dominated a narrow face. He was delighted to meet Davidson again and proud to show his workshop to a fellow-craftsman. On her way out with a batch of rising dough, Mrs Boulton agreed to provide three nights' room and board to Mr Tidd. She said she trusted the men had more sense than to attend the Manchester meeting on Monday. Her husband laughed and replied that Henry Hunt was a champion of peace, and his rally would be no different from any Whitsun Parade, except that it would go down in history.

"The only history I want is the day my pantry's full again!" replied Mrs Boulton.

When she had set off for the bake-house, her husband informed Tidd and Davidson that unfortunately, the rally had been delayed. Tidd, who had little to lose but his wife's good temper, was disappointed, but if the Boultons could spare the billet, preferred to wait in Stockport than return home. Davidson's quandary was more challenging. If he failed to return to Sandon before the timber delivery on Thursday, he could lose his job and his professional standing. His family's livelihood was at risk, and yet, for all the spice in Jamaica, he did not want to miss the Manchester meeting. Tidd advised him to consider the dilemma in peace, and for today, at least, enjoy his holiday.

That afternoon, they attended the Windmill Rooms for a meeting of Parson Harrison's Union for the Promotion of Human Happiness. After prayers, Harrison reported that Home Secretary, Sidmouth had again refused to pass the Union's petitions to the Prince Regent. The refusal confirmed, once more, that the government was in defiance of the Magna Carta.

"Here, here!" shouted Will Davidson and asked to recite the relevant passage of the charter.

"Thank you, Will Davidson," replied the parson. "Another time. Our priority today is the rally, and first of all to give notice that Henry Hunt has promised, immediately after the Manchester Meeting, to return to London and deliver, in person, a similar document to His Royal Highness.

There were cheers and then Tidd raised his hand, nervously.

"Welcome, stranger!" said Parson Harrison.

"Richard Tidd, sir, bootmaker of Grantham and London, who once met Jeremy Bentham, the man responsible for your philosophy of Happiness, and lent his name to my first-born son.

The congregation applauded.

"I'm sure Dr Bentham was honoured," replied the parson. "However, his philosophy and ours has a far longer heritage than the current century, or indeed the last."

"That's as maybe" said Tidd, "but I was present at Smithfield on 't day of your arrest, Reverence, and very much opposed it."

The congregation applauded again.

"Thank you, Mr Tidd," replied the parson.

"I ain't done, sir," said Tidd. "If I may, I have a question, of a sensitive nature. In 't first instance, I want to convey that Richard Tidd is a man of peace, who wishes he had Happiness in his hands, and could distribute it fairly to all God's creatures!"

Some in the congregation laughed appreciatively.

"As you see, Mr Tidd," replied Harrison, "you're among friends. Stand on a chair, sir, and everyone will hear you."

Tidd climbed on to his chair and cleared his throat. He had waited long to say these words, and in a room of strangers, whose knowledge of Westminster, for reasons of geography and perhaps more, was inferior to his own, his confidence soared.

"Thank you, Reverence," he began. "My question is this; why do you suppose that 't damned Regent will be more sympathetic to your petition than Sidmouth was, when His Highness is 't greediest of all 't pigs what call themselves Dukes?"

Davidson gasped at his guest's outburst and the room fell silent. Parson Harrison responded calmly, without signs of condemnation, that in his community, rough language was considered unproductive. Further, the issue at hand was not the personal failings of any one person, but a principle of law. A Head of State who is kept in ignorance cannot reasonably be expected to authorize change. It was therefore the legal responsibility of any government to keep the King or his Regent properly informed. In domestic matters, that duty fell to the Home Secretary. By denying the Regent of information, the Minister was guilty of Treason.

"Here, here!" cried Davidson.

Tidd, on his chair, seemed not to have listened attentively, but he was aware that all eyes in the hall were turned to him and sensed that a response was due.

"Shall we not track 't tyrant down and hang him?" he called, loudly. "Hang draw and quarter him!"

Instead of the cheers Tidd expected, a mutter of discontent flickered through the room, which stopped when Parson Harrison spoke.

"Dissenters we may be, Mr Tidd," he said, "but the Ten Commandments are revered by our congregation, as is the principle that criminals, however provocative, should be tried in a court of law. We understood that you have travelled far and may have reasons to unburden yourself of private anger. Equally, we are pleased to have given you the opportunity to so in a protected environment. But time is short, Mr Tidd, and this meeting must turn to its proper theme, the postponed meeting in Manchester."

Persuaded that the people of Stockport were too meek for their own good and more embarrassed than he would ever admit, Tidd climbed down from the chair, which Davidson held steady, although he would not meet his companion's eyes. The remainder of the meeting focused on the Stockport processions; details of the route, who had been chosen to carry which banners, problems arising from sickness among the musicians and the shortage of transport for the elderly and infirm. When the formalities were done, wives of the Stockport Potato Traders provided a salty tater broth. As Tidd and Davison filled their mugs, Harrison approached them, smiling, as if Tidd had never made his blunder. He would enjoy spending time with his guests, he said, but his wife had prepared supper, and he must write tomorrow's sermon. He recommended they stroll along the Mersey, and meet him at the chapel in two hours' time. With that, Harrison hurried to the back door and away. As they left by the main entrance, Tidd and Davidson were obliged to squeeze through a great quantity of women.

"That explains why His Reverence rushed out 't back!" surmised Tidd, with a twinkle.

"He's a busy man" said Davidson, "and there are only so many opinions one person, even as noble as Parson Harrison, can digest in a single afternoon!"

"Who are they?" asked Tidd.

"A union for radical women," said Davidson.

"Surely not!" said Tidd. "How can so many husbands and fathers tolerate distraction from 't domestic sphere?"

"Women's groups are becoming common in northern towns," replied Davidson.

"I'll be damned if my wife possessed any ideals beyond John Bunyan and certain expectations for 't family!" said Tidd.

"The best of women are spirited, like my Sarah," replied Davidson. "She never had much schooling in Devon, but her attitudes are flexible, and she'll enter a discussion on any subject you care to mention. If she weren't so busy with our boys, I swear Sara'd start a group in London."

"Mrs Tidd is a holder of opinions," said Tidd. "I seldom oppose her, but at 't end of a hard day's work, I'd find a clever woman tiresome."

"You mean you're frightened they'd get the better of you!" said Davidson.

"Not at all!" replied Tidd. he turned as if to re-enter the Windmill Rooms. "Come, let's hear what 't women reformers have to say."

"No men are admitted," said Davidson with a chuckle, "and you've caused enough sensation for one day with your premature opinions. Give it a try, Tiddy, if you must, but you'll be ducked in the Mersey till you find your senses!"

"Where are your ten commandments now, Will Davidson?"

"You name the commandment that forbids the dousing of a fool!"

The two men laughed and were friends again.

Later that evening, William Beard's weariness after a long day at the loom was forgotten, when he saw his dear friend, Will at the door with his rucksack and a bucket of tater broth for the family. When Davidson explained the personal predicament emerging from the delay, Beard said that the radical cause depended on fellows with brains greater than a poor weaver's. Will's understanding of the law, experience of the world and of both the upper and the lower classes, made him an ideal candidate for Parliament, and he should not consider, for a single moment, missing such an historic occasion. Davidson was grateful for his friend's faith, but he knew that because of the delay, on Monday, for Sarah's sake, and their sons', instead of marching into history, he must begin the long, honourable walk back to Staffordshire.

EDWARDS

Fleet Street, London

On that same Saturday afternoon, Cornelius Thwaite stood on the corner of Fetter Lane, in his best hat and coat, watching out for a short, pock-marked fellow pulling a butcher's cart and answering to the name Thomas Brunt. In the sculptor's coat pocket were the keys of George Edwards's former dwelling in Johnson's Court. Thwaite had acquired them by bribing a former associate, a clerk at the Admiralty, who had lost his job as part of the navy's cost-cutting exercise. The intention was to retrieve Edwards's personal effects, including art materials and the parts of a small printing press, from the apartment which the faithless Tilly now shared with a Sea Lord, and to transport them to a property Edwards had inherited from a Bavarian cousin from his father's side. Mrs G must be told nothing, Edwards had insisted, about either the inheritance or the new premises. Thwaite longed to see how his darling protégé lived these days, and he had been promised a treat, should the removal run smoothly.

Brunt's progress with the cart was slow because of his swollen ankle, but soon he sat with Cornelius Thwaite at the Mitre Inn, where Edwards stood them a dinner of liver and bacon. When Brunt explained that he was not fit for the stairs, Edwards employed an old soldier, who generally played his whistle in Mitre Court and had been reliable in the past. Brunt must guard the cart during the removal, while Thwaite distracted Tilly for a couple of hours.

When Cornelius Thwaite knocked grandly at her door, Tilly was engaged in beauty treatment and feeling fragile on account of her condition. With a little persuasion, she welcomed Sir Josiah Bacon and was amused by his plan to accompany her to St Paul's garden, where she might pleasure him behind the walnut tree.

"I know some gentlemen is only satisfied by risky tricks, Josiah," she said. "I'm afraid I've stopped all that since being a married lady, what don't need no extra clink."

"That's a proper shame," said Thwaite, hoping he could keep the grand voice going all afternoon. "However, with the

Admiral aboard a ship to India, I'm finding life a little dull. I've no objection to a respectable walk out, Josiah, especially if there's a new'at in it."

As they descended the staircase, Cornelius Thwaite found strange delight in the proximity to a woman once loved by his precious boy. Tilly was easy company, but there was a challenge ahead. Georgie had provided cash for a few shots of gin or tea with cake, but not enough to buy a hat as well.

The removal party busied itself dismantling the printing press. The components were heavy, but after four trips up and down the stairs, Edwards's possessions filled the cart, including the baubles he had given to Tilly. Edwards did not especially want them, but he enjoyed envisaging the tantrum when she found them gone.

When everything was unloaded at New Fish Street, the press was installed, and the soldier had left with his fee and a pretty silk scarf to sell, Edwards invited Brunt to rest his leg and take some ale.

"What do you think of my new house?" he asked

"It's seen better days," said Brunt, "and it's fancy enough, but since you ask, on the large side, for a single fellow."

"I may work here sometimes," said Edwards, "but I shall be living elsewhere."

"I see," replied Brunt, although he did not.

Edwards looked at him steadily, took Brunt's mug and turned to fill it again.

"I need someone on the premises"

"Understandable."

"You don't have a home to go to, do you, Brunt?"

Brunt was astounded. The best he had hoped for was the bed vacated by Julian Thistlewood.

"What about it?" asked Edwards.

"I have a family and an apprentice to think about," said Brunt.

"There's room for all of you" said Edwards, "I shall provide furniture, and there'll be no rent to pay."

"Where's the catch?" asked Brunt, cautious, as usual, with Edwards's propositions.

"There is none!" said Edwards. "It's all for the cause. If, as I believe, Arthur wants us to follow our own path, the contents of those teeny-tiny barrels at the Black Lion won't help us hardly at all. On the other hand, beneath our feet is a spacious basement."

Brunt fell quiet, as the implication took shape.

"Is that why you've taken the house?" he asked.

"I inherited the property from my Bavarian relation" replied Edwards. "If he lived, he would be delighted to lend it to the cause of reform."

Later that evening, Cornelius Thwaite arrived at New Fish Street to view his angel's new premises. His time with Tilly, he revealed, had been enchanting, although, regrettably, entirely respectable. He produced the receipt for her new hat from March's on the Strand, to which, he assumed, the Bavarian baron would have no objection. Having walked the lady home again, and then alone from Fleet Street, to New Fish Street, Thwaite felt deserving of refreshment.

"Where shall we dine?" he asked.

"Wherever you wish" replied Edwards. "But first come with me. There's one more staircase for you to climb, Uncle Con, and you'll have a visual feast, such as you never had in your life."

It was only a few yards from Edwards's new house to the Monument. Three hundred and eleven more steps they climbed that day, all the way up to the public gallery. At the summit, Thwaite's said his knees felt softer than raw eggs, but his weariness was forgotten, when he looked out over the most beautiful city on earth. At last he knew, he said, how it felt to be a bird, soaring above the roof-tops. He gasped at the twists and turns of the amaranthine Thames and sighed at the slow descent of the sun in the vermilion sky above Hyde Park. Thwaite was ecstatic. With tears in his eyes, he thanked George for the best treat of his life, and for being a greater friend than a miserable donkey deserved.

"Shut your eyes," said Edwards, closing an arm around his tormentor's waist, "and dream!"

Blissfully, Cornelius Thwaite submitted. Edwards heaved him up and gave an almighty shove. Before the miserable donkey could make sense of it, he was, indeed, flying. His body flipped over and over and landed on the ornamental base of the Monument, where Uncle Cornelius's skull smashed against the tail of a griffin, and between its cold, hard wings, his satanic heart beat for the last time.

George Edwards hurried down the spiral staircase, and after viewing the evidence and comforting the assembled crowd, he took a cab to Bow Street to report a tragedy at London's best-known suicide destination.

CHAPTER FIFTEEN

Sunday, 8ᵗʰ August, 1819

INGS

Bullocksmithy, Cheshire

If Ings had flown into the sky and landed on one of the twinkly stars above, he would not have expected a world more alien than the north of England. The factories were less densely built than in London, the meadows a bluer kind of green than any in Hampshire, and the livestock half-starved. The greater strangeness was in the people, whose speech patterns, dress and plain manners distinguished them from anyone he had met in the south. Tidd had drawn his attention to the shoes, which were almost exclusively the kind with a wooden sole, fixed with nails, and sometimes fitted with iron in the toe. They were known, he said, all over the north as clogs.

The innkeeper's wife at Bullocksmithy wore clogs. With her round, pale face and flattish nose, she reminded him of his cousin's wife Lizzie, only with wisps of brown hair that strayed out of a woollen bonnet. She spoke in a dialect that was challenging for Ings, especially as she seemed starved of conversation and spoke too much. It appeared there had been a disagreement at the inn.

"Mr Hunt were reet razzored!" she said. "Chastising th' occard young noddy, till I didn't know where to point my eyes!"

"Do you mean Mr Hunt's colleague?" asked Ings, who had the gist of it.

"Not Mr Carlile, no. Th 'other fellow; scarce owd enough to ow' whiskers, let alo' a factory, and - if tha can stummock it - hauf a newspaper. Johnson, he were called; Joseph Johnson."

Ings had come across that name in the coffee shop.

"Joseph Johnson as writes for *The Black Dwarf?*" he asked.

"Tha'rt talking wi' th' innkeeper's wife, not th' bloody schoo-teacher! He were a local mon, local to Salford any road, wi' a too high opinion of his-sell. More I cannot tell thee, except there's egg on his face, th' Orator's terrible twarly and th' meeting's been backened."

"Backened?" asked Ings.

"Put off, Mr Ings; delayed! That's what th' gentlemen were accussing. I shall lay thee a place at table, and tha shalt find out tha-sell."

Ings considered the price of dinner, and - if only to meet Mr Carlile and ask whether to travel north or south after break-fast tomorrow – he decided to pay up.

"Fitchet pie," said the wife, by way of a receipt.

Ings spent a pleasant afternoon with the local butcher, who told him trade was middling, with local inns serving the traffic into Liverpool and Manchester. Ings reckoned that business was better than middling, because at three o'clock, the butcher closed up shop and took him on a tour of the factory next door. The workers were curious to meet a visitor from Hampshire and marked the occasion by presenting Ings with his first top-hat. The item had been made to measure, they said, for some Lud-ship who'd failed to pay up, and he had the same head size. Never a man to accept gifts from strangers, Ings dug out the taters in the manager's garden as fair exchange.

When he returned to the inn, the same keeper's wife helped with materials to polish his boots, but said she was too busy cooking for chat. He washed his face, combed his hair and whiskers, and then, clutching his hat as nervously as the new boy at school, Ings entered the dining room.

Mr Carlile and Mr Hunt seemed uncommonly pleased to see him, congratulated him on the new hat and introduced him to Mr Johnson, who was so flattered that Mr Ings knew his writing that he invited him to stay at his comfortable cottage in Cheetham, alongside Mr Hunt and Mr Carlile, who had already accepted.

"There, Mr Ings!" said the Orator. "We shall be together for a whole week! What do you say?"

Ings had never met the Orator face to face and was perplexed that such a celebrity should know him.

"Mr Hunt, I'm lost for words," he said, "at the warm welcome into the company of gentlemen. May I ask, sir, why the rally is delayed?"

"Let Mr Johnson tell you!" said Hunt, his smile transforming into a snarl. "He invited me here, and now his carelessness has cost a week of my time!"

"The new date is agreed," said Johnson, his face quite scarlet, "and if may I say, Mr Hunt, The Patriotic Union Society, of which I am chairman, was unanimous in selecting the speakers and composing the advertisement, which they regret no less than I."

Johnson was spared further humiliation by the arrival of soup. It was cabbage, and once Hunt had finished Grace, it was enjoyed without conversation. When the china was gathered up, Joseph Johnson cleared his throat.

"Mr Hunt," he began. "There's no need to waste your time. I shall arrange a series of visits."

"I have seen your factory on Shude Hill, Mr Johnson, thank you," came the sharp reply, "most efficient."

"Forgive me sir, and thank you for the compliment," said Johnson, in none of his dealings acquainted with irony. "No,

I imagined you making addresses in halls and taverns all over Lancashire, which I am happy to facilitate. Would that suit?"

"No, Mr Johnson!" cried Hunt. "Emphatically it would not! I am not the servant of your ambitions, sir, and neither will I walk into a charge of conspiracy. The Magistrates are as jumpy as fleas. Nothing would please them more than an excuse to ban the rally altogether."

"Then I hope, Mr Hunt" said Johnson, with a note of quiet defiance, "that you may profit in other ways from a week in Salford."

"Perhaps I shall," said Hunt, "if you will stop chewing at my ankles like an untrained puppy! Concentrate on the pursuit of truth, Mr Johnson! Can you imagine Richard Carlile printing anything without first checking his facts?"

Carlile salvaged the peace by asking Ings to describe his afternoon and explain his new hat. Overcoming some initial anxiety, Ings concluded that the occasion was no different from a family gathering in Portsea, when everyone put their problems aside, and by the time the fitchet pie arrived, the company was laughing as merrily as at a wedding. Ings took a note of the contents of the pie - bacon, onions and apples, and speculated how tickled Celia might be, if he could write out the method and send it to Portsea.

When the brandy was carried in and Carlile wished everyone a goodnight, and Ings followed him into the hall and asked if he'd kindly explain the postponement.

"Johnson placed an advertisement in *The Observer,* of which he is a director," said Carlile. "Unfortunately, it connected the rally to the people's demand for representation in Parliament. Because the wording defied a Royal Proclamation, Hunt was forced to apologise to the Magistrates, and there's nothing the Orator hates more than being made to look a fool."

"I see," said Ings, adding, as Carlile turned toward the stairs, "My own predicament, sir, is less momentous, but painful, all the same."

"Namely?" asked Carlile, turning to look at him.

"I must decline Mr Johnson's invitation," replied Ings, "on account of my employment at the coffee shop."

"Don't worry. I'll write to Edwards," said Carlile. "I need you here."

"You do?"

"You keep me sane, Ings!" said Carlile, climbing up to his room, where he would work half the night.

The inn stood on a corner plot and boasted an enormous garden, which, for the most was not overlooked. Ings plucked a few pea pods from the vegetable patch and put them in his sack for tomorrow. Then, seeking out a mossy place between night-scented stocks and the Sweet William (a sore reminder of his son), he settled on his back. With his sack and his new top hat at his side and his belly fuller than he could remember, Ings looked at the speckled sky and the bright moon that had begun to wane. Contemplating the history that might be made this week, he thought how proud of him Cousin Jack would be. Then, Ings wondered where Tidd and Davidson were sleeping tonight, whether they knew about the delay and would stay up north, and, either way, whether he would ever see Will Davidson again.

Wednesday, 11th August, 1819

ELIZA TIDD / HARRY BRUNT
Hole-in-the-Wall Passage, Holborn

On Wednesday morning, the bustle of Brooke's Market was suspended by a jaunty hand-bell. Quick as a flash, the trader whose front window flaunted the purses and pocket watches trafficked in his back room, closed his shutters. The spinster sisters, squabbling with the fishmonger over yesterday's sprats, turned in surprise. Even the wire-faced ironmonger, whose sons never returned from France, and whose wife died of grief, stopped brushing his dog and stood up smart, while the children dropped their skipping ropes and skittles to run and investigate.

The visitor wore a red military coat and smart beaver hat. He carried the bell in one hand and the handle of a thin box in the other. He ordered the children to stop shouting so he could hear himself speak. When order was restored, he said he had nothing to give them, and he would talk to nobody but Mrs Richard Tidd of Hole in the Wall Passage. Red-haired Marjorie, the canniest of the twins, said she knew the lady in question and was it was worth three farthings to fetch her? Glaring at the skinny little imp, the stranger growled that he was a servant of His Majesty's Post Office and obliged to punish anyone who impeded his duty. Marjorie fled.

"Ma! The letter carrier is here, and he'll only talk to you!" she called from half way up the stairs. Eliza Tidd, scraping taters in the kitchen, was astounded. She had never received a letter in her life.

"Get away with your nonsense!" she said.

"Suit yourself, ma" said the cheeky lass, grimacing and dodging the wallop as she hurried back to her friends.

Hearing the commotion outside, Mrs Tidd wiped her hands on her apron and looked over the railings. There, in the passage, was indeed the letter-carrier. He was looking up at her, surrounded by neighbours with their sympathetic faces on.

"Come down quick, Eliza!" called Mrs Pratt, the widow from Baldwyn Gardens. "Something must have happened to Richard!" said Mrs Dunlop, the hunch-backed gossip from Leather Lane.

Maybe it has, and maybe it hasn't," replied Mrs Tidd, who refused to share her news unfiltered, and summoned the letter-carrier upstairs. She shooed away the children and Mrs Dunlop, too, despite the dame's insistence that Eliza needed a friend in moments like this.

When they were in her kitchen, and Eliza reached for her letter, His Majesty's servant refused to submit without a florin.

"This item has travelled near two hundred miles, Mrs Tidd, and the passage must be paid for."

"Where am I to find a florin?" demanded Mrs Tidd, "when all I have of value is a half sack of oats and cooking pot?

"The Post Office cannot accept your property," said the letter carrier, "and I shall not part with this letter without a florin or coins to that effect."

Eliza considered the consequences of sending the fellow away. What if Richard was taken ill or worse? Or perhaps he had sent money, and the lost florin, if she had one, would be of no consequence. Either way, ignorance would leave her no peace. The fellow was growing impatient.

"I have work to do, Mrs Tidd," he said. "What's it to be?"

"We keep a shilling for the doctor," said Eliza, "and not a penny more, I swear to God."

"It's irregular," said the letter carrier, "but His Majesty's Post Office is not without compassion."

As soon as he was gone, with her heart beating faster than she could whisk an egg, Eliza took her knife and opened the envelope. Hope capsized at the sight, not of a bank note, but of a sheet of paper covered in words she had no hope of reading. Perhaps they contained a promise that could be exchanged by a bank or a customer. The signature at the bottom of the page was exactly the same as on her marriage licence. If Richard could write his name that fluently, she was not widowed yet.

Still, without knowing the contents of the message, Eliza was unsure who could be trusted to read it. Unless she trusted somebody, she would never what the words were telling her. As a professional clerk, her new son-in-law would be accustomed to keeping secrets, even from his wife, but no date had been given for the newly-weds' return from Folkestone.

She might be forced to ask Mr Brunt, who, after all, was her husband's closest friend and business partner. Unfortunately, Mr Brunt had not been seen since their quarrel, and Eliza had no idea where to find him. She turned her letter this way and that, trying to make out any words beyond her own name and Richard's. Perhaps her husband had been given work by associates in Grantham or Nottingham? They would move away, find a new home with land enough to grow vegetables, keep a couple of pigs and some poultry. The children would eat well, go to a proper school and breathe fresh country air.

For a time, it pleased Mrs Tidd to indulge in such dreams, and as long as her letter remained a mystery, anything was possible. Then, as it often does, reality intervened in an unexpected way. Carrying the canary in its cage, his drum over one shoulder and his sack over the other, clever Harry Brunt was just then making his way up Grays Inn Lane.

His ma had fallen ill again, just as she had when pa and his older brother were in France. Molly's cousin, the tanner had been sympathetic, but after two days, Mrs Welch was at her wits' end and put Molly on the coach to her family at Derby. The lad, Mrs Welch had said, could stay, as long as he worked for his supper. She had no objection to Mrs Brunt's canary neither, which had no appetite to speak of and would not scream the place down all hours of the day and night like poor Molly. Harry, who had a mind of his own and was ill-disposed to tanning work, preferred to return to his father.

When he found the premises at Fox Court locked up, and their land-lady in a stupor, Harry Brunt made his way to Hole in the Wall Passage. He took the longer route to avoid Brooke's Market, where the drum and the canary would provoke unnecessary questions. Mrs Tidd answered her door, and, instead of the onslaught Harry expected, she smiled and invited him into her kitchen where there was sure to be a biscuit somewhere, she said, as well as crumbs for the bird.

Without the details, Harry explained that his ma was visiting her sister in Derby and had instructed him to join his pa. Mrs Tidd looked sympathetic and explained that unfortunately, Mr Brunt had gone missing, and had left no key.

"Don't you worry, my lad," she said, with an alarming smile. "He'll be back and until he is, you can stay here, with me."

"How kind, Mrs Tidd," said Harry, exactly as if he meant it.

"I could do with a helping hand," she said, "and the twins will be happy to see you."

When Harry had finished two biscuits and the scrapings of the porridge, Mrs Tidd wiped the table and told him to clean his hands. Then she climbed on a chair and reached for the gilt-encrusted Bible that stayed on top of the cupboard. Harry Brunt must place his hands on it, she said and swear an oath of secrecy.

"My dearest Eliza," read Harry from the letter. "I have arrived at a town that is the nearest I have been to paradise. The people are friendly and kind to each other in ways they rarely are in London. Every other building is a place of work. The footwear is disappointing, and I suppose there to be a shortage of good bootmakers. For that reason, I shall stay a week or two longer to discover what opportunities our family may pursue. I trust that Mary will read this news to you, and implore you both, on no account to reveal it to Mr Brunt, who, in these harsh times, must make the best of his own future".

Harry looked at Mrs Tidd's embarrassment.

"Don't you worry," he said. "Pa is by nature strong and in-dependent."

"You won't tell him?"

"Have I not sworn an oath, Mrs Tidd?"

Behind the solemn expression, Harry's young heart was singing that he would forever be free of the pesky twins.

"Is that the end of the letter?" asked Mrs Tidd.

"Not quite," said Harry, and continued; "I shall return to our too humble abode as soon as I can. Until then, beloved wife, fare well. Kiss the children for me. Your affectionate husband, Richard Tidd."

Precisely as Tidd had calculated, his wife was pacified, and there would be no sour face when he returned to Holborn. In the meantime, the short letter had brought light into the bleakness of Eliza's world, and, since His Majesty's letter-carrier was rarely seen in these parts, a degree of celebrity too.

Mrs Tidd decided to visit the market at once and impart some of the content of her letter. She told Harry she would be back in ten minutes, in which time, he could make a start on the hearth which hadn't been swept for days and carry the ash bucket down the steps to save her poorly back. There was an awful lot of ash, and when Harry had carried the first buck-et-load down, the yard was empty. The twins and all the neigh-bours must have followed Eliza, like the Pied Piper, to hear her news. If he left now, Harry thought, there would be nobody to ask questions or report his escape. He ran up to the kitchen, picked up his sack and the cage and hurried away.

Harry's first destination was Mr Carlile's premises on Fleet Street. The coffee shop was closed, and with Mr Carlile away on business, his duties were conducted by Mrs Carlile and her sister-in-law. As well as noisy machines, the women were surrounded by towers of paper and three infants. When the polite young man arrived to enquire after the whereabouts of his father, the poet and bootmaker Tom Brunt, the ladies admired his canary and directed him to the Black Lion, where Mr Brunt was most likely in a meeting.

That evening, Harry was treated to supper with his pa, Thistlewood and Edwards. Everyone chose whiting and chips, except Edwards, who could never stomach fish and demanded mutton instead. The meals were a parting gift from Mr Cooper, who regretted that no further meetings would be held either at the Black Lion or at his hotel on Bouverie Street. A new Home Department initiative promised to withdraw the licence of any tavern-keeper, who allowed known activists to assemble on his premises.

Thursday 12ᵗʰ August, 1819

EDWARDS

The Black Dog, St Clements Lane, Strand

Before visiting Thistlewood on Thursday, George Edwards returned the keys of Tilly's apartment to the redundant clerk, who doubted that the Admiral had noticed they were missing. Edwards stood the fellow a plate of bread and cheese and described the tragic death of their mutual friend, Mr Thwaite. The clerk, who knew George Edwards as Mr Wards, was sympathetic.

"To have known and lost artistic glory," he surmised, "to have descended from the pinnacle of society into its gutter, is enough to drive any man to fanatical acts!"

"Our friend's fate was no less calamitous than losing a good position at Whitehall." replied Edwards.

"You'll never find me succumbing to despair, Mr Wards," said the clerk. "Writing is my trade, but my nature, sir, is not poetic. Having a wife, two mothers and seven children, I'm forced to be a pragmatist."

Fifteen minutes later, the clerk had promised, for a guinea, to produce another, more permanent set of keys. He would acquire, on Mr Wards' behalf, a lease on a small house in Ranelagh Place, the property of another Sea Lord, believed to have drowned without heirs. Edwards was delighted. Verdant Pimlico would become his refuge, where he would prepare for the life of luxury that, one day soon, would be his. It was small compensation for the corruption of his soul by Cornelius Thwaite.

Far from ceasing, Edwards's nightmares had multiplied since the death of his tormentor. Perceiving there would be no return to purity and peace of mind, he had resolved instead to enjoy life more and grasp every advantage his situation offered. He arranged, a week from now, to stand the clerk dinner at the Bag o' Nails on King's Row and then took a cab to Stanhope Street, where Arthur Thistlewood was in need of encouragement.

The Water Lane Group was still the most active in London, and a small executive, representing the committee, met daily at the coffee shop, where Edwards had installed his brother during Ings's absence. The delay in Manchester had provided time to galvanize four simultaneous parades in the capital on the day before Hunt's rally. The London marches would express a degree of alignment with Henry Hunt, while leaving no doubt that the mood in London was incendiary.

Thistlewood had developed an interest in the changes, recently imposed by local Aldermen on the working conditions of weavers in Spitalfields. The profession was already on the brink of collapse in London, and since the new regulations were published in language likely to confuse the few remaining practitioners, Thistlewood intended to use the Spitalfields meeting to explain the changes and assess their potential impact. He also planned to commemorate the weavers' riots of fifty years ago, the men who died and those wrongfully hanged. As always, Edwards encouraged Thistlewood in his ambitions, advising on strategy and erasing any doubt about his interpretation of the facts. It was as easy as spreading warm butter.

INGS

Cheetham, Lancashire

At Smedley Cottage, Ings shared an attic bedroom with Mr Hunt's elderly manservant. Lean and neat as a dragon-fly, but, alas, no longer as speedy, Mr Godfrey suffered with his knees, and Ings took pains always to climb the steep, narrow stairs ahead of him. Joseph Johnson was out on business most of the time, to the evident relief of Orator Hunt, whose fame obliged him to stay indoors. Richard Carlile's writing and opinions were well known in the north, but his face was unfamiliar, and he could come and go as he pleased. He always seemed busy and retired every afternoon to compose, Ings supposed, another torrent of words.

The Orator was restless and, when he wasn't receiving dignitaries, issued instructions here, there and everywhere. He treated Ings as Mr Godfrey's deputy, and allotted to him any tasks requiring foot-work. Ings was grateful to escape the tension and soon accustomed himself to the local hills, and sometimes to Mrs Johnson's cart and a cantankerous donkey, known as Mr Pitt.

At dinner on Wednesday night (Mrs Johnson's own hot-pot, with Westmoreland lamb), Richard Carlile had reported, up on the moors, military-style drilling under the instruction of Waterloo veterans. Hunt flew into a temper.

"The monumental fools!" he raged. "We shall see how fast the magistrates cancel my rally!"

"It's a most uncommon occasion," replied Joe Johnson with confidence. "My sources assure me that all such activity stopped weeks ago."

"Your sources have eyes on every moor in Lancashire, do they?" roared Hunt.

Johnson's smile vanished.

"You are naïve, sir!" continued Hunt. "Make them stop, or I shall return to London tomorrow."

There was further cause for alarm when, on Thursday afternoon, Ings was dispatched, with the donkey cart, to Manchester to replenish the stationery supply. Turning off Deansgate, he drove into a gang of uniformed men, who were ripping out the railings from a terrace of houses. A cluster of residents stood resentfully by. After taking measure of the situation, Ings asked in a respectful tone, on whose authority the officers were damaging property.

"That's not for me to say nor tha' to ask," replied an officer.

"Shift tha-sell!" bellowed another, directing a length of iron at Ings's head. "Afore I knock thee all 't way to Blackburn!"

As Ings drove on, he observed, pasted to various walls and windows, notices instructing peace-loving residents to ban their servants and families from attending Monday's Meeting. He tore down a dozen or so and returned to the cottage as hurriedly as he could get Mr Pitt to climb that hill. With a degree of trepidation, he showed an intact sample to the Orator. The response was astonishing.

"Your diligence his week has been noticed, Mr Ings," said Hunt. "And you have witnessed the people's mood at first hand. If I were to ask for your advice, regarding a message of encouragement, what would it be?"

Ings had come to the conclusion that the Orator underestimated the fear of the authorities, but it would take a bolder man to say so.

"In what respect, sir?" he asked.

"Style. You're a man of the people, Ings. How you would phrase a message, urging the local population to abandon their worries and come out to hear the speeches?"

"It is my observation," replied Ings, "that plain folk respect plain language. No frills, no Latin and no odour of wealth. Is that what you mean, sir?"

Hunt nodded, gave thanks and went to his room. Ings's wisdom cost him a good deal more walking. That evening, the Orator put the entire household to work copying it out. It was a message again, of peace, and Ings wrote out the words at least forty times himself, and on Friday, during the delivery, which, to spare Mr Godfrey's knees, he undertook alone, recited them to so many parties who could not read, that they stayed fresh in his mind to the end of his days.

The inflammatory posters were not the last of Hunt's impediments. On Saturday morning, he planned a journey with his retinue to agree the route to St Peter's Field, and the precise position of the hustings. A member of the escort said there were rumours of a warrant for the Orator's arrest. How Ings admired Henry Hunt when the party arrived at The New Bayley in Salford. Proud as Punch, he dismounted, walked into the prison and offered himself for arrest, as soon as the officers produced their warrant. Forty minutes later, he emerged triumphant, shouting "God Save the King!" His entire retinue and the gathering crowd cheered, three times the three (even Mr Carlile, who generally had no truck with His Majesty) and continued the navigation of Manchester, their hearts filled again with optimism.

Sunday, 15*th* August, 1819

Chadderton, Lancashire

On Sunday, while Hunt and Carlile were busy revising their speeches, Ings accepted an opportunity, declined by Mr Godfrey, to attend a rehearsal for the procession from White Moss Field near Chadderton, north of Cheetham. He hesitated on learning that his transport must be that wretched donkey and trap, but he was curious, and after all the hard work, welcomed an outing with no responsibilities attached.

A servant arrived at nine o'clock to escort Ings to a ginger-bread shop, of which the proprietor would be Ings's companion for the day. Mr Murray's bag of stale biscuits delighted Mr Pitt, who pulled them gaily all the way up the hill to Chadderton. Naturally, Mr Murray was curious about the visiting celebrities, and Ings parted with a few practised titbits, but gave no undue information and focused instead on his business at Portsea. Ings found the gingerbread maker too earnest for a friend, but as fellow shop-keepers, they found similar pleasures and complaints in their work.

When the cart arrived at White Moss, Murray suggested parking in a corner of the field, from which they might join the line when it passed by. It was a ragged formation of about sixty persons, including a good number of girls and women. The untrained youngsters found it difficult to walk to the rhythm of the band, a failing which annoyed the veterans. The louder and more frequently the commander shouted, the more the females giggled and provoked the lads to act the fool. When the joyful chaos infected the drummers, the beat collapsed, the pipes stopped too and the procession came to a messy halt.

How different Ings's history might have been, had Mr Pitt not chosen that moment to begin braying, thus drawing some sixty pairs of eyes to their corner. While most seemed unconcerned by the presence of strangers, three burly men approached in postures that Ings did not consider welcoming. When he turned to ask if Mr Murray knew them, the baker was already in the cart, preparing to flee. Mr Pitt refused to move, and one of the men grabbed the driving stick and threatened to beat Murray to a pulp, unless he accounted for his actions.

"Citizens! My friends!" cried Ings. "The Orator has urged us to refrain from violence."

The words, or Ings's southern way of saying them, only enraged the ruffian, who jumped down and set about the Hampshire butcher. A hand, greater than Uncle Percy's, covered his face, a clog hit the back of his knees, and Ings fell to the ground, where his left kidney was pummelled by more wooden shoes. Between blows, Ings shouted that he was a friend of Mr Hunt; and a private guest of Joseph Johnson. His voice must have been drowned by the noisy donkey and the shouts of the crowd, because the man only kicked harder and then started on the other side. Ings felt a crack in his ribs and begged his attacker to stop and hear him out.

Dazed though he was, Ings heard women shrieking; no special constable was worth the price, they cried, and how would their children survive, with their fathers transported or hanged by the neck? When Ings tried to protest that he was not, nor never had been, a constable, special or otherwise, his assailant only kicked him again with his clogs, and for a time, Ings knew nothing at all.

If he still believed in such creatures, Ings would call Margaret his Guardian Angel. She was about thirty years old, with curly brown hair and the softest hands that ever touched his skin. Except for his ma, or his wife in younger days, no woman had ever evoked such tender feelings. Much later, in his prison cell, Ings would recall the gentle splashes, as his angel washed the dirt from his cuts and bruises. A miner's widow, Margaret said she worked at Johnson's brush factory in Shude Hill. She knew the trap and Mr Pitt, she said, and her boss must have been tricked into lending them to the gingerbread maker, who was not the man he seemed. Murray had once been discovered breaking into Henry Hunt's hotel room and searching his papers. He had been hated ever since, as a spy of the magistrates.

Margaret put a cup of fruit brandy to his lips and begged Mr Ings to forgive her brothers, who had mistaken him for Murray's accomplice.

Ings could feel her soft breath on his cheek. Her eyes were more golden than twice-turned honey, and when he dared to look into them, deeper and more mysterious than pools. He tried to remember how long it was since another body held his as close as this. With all his might, Ings wished for the strength and boldness to kiss Margaret. He even thought he would abandon the cause, if only Margaret would lie by his side a while.

That he remained true to Celia may be connected to his temporary delirium, or possibly to the widow's modesty, but Ings always preferred to believe that he battled temptation in that cottage near Chadderton and emerged triumphant.

Ings neither knew nor cared what became of the gingerbread baker that day, but when night began to fall, Margaret's three brothers carried him to the donkey cart as tenderly as if he were their dying child. They drove him down to Cheetham, where, on hearing the story, Mr Hunt and Mr Carlile welcomed all four men as heroes, and Mr Johnson promised to advance Margaret's prospects, when the factory reopened on Tuesday.

The brothers stayed for supper (Lancashire cheeses, parkin and fruits), and when they had left, Carlile retreated, as usual, to his desk, Johnson went to his pregnant wife, and Godfrey to his Bible. Hunt asked Ings to stay a while, and described his regret that Mr Johnson had not forewarned them about the gingerbread man. Then, in a blow, more bitter than any delivered by the Chadderton lads, Henry Hunt announced, with regret, that Mr Ings was unfit to attend the rally. Ings begged to disagree; as – in all likelihood – the sole representative of the county of Hampshire, his attendance was essential. Why, he would even travel on the back of that blessed donkey, with a sack of Mr Carlile's pamphlets to distribute. The Orator was not for turning. The presence of an injured man was too great a risk, he said, and Ings must remain at Smedley Cottage. When Mr Hunt proposed, in compensation, to rehearse the speech for his ears alone, Ings was more than happy to oblige.

Neither man suspected that it would be the only time that eloquent speech would be heard. Instead, they awaited the making of history. In that aspiration, at least, they would not be disappointed.

THE PRINCE REGENT

HMY The Royal George, The Solent.

There were few occasions at which he craved the company of his brother, Billy, but on Sunday, moored off the coast of Hampshire, His Royal Highness would have parted with a minor colony to have the Duke of Clarence at the dinner table. The cruise around the Isle of Wight had, so far, been a happy affair. Isabella, Lady Hertford, was, for the most part, in good humour, the company was cheerful and the music charming. Sumptuous dinners were served on the Regent's nautical china, while his secretary and Charlie Anderson-Pelham (his host at Cowes) had spared him from troublesome dispatches about the manufacturing towns up north.

Festivities were temporarily suspended on the arrival, direct from Sierra Leone, of Commodore Sir George Collier, whose credentials included a distinguished record in the Bay of Biscay and an extensive knowledge of astronomy. The Prince Regent anticipated sparkling tales of nautical daring and new insights into the skies above, but Sir George, who had recently been commissioned to uphold the abolition of slavery, would talk of nothing but the betterment of Africans since their protection by the British government.

The only and most excellent advantage of the Commodore's visit was in the hold, paddling in an enormous tub of sea water. Sir George had transported, all the way from Sherbro Island, a green sea turtle of exceptional size, with a weight of nearly seven hundred pounds. There had been trinkets of gold and ivory, of course, crocodile skins and a set of elephant's teeth, but nothing set His Royal Highness's heart racing faster than the anticipation of a dozen Chinese tureens, each brimming with turtle soup, laced with asparagus, lemons and cayenne pepper. Seventy guests were expected from houses in Hampshire and Wiltshire on Monday. Until then, the turtle would remain in its tub, with a footman to guard it and supply, as necessary, fresh sea water and a proper diet of jellyfish.

Had the Regent permitted himself an opinion about slavery, it might have favoured continuation of the trade;

his ministers moaned perpetually about economic depression, and yet had outlawed a perfectly efficient and profitable business. Worse, the Spaniards and Portuguese had begun to profit to the detriment of Great Britain. As a sailor with vast experience of the Caribbean and an ebullient opponent of abolition, the Regent's brother would have occupied the Commodore with argument, leaving Prinny and his friends to their merriment.

Lady Hertford was absent tonight, having taken offence at his harmless remarks to the female harpist. The Rt. Hon. Charles Anderson-Pelham, who served, with no discernible enthusiasm, as Whig Member of Parliament for Lincolnshire, had been known to favour abolition, but since the Prince Regent had, for the first time, been his guest on the Isle of Wight, he preferred to avoid the subject of slavery. In a moment of impulsive inspiration, the Regent had invited the vicar from the Royal Garrison Church in Portsmouth, who had conducted Holy Communion that morning, to dine aboard the royal yacht. Overwhelmed by the occasion and nervous, on his wife's behalf, of being sent to Africa, the Reverend said hardly a word to the Commodore or anyone else, only nodding frequently until he tasted snails in brandy and had to be escorted early to his cabin.

As a result, the Regent was obliged to endure Sir George's tediously expressed gratification at so many young, smiling black faces, doing very well at school and singing praises to the Lord every Sunday, as well as his extensive ambition to send missionaries to remoter regions to learn local languages and translate the scriptures for the benefit of all.

Eventually, Prinny proposed a competition, which the present company would be divided into groups. Each was allotted two musicians and the task of composing a Glee on the subject of the Constitution. To the uninformed courtiers and musicians, the idea promised entertainment, to the ship's crew and Sir George himself, an act of petty spite. Towards the end of the American conflict, the Commodore's floundering attempts to capture the enemy vessel, Constitution had been thwarted by the signing of the treaty that ended the war. After a career of high distinction, Collier was branded a coward by men who had never seen the Atlantic. The matter would eventually contribute to his suicide, but today, the Commodore applied his British fortitude and his stiff upper lip and refused to gratify the damned-fool Regent by displaying his discomfort.

An hour and a half later, hoarse from singing and from laughter, the Regent's thoughts were directed again to his mistress and his belly.

"God Bless you all," he said, and, issuing his usual little wave, the Regent drifted away to his quarters, with Charlie Anderson-Pelham attached to his arm and a mind stuffed with Isabella's plump limbs and the prospect of turtle soup tomorrow.

CHAPTER SIXTEEN

Sunday, 15ᵗʰ August, 1819

BRUNT / THISTLEWOOD / EDWARDS
New Fish Street, City of London

"That drum," declared Brunt, as Harry adjusted the sling buckle, "is an historical instrument."

"It will be historic," replied Harry, "by the end of today."

He pulled out his sticks and demonstrated his five-stroke roll.

"That's practice for you!" said Brunt, heaving his sack on to his back.

It was Sunday morning, and they were in the hallway of their new home. Edwards's property was spacious, but dark inside, and as they stepped out to the street, the sun, in a flash of heat and light, lifted the hope in their hearts. As they set off towards Spitalfields, Brunt distracted his son with history.

"There's more to that drum than you can guess at," he began.

"Yes," said clever Harry. "It came from the Military Academy."

"That's just the sticks," said Brunt. "See, ma never wanted you to hear the truth."

"Was it grandpa's?" asked Harry, excited at the possibility. "Did it go with Grandpa Moreton to India?

"No, but it's a tragedy all the same, and if you're man enough to join us today, you're man enough to hear it."

Brunt told Harry the story of a boy soldier, who drummed right up until two days before Waterloo, when his skinny little frame was sliced in half at Quatre Bras. The sticks stayed with the corpse, but the drum fell into the possession of Brunt who was responsible, at the time, for regimental foot-wear, and knew the lad's family well.

"They had Quirke's wash house on Union Street," continued Brunt. "His pa, my old playmate, cried, when I give him the drum. See, Daniel was his only living child, and he'd ran off to enlist, without telling nobody. What a price he paid for that sin, Harry! He sent his shilling to his ma, not knowing she'd thrown herself off the bridge already for missing him so terrible."

"Didn't Mr Quirke want to keep the drum?" asked Harry.

"The sight of it made him miserable," replied Brunt, "but he couldn't bear to throw it out. After a month, he sent it back to me with a messenger, who left it with ma, about the time you was polishing boots at the Academy."

"That's why they gave me free lessons?"

"You worked for them lessons, Harry; every last one; don't you forget it."

They continued northwards to Spitalfields, and as the sun grew hotter and his ankle more troublesome, Brunt was grateful for the loan of the walking stick. Harry fell unusually silent, occupied by the seeds of an idea and the conviction that whatever glory was bestowed on him in the coming hours, it must serve the honour of Drummer Daniel Quirke.

The Dolphin Ale House, Cock Lane, Spitalfields

Apart from a few uniformed officers, wilting on horse-back, Spitalfields seemed eerily quiet, as, a little ahead of the Brunts, Thistlewood and Edwards approached the Dolphin Ale House. Thistlewood's contact, known as V, had promised a resounding welcome, but the streets were as empty as if the plague had fallen. Edwards proposed a cab to Kennington or Deptford, where there might be more action and some reporters. Thistlewood refused. Firstly, he had promised to meet Brunt. Secondly, his speech was written down and regardless of crowd or no crowd, would achieve lasting momentum for the history of the Spitalfields weavers, both today and fifty years ago. In that respect, even if more participants had gathered there – which was by no means certain - neither Deptford nor Kennington could compare.

"Very philosophical," replied Edwards, scarcely curbing his irritation and cursing himself for diverting the press to the other nominated districts, at which, with his enthusiasm for Spitalfields, there would be no time for Thistlewood to speak.

"You disagree?" asked Thistlewood.

"Look around you, Arthur! Spitalfields was a mistake."

"Five harmless weavers were hanged, George, by tyrants, right here, in the heart of their community!"

"This country needs change, Arthur, not a history lesson," said Edwards. "Even Henry Hunt understands that."

"Damn Henry Hunt!" said Thistlewood. "We forget history at our peril, George, and I shall not change my mind. Today, we shall remember the suffering weavers, and illuminate the destruction of their trade."

They arrived at the Dolphin, where a few flags and banners rested at the entrance, but there was no bustle of eager partici-pants. At the top of the crooked, creaking staircase, half a dozen emaciated old fellows waited silently in a corner. When Thistle-wood went to shake their hands, they seemed less impassioned by action or history than by the trouble it took them to get up the stairs and the pint of ale they anticipated for turning out. Only a short, thin man of Gallic appearance seemed enthusiastic. He introduced himself as Gabriel Valline, usually known as V.

"Where's your crowd?" asked Edwards, as he peered through a rear window at the dismal yard, where a family of rats clambered over piles of rubbish and burrowed beneath the back gate.

"They said they'd come," said V, "but it's very hot out, and people are disillusioned. Every decent weaver went north, years ago."

"Where are all your young men?" asked Thistlewood.

"Their spirits are all broken," replied Valline. "They'd rather use their fathers' looms for firewood than serve pointless apprenticeships."

He pressed his bony fingers into Thistlewood's arm. "You won't abandon us, sir?"

Thistlewood sensed his deputy's seething disapproval, but he gave Vallance his promise because there was no alternative.

"Where's the action?" asked Brunt, half way up the stairs.

Thistlewood, was ahead with a jug of ale and Harry at the rear with his drum.

"We're revising the plan," said Thistlewood, darkly.

As the old men sipped their ale and recited their names for Edwards's notebook, Valline welcomed his visitors to the very alcove where the riots began in '69. He was just twelve years old, he said, when his great uncle was hanged; about the age he supposed Master Brunt to be now.

"My son is thirteen," said Brunt. "The men in our family are small, but spirited."

"Musical, too, it seems!" replied V.

"This drum has seen action, citizen," said Harry, reaching for his sticks.

"Patience, my son!" Brunt turned to Thistlewood. "How far is it from here to Deptford?"

"It is not my intention to go either to Deptford or Kennington or Millbank," hissed Thistlewood.

"Please, sir," said Harry brightly, eager to spill his plan. "We don't need to go nowhere!"

When everyone turned to him with expectation in their eyes, Harry's confidence wavered.

"Come on, lad," said Brunt. "If it's worth saying, tell me."

"Pa," said Harry, "If my grandfather had run to another, more exciting battle, would Wandiwash have been won or lost?"

"Lost, my son," replied Brunt proudly, "lost, without a doubt!"

"The tiddler's got spirit!" cried Valline, and his comrades, remembering the Indian conflict, cheered in appreciation.

"I have an idea." said Harry, emboldened.

He had observed, as they approached the ale house, a foundry with a flat roof. He was nimble enough to climb up, he said, and would take his drum and pa's banner, which he could attach to a chimney. The drum would be heard all around, especially by weavers in their attics. The whole neighbourhood would come running to see what the fuss was about, and Mr Thistlewood could deliver his speech.

In the brief silence that followed, Harry thought all was lost, but then Thistlewood smiled broadly and said it was the best idea of the day, and the old men lined up to shake the tiddler's hand. Brunt offered, despite his poorly leg, to keep his son company on the roof, while Edwards, who had no stomach for heights, promised to mind Harry's rucksack, while he joined V in the streets, organizing the crowd.

On the foundry roof, Harry checked his buckle again and positioned his drum, exactly as he was taught. He bent his left knee slightly and placed his left heel steady in the hollow of his right foot. Standing erect, he raised his elbows and began to strike, slowly and evenly, gradually increasing the pace; a five-stroke roll, a nine-stroke roll and a series of paradiddles.

Normally less susceptible than his pa to flights of fancy, Harry Brunt imagined himself ahead of a regiment in some strange and distant land, where the north wind howled across the plains, and he was drumming for the glory of a better England. He beat that drum as if possessed by the air, the spirit and the once supple wrists of the boy-soldier whose instrument he played.

On the roof beside him, Brunt had put aside Farmer John's walking stick to parade the flag he had carried in his rucksack. It was scarlet with a black skull and the brave legend:

LIBERTY OR DEATH.

Two of Valline's grandsons stretched out a battle-scarred banner, that billowed as they turned it this way and that. Fifty years since it was woven, the message was still clear:

WEAVERS ARE NOT SLAVES! SAVE YOUR SILK!

As Harry had predicted, people stared in amazement at the roof, and when the drumming stopped, about two hundred had gathered on the street below. As the people waited for the speeches, they recited their names and addresses for George Edwards's notebook, even those with insufficient eyesight or learning for the circulars he promised to send.

First to speak was Gabriel Valline, who introduced the crowd to the heroic veterans, every one a friend of his late great uncle. With Brunt in their midst and Harry drumming away at the side, the old men held up their flags and banners, their moment of glory reviving for a time their battered spirits. Valline recalled the riots of sixty-nine, and he mourned the decline of the London weaving trade. When he presented Arthur

Thistlewood, a cheer filled the air, as the people's champion climbed on to the table, borrowed from the Dolphin for the hustings.

After a tribute to the martyred weavers, Thistlewood described new changes in the law, which made it impossible for any weaver to survive in London. Let the Aldermen see for themselves, he said, how they had decimated the industry until there was nothing left to destroy. He spoke of the young people who would own London and the world in another fifty years, and who must be encouraged to participate in the struggle for a future that would truly be theirs.

As the Brunts headed back to New Fish Street, Edwards and Thistlewood took a cab to Lincoln's Inn Field. Instead of heaping praise on his friend's energetic speech, Edwards described his misgivings. While the enthusiasm of Gabriel Valline and the Brunts was laudable, passions had been inflamed in Spitalfields that would be forgotten by Tuesday. Nor, beyond an affirmation of their own misery, would the occasion help any weaver still operating in London. While Henry Hunt was certain to bask in glory in Manchester, Thistlewood's speech in Spitalfields would go unreported, and was barely worth the paper to print and distribute it. Regardless of outcomes in other parts of London, today would never be counted among Arthur Thistlewood's finest. Rhetoric would change nothing. The time for action, Edwards concluded with emphasis, was upon them.

They parted at the end of Stanhope Street, from which Edwards would continue, he said, to a meeting about his Bavarian relative's will. Bruised by the criticism and numb with hunger and exhaustion, Thistlewood begged his deputy for protection from future short-comings, stepped on to the street and returned to his lonely apartment.

After a splendid steak and kidney pudding at the Bag o'Nails, Edwards walked through the fading light of Pimlico to his new home. Savouring his gin, he congratulated himself on a not entirely fruitless day; the notebook, once copied out, would secure a neat bonus from Bow Street, and he had guided his choicest victim a little closer to his destiny.

Monday, 16*th* August, 1819

TIDD

Stockport, Cheshire

Shortly after ten o'clock, the big bass drum of the Union Society Band boomed in the market place. One and a half thousand souls stopped their chatter and shuffled into line. Banners were raised, and the marshals hurried back and forth, chiding wherever they found discipline broken. The side drums took up the beat, the pipes and piccolos trilled and the six-mile procession to Manchester was underway. For some it was a jubilee, a rare holiday in the sunshine, while others hoped that the desperate plight of working people would be acknowledged, and history would be made. Walking with Stockport's boot- and shoemakers, Richard Tidd abandoned his customary scepticism. Boulton's wife had stayed at home to pickle onions, but his daughters joined him behind the Guild's own banner and another, especially stitched for today:

NO TAXATION WITHOUT REPRESENTATION

Boulton's older grandchildren, in their Sunday best and garlanded with flowers, skipped with their school-friends behind Parson Harrison and his teaching staff, who marched behind the band. Next, all dressed in white, and watching out for tired or unruly children, came the female reformers beneath their sparkling new banner:

SISTERS OF THE EARTH UNITE!

The women were followed by the weavers and spinners:

AWAY WITH POWER LOOMS!

A company of hatters ignored the band and belted out a lusty repertoire of its own. Each man wore an identical top hat, decorated with sprigs of laurel for peace and each carried a red flag, embroidered in yellow thread:

UNITE AND BE FREE!

As the procession passed Heaton Lane, an elderly spinner was overwhelmed by the occasion and suffered a seizure. His friends fetched Parson Harrison, who regretted that no doctor could help the old man now. After prayers for the life and soul of Gideon Thorpe, the parson stayed with the family, whose peace of mind was more important than glory on the hustings.

As the band started up again and the ramshackle parade moved forward, Tidd leaned towards Boulton.

"I never knew Mr Thorpe, but I shall mourn him," he said, "and I tell you summat else, Boulton; I feel more akin to folk here than I ever did down south, and if every march is half as sensible and good humoured as this, 't Orator can expect a triumph!"

Tidd might have drawn different conclusions, had he been at the Star Inn on Deansgate, where the Manchester Magistrates had gathered, each as jittery as a frog in a hot pan. They had invited sufficient loyalists to sign the necessary documents, should any identifiable regulation be broken. With an armed guard, led by the fearsome Deputy Constable Nadin, they set off for the borrowed house on Mount Street, which, from the first floor, offered a clear view of the hustings. St Peter's Field was empty, but for a few youngsters who stopped playing tag to marvel at the officers and the fur-lined robes and wonder which of the gents might be Orator Hunt.

Meanwhile at the Manchester Exchange, four hundred shopkeepers and property owners were being sworn in as special constables, while at Pickford's Yard, sixty Manchester and Salford Yeomen, volunteers from the nobility and wealthy manufacturing class, sipped brandy as their manservants polished boots and brushed the horses. At the same time, out of sight, on the outskirts of Manchester, to the north, south, east and west, a thousand professional soldiers awaited orders.

The volunteer constables and yeomen heard, as they drank their beer, instructions not to use weapons without provocation, and only to employ the blunt side of their blades. Their contempt for the ungrateful working class had been made chronic by articles in the *Manchester Mercury*. Not one of them doubted that missiles were stitched into every rogue's clothing and the hems of their wives' and sisters' dresses, and that any attending female had forfeited her right to courtesy.

The Stockport procession was among the first to arrive. Children were marshalled to the edges of St Peter's Field, while committed reformers, male and female, followed their banners to the centre. Tidd and Boulton moved as close as they could to the hustings. From all around, they heard the celebratory blasts of clarinets, pipes and bugles and waves of patriotic song that moved from one section of the crowd to another. On higher ground, beyond the hustings, and in a holiday mood, families laughed and held hands, swaying as they sang *God Save the King*. Tidd thought of his own wife and children and strengthened his resolve to bring them all to Stockport. They would be a proper family again, with happiness and holidays and a vegetable plot like the Boultons.

The Manchester Magistrates peered out of their window. They reckoned the crowd at over fifty thousand, but eighty minutes after his scheduled arrival, there was still no sign of Henry Hunt's party. Lord Sidmouth's correspondent, the Reverend Hay pointed with alarm at a banner, making its way towards the hustings.

EQUAL REPRESENTATION OR DEATH

A moment later, a messenger left a back door of Mount Street with an instruction that Deputy Constable Nadin had received from the magistrates. Almost at once, Tidd sensed a change in the mood behind him. He could not turn around because his chest was tight against the hustings, and he was jostled from three sides. The singing slurred to a halt and was replaced by slow hand claps. As the crowd hissed and clapped, someone tried to raise the national anthem, but the words went no further than *Send him victorious.*

He felt a grip on his shoulder and a voice barked at him to stand off or take a beating. Tidd saw the twisted face of a special constable, who snarled and flaunted a baton. The stench of ale was on his breath and a gleam in the oaf's eyes of a loathing that Tidd had not seen since Nottingham Gaol. Ignoring the provocation, Tidd shuffled sideways.

"Make no mistake," said Boulton, tight against him. "This battle is personal. God help anybody comes face to face with his employer."

As more constables pushed towards the hustings, Tidd thought the air would be crushed from his lungs. Then, a mighty roar lashed the air and behind him, a song began; *See the Conquering Hero Comes.* Far behind, the crowd pulled aside to make a path for Henry Hunt's barouche, with its special guard ahead and a line of women, all in white, behind. As the Orator's party inched towards the hustings, wild jubilation erupted. From their room on Mount Street, the Magistrates saw only pandemonium. Reverend Charles Wickstead Ethelston stood at a window and read the Riot Act in a voice that was heard by nobody but himself.

When, at last, the Orator climbed the ladder to the hustings, the taunts of the special constables were lost in the thunder of applause. On the outskirts of town, restless regiments heard the commotion and officers exchanged eloquent looks, but would do nothing without orders.

Henry Hunt raised his arms to silence the crowd and praise its peaceful conduct, but his words were indistinguishable, even to men as close as Tidd and Boulton. In the house on Mount Street, the Magistrates agreed that sixty amateur yeomen would never stem the tumult, in which they, the chief keepers of peace and prosperity in Manchester, were certain to die. Nadin was given his signed warrants of arrest, and messengers were dispatched to inform the yeomen and order the professional soldiers to stand by.

On the hustings, when Henry Hunt saw the advance of the mounted yeomen, he urged the crowd to sing a song of welcome to their fellow Mancunians. It was hopeless. Fired by scorn and brandy, the aggressors were amateurs, most with no idea - or care - whether the blunt or the sharp end of their swords was forward. Many rode borrowed horses, which had not been trained for combat. Terrified, the animals retreated to the herd instinct and charged, crushing anyone who had been knocked to the ground. Only the most competent and sober horsemen stayed in their saddles. Amid the chaos of dust, glinting steel and visceral screams that followed, the first death was of a two-year-old child, who fell from his mother's arms in the crush.

Tidd aimed a punch at a pair of constables who were tugging the white skirts of a female reformer on the hustings. They lunged at Tidd with their batons, and he fell backwards into the side of a horse, which reared up, unseating the yeoman. Tidd staggered forward, but someone hit his head with the butt of a musket, and he was down, too.

With hooves and boots and dust all around, and no air to breathe, Tidd thought his time had come. He was not ready to die; please, not like this! His head was on fire, his mouth, eyes and ears full of earth and grit. He tried to crawl into an empty space beneath the hustings, and he vomited. Above the rumble of hooves, he heard the piteous cries of the injured, and then, on the ground nearby, he made out the silent, crumpled form of John Boulton. Tidd stretched out his arms and dragged the body, dead or alive, to safety under the platform. He felt Boulton's chest and knew that his friend was breathing. As he stretched his long legs, as best he could, Tidd wondered if this was the revenge for all the battles he had missed and all the bounty he had stolen on behalf of Tom Spence or his own swinish appetites. Then he lay still, too and as his pain and the bedlam seemed to retreat, Tidd surrendered to the soft earth.

And, as I slept, I dreamed a dream, said the soft clear voice of his daughter, Mary, and Tidd was gone.

INGS

Cheetham, Lancashire

Ings spent the fateful morning in the shade of Mr Johnson's pear trees, on which the fruit was plentiful, each the size of a bull's eye. On one side sat Mrs Johnson, trimming a bonnet for her imminent baby. On the other, Hunt's elderly servant, Godfrey snoozed in his chair, grunting now and then, as if he had not a care in the world. After the second knot, Mrs Johnson pushed her needle into its cushion and implored Ings to distract her. He chose a version of the royal family's visit to Portsmouth, adjusted to protect Princess Amelia's secret.

"I was a small boy" he began, "with my brothers, a union flag and a posy for the queen. When the coach stopped, but the queen didn't look my way, I offered my flowers to Princess Amelia. She scolded me for being too shy to lift my eyes. When I looked up, Mrs Johnson, the princess, God rest her soul, was the most beautiful creature I had seen, before or since – apart, of course, from my wife and your good self, dear lady."

Mrs Johnson laughed at the story, which Ings elaborated for another five minutes. She hoped that little Freddie's knee had suffered no permanent damage and said that the story had moved her to an unusual urge.

"I should very much like to tickle Mr Godfrey's nose with a daisy," she said, "if only I were fit to bend and pick one."

"If you'd asked me yesterday," replied Ings, "I'd have picked it for you, but today, I cannot, and I beg you to stop your mischief, because laughter is more painful than bending down!"

They were chuckling away like naughty infants, when a horse came to a stop at the garden gate. The whinnying woke Godfrey who jumped up, like a startled squirrel, anticipating Mr Hunt's return. The rider wore a yeoman's uniform. He looked anxious and dishevelled, and called that he was in a great hurry, but he had an important message for the residents of Smedley Cottage. Ings and Mrs Johnson hurried towards the gate.

"Is it from my husband?" she asked.

"If your husband is a southern person and soft spoken" said the messenger. "then perhaps."

"I know the gentleman!" said Ings, anxious, in case of trickery, to offer neither opinion nor information. "Is he well?"

"He gives the impression of a fortunate escape," replied the yeoman.

"What is his message?" asked Ings,

"That his friends should go at once to the place where J.I. was given his hat."

"I see" said Ings. "I shall inform the gentleman's friends at once."

"Is there news of any other person?" asked Mrs Johnson, paler now than her needlework.

"Madam; it is no secret that Mr Hunt has been staying at this address. The Orator and his party, including his host, were taken - safe and sound, by all accounts - to the New Bayley."

The rider would tell them no more, except that he had seen sights in Manchester that would curdle their eyes and had made him ashamed to call himself English and a yeoman.

When the fellow had galloped off to another address, Mrs Johnson offered, at once, her gig and two ponies, if Mr Godfrey cared to drive a few items of comfort to the New Bayley. When Ings explained that he was required urgently in a village south of Manchester, Godfrey offered to drive him there from Salford.

Ings was waiting by the gate, with his haversack and Mr Carlile's valise, when three burly figures approached, and he recognised Margaret's brothers. They took off their caps and asked for Mr Johnson.

"The master's not here," said Ings, cautiously, "and Mrs Johnson's busy. Is there a message?"

"Tell him our Margaret bain't goin' down to 't factory to-morrow," said the oldest brother.

"Nor never again," said the second, mournfully.

"Wait!" cried Ings, as they turned to leave "What has happened!"

The brothers stared at the grass and the gate, their hands gripping their caps. They stumbled over their words, one speaking a phrase or two, and another the next.

When the White Moss procession arrived in Manchester, Margaret went to celebrate with her friends. At the first signs of trouble, they tried to leave St Peter's Field, but all the exits were blocked. They huddled against the railings on Windmill Street, and prayed for the violence to end. But the Hussars galloped towards them and Margaret was struck in the breast by a sabre. As she stumbled, the Cavalry charged from another direction, forcing the revellers hard against the railings. The railings collapsed and three women plunged into the stairwell below. Margaret was still living when her brothers arrived to carry her home, but she took her last breath outside the gingerbread bakery on Withy Grove. In the first discharge of their grief, they had smashed Murray's windows in, and they did not care who knew it.

The news of Margaret's death unmanned Ings; he could find no words. The youngest brother nodded in his curt, northern way and said that Ings's hat had turned up in the corner of White Moss Field. It was crumpled, said the second brother, beyond decency, but they would be pleased if he would call by and collect it. Ings explained that he had orders to leave Manchester, and wished them to keep the hat in affectionate memory.

"My friends," he said, "it's not safe to reveal my involvement in these matters, but I shall always regret that I was unable to defend your sister today. As long as this heart of mine beats, I shall seek vengeance for her death."

With the reins of Mrs Johnson's ponies in his hands, God-frey was a different man. He drove with all the vigour of a twenty-year old. The clerk at the New Bayley denied them access to the prisoners and would give no hope of early release. On receipt of a sound florin, he agreed to deliver the personal items and good wishes, and suggested a route to Stockport that avoided the principal trouble spots.

Among the bedraggled parties that trudged along the Stockport road, Ings and Godfrey saw a couple, limping badly, and offered them a ride as far as their home in Levenshulme. It was a lad of Bill Ings's age, with his mother, who had been attacked by a constable and said the monsters had sought out the women for the worst beatings.

After Levenshulme, as the gig gathered speed towards Bullocks Smithy, an unfamiliar feeling grew in the pit of Ings's belly. It was rage, and it was directed towards one man, who had enticed thousands of people to walk defenceless and unpro-tected into a battle that was none of their making. A gentleman of privilege, who had never experienced a day without food, warmth, fine clothes or the submission of servants. Mr Henry Hunt had summoned the innocent poor to their destruction with a weapon no less deadly than the sword; his own tongue, powered by privilege and the clever use of words.

Nobody will ever know the precise numbers, but on the 16th August 1819 some seven hundred unarmed people were injured in Manchester, at least eighteen fatally, and almost every one at the hands of compatriots charged with keeping the peace. At least twenty horses died too, with many more were injured and traumatised, Ings could not know the scale of the massacre, but he did know that he would never waste another day in fri-volity or idleness. His every hour would be committed to the service of honest British people, who were suffering because a greedy few preferred to commit murder than to contemplate sharing their advantages, and because another of their kind assumed command of the common man, but was blind to the depravity of which the tyrants among his own class were capable.

TIDD / DAVIDSON

St Peter's Field, Manchester

With his head in the mud and his eyes still closed, Tidd heard a song, and he thought he was dreaming. The tune was of the hymn, *Love Divine, all Loves Excelling*, but the words were patriotic.

Fairest Isle, all isles excelling,

Seat of pleasures, and of loves;

The voice was deep and passionate, and Tidd had heard it before. After a moment, it came to him. Will Davidson was here! Joyful that his friend was alive and so was he, Tidd opened his eyes. Daylight streamed between the planks, a few inches above his face. He looked sideways, and John Boulton had disappeared.

Beyond the uplifting song, Tidd heard a chorus of groans, and somewhere to the left, the drone of a Latin prayer. He shuffled towards the light and hauled himself to his feet. All around was unbearable, bloody mayhem. And there, atop the hustings, stood Will Davidson, clutching his hat and singing his heart out. Tidd was alarmed, but sufficiently alert not to reveal his friend's name.

"Oy!" he shouted, "You'll get shot! Get down!"

When he saw Tidd, Davidson smiled broadly and hurried down the ladder to embrace him. He had been singing, he said, to comfort the wounded and in the hope that friends might make themselves known. As if to order, William Beard, the

350

weaver approached, half naked, drenched in blood, with both arms wrapped in the shreds of his shirt. He smiled to see the familiar face and asked,

"Did I not send thee on th' road to Stafford, Will Davidson?"

"These feet don't listen to reason, Will Beard!" replied Davidson. "I got as far as Macclesfield and picked berries for a week."

It was the partial truth. Fellow labourers, who distrusted Davidson's looks and unfamiliar manners, had trussed him up on a pole to roast in the sun and shiver all night. and threatened to drag him to the docks at Liverpool and ship him back to wherever he belonged. Fortunately, the bell-ringer was out walking after Evensong with his new wife, who screamed when she saw the scarecrow move. They fetched him down, nursed him fed him bread and milk, let him sleep a while and drove like maniacs to Stockport. Too late for the march, Davidson had arrived at St Peters Field, when the assault was over and headed straight to the hustings.

There was no need to complicate the current situation, so he said no more and took the measure of his friend's injuries.

"Trampled by a horse," explained Beard. "I'm wrecked."

Tidd and Davidson understood that he would never weave again.

"We must take you to the Infirmary," said Davidson.

"Never!" said Beard. "They'll arrest me sooner than find a pin for a bandage."

"Where's your family?" asked Tidd.

"Home, thank God," said Beard. "Without shoes, what child can walk so far? And I'd never leave 't loom idle."

Cautiously the three men stepped through the nightmare. Survivors were helping the injured into carts and barrows. The ground was littered with detritus; abandoned scarves, flags, drumsticks, a

twisted clarinet. They saw Parson Harrison, crouching over an injured woman, speaking of the sweet mercy of Jesus. He had passed
John Boulton and his children, he said, walking home, as he rode
into Manchester, too late, after the spinner died.

At Piccadilly, they came across a pair of runaway stallions,
which, after reassurance, seemed content to carry them, with Beard
tight in front of Tidd, while Davidson, defying the aches and
bruises from his own misadventure, led the way. Gunshots echoed
in the distance and the horses reared up, but did not shed their
passengers. At last, the little party reached the arms and the tears
of Mrs Beard, who had feared the worst and now stood before it.

Mrs Boulton buckled to see Tidd at her door.

"Our John thought tha' wert a goner," she said. "He were
all of a dither, leaving thee. But he had to look aht for 't childer
fust."

"Are they all well?" asked Tidd.

"No harm's come to any o' mine," said Mrs Boulton. "Come
in, Mr Tidd, Tha'rt welcome."

That night, while Tidd and Davidson slept unevenly in
their borrowed cots, the young men of Stockport were consumed by rage and disappointment, and the cheerful hope of
that Monday morning was defiled by a riot in the streets, and,
more privately, by the weeping of Parson Harrison.

Tuesday 17ᵗʰ August, 1819

The road south

They had agreed to leave the horses with Beard and Boulton,
but neither family wanted them.

"Even if we could afford to feed him," said Mrs Beard, "fine beast like that, prancing round Heaton Norris would bring nowt but trouble.

"We've had enough grief, wi'out my man arrested for horse-stealing!" cried Mrs Boulton.

Davidson's proposal of auctioning the animals to help the wounded of Stockport was accepted by Mrs Boulton, on condition the sale occurred in London, where the animals were less likely to be identified. Her husband advised Tidd and Davidson to leave the area quickly, before the authorities came looking.

"The so-called authorities have breached the Magna Carta," replied Davidson, "thereby surrendering the right to arrest us."

"I should like to see thee tell 'em so!" said Mrs Boulton.

"Do not doubt it, madam" said Davidson, "I shall."

During the first and most leisurely part of their journey, they speculated what might have happened to Ings and Tidd told Davidson about the Water Lane Group and its connection to the coffee shop on Fleet Street where Jimmy lived and worked. Davidson was grateful for Tidd's promise of an introduction to his poetic partner, Brunt and to the group chairman, Arthur Thistlewood.

In the flat, open country of Cheshire, they gathered speed for a time and then sat by a pond to give the horses a break. They washed themselves in the cool water, swore an oath of eternal friendship, forged on St Peter's Field. Then they opened their rucksacks to enjoy Mrs Boulton's picnic, the bread being preferable to the pickled onions, which, being fresh, were very sour.

As they exchanged private histories, Tidd asked Davidson how a man from a colonial background had been drawn into radical politics. Two Scotsmen were responsible, Davidson explained, and both had died before he left Jamaica. One was the poet,

Rabbie Burns, and the other Deacon Brodie, a city councillor in Edinburgh, and senior official of the Cabinet-makers' Guild.

"To the suffering poor, Brodie was an angel of God," he declared, "but to the rich men, whose keys he copied and whose money he stole, he was the devil incarnate."

"They hanged him?" asked Tidd.

"Aye."

After studying a new edition of the Magna Carta, Davidson had informed his teachers in Edinburgh that he declined to pursue a profession in law, because the present system deviated too far from the principles laid out in 1215. After the inevitable fall-out, Will's father, the Attorney General of Jamaica, sent his son to Liverpool, where a study of English law would prepare him more usefully for a future back in the West Indies. But Mrs Davidson, who was Jamaican and considerably younger than her husband, planned to spend her later life as a refined English widow. When Will continued to rebel and - in secret honour of Deacon Brodie - became apprenticed to a cabinet-maker in Liverpool, his mother indulged his every decision, furtively boosting Will's income so that he might succeed in business and provide her with fine accommodation in England, when the unhappy time came.

"Your ma's in for a grand disappointment!" said Tidd.

"Perhaps I should'nae take her money," replied Davidson, "but she has plenty of it, and how can I explain that the Britain known to you and me is not the paradise of her imagination?"

"She's sending you money still?" asked Tidd, startled that a tradesman like himself had an income, to which no effort was attached.

"Now and then," admitted Davidson. "We had a hollow time when papa found out, but mama convinced him, and there's enough, with my wage, to feed the boys till Christmas."

"Do your parents know you're married?" enquired Tidd.

"Aye, and that my good wife has given them a grandson. I thought it wise to keep quiet about the weans Sarah brought me ready-made."

"How many?" asked Tidd.

"Five," said Davidson, "including mah ain."

"Same here," replied Tidd, sympathetically.

On this count, Tidd and Davidson were both entirely wrong.

Friday, 20ᵗʰ August, 1819

SARAH DAVIDSON

St Marylebone, London

It was just over a year since she held a husband in her arms, a year in which events had unfurled of which Will Davidson knew nothing. When Sarah was certain there would be another baby, she had considered various methods to prevent the birth, but feared for the fate of the other boys, if she died. She wrote secretly to her mother-in-law in Kingston, but when she went to collect the usual payment eight weeks later, the bank clerk had firm instructions to withhold it. Sarah had no heart to inform her husband, either of her correspondence or of its consequences.

Will's journeyman wage, which she collected weekly from the housekeeper at Grosvenor Square, was not enough to support herself and the five boys she already had. Sarah had taken stitching jobs from a milliner, and she worked at home every night until her fingers bled. When she asked to take more, the milliner said Sarah was still pretty enough to do "upstairs work," which would earn more money for less effort. Sarah Davidson said she was no whore, and the milliner could keep his wages. Two days later, the nasty man knocked at her door and threatened to send the patrole, because Sarah Davidson had stolen a box of feathers and her eldest, Abraham, had been witnessed outside the Yorkshire Stingo, selling them from a box round his neck. The milliner promised to retract his false accusations, only if she agreed to the upstairs work. He had underestimated the spirt of Sarah Davidson, who arranged for the entire Sunday school to gather outside his premises and sing wholesome songs. When the pastor stood at the door, issued his lecture on temperate morality, and offered to do so on a daily basis, the milliner promised to leave Sarah and her sons in peace.

In weekly letters to her husband, Sarah wrote nothing of her troubles, but described how bravely the boys were facing life without him and what flowers were showing in the verges today. If he knew the truth, Will would come running home, and without his job at Sandon, all would be lost. When there was still no money from Jamaica, Sarah wrote a second letter that was not for her husband's eyes.

12, Elliot's Row,
Lords Old Cricket Ground,
St Marylebone New Road,
London
Sunday, 13th December, 1818

Dear Mrs Davidson,

I trust that you and my father-in-law continue to enjoy good health and have avoided the yellow fever epidemic that has concerned us all, and that Kingston has not been troubled by further tempests.

I am happy to tell you that William still has good work with Lord Harrowby, and that your grandson John Davidson is in the rudest health. He is two years old, the image of his papa, especially about the nose and chin, and just as charming. John is a chatterbox and yet he is very attentive. He stays by my side whenever we go out, and I never need fear that he will run into the path of a horse or splash about in the mud like other children.

Dearest mother-in-law, when I wrote to you in October, I trust that I did not offend you, as nothing could be further from my intention. Perhaps my letter was spoilt in stormy weather and you never saw it. In either case, since I have received no reply, I take it upon myself to write again.

God willing, your new grandchild will be born at about the middle of April. William and I write to each other every week, but in short, I have been reluctant to increase his worries with news of the impending birth. For a time, I worked for a milliner and my son, Abraham, who is thirteen, has a good reputation in the neighbourhood for shining shoes, but he must stand outside without a warm coat, and the English winter is cruel.

Dear mother-in-law, the situation in London is dreadful. William is doing all he can to help his family, but our lives more pitiful than I could ever have imagined, and the children rarely eat more than watery porridge, and no meat or greens at all. As you know, my parents in Devon are deceased, and my only sister lives in difficult circumstances. I cannot tolerate taking the boys into the workhouse, where we would face separation. Nor would I ever hand William Davidson's new baby to a stranger, no matter how well she may care for it.

May I encroach upon your generosity to help us until such time as we are better able to restore our former lives? We do not seek riches, and neither are we idle. In precisely three months' time, I shall visit Mr Coutts's bank in the hope of a note from you.

With my regards to you and, if they are appreciated, to Mr Davidson and to my husband's brothers.

I am

Your affectionate daughter-in-law,

Sarah Davidson

In the middle of April, the letter carrier had visited Elliot's Row, St and, in exchange for Sarah's wedding veil, provided her with two letters; the usual affectionate note from her husband, and another, with less familiar handwriting.

Duke Street,
Kingston,
Jamaica
Friday, 5ᵗʰ February 1819

Dear Sarah,

Thank you for your letter. I pity you, but my husband forbids me to forward any further monies in support of children who do not bear the name Davidson. When he is satisfied of the facts by a letter from William, he will reconsider the position with regard to our son's children.

In the meantime, I will make arrangements for the new baby to be examined by a doctor of our acquaintance, a good Christian. If it appears to be a grand-child of mine and is in good health, the same doctor will carry the baby to Kingston, where it will be tenderly cared for under my direct instruction.

You may expect the doctor (a citizen of Aberdeen by the name of Duncan Mennie) to visit you soon, since he is travelling to London and will post this letter there and visit you one week later. May God Bless You and your family.

Yours sincerely,

Phoebe Davidson

A kind and perceptive man of forty-five, Dr Mennie was enchanted by the Lane-Davidson boys and, on the very first day, gave Sarah a guinea from his pocket. He told her not to resent Phoebe Davidson, who had no overseas experience, and could not be moved from the opinion that Britain was a land of milk and honey, in which only the lazy and the sinful suffered hardship. Dr Mennie was in London for business, and he planned to visit relations in Scotland, but would do so only after the baby was safely delivered. Having no children of his own, the doctor said he would welcome further acquaintance with the young Davidsons and would ensure their good health and security during his stay in Britain.

Dr Mennie confirmed that Sarah's baby had turned and would be born within a week. When the time approached, young Abraham must hurry to his hotel, and he would assist at the birth, free of charge. He would carry no child into the tropics unless it was at least fourteen weeks old and thriving.

By the middle of August 1819, little Duncan Davidson had a firm, round tummy and sturdy limbs that kicked and punched just as they should. He slept quite well, grinned often at his mother and brothers and knew his god-father, the doctor too.

In one of those strange turns that history produces, the date on which the doctor came to carry Duncan away, was also the day on which Will Davidson expected to surprise his family. With his heart aflame, he approached Elliot's Row, paying no attention to the carriage, parked outside their cottage. He tied his horse, dropped his rucksack on the step and knocked at the door. The commotion inside was natural for a family of five boys, and he knocked hard until he heard the door handle turn. In a moment, he would hold Sarah tight, and the boys would shout for joy.

Sarah fainted. As he caught her in his arms, Davidson knew that her tears were not of joy. The two younger boys were clinging to her skirts. Will tried to comfort them, but they only wailed louder and pushed the strange man away. Abraham and his two brothers, who had always adored him, only stared at their stepfather with blank eyes. As Davidson looked around in bewilderment, he noticed the well-dressed gentleman and the nurse with a baby in her arms.

Dr Mennie was not unmoved by the circumstances. Already late for his journey to the docks, he granted the parents a few moments alone to kiss their child and consider the matter. If Will Davidson accepted his mother's offer, the doctor promised a first-class account of the family to their relations in Jamaica, and he vowed to return in two years, with or without little Duncan, whichever the little boy's parents desired.

TIDD

Grays Inn Lane, Holborn

His legs had rarely been so sore, even after walking from Nottingham to Mansfield in faulty boots. Nevertheless, Tidd was mindful of the consequences of arriving at Hole-in-the-Wall Passage on a stallion worthy of a Duke. Fortunately, a watchman at the livery on Grays Inn Lane was sympathetic. Hearing that Tidd and his mount had ridden directly from the Manchester Meeting, he promised, for a shilling from the anticipated profit, to ensure the animal was properly fed, rested and groomed before morning. For another shilling, he might introduce Mr Tidd to a gentleman whose own mount was lamed on Monday. Too weary to show either gratitude or resentment, Tidd said he would return tomorrow and made his way to the familiar passageway, hoping, once the joyful reunions were done, for soup in Eliza's pan, water for washing, and a long sleep on a mattress free of bugs and wriggling kids.

The neighbours stared, when Richard Tidd, unshaven and tired, trudged into Hole-in-the-Wall Passage, towards his staircase. Some had suspicions about his absence, but Tidd's fixed expression reminded them of returning soldiers, and they kept a respectful distance.

In anticipation of, at least, temporary rejoicing, Tidd opened his front door to find the apartment empty. He laid down his sack and searched for food. There were no biscuits in the tin, bread in the box nor taters in the pan. Speculating that his family might be combining their meals with the Brunts, Tidd trudged down the steps again and headed to Fox Court. When he reached his partner's apartment, the door was opened not by Mr or Mrs Brunt, but by the bespectacled clerk who had been courting Mary these last months (and thought her pa had not noticed). Mr Barker welcomed Mr Tidd brightly, explained that Mrs Tidd had gone foraging with the twins, and he had important news to impart.

In this manner, Richard Tidd discovered that his own Mary, whom he had first known as curly-haired baby, and always loved as a father, had married Gerald Barker. There was more. During their honeymoon with relations in Folkestone, Gerald had been reunited with his own two children, whose mother died at sea last March. Six and eight years old, Ellen and Horace Barker peeped shyly from behind their papa.

"You have work, I suppose, Mr Barker?" asked Tidd.

"I do, father" said the clerk, ever so politely, "to a degree."

CHAPTER SEVENTEEN

Sunday, 21ˢᵗ November, 1819

CARLILE / EDWARDS
Blackfriars Bridge, London

Rain had fallen since Friday, and at about two o'clock on that frosty Sunday afternoon, a coach with covered windows hurtled over a cavity on Blackfriars Bridge, raising a mighty splash that drenched a pedestrian, who was hurrying in the opposite direction. The pedestrian turned to pursue the vehicle, cursing and banging on the side, intent on demanding compensation for the damage to his clothing. When he saw the crest and knew that the coach came from the Old Bailey, he decided that his effort would be better spent on a complaint to the Court Administrator, when he was warm and dry and had gathered his wits. As the coach rattled onwards, what George Edwards could not know was that its principal passenger, newly convicted of sedition and blasphemy, was Richard Carlile, on his way to Dorchester Gaol.

Carlile's reports from Manchester had shaken the nation and intensified the excitement surrounding his trial for seditious libel which, after half a year of speculation, began in October, when London was prematurely covered by a couple of inches of snow. He had never pretended to be a skilled public speaker, but the lacklustre self-defence in court disappointed a public hungry for sensation. Then, amid the frenzy surrounding the opening of Parliament, Richard Carlile vanished from scrutiny like a feather in the wind.

Publicity was a process that he had manipulated brilliantly during his ascendancy. Today, as he bounced across the mighty Thames, manacled to a haughty officer in a coach with no springs, Carlile was its latest victim, and he knew it. A similar process had all but destroyed Henry Hunt. Out on bail and fearful of imminent obscurity, the Orator had forfeited much of his support in a battery of public bickering with Thistlewood that had titillated readers and sold tens of thousands of newspapers.

When Carlile heard the angry thumps and the shouts outside, he presumed himself mocked by one of the poor wretches whose life he had intended to improve. Rarely, Carlile thought, had his skills been more necessary than now.

Since Peterloo, workers' unions had grown rapidly in strength and numbers. Fearful of attack, reformers carried bricks and stones to their meetings, and were not afraid to use them. Equally fearful of Revolution, government ministers failed to control the reformers, and were mocked as ineffectual by the press. As a result, Lord Sidmouth was expected, in the Regent's Speech on Tuesday, to reveal new and oppressive measures.

On their visits to Newgate, Carlile's family had promised, should he be convicted, to continue his work. His sister was clever and resourceful, but his wife, though committed to the cause, was insufficiently educated and burdened with three small children. How would two inexperienced young women cope in an environment that was bewildering enough without the complication of further constraint. Would his printing press be silenced, his archive destroyed? Worst of all, there was nothing Richard Carlile could do, no phrases he could invent or vocabulary deploy that would prevent the catastrophe that, without the voice of reason to restrain it, must lie in store for his beloved country.

George Edwards quickened his pace until he reached the Old Bell, where Mrs Harding gasped at the sight of him and his beautiful greatcoat. She sat him by the fire, and reckoned the muck would brush off when it dried, and there was a hundred tailors in London ready to attach a new velvet collar. She lent him a gown and a blanket and went to fetch his suet pudding and a small gin.

He had left Thistlewood under a canvas shelter at Kennington Common, addressing a huddle of Irish labourers who would, they hoped, bring thousands to Smithfield, where a grand Meeting was scheduled to respond to Sidmouth's proposals. On a late November day, there would be no sunshine to tempt the people out, and there were no outside speakers. It would be a useful measure of Arthur Thistlewood's influence.

Since a spate of bickering with Hunt in the press, Thistlewood was popular with the public, and he was no longer as pliable as in the aftermath of his failure at Spitalfields. The Water Lane Group had quadrupled in number. The core membership had elected an Executive Committee, with Thistlewood as captain and Edwards his aide de camp. But Edwards had failed to identify an opportunity that might lead to the ultimate result. The regular payments continued, but he had not anticipated such a long a wait for the grand reward. With the house in Pimlico, the headquarters at New Fish Street and a needy mother in Cripplegate, Edwards was accruing debts.

He knew that he must proceed with caution. He understood that as pressure mounted, Thistlewood would become increasingly mercurial. For all his insight into human nature and its underbelly, Edwards was unsettled by volatility, and he could not always predict Thistlewood's reactions. He awaited Sidmouth's proposals with interest. Properly combined with persuasion and a new supply of absinthe, they might provoke Thistlewood towards extreme action.

The necessity for a new greatcoat was an irritant, certain to invite queries from every ragamuffin in the Group and from his ma, but Edwards could not stomach dishevelment, and the winter promised to get colder. Since it was Sunday and no new coat was to be had anywhere, he paid for his gin and his pudding and asked Mrs Harding to secure him a cab for the short distance to St Magnus the Martyr.

When the coffee shop closed and Carlile's family needed the apartment, George Edwards offered the Hampshire butcher a room at New Fish Street, and an executive role as caretaker and controller of the armoury. Ings seemed content to continue his duties all day, every day, as long as his ale was topped up regular, and there was always fat tater on the fire. He was as biddable as clay, Edwards thought, and invaluable for his knife skills and steady nerve with blood and guts.

The weapon store had expanded rapidly thanks to the younger members, consisting of Harry Brunt, the apprentice, Joe Hale and the older sons of Thistlewood, Tidd and Davidson, who worked at night, had perfected the arts of scavenging and pulling out railings in near silence. None of the lads believed the official story about building a House of Liberty in Nottingham, but all respected the instruction for sealed lips, even amongst themselves.

There was sufficient distance between the church and his headquarters for Edwards to appear damp, when he arrived to inspect the armoury. The lads were playing marbles, relaxing after a busy night, and Ings was down in the back room, filing pike-heads.

"Good man!" said Edwards. "We'll have enough of those soon to fight off a battalion!"

"Thank you, sir," replied Ings, cheerfully, "and a very good afternoon to you!"

Edwards intended to have an extremely good afternoon. A committee meeting had been called at Stanhope Street, and he planned to arrive early and see a special lady before her husband came home. The rain had stopped, a fresh breeze was blowing, and a walk would save the fare and clear his mind for Susan. As always, Edwards hurried past the Monument, head down to avoid the griffins, whose accusing grimaces unsettled him. On Fleet Street, he was gratified to observe that his own bust of Tom Paine still dominated Carlile's print-shop window. From a bucket in Wych Street, when the florist turned away, he lifted a bundle of autumn leaves and berries and darted into a yard to bind them into a posy.

SUSAN THISTLEWOOD / EDWARDS

Stanhope Street, Lincolns Inn Fields

Susan Thistlewood, busy baking oat-cakes for the committee, blushed as she thanked George for the gift, and insisted he sit in her warm kitchen, and she would see what could be done with his poor coat.

Edwards had learnt, from observing Susan, that not all independent minded women were as intent as his mother and Tilly on identifying a man's weakness and taking advantage. He understood, through Susan, that a woman could have interests of her own and still be committed to a marriage. What

Edwards had not perceived was that a good marriage was not a stroke of luck, nor was it effortless, like the rising of the sun, and any wife, of any degree of intelligence, might struggle with a husband consumed by noble ambition.

The truth was that since their joy at her return from Lincolnshire in September, Arthur and Susan Thistlewood rarely exchanged more than functional phrases. Little more than the essence of their previous intimacy had survived. Susan was fully informed of her husband's activities and ambitions, and they trusted each other. There was no animosity, but no identifiable joy either, apart from the shared pride in Julian. At night, Susan and Arthur Thistlewood were too busy, or too exhausted even to imagine any pleasure of the flesh.

With Julian's education, her domestic duties and clerical support for the committee, Susan Thistlewood's personal ambition to improve the lives of ordinary women was postponed. Her spirit was lonely, and when her husband's closest ally asked about the family in Lincolnshire, she found herself confiding in him, as she washed his velvet collar.

Sitting back and listening in that expert way of his, George Edwards learnt everything that Aunt Mary had disclosed, while Julian was out riding with his friend. Arthur's invalid father was plagued by terrible moods and episodes of violence. Arthur's Uncle John had died young in Jamaica, possibly in revenge for brutality while visiting Thomas Thistlewood, Arthur's great uncle, a notoriously cruel slave-driver.

"Do you believe, George, that a sane and reasonable person is capable of evil?" she asked, her eyes appealingly wide.

"Mankind is infinitely variable," replied Edwards coolly. "Those of us fortunate enough to live in civilized nations, in accordance with a decent moral order, are perhaps better able to protect ourselves from the exertions of the devil."

"How wise you are!" said Susan. "But have you considered the difference between evil and madness? Take the old King. Do you believe he's mad, or do you suppose his condition to be the consequence of past actions? Or could there be illness in the family? I've read the rumours about his children, and is His Majesty not closely related to the Brunswicks, who are reputedly more than unstable?"

Edwards's expression of concerned enquiry was rewarded.

"You see, George," she continued, "I wonder sometimes if there's a similar frailty in my husband's family. Of course, I dread his capture by one of Sidmouth's toadies, but what keeps me awake, as he sits all night at his desk, is the fear of madness."

Edwards replied that Julian seemed an even-tempered young man, and he had seen no evidence of instability in his father. A degree of melancholy could be expected in the most even-tempered fellow, faced with the current circumstances.

"My husband suffers more than melancholy. There are rages, George. Can they be explained by the liquor and the laudanum he consumes almost daily."

"If they ease his hunger and his sleeplessness," asked Edwards, "and they pass by, why not simply ignore the rages?"

"Not if there's a chance of something more sinister at play. Arthur would prefer to die, George, than exist in the living hell that, by all accounts, plagued his father."

Susan looked away, the pain almost beyond endurance, and Edwards, so rarely moved by another human being, was shaken out of his pretence.

"Susan," he said. "I don't know how, but this radical business will end badly. Whatever you and I do to support him, Arthur is unstoppable, and he will take whatever the future brings. For your own sake, keep yourself wholesome, and your time will come."

"I don't understand you, George," she said quietly. "What time? What do you mean by wholesome?"

George Edwards gazed at the rag rug on the floor and could say no more. Susan Thistlewood could not know that he had attempted the most honest statement of his life and that his usual clarity of thought had failed him.

As she hung Edwards's great-coat on a hook by the fire and turned to retrieve her oat-cakes from the stove, Susan This- tlewood wondered if she had said too much. It was a relief to share her fear with a trusted friend, even though his reaction was strange. Perhaps, she speculated, George is unused to the ways and worries of women, and she focused her attention on the imminent committee meeting.

Edwards had moved to the sitting room, and there, on the yellow settee, his equilibrium returned. He was armed with the certainty that Thistlewood's greatest fear was insanity, and his angel had confided in nobody else, but him. In the short time alone with Susan Thistlewood, the icy cage round Edwards's heart had melted a little, and now granted him a blast of jubilation.

Tuesday, 23rd November, 1819

THE SCOTCH ARMS

New Round Court, The Strand, London

Early on the frosty morning when the Regent would recite his government's new proposals, a chattering crowd squeezed into the tangle of alleys at the St Martin's end of the Strand. While the Prince's private table at Carlton House was laid out with pigeons, beef-steak and brandy, each of these citizens carried a wooden basin and a spoon in anticipation of a decent meal at last.

Will Davidson, recently appointed secretary of the New Shoemakers' Union, had conceived the idea of a communal breakfast. The involvement of their families would lift members' spirits before Smithfield and remind them of the rally's proper purpose. Davidson's petition had so impressed the philanthropic lawyer and philosopher, Jeremy Bentham, that he had promised enough cheese for one hundred people and contributed two crates each of apples and pears from his own cellar, with half a dozen oranges for the committee.

Naturally, when news leaked of free food, families with no connection, either to the politics or to shoemaking, set out for the Scotch Arms to swear allegiance to this most radical of unions. Mary Tidd Barker, carrying warm bread from the bakehouse, saw how frisky the people were, and that the numbers were far greater than expected. She advised the women to make the portions smaller, so that more men would be encouraged to join to the rally.

Organizing the food was a timely distraction for Mary. The banker's clerk had vanished six weeks after fetching his children from the workhouse. When the abandoned bride said that she could no more give up Horace and Ellen than her pa could have rejected her, when he married ma, Richard Tidd had sighed and asked what harm two little orphans could do to a family of seven? His wife, unexpectedly, had agreed without contest.

Eliza Tidd's epiphany had occurred after she connected her husband's absence last August to the talk of a massacre at Manchester. The conjugal row was heard all along Hole in the Wall Passage, but soon afterwards, Eliza rejoiced that she was not a widow and nursed no greater wish than to support her husband in his heroic efforts. When Susan Thistlewood made Mrs Tidd welcome to the new women's club and presented her with a book, Eliza said that her daughter would read it aloud in the evenings. Slowly but surely, extracts from Thomas Paine's *Age of Reason* had weaned Mrs Tidd from two and a half decades of John Bunyan and launched a month of ruthless questions.

Now the proud consort of a Union Official, Eliza Tidd was instructing the Barker orphans and her younger twins in the correct setting out of trestle tables and chairs. Mrs Thistlewood stood in a corner of the Scotch Arms with the lads, explaining how the government's proposals were to arrive promptly at Smithfield Square.

The moment The Regent stopped speaking, copies of his speech would be carried out by a regiment of clerks and sold for a shilling a piece in the Old Palace Yard, but because those copies were unreliable, Susan preferred to pay a penny to listen to the official reading, of which she would quickly write a précis for her husband and Mr Edwards. The quickest way to transfer the notebook was by a relay, in which each lad would run as fast as he could to the next. They had been shown the route and must agree where each boy's station would be. It was also important to have plausible explanations, should any officer enquire why the young man was loitering on a corner, or running so fast with a lady's notebook.

Tidd was standing sentry at the door with Davidson, when James Ings arrived, flustered, from Dr Bentham's house in Westminster. Thrusting a crate of oranges and cheese into the arms of Tidd, he explained that on account of a past insult to his wife and daughter, presently in Hampshire, nothing would induce him to enter the Scotch Arms.

"Nobody wants to force you," said Davidson as Tidd carried the crate away. "You can have your breakfast out in the cold."

"Ain't no time for breakfast!" replied Ings. "Not when there's cattle to be calmed and milking to be done."

Instead of transporting full churns, Hyden and Firth, cowmen from Hyde Park, had preferred to drive the cattle along Oxford Street and down to the Strand. The plan succeeded until they met the throng of people at the corner. The cows had become nervous, and as a countryman accustomed to livestock, Ings's assistance had been requested.

"I tell you, Will Davidson," he said, "nervous cattle means kicking cattle that are more likely to shit everywhere than provide milk. I shall assist the cowmen before anyone gets hurt. Furthermore, since I was obliged to park my cart in The Strand, where the apples and pears are at risk of filching, it must be someone else's responsibility to protect my property and carry the fruit inside."

The lads were summoned to help with Ings's cart, and Davidson asked the crowd to stand back and stay respectful, as Ings and the cowmen herded the growling animals into the yard and began the milking.

When the job was done, Mary Tidd Barker, who had enjoyed the spectacle from the kitchen window, urged Ings to forget his grudge. The Scotch Arms had new management, she said, and he needed his strength today, and should enjoy a good breakfast like everyone else, before the day turned serious. Often weakened by a pretty smile, Ings allowed himself to be led, with Tom Hyden through the kitchen door to the committee table, while Elias Firth chewed on an apple and kept the cows from straying.

At last, and with due ceremony, Eliza Tidd opened the doors to the public and in her best, market Duchess voice, announced that, in single file, and on strict condition of no fighting, the guests should take their spoons and basins and line up at the table.

When the feast was over, Will Davidson stood to give thanks and led the community in the lines of a poem by William Blake.

Bring me my bow of burning gold!
Bring me my arrows of desire!
Bring me my spear: o clouds unfold!
Bring me my chariots of fire!

"God Save the King!" called Tom Hyden, when the song was done.

Despite His Majesty's fast-failing health, the response was half-hearted. There were even boos and hisses until Davidson and Tidd unfurled a black banner. The centrepiece was a skull with crossbones and above it, Mary Tidd Barker had stitched the stark motto;

Let us Die like Men
and not be
Sold like Slaves!

The community cheered and Davidson's plea for three times, "Reform Now!" raised the roof. Then, leaving the women and the younger children to the warmth and safety of the Scotch Arms, or at least to the clearing up, Davidson, Tidd and Ings led the march to Smithfield Square.

SMITHFIELD SQUARE

It was ten to eleven by St Bartholomew's clock when Thistlewood and Edwards arrived. The ground was hard with frost, and the air pinched their faces and numbed their thighs. Smithfield Square, so jubilant at the rally in July, seemed grey and dismal in late November. No flags were waved from crowded windows and roof tops and without a single pipe or drum, there was no sense of either jubilation or expectation. Apart from Brunt, who waited by the hustings, the only signs of life were the barking of dogs and the rumble of the market, close by. Brunt said that the hustings were not secure, and that Hale and the stewards were looking for rope.

At about eleven fifteen, a group of some twenty men approached. Dock-workers from Deptford, they showed Thistlewood how cleverly their wives and sisters had stitched stones into their hems.

"We can't hardly wait for sparks to start flying!" said one.

"Not before we're provoked," replied Thistlewood. "Your stones may have greater purpose on another day."

Muttering about the waste of bloody time, the men sauntered away. Their leader, John Gast, stopped to shake Thistlewood's hand.

"You have thousands of sympathizers in Deptford, Thistlewood. Most of 'em got no fight left. This is all I could fetch out and every last one of 'em battle hungry."

"Thank you for your loyalty, Gast," said Thistlewood. "If you can, take the men to The Ram and divert them from violence. We need their ideas. We will not fight off the tyrants to become dictators ourselves. The new society will be built on shared opinion, and they must tell us what they want."

"Aye aye sir."

As he limped after his men, Thistlewood indicated John Gast's shoes; nothing but shreds and patches, barely covering his feet.

"Without food in his belly, or coat on his back," said Edwards, "what man will come out on a freezing day to hear that his last hopes are damned?"

Apart from the Deptford dockers, heading for The Ram, the only men in sight were Joe Hale and a few stewards, scouting for military.

"They'd have come out in a blizzard for Hunt!" said Thistlewood.

"Don't be despondent," replied Edwards. "Hunt is the past. You are the future, and we have assurances from Vauxhall, Kennington, Spitalfields and the barracks."

"The Scotch Arms contingent should be here by now," said Thistlewood, as Brunt approached to say the repairs were done and the committee would have a clear view across Smithfield Square.

As he and Edwards mounted the ladder, Thistlewood sighed and looked up, as Farmer John had always looked up at moments of uncertainty. The sky was a dull, whitish grey, broken to the south by narrow blue streaks. The clouds were on the move.

"The weather will improve in an hour."

"That's when they'll come," said Edwards.

Edwards was quietly persuading himself that the disappointing turnout could be an advantage. He would not have to suffer the sight and smell of bloodshed, and Thistlewood, with his confidence knocked, would become more malleable.

Then Brunt approached, the excitement cracking his voice.

"They're here!" he cried. "A great crowd, marching up Giltspur Street! Listen!"

They heard the steady beat of side drums, and men's voices. singing *Rule Britannia,* and around the corner, with his skull banner, came Davidson, with Tidd on one side, and Ings, with his cart on the other, followed by a hundred well-fed and lusty men.

As Thistlewood and Edwards applauded the arrivals, Brunt climbed up to the platform, and then, Ings called up, food parcels under his arm.

"Park under the platform, Jimmy," said Thistlewood, "and come up! Breakfast can wait."

"I'm too private for hustings," said Ings, "and I'll not be parted from my cart. There'll be men at the market I can rally up; Smithfield's half dead on a Tuesday."

As Tidd and Davidson fixed the banner to a stake on the hustings, more men began to stream into the square from all directions.

"What took so long?" asked Thistlewood.

"We was passing 't Old Bailey," said Tidd, "when a line of officers approached, meek as you like, telling 't crowd to disperse. They said Will's banner was illegal, and asked him to give it up."

"I could have lifted any of those kitten-livered officers by the ear," added Davidson, "and tossed him in the ditch. But the ninnyhammers felt the mood of the people and ran for their lives!"

At Thistlewood's word, Davidson moved to the front of the platform and raised his arm. The crowd quietened, and he thanked them for making the journey in such difficult circumstances.

"While you freeze out here in the open air," he continued, "The Regent is all tucked up at the Palace at Westminster, in his ermine robes, issuing the words that, unless we take action, will define our fate. Until the report arrives, citizens, until we know its contents, I urge you to remain calm and hopeful. While you wait, it will be the committee's pleasure to present an eye witness account of the Battle of Peterloo. Let us begin with the words Jesus taught us."

At Davidson's command, every man (or almost) bowed his head and closed his eyes.

Forgive us our trespasses
As we forgive those who have trespassed against us.

If, in all his life, Richard Tidd experienced a moment of glory, it was during Will Davidson's impassioned account of their experiences in Manchester. When the report was done, the people chanted Tidd's name, and Davidson pulled him to the front of the platform, too. Tidd said he was a modest bootmaker from Grantham, and not built for speeches, but he was prepared to die for the cause, and he knew better than most that the time had come for vengeance.

Thistlewood's disapproval was lost in a great howl of assent. Even the saddler, the farrier and the stable-boy, listless when the Hampshire butcher cajoled them to come and watch history taking a twist, joined the crowd as it whooped and frolicked like wild men, without quite knowing why.

Ings, at the corner, watched, but he did not dance. Instead, he imagined he saw in his cart, among the crates and the last of the breakfast parcels, a pale face with eyes, soft as twice-turned honey, that had once brought him comfort, but shone no more. Suddenly, everything around him, the crowd and its evident unity, Thistlewood, Tidd and Davidson waving their arms on the hustings, the dank, dark houses all around, the church clock, the freezing air and even his trusty cart seemed futile. He thought of his innocent family in Portsea, and of the troubles to come, if Thistlewood's still undefined mission collapsed, and Ings, too sensed the breath of delirium, but his was as cold as a dungeon, and he knew no escape.

POLITICS

The crowd was calmed again by song until Harry Brunt arrived with Mrs Thistlewood's notebook. It was his father's respon-sibility to address the crowd, while the captain and his aide studied the report, and Tidd and Davidson stayed alert for approaching officers. Brunt searched in his pocket, but the poem he had so lovingly prepared had vanished! He looked down at the expectant crowd and saw nothing but a haze. His grandfather, in the grip of the tiger's claws, must have felt the same. The men were chanting his name.

"You can do it, pa!" said Harry, still on the platform behind him.

"Thank you, citizens!" began Brunt, but his voice could summon no strength. "My heart is too full of hope and fellowship to find the words I so fervently wish to speak!"

There were jocular shouts of "Speak up" and "It ain't rhyming, Thomas!" Instead of unnerving him, the mockery inflamed Brunt and spurred his confidence. The words seemed to come from nowhere, and they came out loud and clear.

"On behalf of Mr Thistlewood and the Executive Committee, I wish to thank you, citizens, for walking so far on this cold winter's day. We welcome you all to the historic site where in 1381, the peasants' leader, Wat Tyler was slaughtered by officers of King Richard, and where only four months ago, under my own eyes and those of many of you, the tyrants arrested an innocent friend of the people. Today, once again, citizens, history will be made in Smithfield Square, and this time, its spokesman will be Arthur Thistlewood!"

The applause grew, but Brunt waved his arms; he had not quite finished.

"Fellow citizens," he said. "I hope these few words make as much sense as my poem on the same theme that has gone missing today. If anyone finds it, they might deliver it, with my regards, to Mrs Carlile at 55, Fleet Street. Thank you."

The cheers swelled again, as Thistlewood took the platform, holding his wife's notebook high.

"Citizens," he began. "I shall not keep you waiting a moment longer than necessary, neither in today's biting frost, nor in the poverty into which a debauched government has driven our families. The committee's policy of reform will be inspired by your needs and by your response to the Home Department's plans, whatever shape they may take. Are you ready now to hear what they have to say to us?"

"Aye!" came the thunderous, exhilarating reply.

Deep inside Thistlewood was like a child, made giddy when his kite flies high. He did not suppress the feeling, but allowed it to flourish and provide the strength to fulfil his burning duty. He looked round at the expectant faces and beamed with pride and hope.

"And when we know the worst, how will My Lord Sidmouth and his flunkies stop us?"

The round of laughter was followed by a blast, as a musket was fired into the air. Thistlewood shook his head grimly.

"Hold your fire!" called Tidd.

"Keep the peace!" called Davidson "In the name of those who died at Manchester!"

"Good citizens of London," continued Thistlewood, "now is no time for violence. Listen carefully, then have your say, and we shall prepare our response according to your will."

The news was brief and explicit. In six new Acts of Parliament, the Home Secretary proposed to increase the restraints on political and religious activity. A new tax on the radical press would make political pamphlets unaffordable to the majority, while trials for sedition and blasphemy would be speeded through the system to limit the abuse of publicity.

When he had finished, he looked out into the silence, and every man looked back at him, waiting, in his own way, for salvation, each certain that somehow, Arthur Thistlewood would produce it. Bewildered and disappointed though he was, Thistlewood felt as responsible for these few hundred men as Farmer John had for the tenants at Gautby. He looked around, still hoping for some response to the outrage he had just described, but not a single word came.

"My friends and brothers," he continued. "We must re-member that these proposals are not yet Acts of Parliament. However, as you know, the Opposition is too weak to stop them becoming law. That task must fall to every one of us. The committee will consider action on your behalf, but we cannot proceed without your ideas. Now, who has something to say?"

Michael O'Flynn, labourer from Vauxhall wondered if Mr Thistlewood knew what time My Lord Castlereagh would ride out of Westminster today, and by which route, because he had a bullet for his head.

Thistlewood replied that wanton assassination would not help the cause of reform. While Castlereagh's decisions in the past had resulted in the deaths of many Irishmen, as Foreign Secretary, he was not responsible, either for the massacre in Manchester, or for the proposed new laws.

There were angry hisses and another musket blast. Thistle-wood threw a loaded glance at Davidson, who, at once, began to sing. The crowd joined his sonorous voice.

Amazing grace! How sweet the sound
That saved a wretch like me!

When the song had calmed the crowd, Thistlewood asked again for ideas or questions. James Fullwell, anchor-smith of Southwark said that most of his friends had lost infants or old folk since the cold weather set in, and they would do anything for an honest day's pay. Could any gentleman on the hustings offer practical advice or suggestions? Will Davidson suggested Mr Fullwell put his faith in God and all true patriots of Great Britain. With the committee's help, liberation was at hand.

There were cheers, and when no further questions fol-lowed, Thistlewood thanked the men for their attendance and urged them to return peacefully to their homes. The Meeting ended with a round of *Should Auld Acquaintance be Forgot,* and the men filed peacefully away. A few lingered, eager to shake Thistlewood's hand, while one of the Deptford dockers complained to Edwards that their wives' stitching had been pointless.

"Save your stones," replied Edwards, "We are not finished yet."

The Ram Tavern, Smithfield

"I suppose about three hundred turned out," said Thistlewood at the Ram, as he and Edwards enjoyed Jeremy Bentham's breakfast at last, "but apart from Davidson's minor tussle at Newgate, His Majesty's gutterpups showed no interest whatsoever."

"Sidmouth needs the press to report his glory at Westminster," replied Edwards. He ignored us because he can't afford another Peterloo. If we want to provoke them, we'll need to think again."

"Provocation," said Thistlewood, "is not my principal concern. The people deserve a say in how Britain is run, but they have no fire! Instead of offering opinions we can work with, they repeated the same old complaints, as if we're some divine oracle, capable of instant solutions. Are my blood and bones not plagued by the same hunger and the same desperation as theirs?"

"The people do not have your insight, Arthur, nor your passion and your innate capacity to inspire others," said Edwards. "They're powerless, and they crave leadership. The only man in England who can help them is you."

"You're not suggesting we act on the people's behalf?" asked Thistlewood.

"As your aide, Arthur, that's exactly what I advise," replied Edwards. "Your committee is ready for action."

"And a captain must lead," said Thistlewood.

"And when reasonable argument fails", said Edwards, "what other means do we have?"

His voice was as cold as the ocean floor. He filled Thistlewood's glass.

"Drink to it. There must be no half-measures."

"You're right," said Thistlewood, raising his glass. "Perhaps my sword has been paralyzed for too long."

"Indeed, Arthur, perhaps it has."

CHAPTER EIGHTEEN

Sunday, 12ᵗʰ December, 1819

INGS

New Fish Street

On the third Sunday in Advent, Ings and Brunt were making wax ends for the knives and daggers, a process that became necessary when Davidson cut himself, practising on a wilful piglet. As they twisted twine around the handles, Ings sighed.

"What's up?" asked Brunt.

"Thinking how my little ones must have growed since I saw them last."

"They're lucky to be out of London!" said Brunt.

"It's alright for you to say that," muttered Ings, "with a son beside you day and night."

"And another one I ain't seen in a year, and my Molly in Derby" said Brunt. "Just imagine Davidson, with his baby took across the Atlantic!"

"Will's not been left all alone, though, has he?" said Ings.

"Cheer up Jimmy!" said Brunt. "What are a few months' separation, compared with the suffering at St Peter's Field?"

"That's rich, coming from you," said Ings, "who wasn't in a hundred miles of Manchester!"

Brunt thought it a haughty response, but said no more, and went to the fire to check the pan. Too much heat and the mixture might flare up and scald them, while too little and the wax would spread unevenly.

Planning was still in its early stages, but the campaign had two fixed intentions; to hurt no innocent bystanders and to separate His Majesty's Cabinet, first and foremost, Sidmouth and, the Irish membership had insisted, Castlereagh, from their heads. Those items would subsequently be mounted for public display, and those members of the committee, selected to perform the dynamic action, required specialist training to make a tidy cut. An invaluable consultant, James Ings supervised the training. As resident armoury manager, he also coordinated all works related to the offensive and its immediate aftermath, from the production of spikes to Edwards's revived experiments with combustibles.

A long-ago kiln injury had rendered Edwards's hands unreliable with knives, or so he said, but everyone else learnt how to make a quick, clean cut along the throat. Ings began the training with dead cats and dogs, of which the lads found most, while out scavenging for iron. When the skinny carcasses stank and brought flees and worms into the house, Edwards took to sending Brunt and Tidd up to Smithfield with the butcher's cart. The first time they returned with half a dozen tied rabbits, afterwards it was usually a live hog or a sheep. It would be exactly the same process with the tyrants, Ings advised, and the committee must expect their Ludships to struggle and squeal, just the same. At fifty, Lord Wellington was still likely to put up a fight; he supposed, but the rest had less muscle between them than a snowman.

When the wax was sufficiently heated, Ings gave Brunt a cloth to hold the pan steady, while, one after the other, he gripped the blades and plunged the handles into the hot pan. The fire crackled with tiny explosions at every spillage. Otherwise, apart from the refrains of Mrs Brunt's canary (which also resided in New Fish Street), they continued working in silence until Brunt hurried away to his correspondence meeting with Mrs T.

Alone at last, Ings covered the hot pan, went to his private cupboard and fetched, from behind his haversack, the little package he had longed, all morning, to open.

It was one of five items, each wrapped in brown paper, contained in a parcel that Celia had sent to his former address and Ings had collected from Mrs Carlile at the end of November. The contents were numbered one to five, with an instruction from Celia to open one on each of the four Sundays of Advent, and the fifth on Christmas Day. When the first Sunday came, and Ings had opened his first packet, his fingers were out of control. Inside, wrapped in muslin, was a real Hampshire pine-cone. It smelt of the woods, and there was a message from his son.

> Dearest Pa,
>
> *On this first Sunday in Advent, please know that your family hopes to be reunited soon. Ma says to tell you that Thirza is learning to make pastry and has good cool hands. I remain, in hope, your sincere and only son, William Stone Ings.*

The package for the Second Advent Sunday, came from Annie, who had stitched her numbers for him, ever so neat on flannel, and wrote a message in ink.

> Dearest Pa,
>
> *On this second Sunday in Advent, please know that your family remembers you every day and loves you. Ma*

said to tell you Billy's voice is dropping fast. Yours in hope
and love, from your own, sincere daughter, Celia-Ann
Ings the second.

On this third Advent Sunday, when Ings opened his third
packet, he reached for the letter first, and recited it to his principal companion at the time, the canary. (The name Lottie had
been dismissed for its royal connections, and since Brunt could
offer no proof that the bird was female, the name Boney had
been selected in honour of the French general.)

Dearest Pa,
(wrote Thirza's pencil, in straight, childish letters)

On this third Sunday in Advent, I wish you joy in
whatever you do down London. Ma said to tell you I
helped Aunt Lizzie with the Christmas pud and we hid
a farthing in it for the lucky one to find on Christmas
Day.

In hope, love and joy, I am Yours Most Sincerely,

Thirza Ings.

The packet contained, wrapped in muslin, a curl of his
little girl's brown hair, tied with a ribbon, exactly the colour
of Thirza's eyes. Ings decided to carry them next to his heart,
but he showed them to Boney first, and then, to overcome the
threat of tears, he sang the song about *Widdicombe Fair*, and
was soon fit to return to work.

The canary was still singing, when Ings heard loud banging
at the outside door. There was no code in the banging, and he
tried to ignore it, but the noise persisted, and it upset Boney,

who began to squawk. Quickly, Ings wiped his hands, covered the hot pan, locked the knives away, ensured there was neither blood nor weapon about his person and went to investigate.

In all his life, Ings had never seen such a vision of indignation as stood on the doorstep that Sunday. A small, dark-haired woman, not long out of her prettiest days, she had a narrow, drawn face beneath a yellow hat. She was thin as a stick, but her belly was unmistakably swollen. Seeing no pity on the country fellow's face, she tried one of those appealing smiles that turn men's heads. Ings, usually susceptible to such tricks, was not impressed.

"Good Day Madam," he said. "Please tell me, with all your violent knocking, what you are so desperate to say."

"Is my husband at home?" she asked.

At first, Ings presumed that Mrs Brunt had returned from Derby. He thought how young she looked to have a strapping son like Harry, and an older one besides, and wondered whether Brunt would be alarmed or pleased that a third was on its way.

"There's nobody home but me and my canary," he said.

"Oh," said the woman, with a frown.

Ings reckoned the real Mrs Brunt would have responded differently to the mention of the canary. Perhaps young Hale had a clandestine wife. He asked the woman for her husband's name. The reply was shocking.

"George Edwards," she said tearfully. "My Georgie! You must find him!"

Ings had never been equipped for weeping females. He knew that whoever the woman was, there would be trouble if he gave out any information. He offered to take note of the lady's name and address, which he would pass on, should anyone with the name Edwards come by.

"I know my husband lives here. I've seen his comings and goings," she said, cocking her head to one side, like a hen. "Tell him his girl has come home. She ain't got no address but this, and she'll stand on the north-east corner of London Bridge until seven o'clock, at which time precisely, she'll throw herself and their unborn child into the river!"

Ings tried to persuade the young woman that although life has a habit of being awkward, it is a more certain arrangement than death. Before the sentence was finished, she had walked off with more flounce, he thought, than despondency. It was strictly forbidden to leave the house empty, but the young woman's threat weighed heavily on his conscience. He pulled the wax pan and his tater from the fire, checked Boney's water and found a crust for the bird to tussle with, locked everything that needed to be locked, pulled on his boots and left the house for the first time in weeks. Observing that despite its proximity to Billingsgate, the air on New Fish Street smelt exceptionally sweet – it resembled nothing so much as jasmine - Ings set off in search of George Edwards.

Saturday, 18th December, 1819

EDWARDS

Ranelagh Place, Pimlico, London

Edwards poured himself a gin, sat on his new yellow settee and admired his view. Simply by looking through the large south-facing window, he could forget the clamour of town and enjoy the market garden, which, though plain in winter, could always be relied upon to ignite an artist's imagination. There was delight in the patterns of frost, dripping infinitely slowly from thin, gnarled branches, in the anxious flutter of birds or, sometimes, in the toil of a muscular labourer, digging the un-forgiving clay. Indoors, the polished floors, the fine trimmings and furnishings were unblemished by the mucky business of earning a living. Edwards's activities, the preparation for the luxurious life he deserved, were no better or worse, he surmised, than the offences committed by the half-wits who inherit their wealth without a single day's effort.

His principal headache had been Tilly's enquiring mind. Somehow, she had located his operational base, and although she understood never to enquire about his business affairs, Tilly was mischievous, and she was stupid. Unless he managed her wisely, she would devastate his plans. Edwards could not stomach the prospect of another murder, nor of entrusting anyone else with the task. On Monday, therefore, during the usual business at Bow Street, "Henry Ward" explained to the chief clerk that he needed another advance and a special favour. On Tuesday morning, he visited Tilly. Correct in the assumption that she had been abandoned by the Admiral and the lease on Johnson's Court was out, Edwards swore to a change of heart and to his undying devotion to Tilly and the forthcoming infant. On Tuesday afternoon, he rented a house in St John's Street, Clerkenwell, and on Wednesday, by special licence, Miss Matilda Buck became Mrs George Edwards.

On Thursday, Tilly's mother, Harriot Parker, a native of County Kerry, appeared at the new premises. Mrs Parker was not alone. Three-year-old Hattie was a tiny replica of Mrs G, and Edwards could scarcely deny her as his own. There were two further infants; the progeny, Mrs Parker explained, of the nephew she lost at Waterloo. The new Mrs Edwards was happy to accept her husband's terms that Mrs G must never be informed of the new household, and that enquiries by his mother-in-law about his trade and income should be explained, if at all, by his success at model making and printing, and inheritances from a Bavarian cousin and the celebrated artist, Cornelius Thwaite.

Despite the extra expense, the arrival of Mrs Parker was a blessing. Clean, competent and a committed Catholic, she would keep a beady eye on Tilly, take little Hattie regularly to St Etheldreda's and be content to leave George Edwards in peace.

Still, his debts had increased and the unexpected expense of a family meant that the regular payments would be swallowed by the bank with little left for the pleasures in life. More than ever, Edwards needed the refuge of Ranelagh Place, of which none of his associates knew and certainly not his family. Since Tilly could not be relied upon to ignore the activities at New Fish Street, that property had become an encumbrance. With all London ready to turn a blind eye for a little rent, he would easily find somewhere else to store the weapons. On the other hand, Thistlewood's gang must start fending for itself. Why waste money on fellows who were already dancing to his tune as eagerly as puppets at Covent Garden?

Edwards sipped his gin and turned to admire the figurine of Susan Thistlewood, which he had decorated in the style of a Countess, and which stood on top of an inlaid cabinet. He put down his glass and lifted his one true angel, caressed the elegant neck with his fore-finger, brushed his thumb slowly across her breast, closed his eyes and breathed in the fullness of the life he desired.

Wednesday, 22ⁿᵈ December, 1819

BRUNT /TIDD

New Fish Street

Two particular responsibilities dominated Tom Brunt's time and attention; helping Mr Edwards with his experiments and assisting Mrs Thistlewood with clerical duties. There had been no time to miss Molly, and if he thought about his wife at all, it was with gratitude that the relations in Derby were dependable, and he had his peace in these important times. Edwards seemed pleased by his fearlessness with fire, and Mrs T had loaned him a thick novel by Walter Scott to read with Harry at night. She also advised on the new stanzas for Brunt's personal protest at the tyrants' decision to ramp up stamp duty and clamp political opinion. Mrs Carlile had promised, when Mr Brunt had finished the poem to his satisfaction, to consider it for *The Republican* (*Sherwin's Weekly* having closed after Peterloo), although very few columns remained available before the Six Acts became law, when the new journal seemed likely to perish, too.

On Wednesday morning, when he joined Thistlewood to inspect the armoury, Edwards explained that the house on New Fish Street was being watched and must be vacated at once. Brunt wondered where he and Harry would sleep at night. He could not depend on Tidd, whose warmth had faltered since the misunderstanding with Eliza, and who had aligned himself closely to Davidson.

Harry was dispatched to investigate Fox Court and returned with good news; the only changes were a damp smell in the air, a layer of dust and a few extra spiders. Mrs Rogers, Harry reported, was soaked in liquor, seemed not to have noticed the Brunts' absence and made no awkward enquiries about rent.

While Harry carried his drum, his rucksack and the canary's cage back to Holborn, Edwards, Hale and Ings dismantled Edwards's printing press. Julian Thistlewood and Abraham Lane-Davidson were on look-out duty, and when they gave the nod, the components were lifted on to the butcher's cart, covered over and transported by Ings to Mrs. Edwards's home in Clerkenwell. The more delicate duty of moving all the weapons was entrusted to Brunt and Tidd. When Brunt proposed a re-enactment of the barrel trick, Tidd was glad of an opportunity to spend time with his old partner, especially if they were to be neighbours again and, quite possibly, colleagues. Brunt reminded him that, with the weather cooler, there would be less of a stink and no flies to speak of, and Tidd replied that he was more than amenable.

Brunt's old friends at Billingsgate were pleased to help again, and everything ran smoothly until the third and most perilous trip. The flannel cartridges were stowed at the bottom of the cart, beneath the barrels, which were stuffed full of pike handles, all topped with a thin camouflage of seasonal fish.

On Newgate Street, a constable emerging suddenly from the Bull's Head gave them a fright when he ordered them to halt.

"I am investigating the theft of domestic gates and railings" he said, "of which there has recently been a spate in these parts."

The pompous tone irritated Tidd and Brunt almost as much as the prospect of discovery frightened them, but they maintained expressions pertinent to a pair of carefree fish-mongers.

"While you've been going about your business," the constable continued, "'Ave you seen any suspicious behaviour, though how a willan can profit off old iron, when no-one's buying it no more, is a mystery to me."

"We ain't seen nuffink," said Tidd, in a fair attempt at a London drawl, 'ave we Bert?"

"No," said Brunt, moving his head to indicate the back of the cart. "Treat the wife, officer. Take a mackerel home."

"'Ere, 'ave two big 'uns!" added Tidd, wisely turning to make the selection himself.

"Thank you, I accept!" said the constable, "and I wish you gentlemen a prosperous onward journey!"

By late afternoon, the weapon store had been resurrected in the old workshop at Fox Court, and the alliance of the boot-makers was fully restored. Eliza Tidd cooked a feast of fish and opined that Mr Brunt's apprentice looked chubbier since they'd been gorging at someone else's expense. The Tidd family had not been indulged by no-one, she continued, Mr Ings and Joe must live with the Brunts, and none of them must expect her husband to bail them out of misery.

Later, as Hale and Ings settled on their mat behind a curtain in the store-room, Brunt and Harry rested in the old cot and read a chapter of Walter Scott. When Brunt had blown out the candle, he whispered that until they could find paid work, he would need to visit the pawn shop. He was hoping very much not to take Harry's drum. There was a long pause before Harry spoke.

"Tidds have got a gilded Bible," he said, with a tone. "I know because I swore on it".

"What did you swear?"

"If I told you, I'd be breaking an oath, wouldn't I?"

Brunt replied the boy was too clever for his own good.

"You should see them pages glitter, pa, "whispered Harry. "Like the chains round a Turkish trollop's ankles."

"Where did you see a Turkish trollop's ankles?"

"Nowhere."

"Don't lie to me, Harry Brunt!"

"In a book shop down Wych Street. Julian showed me. Full of trollops, not just from Turkey. You should see them! Not a stitch on 'em but bells and glittering chains!"

Brunt considered his response and then said, "Don't you go anywhere near that Bible, Harry!"

"Five pound the trollop book cost," continued Harry, "Think what you'd fetch for that Bible! We could share it out, fair and square."

"I would rather sell my fingers one by one than take a single button from my dearest friend and partner," whispered Brunt.

"Who is there, pa, wants to buy your fingers?"

Thursday, 23rd December, 1819

BRUNT

Streets of London

On Thursday morning, as Brunt strolled down Fetter Lane, he filled his mind with Molly's best dumplings, piled high on plates and steaming beside chunks of boiled bacon and with grandpa's favourite, the rabbit pie they always had on Saturdays with mash.

At the print shop on Fleet Street, Mrs Carlile was surrounded by paper and mewling infants, but when Brunt offered his new poem to peruse in her own time, she said it would be a pleasure. He crossed to the pawn shop on the corner and produced, from his sack, the dress, the shawl and the bonnet that Molly wore on the day they met. As he shook the items out for display, Brunt sighed at the memory, admitted they were musty and pledged the lot, without argument, for two shillings and sixpence.

As he walked back up Fetter Lane, the coins in his pocket, the delivery of his poem, the triumph of the fake fishmongers and the restoration of his home at Fox Court made an exhilarating combination. As he passed the Moravian chapel, his joy inspired a new idea, perhaps his best since the herrings, and when he turned on to Grays Inn Lane, instead of going straight home, Brunt continued up to the Military Training School. Two days before Christmas, the premises would be almost empty.

Military Academy, Grays Inn Lane

A labourer, not much older than Harry, was busily scraping ice off the bunk-house windows. Brunt wished him warmth in his hands and joy in his work. When the lad turned to return the greeting, Brunt revealed that contrary to appearances, he was a surveyor, sent under cover. As a result of widespread activity by radicals, he explained, there was a plan to increase security at all defence establishments. It was his responsibility to inspect the Training School and recommend improvements. The labourer seemed indifferent until Brunt gave up his sixpence, upon which the lad shrugged and unlocked the bunk-house door. The lad must have gone straight off to report the incident because a few moments later, Brunt was confronted by a sneering non-commissioned officer, who demanded to know why he had not been informed of the visit. Brunt, who had experience of precisely such fellows in France, saw that this one was half cut.

"I should have thought that was obvious. It's orders! With all the spies and agents operating these days, any warning could prejudice my findings, and I must be allowed to proceed without impediment."

The silly young man saluted and returned to his liquor and his card game. In no time, Brunt had memorized the layout of the Military Training School. He had pocketed a bundle of keys and identified a dozen useful sources. He knew which of Edwards's combustibles would be most suitable for which obstacles and even made plans for the pair of canons in the garden. Walking back down Grays Inn Lane, it pleased Brunt to imagine the praise that would be heaped upon him at tonight's meeting.

Brooke's Market / Fox Court

During Brunt's private reconnaissance, George Edwards had taken a cab to Grays Inn Lane in order to inspect the weapon store, now restored at Fox Court. Arriving early, he decided to investigate Brooke's Market. The ironmonger's store looked interesting, but the owner's gaunt, grey dog sprawling beside the stove, unnerved him, as it raised its dark, inquisitive eyes and snarled. With a sharp word from its owner, the dog slumped back to its reverie, and Edwards explained that he was an agent, enquiring after additions to a client's collection of historic pistols. The ironmonger's eyes lit up.

Half an hour later, after recommending a more organized layout for the weapon store, Edwards gave Brunt half a crown to buy a pair of pistols he had seen in the market. He had not purchased them himself for lack of a big enough sack, in which to conceal them. The ironmonger would be a discreet ally, and the subject of similar opportunities would be discussed at The White Hart, where Mr Hobbs had agreed, by special arrangement, to accommodate a meeting.

"Can I come?" asked Harry Brunt. "I'm practically one of the men."

"Certainly not!" retorted Brunt.

"I bet Joe Hale's allowed!" protested Harry.

"Joe's not in the committee neither, so he'll stay here and finish arranging the store."

"I'll help Joe, then."

"No," said Brunt. "You may be bright as a button, Harry Brunt, but you're still only thirteen."

"In that case, give us another candle, so I can read my book instead of sitting alone in the dark while you all have fun".

"What book?" asked Brunt, mindful of the trollops.

"The novel Mrs T gave us."

"Good," said Brunt, "and let me remind you that far from having fun, we men are building a better world for cheeky blighters like you!"

"Yes, pa" said Harry. "Thank you."

Edwards gave the boy sixpence for knowing the importance of self-improvement and said Harry must burn as many candles as he liked, but not take them near the weapons, and buy more tomorrow at the market. Brunt would have preferred the sixpence for bread, but he kept that protest private and shooed smug Harry away.

White Hart, Brooke's Market

George Edwards had described his plan for a raid on Parliament in the new year which, in the absence of better suggestions, Thistlewood had promised to reconsider. For his plan to be effective, Edwards said, they needed at least two hundred men. Tidd, the deputy responsible for recruitment, disclosed that despite his best efforts, only thirty-seven men had so far pledged their names.

"If we find a way of promising anonymity," he said, "the numbers will increase tenfold."

"Why should we take all the risks" asked Ings, "and die for the sake of cowards?"

"Any man too frightened to give his name should forfeit his right to liberty and equality," added Davidson.

"Agreed!" said Ings. "

"Enough!" said Thistlewood. "If we go round, shouting that kind of slogan, we'll never attract new members."

Brunt seized his opportunity.

"I sympathize with Tiddy's recruitment problems," he said. "Indeed, I have a proposal that will alleviate it!

"Hallelujah!" said Thistlewood. "Out with it!"

"During a recent reconnoitre of the Military Training School," said Brunt, "I saw a room full of uniforms, and in my pocket are the keys that will take us to them. If those garments are requisitioned, fifty men disguised as soldiers, would suffice to take Parliament, isolate the tyrants and bring the plan to its fulfilment."

Thistlewood and Edwards looked at each other and could find no objection. Ings thought the plan worthy of a genius, while Davidson's approval depended, he said, on examination of finer points, especially the risk to innocent lives. Thistlewood agreed that details were open for discussion, but for the moment, he was happy to congratulate Tom Brunt on a potentially first-class idea.

Fox Court, Brooke's Market

Returning from the meeting, Brunt and Ings climbed the staircase in high spirits. A light was burning in the workshop, where Joe Hale was still busy rearranging the new armoury. He stiffened when he saw them because he had prepared a speech.

"I wish I had beer in my belly and a merry grin on my chops like you two," he said, "but I have a trade to learn, and no political campaign is about to stop that. Mr Brunt, I should like to know your plans for my future."

"Not now, Joe" said Brunt.

"That's not all!" said Hale. "The workshop's far too cramped; there's scarcely room for the tools of my trade, let alone the mat I have to sleep on beside Mr Ings."

Brunt chuckled and said it was as well Ings wasn't getting stout on his wife's pies.

"Where's Harry?" asked Hale suddenly.

"Reading his book," replied Brunt.

"No, he's not." said Hale. "He went off to find you."

"You let him go?" asked Brunt.

"There was no stopping him!" replied Hale.

Brunt hurried to the back room. There was a note on the pillow.

Dear Pa,

I am going to see ma's alright. Somebody's got to, and you're too busy. I took the book, the blue rug and the sixpence Mr E gave me.

Don't worry, Pa. I only used a bit of the candle.

I am Yours Faithfully,

Harold Moreton Brunt

DAVIDSON

Elliot's Row, Lords Old Cricket Ground, St Marylebone

On Thursday night, while Will Davidson attended the meeting at the White Hart, his wife, searching for stockings that might fit three-year-old John, came across an old blunderbuss. As she fumbled at the back of the cupboard, she felt the cold metal against her fingertips. She tore at the softer contents of the cupboard, and when she saw the unmistakable form of a gun, her heart missed a beat. The barrel was long and it flared. In horror, she pushed the clothes back over it, shut the cupboard and leaned hard against the door, as if to protect her memory and her sleeping boys from what she had seen.

Sarah Davidson knew vaguely about her husband's mission. She had asked to be kept ignorant, so that she must tell no lies when the time came for her baby to be returned from Jamaica. She had not attended the breakfast arranged by her husband at Scotch Arms, and she had continued to stay away from the other families. When Will hosted meetings at Elliot's Row, she always took the children for a walk or visited their friends from Sunday School. She opposed Will's argument that if they lived closer to the other committee members, he could spend less time wearing out his shoes and more at home with the children. In short, she preferred to conduct her life as if her husband were not a political activist. The discovery of a gun was clear evidence that her husband's plans included violence, and Sarah Davidson could no longer hide from the truth.

When he fell on to the mat beside her, Sarah knew from his slowness how tired her husband was, and from his breath that he had been drinking, but she decided to disclose her find at once.

"It's an investment," explained Davidson. "I shall sell it, and we shall have food for three months, my sweet, and you shall have shoes again. There's no need to worry."

Sarah was not satisfied.

"Where did you get it?" she asked, "and why, when we're so desperate, have you not sold it already?"

"You shouldn't be troubled with any of this," said Davidson, who was weary after the walk from Brooke's Market and longed for sleep.

Sarah sat up, reaching for her fine brown shawl, knitted a decade ago with Dartmoor wool and darned a dozen times since.

"My father taught me that husbands must have their secrets," she said, "but the man I married is an enemy to deceit."

"Who has nonetheless respected your preference to know nothing," replied Davidson.

"I never expected a gun!" exclaimed Sarah. "Whatever the cost to my peace of mind, ignorance has become the worse option. Husband, the time has come to explain."

"Tomorrow morning?"

"Now."

Davidson rolled over on the mat and looked up at his wife. She was thinner than he had ever seen her, her usually soft, forgiving body as stiff as a beam, her eyes riven with fear of the unknown and the possible. Confronting his shame, Davidson sensed again the tears of his mother, the rage and disappointment of his father, when he abandoned the study of law.

"Now," said Sarah again.

"A few days ago," he began, "I bumped into Goldworthy, my old master. He and his colleague were struggling in Liverpool and thought they'd try their luck in London. Then, the colleague, a Mr Williamson, had a chance to sail to the Cape of Good Hope. He needed money for the deposit and supplies and for the journey. He offered the blunderbuss for a fiver, and promised that when it was cleaned and polished, it would fetch ten at auction."

"Where on God's earth did you find five pounds?" asked Susan.

"George Edwards bought the gun, passed it to me for cleaning and said I could return the money, when the item was sold. Unfortunately, it failed at auction, and he advised me to wait until New Year when the firearms market generally improves.

"We owe Mr Edwards five pounds?" asked Sarah in horror, "and the only means of repaying it is a useless old gun!"

"It's not useless! Did you not make a delicious pie on Sunday?"

"You shot those pigeons with a blunderbuss?" asked Sarah.

"I was testing it," said Davidson. "Oh smile, Sarah, smile! I shall sell the item tomorrow, if you wish, the boys shall eat beef for Christmas, and we shall sing together all day long."

He was smiling now and stroking her arm, but Sarah Davidson left their mat and pulled her shawl tightly around her shoulders. She had no intention of singing at Christmas, she said, or possibly ever again. She cursed herself for being so blinded by Will Davidson's good looks and fine brain that she had not seen how thoughtless he was and taken her boys back to Devon to the nice farmer who had courted her for months. For all Will's philosophy, his recitations and high and mighty moralizing, he understood nothing about family responsibility. He had embroiled her first-born, an innocent youth in his dangerous activities at goodness knows what cost to his future. Her youngest was taken far away to what life she could not imagine. They were starving, they had nothing, and Will had been tricked into an impossible debt by men he called his friends. Anyone who believed an old blunderbuss to be worth more than a few shillings was a fool. Her husband's failings had knocked all the joy and the spirit out of her, and she was going to sleep on the kitchen chair because she could no longer bear the presence of him or his ale-drenched breath.

CHAPTER NINETEEN

Friday, 24ᵗʰ December, 1819

THISTLEWOOD

Stanhope Street

With very few tavern landlords brave enough to welcome Arthur Thistlewood, his apartment had become the most frequent location for meetings, alternating with the homes of other committee members. The ragamuffins, who hovered in the area, believing themselves unnoticed, were undoubtedly policemen in disguise. Susan confounded them by ensuring that the rota was irregular and engaging less well-known members to distract the constables, shortly before the committee was expected and again, when proceedings finished.

Even when there were no formal meetings, the apartment on Stanhope Street was a hub of activity. Thistlewood trained the older lads in swordsmanship, discussed recruitment with Tidd, advised Edwards on the chemistry of explosions and compiled, with Davidson's assistance, complex texts for the new constitution. Mrs Thistlewood coordinated donations, assisted Brunt with communications to the membership and baked endless supplies of biscuits. Julian's sketch book was rarely opened. Instead, he kept neat records of the streets from which iron railings and the like were taken. When his help was not required elsewhere, the lad challenged himself with a private study from his school-books of the tactics of Julius Caesar.

Tidd had requested a Friday meeting for all members to be held at the Pontefract Castle in St Marylebone, which was always packed at Christmas. Of the committee, only Will Davidson, who lived locally, was known, and not in any political context. Since no other activity had been planned during the holiday, the Thistlewood family found itself, on Christmas Eve morning, for once, alone.

Arthur stoked the fire, while his wife fixed small candles to the sprigs of holly she had foraged. When she suggested brightening the mood with a game or a song, there was a strained silence until Julian said, "Aunt Mary told me you can play the spoons."

"Did she now?" replied Arthur.

"She said the Horsington grandfather was famous for it, and he taught you."

"So he did," said Arthur, "not today."

"When?"

"When we have reason to make merry," replied Arthur.

"It's Christmas Arthur," said Susan, "and there is nobody here but your family. Is that not reason enough?"

"Tell us about your adventures, pa, when you dodged the bows and arrows on the beach at Haiti."

Arthur looked at his son with solemn eyes and said there would be better grounds for celebration when the operation was done.

"What operation, papa and when will it be?" asked Julian.

Susan had asked herself the same questions on an hourly basis for weeks. If ever she mentioned it, Arthur would always that say he was not sure, but he sensed, and George agreed, that an opportunity would arise soon.

"I cannot answer you now, Julian," Arthur replied, "but it would certainly please me to hear your account of the Gallic Wars."

Susan understood that her stepson's preoccupation with Caesar was a struggle, undertaken solely to please his father. A stammered recitation would impose an unnecessary strain on a boy, whose heart yearned for Christmas.

"Come! said Susan. "Let us abandon strategy for once and attempt something joyful!"

Try as they might, neither Arthur nor Julian nor even Susan Thistlewood could animate a feeling of joy, even at the birth, for which this date was set aside to celebrate.

DAVIDSON

Streets of London

On the morning of Christmas Eve, Will Davidson left his mat before the boys awoke and became the day's first customer for James Aldous, pawnbroker of Berwick Street. He pledged his precious tools and his trolley for thirteen shillings, the old blunderbuss for seven and his boots for one and six. He thought of going straight to the butcher's on Oxford Street for a cut of beef, but instead bought a currant bun against the clawing in his belly and walked down to the Scotch Arms in the hope of a fire and some manly conversation. The landlord, Mr Brown was alarmed by his feet, which were blue with cold, filthy and bleeding. He fetched warm water, spirit and rags and advised him to bind them well; Mr Davidson would not be the first or the last to lose the use of his feet this winter, if he failed to take care of them.

As he passed through the dingy alleys into the Strand, Davidson considered Edwards's reasoning in the matter of the blunderbuss. Why would he donate five pounds so that a remote acquaintance could sail to Africa? Edwards was generous, but he was not easily duped. Davidson could not recall him mentioning military service; perhaps he knew nothing about firearms, and Williamson had taken him for a fool. Whether or not George Edwards knew the gun was useless, why involve Davidson?

Tidd had once remarked on Edward's habit of under-mining any opinion expressed by the committee, especially Davidson. They had dismissed the habit as misplaced jealousy, but it did not explain the riddle of the gun. For the moment, Davidson's priority must be to retrieve the debt. With tuppence spent on the bun and the small beer, he needed to find three pounds, eighteen shillings and four pence. It might just as well be a king's ransom.

Williamson was due to sail from Deptford today aboard the Belle Alliance. If departure were delayed by the tide, there was a chance Davidson might catch the fellow and confront him. There would be a long, freezing walk to the dock, with frustration the most likely outcome. If he caught a chill on the road and died, who would look after his family? Was it better to do nothing and regret it forever more? Was there truly a chance that the price of guns would rise in the new year, as Edwards supposed? Then Davidson remembered that he had left the blunderbuss in Berwick Street, and he was not fit for that short journey, let alone a perilous walk to Deptford, with little hope of a result.

As he trudged along the Strand, Davidson tried to recall his favourite poems by Rabbie Burns and Rab Tannahill, the weaver poet, but even their words failed him. He was consid-ering which portion of the Bible might support him, when there was a tap on his shoulder.

"Good day, sir," said a small, well-dressed gentleman with a tall hat that reminded Davidson of his own which, in another life, had been spoilt by a bullet. Instead of averting his eyes as soon as he saw Davidson's face, the man smiled and asked for his name and what troubled him. Davidson confessed that he had a wife and five sons, with a baby taken away to Jamaica, and he could neither feed nor shod any of them. He was an educated man; a Sunday school teacher and a cabinet-maker of note, who had not found a day's work since August, and had been cheated of his last five pounds. The prospect of his family facing a barren Christmas was breaking his heart.

The stranger looked sympathetically at Will Davidson, gave him a ticket and asked him to continue to St Clements Church and go into the Crown and Anchor, where an officer of the Mendicity Society would be waiting on the first floor. There would be no tricks and no unpleasant surprises, only a few questions to answer and a form to write up, before his family's needs were met.

In a parlour above the ballroom of the Crown and Anchor, a spinster with white hair and watery blue eyes settled him by a roaring fire and gave him gingerbread and hot milk. For a moment, Davidson was transported to the afternoon parties at Lichfield, and he saw, starkly, how far he had fallen since those times. The spinster explained that the Society tried to identify individuals and families in most need. Sometimes they might be given a new home in the workhouse, but where a man was capable of work, he might be eligible for a loan to re-establish himself in paid employment. Should Mr Davidson take such a path, he must understand that if were discovered begging in London again, he would be punished, perhaps by a public whipping or a prison sentence. Davidson decided against correcting a point of law and replied only that he had not been begging today, had never begged in his life and never expected to. The spinster only smiled and handed him a form, on which Davidson wrote out his name and address, his family's names, his qualifications and his means of earning a living, should his boots and his equipment be restored.

At two o'clock on Christmas Eve, when Will Davidson walked on to the Strand again, the air was so cold that he that could see the puffs of his breath, but his heart was lighter and his pocket heavier by two pounds, four shillings and sixpence. He walked to Berwick Street, where Mr Aldous returned the boots, the tool box and the trolley. The blunderbuss he would leave with the pawnbroker, Davidson decided, rather than take it home to his sensitive wife. He walked down to Oxford Street and had soon filled his trolley with firewood, a new handle for the broken pan and sweetmeats for the boys. At the butcher's, he met the cowman, Tom Hyden, who gave him a left-over can of cream and accompanied him to the meeting. They strolled through Gee's Court, already milling with Irishmen, some heading south to get a good seat at St Patrick's for Mass and some, like themselves, into The Pontefract Castle.

The landlady knew Will Davidson and offered, if he treated her customers to *Come, thou Long-awaited Jesus*, to keep his tool trolley behind lock and key. When Hyden offered to sing along too, she filled their pots with free beer and was rewarded by half a dozen Christmas carols, until Arthur Thistlewood slipped, unnoticed, into the tavern with Edwards and summoned them away.

INGS

Fox Court, Holborn

On Christmas Eve, Ings submitted to melancholia. On the previous Sunday, he had opened his fourth Advent package. There was no letter, but a picture, evidently in the hand of their youngest, sweet, curly-topped Emeline. She had drawn the whole family, including his absent self, with the wavy sea behind and a great sailing ship. Above the drawing were seven words in childish disarray:

To Pa, H o p e L o v e J o y P e e s E m e l i n e

Ings had almost wept, but in keeping with the committee's resolution, endeavoured, as he broke his daily bread with Brunt and Hale, to keep his private troubles to himself. Since moving to Fox Court, Ings had suffered less with the loneliness and felt quite well, despite the hunger, the cramped conditions and his close proximity, night and day, to instruments of death.

That evening, Brunt took the coach to his wife and son in Derby, Hale went off to his mother in St Giles, and Ings was alone again with the canary. Boney must have soaked up his despair, because he did not sing a note all afternoon.

When Tidd arrived, Ings was studying Emeline's letter. He looked up and explained that neither he nor Brunt would attend.

"Thomas has gone to his wife and sons in Derby," he explained. "He pledged Molly's wedding skirt to pay for the passage, which indicates a serious mission."

Tidd scowled. "What have you pledged," he asked, "for the journey to Hampshire?"

"My family must do without me," replied Ings, curbing his indignation. "If you want the truth, Tiddy, I am unwell this evening, and the meeting will succeed better without me."

Tidd's good eye fell on Ings's letter. He turned it round with those long fingers of his and studied the portraits and the writing. He was not without a heart.

"If it's gentle company you're in need of, Jimmy, my wife and daughter will be sympathetic."

As he turned to leave, Tidd took the flask from his breeches pocket, placed it on the table. If a taste of Edwards's best gin would make Jimmy more resolute, he said, they might see him later at the Pontefract Castle.

Ings would not have been more surprised, if Tidd had turned into a goblin. In all their adventures and confidences on the journey to Manchester, he had never seen the tender side of his friend's nature. What powerful magic Emeline's picture must contain! Ings resigned to keep it, with Annie's embroidered flannel and the lock of Thirza's hair, and, when the time came, to be buried with them.

Half an hour later, with even the canary silent, Ings opened the flask and sniffed. The last gin he had tasted was Philbin's. He took a swig now for his lost Irish friend, a swig for each of the children, another for Celia and old Ma and Pa Ings and Lizzie, and finally, for sweet Margaret. Then James Ings knew nothing until a distant bell woke him to the dawn of Christmas Day.

THE PONTEFRACT CASTLE

Wigmore Street, London

Tidd's principal reason for proposing the Pontefract Castle Tavern was recruitment. A more productive source than the population at large, the local Irish population would, he argued, come out in full on Christmas Eve. In the inevitably festive crowd, nobody would suspect that a notorious English radical and his gang were mingling there.

Music and customers were spilling on to the frosty courtyard, and when Davidson asked the landlady if he and a few peace-loving English friends might occupy a quieter room upstairs, there was no reason to object, so long as they purchased some drinks and he promised to sing again later.

Less than twenty members, including Tom Hyden, made the journey to the Castle. Given the particular date and the absence of two committee members, Thistlewood considered the number reasonable. With a guard at the door and all formalities completed, he said that he would reveal the exciting objectives so far developed by the committee, but in the first instance, wished to air his reservations about the plan for a raid on Parliament. The new Executive Committee which would replace Lord Liverpool's cabinet was passionate in its intent, but for obvious reasons, lacked know-how, and the country would not thrive without the contributions of middle-ranking and junior civil servant, the higher echelons being largely disposable.

"To avoid the slaughter of useful men and innocent bystanders," said Thistlewood, "I strongly advise against the raid. Instead, I suggest that we identify an occasion when the eagles of destruction are assembled alone."

"It's not impossible," said Edwards, who had been obliged, some days earlier, to accept Thistlewood's veto. "Just like our own committee, Ministers are constantly in contact, even when Parliament is not sitting."

"What we need," said Davidson, "is notice of some private meeting, where access is easier than to the fortresses at Westminster or the clubs of Pall Mall.

"A dance, perhaps, or some other seasonal occasion?" suggested Tidd.

"No," replied Thistlewood, "We can presume the wives to be faultless, since most were provided in financial transactions by their fathers."

"Here, here!" said Davidson.

"It's an established fact," said Edwards, "that Ministers meet every week for a working dinner. That might provide our best opportunity."

"Aye" said Tidd, "well said, Edwards."

"We'd have to act quickly" added Thistlewood. "There are plenty in Westminster ready to fill the tyrants' places, unless we restore a proper order first."

Since nobody in the room had grounds to reject the idea or could suggest an alternative, the plan was put aside for formal agreement by the full committee.

There was a pause for pots to be filled with ale (a gift, Edwards explained, from Bavaria). Then Thistlewood asked for quiet while he outlined the provisional plans drawn up by himself, Edwards and Davidson.

1. Until the first annual election, a Provisional Government would be based at Mansion House, protected by the canons observed lately by Mr Brunt at the Military Training School on Grays Inn Lane and at the Royal Artillery Ground at Bunhill Row.
2. A provisional constitution on the Saxon model was being drafted by Will Davidson, based on his study of Scottish and English law and particularly his knowledge of the Magna Carta.
3. George Edwards was planning the redistribution of wealth, although details were not forthcoming until a raid on the Bank of England revealed the secrets of the Treasury.
4. Arthur Thistlewood would oversee the equal division of land on Spencean principles. Again, details were unavailable until records of land and property-ownership had been liberated from Chancery.
5. Richard Tidd, with proper support from the civil service, would be responsible for security and defence, similarly, Brunt for national employment and Ings for trade.

6. To service the new Executive Committee, a special unit, drawn from the wider membership, would oversee other sectors of the economy, for instance, agriculture, fishing, distribution and transport, health, education, science, manufacture, building and foreign affairs."

The applause was enthusiastic, and the men banged their pots on the table until Thistlewood commanded them to hush and offer any objections or questions. Tidd was anxious to know what plans were afoot for the royal family.

It was a complex matter, Thistlewood told him. As long as they stopped draining the resources of state, those people were of no consequence. A king was no more responsible for the circumstance of his birth than any man in this room and no less responsible for his own behaviour. However, note must be taken of the constitutional role. The old King's health was deteriorating rapidly, and if the current system survived his death, a traditional election would be called and a new Cabinet formed. Further, the Regent's estranged wife had expressed allegiance for the radical cause. She was popular with the people and it would be foolish to disregard Caroline if she returned to England to see the King, who, after all, was her uncle and guardian, or when, eventually, she became Queen.

These were decisions in waiting, Thistlewood continued, but for the time being, he was less interested in a few pampered figureheads than in his plan for the purification of water.

"Clean water will put an end to the disease of drunkenness and all its social consequences. It will vastly improve health and transform the cities. In the first week of our ascendancy, a national competition will be launched and the engineer who most successfully designs such a machine will be rewarded with a wing of Windsor Castle.

"Bravo, Thistlewood!" called Tidd, "and if any royals remain, let's give 'em a life in service!"

"Let them clean grates!" said Davidson.

"Send 'em up the chimney!" cried Tidd.

Amid the softening of solemnity, the members; meeting was adjourned. Edwards chatted with Tidd for a while and bought a jug of ale for Davidson and Tom Hyden, who had offered to stay an hour or two longer at the Castle for recruitment purposes.

Too well-known to linger at the tavern, Thistlewood made his way back to Stanhope Street, pleased to devote an hour to clear thinking. He knew, of course, that achieving change in the government of an ancient state depended on more than an attack on a few old men and the institutions they treated as their private property. The committee's lack of experience, even naïveté, must be regarded as a benefit to be transformed by the support of university men, who lacked the liver for violence or the pursuit of power, and would easily be persuaded to common sense, once the change was underway.

As he turned on to Stanhope Street, he glanced up at the sky. The narrow, waxing crescent of the moon pierced the clouds above, just for a second or two, and Arthur Thistlewood wondered whether by the next full moon, his plans would be complete, and there would be hope, at last, for Great Britain.

TIDD

Hole in the Wall Passage, Holborn

Tidd was making a small living by mending the decorative silk covers of ladies' shoes, which were frequently damaged by over-enthusiastic dancing or clumsy partners. Since most of the ladies were haughty and spoilt, Tidd found it impossible to stay civil in their company. He was relieved when his daughter offered to collect and deliver the shoes. On one such errand, Mary happened to meet a manufacturer and solicited work for herself, sewing up the steams of stockings. On Christmas Eve, she was busy with an order that needed to be returned early on Monday. She was determined to finish tonight and spend Christmas Day entertaining the children. Eliza was asleep, having finished all she could in the kitchen, put six kiddies to bed and helped her daughter out by stitching for an hour. Mary, whose eyes were younger, was still working when her father returned with Mr Edwards. The night was black, Edwards had said; there were armed robbers about at Christmas, and Tiddy's weary legs would be spared if he accepted a ride in his cab. Besides, there was something particular he wanted to discuss, where there would be no danger of listening ears.

"There's nought you can't say in front of our Mary," said Tidd proudly when Edwards seemed surprised that instead of modestly leaving the room, Mrs Barker continued stitching.

"My daughter is a patriot," explained Tidd. "If there were less to do at home, I'd have her running a committee."

"Which committee would that be?" asked Edwards, enjoying the young woman's up-turned nose and the earnest arch of her eyebrows.

"The committee for the care of unwanted children and orphans," replied Mary in a flash.

"All yours!" said Edwards in a tone that implied a jest.

"She means it!" said Tidd.

Edwards shook his head and said no more.

"Right then, George" said Tidd. "I'm about ready for bed. What is it you wanted? There's precious little in 't pantry, but, as always, Tiddy will do his best to satisfy."

"No, Tidd; I have something for you!" said Edwards, earnestly. "A precaution."

"Let's have it!" said Tidd, anxious only for his bed.

Edwards opened his haversack, removed a polished wooden box and placed it proudly on the table beside Mary's pile of stockings. Tidd stood there quizzically until Edwards opened the lid to reveal a perfect pair of flintlock duelling pistols and a leather pouch, packed with flints.

"Where in hell did you get those?" asked Tidd, impressed.

"Tut, tut, Tidd; you know I can't reveal my sources! And there's no need to tell anyone else I've done you a favour."

"How is this a favour?" asked Tidd.

"You have a large family, Tidd, and may have occasion to defend them."

"We can't keep no guns here," replied Tidd, "with so many children about, and 't lads acting half like soldiers already."

"When they come to find you, you'll be glad of them!" replied Edwards.

"Forgive me, George" said Tidd, "but I am a man of 't world and 't best judge of how to protect my family. Now then, after a hard day's work, my daughter is tired, and so, am I. I must thank you for 't lift home and wish you good night. Don't forget your box."

"You'll regret it!" said Edwards. "But good night, all the same. Good night Mrs Barker!"

"Good night." said Mary, standing politely. "Merry Christmas, sir!"

Father and daughter stood at the doorway, each holding a candle while Edwards put the box back in his haversack, stepped cautiously down the steps and along the yard to Dorrington Street, where his cab was waiting, and the horse stabbed restlessly at the ice.

"What a loathsome man" thought Mary, as she returned to her stitching, while in the next room, Richard Tidd, whose back was aching like the devil, lowered himself wearily on to the mat without waking Eliza and was soon sound asleep.

DAVIDSON
Streets of St Marylebone

At half past eleven, as the last of the Irish sauntered off to meet their families for Mass at St Patrick's, Davidson and Tom Hyden left the Pontefract Castle and headed for their homes in St Marylebone. They were in high spirits; Hyden because of the mistletoe he had spotted on Manchester Square, and Davidson, because he had eleven new signatures, and he anticipated Sarah's delight at the contents of his trolley. When Hyden asked for the prompt return of his canister, when they'd used the cream up, Davidson invited him to bring his family and share the beef on Christmas Day. The children would enjoy each other's company, and his wife, being a west country girl, with few acquaintances outside Sunday school, was in need of fresh company. Hyden accepted happily. His family was accustomed to meat on account of his trade, he said, but they rarely enjoyed as juicy a cut as that one. Being especially talkative, Mrs Hyden would soon snap Mrs Davidson out of her shyness, and unless she had already wrung its neck, would spare their hen for another occasion.

The sky was dark, but there were gas lights in Manchester Square, and sure enough, on the higher branches of the elm there hung a fat clump of mistletoe, thick with creamy berries. Being the taller man, with longer limbs, Davidson offered to climb the tree with his small saw. Tom Hyden should keep watch, and if the watchman came snooping, he must hoot like an owl. Soon a huge clump of mistletoe came tumbling down, and when, a moment later, Davidson slipped to the ground, there was hardly a scratch on him and only a little tear by his right elbow patch. As they divided the harvest, Hyden said he had not enjoyed himself so much since he was a boy, scrumping apples.

"Just think, Tom!" remarked Davidson, packing his share of the mistletoe into the trolley. "When our business is done, there'll be no need for scrumping! Not for anybody. You'll have a small farm with fruit trees and pasture and cattle you can call your own!"

"I shall not!" replied the cowman. "God has given me daughters, and a farm won't suit my older years. I shall exchange my share of land for a horse and a hansom cab!"

When they reached the street where Hyden lived, the cowman chuckled and said he expected more than a grateful kiss when the missus caught sight of his mistletoe. There would be no scolding for lateness neither, when she knew her hen was spared and she could go to church instead of standing at the stove all Christmas morning.

Hyden vanished into the Manchester Mews, shouting his wife's pet name, as celebrations for the holy birth resounded from the Spanish Chapel ahead. Davidson stood on the corner and listened for a moment or two. He found the worshippers' voices feeble, but was not tempted to join them. As he walked on with his trolley, he forgot Jesus and contemplated the cowman's admission. Even after a life managing another fellow's animals, Hyden had no desire for land of his own. How would that fit with Thistlewood's planning? Had they miscalculated the issue of independent choice? He marked the point for consideration, when he was less weary and his mind was sharper.

As his trolley clattered along the dark streets of St Marylebone, every now and then, a Christmas song burst from a church door or an open window. A small part of Will Davidson wanted to park his trolley and join the celebration. His voice would soar again above the congregation, and he would feel, again, the hand of God. Instead, Davidson turned his thoughts to domestic matters. This morning's sorry parting from his wife would not be appeased by a bunch of mistletoe, perhaps not even by a joint of beef, some cream and a new handle for her pan. Sarah would certainly rejoice in the absence of the blunderbuss, and in the news of a charitable loan, but the intrusion of strangers at Christmas might be more welcome, had the guests been in desperate need, rather than a family who ate meat frequently and had a hen to spare.

As Davidson tried to formulate his explanation, a thin, bright slither of moon pierced the black haze above London. It sparkled for a second or two, as if determined to make an appearance to anybody who sought it this Christmas Eve, and was smothered again. The moment of brightness took Davidson's breath away, and it made him philosophical. How small and remote was the moon's orb, he thought and how immense its impact on nature; how ancient it was and yet how consistent and regular its changes. If history had a rhythm, he speculated, it would be measured not regularly, by the month, but in longer, less mathematical phases. Society had a way of producing, every century or so, extraordinary men and women, who responded to surges of discontent by creating a new age of peace, which was inevitably unsustainable because human nature is flawed. Chaos would ensue, until a new genius reached maturity. It followed, therefore, that man's existence could be reduced to a natural cycle that bore a degree of comparison to the moon. By contrast, he thought, the mysteries of domestic contentment were as complex and elusive as the vast constellations he had seen above Jamaica, Scotland and the ocean in between.

On Christmas morning, the family rejoiced at all the good news. Sarah said she was sorry for being cruel to her husband. Of course, she looked forward to the acquaintance of his good Christian friends, whether or not their home overflowed with milk and honey, and the boys looked forward to playmates, who might fight less than their brothers. When Davidson tried to recall his philosophical insights and explain them to his wife, they were nowhere to be found. It was a brief vision that had sparkled like the silvery moon, illuminating the human condition for a few moments, before vanishing just as fast.

CHAPTER TWENTY

Tuesday, 1ˢᵗ February, 1820

MOLLY BRUNT

Fox Court, Holborn

Mrs Brunt was dividing a flannel sheet into squares, and despite the awkwardness of her scissors, the pile was rising nicely. The sheet, which was pale green, had been part of her dowry, but Mr Brunt had promised that the sacrifice would be worthwhile. Molly was not sure of the purpose of the squares she was cutting, except that they were crucial for the operation that her husband was preparing with Mr Thistlewood and their friends, and which was intended to make them prosper. She wished it would hurry up, because Harry had grown even scraggier since their return from Derby, and Molly herself kept coming over dizzy. Her husband said he took all the nourishment he needed from the task at hand. His breeches wanted taking in every other week, he was coughing more than he ought, and if ever Mr Brunt ran up the steps, his arrival was marked by an indecent amount of puffing.

The Brunts' woes paled, Molly had decided, in comparison to the Royal Family's. A week ago, the old King's third-born son, the Duke of Kent died suddenly of pneumonia, and yesterday Harry came bursting in with news that the King had dropped off his golden perch himself. Though long-expected and merciful, the news was a shock for Molly Brunt, who closed their shutters and covered the canary's cage. Later, while her husband did his business with the iron-monger, and Molly petted the dog he kept on a chain outside, Brooke's Market was full of gossip that the new King was dangerously ill too.

When, at last, her husband emerged from the shop, Molly told him she was glad Queen Charlotte had not lived to see it. She might have been foreign and, by all accounts, perpetually cross, but she had feelings like anyone else, and no mother should lose a husband and two sons in less than a fortnight, with another one on his way. Brunt replied that plenty of women had fared worse in the wars, and if the new King sped early to hell, too, the nation's resources would be spared a glutton. Molly opened her mouth to disagree, but then remembered the terms on which her husband had fetched her home and closed it. Brunt said he would return later with his friends and asked her to take his parcel and leave it unopened by the store-room door. As soon as she was inside the house, Molly could not resist peeping at the contents. She could not imagine any purpose on earth for a bag of rusty nails.

It was Molly's habit, when performing repetitive tasks like cutting squares, to fill her mind with thoughts of her pantry, crammed full, and then to decide how the shelves might be rearranged, what she might cook and what luxuries needed buying in. Her work became less monotonous, and she was able to absent herself mentally from the comings and goings at Fox Court. Instead of trying to decipher the men's whispers, she would translate them, in her mind, to babble, which, when connected to all the other babble, would one day lead to the paradise of which they spoke. On this Tuesday, Molly was imagining herself topping up the vinegar barrel, which was just brimming over, when Tidd, Ings and the apprentice arrived, all at once, each carrying a great sack on his back, which he dumped in the workshop before slumping on one a chair.

"Brought some flour, have you, mi'duck?" asked Molly, knowing full well they had not.

"Don't you try baking that stuff, Mrs B!" warned Hale.

"Why ever not?" asked Molly, who had kept her soft spot for Joe and winked at him.

It was policy to protect, wives and children from the truth, but Tidd was irritated by Molly Brunt. She had an easier life than Eliza, she was irrational and never so provocative when her husband was home.

"The reason it's not for baking" he said, glaring at her with an air of defiance, "is because its gunpowder!"

Molly dropped her scissors. Tidd grinned.

"Heavy as lead, them sacks are," he continued, "And half-starved as we are, we just hauled 'em all the way from the Artillery Ground, ain't that true, Joe?"

"It is," said Joe Hale. "Tiddy's back is breaking Mrs B. And on Charterhouse Lane, the patrole come up and we thought we was done-for. You know what Tiddy says, cool as you like?"

"What?" asked Molly.

"I looks him in 't eye," said Tidd, "and I says, 'it's food for 't poor, Constable,' which in a way it is!"

As Tidd and Hale chuckled, Ings saw how Mrs Brunt struggled to contain her alarm. As she continued cutting, he noticed her lips trembling and her scissors chewing at the flannel. Molly accepted Ings's kind offer to fix her scissors and said she was pleased their little argument was forgotten. (She had taken offence at Mr Ings's renaming of her canary. Mrs Brunt would never call any pet of hers after a Frenchman, no matter how brave or misunderstood. At Harry's suggestion, the bird formerly known as Boney had been renamed, again, Boadicea)

Ings fetched his stone from the store, and as he sharpened her kitchen knife and her scissors, he looked into Mrs Brunt's sad blue eyes, at the trace of freckles on her cheek bones, and at the perpetual frown on her stern. How pretty she would look with a proper smile, when the campaign was over.

"Don't fret, Mrs Brunt" he said. "A brand-new world is on its way, and it is fearless, industrious women like yourself that England will need most when it is reborn."

"How kind you are, Mr Ings," replied Molly. "Perhaps you will explain why England cannot be reborn without destruction."

"Destruction is a last resort" said Ings, "and if we are forced to commit it, it will be born of duty and on behalf of our countrymen."

"That you have sinned, while they have not?" asked Mrs Brunt.

"How clever you are, Molly" said Ings and wondered whether Celia would respond so calmly to what Mrs Brunt had heard today. Molly, who had known few indications of kindness lately, thought that Mr Ings must be lonely without his family, and that by the filtered light of the shutters, he might even be considered handsome.

When Davidson arrived and heaved another heavy bag into the store room (five hundred bullets, each hand-made by John Harris at the letter foundry in Moorfields), Mrs Brunt said they had better watch the floor didn't collapse under the weight of all them sacks. If her family went hungry much longer, she would put some of them in her pan and stew them, even if she blew up the whole of Fox Court and the market, while she was at it. When Ings laughed loudly, Tidd protested that it was not a matter for humour. At the sound of footsteps, they all hushed, but it was only Tom Hyden with a pail of milk and time to spare for weapon duties. Davidson thanked the honest cowman and advised him to make himself comfortable in the corner with Hale. So long as they kept to their oaths of secrecy, there was no reason to go out and suffer the cold during the committee meeting that was about to begin.

When Brunt returned with Thistlewood and Edwards, Mrs Brunt measured a portion of rich, creamy milk into each man's bowl. When the men sat, cross-legged on the floor, she distributed the bowls and then returned to her chair and her flannel. But this time, when the meeting started, instead of retreating to her imagined pantry, Molly kept her hand on her scissors, in case anyone looked her way, and listened very carefully.

THE COMMITTEE

Fox Court, Holborn

Thistlewood was concerned by reports of the new King's failure health. If he died before the coronation, the potential support of Princess Caroline of Brunswick would fly into the wind. Far worse, the next king of England would be the Duke of York, who was the staunchest Tory alive.

"All the more reason to proceed quickly," replied Edwards, "ready or not."

"Agreed," said Thistlewood. "We must act very soon or starve to death waiting. Brothers! Those in favour of immediate action, show your hands."

All hands rose, even the cowman's, who did not belong in the committee. Molly Brunt was spellbound.

Tidd was impatient to speak. "We must strike at the old King's funeral!" he said. "With the military busy in Windsor, London will be ours for the taking!"

There was a murmur of consent, but Thistlewood disagreed.

"Slow down, Tiddy," he said. "The entire Establishment, including the Cabinet will be in Windsor under the protection of His Majesty's forces. What use is taking Mansion House, the Bank and Chancery if the tyrants' hearts are still beating?"

Thunderstruck by the stark disclosure, Molly looked at her husband, who seemed unsurprised and entirely at one with the plan.

"Come, Will Davidson," said Edwards. "Where are your clever ideas now?"

"As it happens" replied Davidson. "There is an alternative."

"Keep it brief, Will," replied Thistlewood. The momentum urgent and, with Edwards in his mocking mood, philosophy was best avoided.

"We might avoid bloodshed and sin by taking their Lordships prisoner and keeping them in the Tower until they can be tried in a court of law; Saxon law of course."

"Here, here!" was Molly's involuntary voice of assent, which was either unheard or ignored.

"Overruled," replied Edwards, firmly.

"Why, Will Davidson, have you never mentioned this position before?" asked Thistlewood.

"Because it's a new position, Arthur, a matter of conscience and of prayer."

"Can you imagine the indecision?" said Thistlewood. "The delays such a process would cause? The cost of it? The retraining of judiciary? How many years, how much disruption, before the tyrants came to court?"

"I will, of course, accept the majority decision," replied Davidson, "though as a rule, I favour debate above autocracy."

"There is and shall be no autocracy here!" replied Thistlewood sharply.

"Then beware of George Edwards!" muttered Davidson, far too softly to be heard.

Edwards took the floor.

"Given that we remain with the plan undersigned by you, Davidson, and the rest of the committee," he said, "and in the light of the new royal situation, we can presume that Cabinet members are especially nervous about their jobs. In sensitive times, they prefer, as we do, to meet in private houses, where conversation may be franker and more private."

"If those meetings are held in private, George," asked Tidd, "how can men like us hope to discover 't when and 't where?"

Edwards admitted that he had no answer yet, but that certain channels might identify an appropriate occasion. For the moment, Thistlewood might wish to confirm the schedule, as far as it had been possible to arrange it.

Giving thanks to his aide, Thistlewood said that it was a matter of great pride to present the plans, which, with George Edwards's help, he had formulated so far.

The disposal of the tyrants would be completed on a date, yet to be arranged, by an elite unit consisting only of the committee. A second unit, led by John Harris, typesetter at Moorfields, would prepare a series of beacons and bonfires to alert the population at large, while a third would remove the canons from The Military Academy and the Artillery Ground and prepare Mansion House for occupation by the Provisional Government. The entire membership would subsequently gather at Mansion House for the Proclamation, of which their old friend, James Watson was busy writing out copies on parchment, under the noses of his guards at White Cross Gaol.

After a round of appreciation for Watson, Thistlewood continued that when their first duty was complete, Edwards, Brunt and Tidd would lead a party to the Bank of England to liberate the nation's finances, while a second squad, led by

Thistlewood, Davidson and Ings, would head for Chancery and procure all documents pertaining to land and property.

Edwards seconded Thistlewood's proposals. Ings, Tidd and Brunt agreed and Davidson conceded to the majority and invited the committee to clasp hands and vow to die, if necessary, for the greatest cause of all, the cause of Liberty.

Fired by mighty expectation, Edwards and Thistlewood left for the Black Dog on Grays Inn Lane to refine the plans, while Tidd returned to his recruitment drive at the barracks, and Davidson to yet another gaol, to convince more prisoners that Freedom would soon be theirs, if they would commit their allegiance and part with another penny or two for the cause.

Molly sat ashen faced at the table, as still as a wax figure. Brunt looked at her and wondered how far, with his political passions, he was responsible for the old girl's fragility, and whether this might send her over the edge again. She blinked, and then she surprised him.

"Mr Brunt," she said, without moving an inch. "I see now the depths of your love for family and the extremes to which you will go to fill my pantry. I cannot say I hate the Queen, not the new one nor the old, for they never asked to be queen, but ever since your experience with the quartermaster, and mine with the regiment, I have felt there is something askew with England. I thank you, Thomas, for your part in improving the lot of our suffering countrymen and women. And I also wish you to know that whatever tyrant puts a knife to my throat or a pistol to my brain, your wife's lips shall remain forever sealed."

"Mrs Brunt," said Brunt. "If I had not already asked you all them years ago, I should bend on my knees now and beg you to be my wife."

"And I should like to see you try, mi'duck!"

They both laughed, and Ings and Hyden, their witnesses, laughed too. Hale was less willing to laugh at the master's expense, but he stopped struggling with his conscience about everything he had heard and drank his milk. Then Brunt wished everyone farewell and hurried away to address a meeting in Gee's Court. His heart was thumping as it never had, at least, not since he first heard the crack of gunfire in France.

Molly removed the cover from Boadicea's cage. The canary rewarded her with a sweet melody, while she cut more boldly into the flannel, Tom Hyden packed her squares with gunpowder and James Ings secured each little device with a butcher's knot.

Monday, 21ˢᵗ February, 1820

TOM HYDEN

Hyde Park, London

As soon as he walked away from the mounted gentleman with the tall hat, Tom Hyden wished that he could swallow the last half hour so that it had never happened. There had been two ladies, the wife, perhaps, and the mother; the two Ladies Ryder, who looked down with faint amusement at the worried cowman with his tattered hat in one hand and his message in the other, to be taken with utmost speed to My Lord Castlereagh. The cowman said he had visited that Minister's house on St James Square, which everyone knew because of all the broken windows, but he had been refused admission. He had decided, despite never having much schooling, to write a letter instead, and here it was. Lord Harrowby had stretched out a gloved hand, his narrow face untouched by emotion, the boyish dimple on his chin softening, slightly, the stern gaze. He opened the letter and read it. He did not seem alarmed by the contents.

"You wrote this, Mr Hyden?"

"Yes, My Lord, it is my own untutored hand."

"Is it not usual to provide an address?" asked Harrowby.

"My Lord, I live humbly with my wife and daughters at 2, Manchester Mews in St Marylebone."

"By Manchester Square?"

"Yes, sir."

"This crime, of which you write," said Harrowby. "Has a time been set?"

"No, sir, but it is expected imminently, I assure you." said Hyden. "Here is my card, sir, which I hope you will convey to My Lord Castlereagh at your soonest convenience."

Harrowby replied that he would do his best. As His Lordship pocketed the letter and the card, Hyden asked for permission to speak. Should the information prove useful, he explained, his family was in need, while he himself desired nothing so much as a Hackney Cab Licence, which would sustain his family through the difficult times ahead.

Acknowledging the request with nothing more than a tilt of his head, Lord Harrowby urged his horse to walk on. After a few steps, His Lordship halted and turned to request a meeting with the cowman at precisely midday on Wednesday. Hyden replied that it might be dangerous to be seen talking to a government minister in the park. If he were observed by an acquaintance, his treachery would be exposed, and his family would be at risk. Harrowby indicated a plantation in another corner of the park, which, he said, would be a safe enough location and urged his horse away.

Hyden had seen them out riding many times while tending his cattle. Lords and Ladies paraded in the park every day, nodding at each other politely, sometimes exchanging news, he supposed, or gentile invitations. Usually at this hour, which was about five in the afternoon, the three Harrowbys rode through Grosvenor Gate, trotting in elegant formation, backs as straight as boards, sometimes laughing, but never noticing the cowman with his ready smile, tapping his cap as they passed. Clip clop, clip clop. How he loathed them for their contempt and their idle wealth, but how he depended on them too, for his living. Now, they would be his salvation.

Hyden knew that the gentleman was Dudley Ryder, first Earl of Harrowby, and a former employer of his friend, Will Davidson. He knew that as Lord President of the Council, Harrowby was a member of the Cabinet, but he did not know that His Lordship was heading home to dress for dinner at Carlton House, where he would meet not only all the other Privy Councillors, but the new King too. Harrowby thought he would take the illiterate message, which seemed unlikely to be more than the figment of some delirious imagination. Either way, it might soften the king's turbulent mood.

Tom Hyden sat on a bench, for once, unaware of either the cold or his hunger. He knew only his aching skull. He tried to think straight. Should he pursue Harrowby, retrieve the letter and pretend it was a mistake? An hour ago, the decision had seemed clear and simple. He tried reminding himself of the reasoning. He had become, through no fault of his own, more deeply involved with the operation than his conscience allowed. The brilliance of Davidson and Thistlewood had dazzled him, but being foremost a practical man, he was less vulnerable than the committee to political passions. He had been flattered by the committee's willingness to befriend a man more accustomed to beasts than philosophy, when in truth, they were probably only after his milk and his cream. Last week, when

Brunt explained that manufacture made him guilty of Treason, Hyden had decided to quit, but feared for his life if he spoke out. Since yesterday, quitting was not enough. A debt collector had visited his wife and threatened her because of a short-fall in his employer's accounts of eighteen shillings.

Hyden had not taken the money with malice. He had been sloppy with measurements, that's all; helped a hungry friend here and there, especially if they belonged to the Union. His employer of twenty years protested that the cowman's suffering acquaintances were not his concern. Times were hard, the accounts were short, and everyone had bills to pay. Even if he pawned every stitch on his family's bodies and every pot and pan he possessed, Tom Hyden could never raise those eighteen shillings.

Darkness was approaching, and he needed to drive his cattle into the shed. He did so efficiently but without the usual banter. Sensing his anxiety, the cows lowed and snorted and pressed against his body until their master reacted; a soothing pat here, a stroke or a whisper there, each beast according to her preference. When they were settled, he said "Good night, my lovelies", as usual, and bolted the cow-shed's ill-matched doors. He walked through the park, weeping shamelessly. A servant, carrying a pitcher of water, saw his distress and offered help, but Hyden shook his head and hurried away.

A new set of doubts began to inflate the last. By talking to Lord Harrowby, he had staked everything and was promised nothing, not even immunity from prosecution, and certainly not the eighteen shillings he needed. Was he too greedy in asking for the Hackney cab? And yet he had signed the death warrants of five excellent men, including his friend, Will Davidson. Their families would forever live in wretchedness, because of Tom Hyden's treachery. What if Thistlewood's men were already captured? How would they react to news of the betrayal? What would be their revenge? Should he have trusted Harrowby? Or was His Lordship, even now, preparing a charge of collaboration, that would send all of them, including himself, to gaol.

In a few moments of madness, Tom Hyden hunted for a pair of heavy stones to tie to his ankles before jumping into the icy Serpentine, but then he thought of his wife and their little ones, and he could not. Instead, he convinced himself that he had spared his country a bloody Revolution, and he ran towards Cumberland Gate. He ran across Oxford Street without a care for traffic, and he did not stop until he reached Manchester Mews, where he gathered his breath before proceeding down to his cottage. Such was the urgency in his voice and in his breath that, for once, his chatterbox wife listened without interruption. He said he knew that it was dark and cold outside, and that little Dorothea was sickly, but if they never did anything else for him, his family must wrap up warm and go hastily to his brother's farm at Islington. They must speak to nobody on the road and must tell his brother that Tom was sorry. He would join them as soon as he could, and if he could not, then he would send an explanation.

That Monday evening, Lord Castlereagh suffered one of his bouts of melancholy and failed to appear at the Carlton House dinner. Lord Harrowby had the strange letter sent, with an explanatory note, straight to the Foreign Office. When, on Tuesday morning, Castlereagh opened his correspondence, he took the cowman's letter to The Home Secretary, and Sidmouth declared it a miracle. The Dairy Iscariot was worth a dozen spies. When the matter came to a head, as soon it would, the reptile known as Henry Ward would be expendable. There was reason to celebrate.

On Tuesday afternoon, George Edwards was summoned to Mr Stafford's office at Bow Street. A note from Henry Hobhouse, acknowledged his latest message to the Home Department, and advised Mr Edwards to purchase *The New Times* tomorrow. Having taken luncheon with that paper's founder and editor, John Stoddart, in Mitre Court, Edwards understood exactly. There would be an announcement in the court pages of The New Times that the Cabinet dinner, delayed by the king's death, would take place at Lord Harrowby's house in Grosvenor Square tomorrow, Wednesday 23rd February, 1820.

Wednesday, 23rd February, 1820

INGS

Fox Court, Holborn, 07.30am

When George Edwards greeted them at Fox Court, there was agitation in his eyes, which were usually as characterless as a china doll's. Ings and Brunt knew at once that there had been developments. He said that for security reasons, he would give each man his instructions separately, beginning with Brunt. Ings must go to the White Hart to order bread and cheese, and Edwards would join him shortly for breakfast.

Mr Hobbs had accommodated the committee on several occasions, and marshalled Ings to a discreet corner, noted that Mr Edwards would foot the bill, and took the order. The cheese and the soft white bread and the accompaniment of pickled onions arrived before the aide de camp, and Ings was obliged to look at them, and smell them for a good quarter of an hour.

"Why, in God's name, did you not start without me?" asked Edwards.

Ings was startled. Edwards carried a tankard of ale and set it beside Ings's plate. As the butcher ate and drank - a slow performance - Edwards issued the orders. Ings must go back to Fox Court and take every knife, dagger and cutlass he could fit into his haversack and take them to the cutler on Drury Lane. A little insulted, Ings enquired whether Thistlewood had been dissatisfied with his own sharpening, which was of the highest professional standard.

"Calmly, Ings, calmly," said Edwards. "Even the best blade in the store can be made a little sharper, a little thinner"

"Why Morrison?" asked Ings. "He's sullen, and he charges extortionate prices for mediocre work. Godbold on Brick Lane is better. he's French, but a perfectionist."

"I'm not here for professional advice," said Edwards, "but to repeat your captain's instructions. Take half a dozen ball cartridges from the store and hide them well in your sack. Wear your butcher's apron under your coat, and for every pocket on your person, you will take thirty bullets, and put a kerchief on top to disguise them. Understood?"

"Daggers, knives, thirty ball-cartridges and a supply of bullets," repeated Ings.

"Correct" said Edwards. "At five o'clock, you will be waiting, with everything we mentioned about your person, at the entrance of Johnson's Court, directly opposite Mr Carlile's shop. Is that clear?"

"Yes, sir, except every kerchief I own is in Portsea. I'll borrow some from Brunt."

"No!" said Edwards. "There must be no conferring."

He dropped two brown pennies on the table.

"The market haberdasher specializes in second-hand."

As commanded, Ings arrived at the entrance of John-son's Court shortly before five, with the cartridges and the sharpened weapons wrapped in paper in his haversack, and his pockets stuffed full of bullets and kerchiefs. A whole hour he stood in the cold, at the limits of nervous suspense, not knowing for what or for whom he waited. When at last Edwards himself arrived, instead of useful information, he provided two empty bags for Ings's haversack. They would serve well, he whispered, when Ings had parted Sidmouth and Castlereagh from their heads. Ings felt his lungs stop, but Edwards would say no more.

He told Ings to follow him and wait while he called on a friend at the St Giles end of Oxford Street to fetch some gin on the sly for their celebration. A whole other hour, Ings shivered outside that house on Oxford Street, but when Edwards emerged, there was no sight of gin nor any mention of gin. He only instructed Ings to proceed to John Street; not St John's Street in Clerkenwell where Edwards's family lived, but another, off the Edgware Road. At John Street, he should enter a mews called Cato Street, where his curiosity would be satisfied. There would be a stable, where, if Ings searched in the straw, he would find something interesting, and soon some friends would arrive.

And so, James Ings marched the whole length of Oxford Street, weighed down by the contents of his haversack and the heavy pockets of apron and his greatcoat, his heart thumping like a big bass drum and still with no indication about where their Ludships would meet the rightful judgment, nor what the other men were up to.

The best thing about that Wednesday was that it was the last time James Ings would ever set eyes on the demon known as George Edwards.

HYDEN / TIDD / BRUNT
Hyde Park, London

As the consequences of his betrayal began to materialize, Tom Hyden was approached by his friend, Elias Firth, as he led his cow across the park. Firth wanted to lodge the beast in Hyden's shed, his own stable on Cato Street and the loft having been requisitioned not half an hour ago by George Edwards. When Firth told Edwards that he could never give over the property without permission from his employer, a hero of the Southern Campaign, Edwards had retorted that since General Tadwell-Watson had retired to France, he need never know. The committee would tolerate no argument, he said, and whatever Firth's objections, he, his family and his cows would find other quarters until Thursday. Without further explanation, Edwards had climbed into a cab and driven off at speed. The story alarmed Tom Hyden, who feared that his letter to Lord Castlereagh had unleashed some urgent activity, but when Firth observed that his friend seemed anxious, Hyden explained that his little girl was unwell.

When they had settled the cattle, Firth and Hyden headed up to Cato Street to satisfy their curiosity. General Watson's property seemed entirely unchanged. There was nobody about but the usual hawkers, and, from his corner, the blacksmith waved and wished them both a good day. Then they saw, pulling the butcher's cart along John Street, the oddly matched figures of Tidd and Brunt. Presuming that the cowmen had been sent to help, Tidd asked if they would lift the tarpaulin cover from the cart to make a curtain. When Firth offered a supply of candles and explained that he was a member of the union, and well known on Cato Street, because he generally kept his cow here, Brunt said that his help was acceptable and discretion would be rewarded.

When the curtain was in place, and the sacks transferred, Tidd explained that while he and Brunt fetched the second load, Firth and Hyden should carry the sacks discreetly up the ladder and lay them out in orderly fashion in the loft. They should, on no account, be opened and under no circumstances, even if a thunderbolt produced pitch darkness, were candles to be lit, until another member of the committee arrived. Any snooping busybodies should be told that General Watson had commissioned improvements to his roof.

Firth was sorry to hear Tom Hyden sighing so frequently about his daughter, and at half past eleven, offered to cheer him up with a pint at the Horse and Groom while they waited for the bootmakers to return. Hyden longed to tell Firth to run as far and as fast as he could, but instead explained that he needed to visit his sick daughter and would be back in time to help with the second load.

The truth was that, with the unexpected distraction, Hyden had almost forgotten his appointment with Lord Harrowby. As he waited for what seemed like a century beneath a young chestnut tree, three sparrows landed in the branches, and knocked fragments of frost on to his cap. Hyden looked up, and seemed to see the mournful faces of Davidson, Brunt and Tidd. He thought he must run and find his dear friends and beg them to alter their arrangements. But his feet were as rooted to the ground as the trees in that plantation. He forced himself to imagine his wife and daughters, who would be playing happily at his brother's farm and longing for his arrival.

Hyden had begun to fear, or perhaps to hope, that the arrangement with Harrowby was a hoax, when he saw two gentlemen approaching on horseback. One of the men, an officer, stopped his horse about fifty yards away and waited while the other, Lord Harrowby, dismounted and walked towards him, shook his hand and wished him a very good day. Tom Hyden begged to be assured of his own safety, not because he cherished life, but so that his children should not suffer from his actions. Harrowby replied that a difficult day lay ahead for everyone, but they were allies now, and Mr Hyden would be taken care of, in due course. For a few short hours, he must pretend to be as committed as ever to the conspiracy.

"I am not a man of violence, My Lord," protested Hyden, "I've never struck another human being except in self-defence."

"You need not discharge any weapon, Mr Hyden, but if your friends become suspicious, all will be lost. You must follow all other instructions, and as soon as you sense danger, take flight."

"You mean desert, like a coward or a traitor?"

"Thomas Hyden," said Harrowby in a reassuring tone, "you are no traitor, but a true friend of your country. It is not your foolish friends you desert, sir, but the ways of wickedness!"

"What then, My Lord? After I have fled?"

"Report to the watch-house on Portman Street, where the officer has my instructions."

Lord Harrowby took a pencil and note book from his pocket and asked for names. When Hyden found his throat paralyzed and could not utter a sound, His Lordship sighed impatiently. "Thomas Hyden. You, not Arthur Thistlewood nor any of his gang, are the hero of the day, and your country will reward you. Think of your Hackney cab and your two fine horses. Think how proud your children and your children's children will be of your heroism, and how bright their future will be, thanks to your bravery now!"

His Lordship's eyes seemed to pierce the cowman's mind. Then, fixing his eyes on his dairy and speaking in a dull monotone, Tom Hyden named the principal activists in a plot to assassinate the Cabinet. He revealed that weapons, stored and, in part, at Fox Court, Holborn were being transferred this hour to a property in Cato Street, whose owner General Watson lived abroad, and whose tenant, Elias Firth was entirely innocent.

Later that day, two constables escorted Thomas Hyden from the watch-house in Portman Street to Bow Street. The Chief Clerk, John Stafford, promised that the cowman's debts would be paid. If the matter was satisfactorily resolved, he would receive his Hackney cab, his pair of horses, a licence and, as a sign of the nation's lasting gratitude, a modest pension. Meanwhile, on the official grounds of the theft of eighteen shillings, Hyden would be taken to the Marshalsea, from which he would be released when his personal safety was assured. As he was driven across the Thames to Southwark and into the safety of gaol, Tom Hyden rejoiced that his wife and daughters would thrive. His private torment would haunt him forever in nightmares, as it did that night on the straw of his cell, when he sat upright in a sweat, terrified by the vengeful fury of his friends and the brittle laugh of a gentleman in a tall hat, with a straight back, a narrow face and eyes that burnt with supercilious scorn.

CHAPTER TWENTY-ONE

Wednesday, 23rd February, 1820
(continued)

DAVIDSON

39, Grosvenor Square, London, 10.00am

John Baker, smiling, white-whiskered, trusty old butler to My Lord Harrowby, said he had often wondered what mischief had found its way to Will Davidson lately, and did not hesitate to invite his old friend to step inside. There was no prospect of employment, he regretted, not in any capacity, neither in London nor Staffordshire, but when Davidson asked if he might remind himself of the craftsmanship of the doors, windows and furniture – some of which he had helped to build – the butler was happy to oblige. The staff would be delighted to see Will Davidson again, he said, but were on no account to be distracted by conversation or song. The household was exceptionally busy in preparation for a formal dinner, which, as so often, the old man explained with a conspiratorial twinkle, had been arranged with too little notice.

Davidson had been given precise instructions for his movements until six o'clock that evening, but he had not been informed about the advertisement in *The New Times*. John Baker had unwittingly confirmed that the operation was imminent.

"Will you be at the dinner, John?" he asked, as casually as he could.

"Between you and me, I'd rather not," replied the butler. "It's Mrs Baker's birthday, and we had plans. You know what she's like; I'm in for a battle!"

"Then battle for your rights, John Baker!" said Davidson. "Tell them your wife is more important than duty!"

The butler laughed at the preposterous notion, and, apart from repeating himself with emphasis, Davidson dared go no further to protect him.

Within an hour, he had sketched the layout of every door, window and staircase of the ground floor of Lord Harrowby's home, and noted obstructions that might cause problems in the dark. John Baker shook his hand, wished Davidson well and hoped he might return on a calmer day to cheer up the staff with a song, like in the old days.

As he walked out into Grosvenor Square, and the spiteful February air blasted his face and hands, Davidson was perplexed. He had agreed to Thistlewood's plan, and to die, if necessary, for liberty, but when he came eye-ball to eye-ball with any man, he wondered whether he had the stomach to kill. If the death of a dozen tyrants released millions of Britons from suffering, would his participation rate as a mortal sin? Must he and his comrades enter the furnace of hell for the sake of future generations? Would their sacrifice be acknowledged by generations to come, or assigned to dust?

Davidson had confronted such questions a dozen times in debate, but never so urgently as now. Did the Magna Carta override the Ten Commandments? If the loyal butler protected Lord Harrowby, would Davidson be forced to kill his kind old friend? If he spared Joe, would the butler be condemned for inviting an assassin into the house? Must an innocent Christian, who had spent his life in servitude, either die by the sword or be humiliated and hanged as a traitor, because he knew and liked Will Davidson?

It would be better, he decided, to run back to St Marylebone, before it was too late. He would take Sarah and the children and, by fair means or foul, sail to Jamaica, where they would be reunited with baby Duncan and lead a carefree life in the sun, far from this blasted cold, the interminable grey and damned political turmoil. He would submit to his father's wish and pursue a career in law, even if that meant a life-time as a humble clerk.

In turmoil, he crossed Oxford Street by Tyburn without checking the traffic. A coach driver, forced to rein in his horses, shouted abuse, wrenching Davidson into the present. He waved an apology to the angry coachman, and then noticed, on the corner, a skinny youth of about fourteen, wrestling with a fellow in baker's garb. The boy gripped a loaf, which the baker seemed determined to reclaim. The youth's tangle-haired sister howled beside the scuffle, while pedestrians, unseeing or uncaring, scurried past.

Davidson's instinct was to snatch the loaf, lift the children and run. But today, when one way or another, history would change, he dared not risk arrest. On the other hand, he could not ignore the suffering of children, whose pitiful faces reminded him of a sermon he once heard at Robert Wedderburn's chapel in Soho.

Without further contemplation, Davidson plunged into the melee and seized the loaf, startling the combatants to submission. He aimed an avuncular wink at the children, whose astonishment had rooted them to the spot. The baker thanked the stranger and asked him to wait, while he fetched the patrole. Assuming his persona as a Sunday School teacher, Davidson replied, in sonorous ones that mankind's only true judge was

God in Heaven, and that presumably, the baker considered himself a Christian.

"Indeed, I do," said the baker, "and as such, it is my duty to see wickedness chastised."

"Do you also believe in Lord Jesus, Our Saviour?" asked Davidson, turning to the children.

"We say our prayers every night, sir, don't we, Clara?"

The little girl nodded as furiously as she had howled a few moments before. Davidson turned to the baker.

"May I remind you of Mathew, chapter eighteen, verse six?"

"You may, but I'd rather have my loaf," replied the baker.

A little crowd was gathering and chuckled at the indignant baker, until Will Davidson struck a pose and declaimed the gospel.

"Whosoever shall offend one of these little ones which believe in me, it were better for him that a millstone were hanged about his neck, and that he were drowned in the depths of the sea.

To the applause of the on-lookers, Will Davidson lifted the loaf and, not without a hint of theatre, broke it into three sections, handing one each to the boy, the girl and the accuser. The children scarpered, but the furious baker demanded that the preacher accompany him to the watch-house. When Davidson asked whether anybody present had witnessed a crime, nobody in the little crowd could say that he had.

Soho Square, London

Davidson's final instruction that Wednesday was to stand on Soho Square at precisely six o'clock, when further information would be forthcoming. By half past six, he had resolved definitely not to back out of the operation, and he was still waiting anxiously, when who should come strolling up, but his former employer from Liverpool. Mr Goldworthy said he was sorry to see an old friend in a state of evident agitation. Without the formality of a greeting, Davidson asked sharply whether his friend, Williamson had ever sailed to the Cape, because he had been cheated out of five pounds.

"Calm yourself, Davidson," said Goldworthy. "You did a good turn to a man, facing an uncertain future. A man of your talents can earn that five pounds in no time."

"I've not earned a farthing since August," replied Davidson.

"I've found plenty of work in London," said Goldworthy, with a reassuring smile.

"As a cabinet-maker?" asked Davidson.

"London is a pot of gold, even in these hard times," said Goldworthy. "It's full of gullible fools, eager to throw their money away. There's enough brain in your head, Davidson, to find a few of your own!"

"I should rather die than behave dishonourably," replied Davidson.

"Your precious morality is more important than your children's survival?" asked Goldworthy. "Tut, tut, Will; you disappoint me."

He looked at Davidson, studying the earnest face, the eyebrows clenched with anxiety, the cheeks all bone and streaked too soon with worry lines.

"What are your plans this evening?" he asked, not unkindly.

"I have no plans," replied Davidson, "beyond finding honest work and feeding my family."

"Then meet me at seven thirty at the Horse and Groom off the Edgware Road. I shall introduce you to a friend, a property-speculator, who needs just such a man as yourself, and will pay you well. Seven thirty. Before the St Marylebone Union meeting at eight. Horse and Groom!"

Will Davidson wondered whether he should continue expecting instruction, or whether, in some strange way, Mr Goldworthy was a messenger for Thistlewood or Edwards. There was time to wait for another few minutes.

At that moment, Ings stood freezing in Oxford Street while Edwards allegedly collected gin, but was, in fact, waiting on another corner for Goldworthy to appear.

"The wind is blowing fair" said Goldworthy, when they met.

"Good" replied Edwards, "and if the ship docks safely, your grubby little secrets will be safe.

"I hope so," said Goldworthy, whose grubby little mind was not in Edwards's league.

George Edwards walked into Soho Square and approached Will Davidson.

"How was the sketching party this morning?" he asked brightly.

"First rate." replied Davidson.

"I have a bargain for you," said Edwards. "I pay seven shillings for the sketches, and you go to Berwick Street to retrieve your property."

"Shall I have use for the blunderbuss tonight?" asked Davidson, confident that no other ears were listening.

Edwards seemed not to hear the question. He stopped to find a coin for a grubby child, who tapped a pair of spoons on an upturned bucket. He dropped a penny into the boy's cap and told him to become a fine drum major.

"Tell me," he said, as he guided Davidson towards Oxford Street. "What are your plans this evening?"

"None so far, except to meet an associate at the Horse and Groom."

"Off the Edgware Road?"

"Aye, at seven thirty," replied Davidson.

"Be sure to take the item with you. You'll soon know if it's needed. Go quickly now, before Mr Aldous closes his shop."

MOLLY BRUNT

Fox Court, Holborn, 6.00pm

Ings's proposal that, on account of her delicate disposition, Mrs Brunt be spared participation in the operation, had been endorsed by the committee, and Molly was instructed by her husband, in any and every circumstance, to stay at home that Wednesday. Her disappointment was intensified by Eliza's gushing preparations for her "indispensable role" in the operation.

In the late afternoon, Molly put her grief aside and parted with tuppence for the letter-carrier, who arrived in Fox Court with an envelope addressed to Thomas Brunt. The hand writing was neat and feminine and like any spouse prone to anxiety, Mrs Brunt was determined to know the contents. She tapped on the store room door and called for Harry's advice on how one might open an envelope surreptitiously. Harry, who was compiling an inventory of the remaining weapons, replied crossly that ma should call him again, when she had boiled some water.

55½, Fleet Street etc

> *Dear Mr Brunt,*
>
> *Thank you for submitting your poetry for possible inclusion in* The Republican, *and I am sorry it has taken so long to reply. We always receive far too many submissions, and on this occasion, we are unable to publish your item. However, I enjoyed your work, and I am sorry to disappoint you.*

Molly was on the brink of throwing the letter on the fire for fear of upsetting her husband over a matter he had probably forgotten, when her eye caught a royal reference in the next paragraph.

However, we are preparing a special pamphlet in which leading radicals express their responses to the death of the late king, the succession of George IV and the anticipated return from exile of his estranged wife. For reasons you will understand, I am inclined to consider those writers who are most confident with the application of metaphor and I consider you to be among that number.

"Harry!" shouted Molly excitedly through the store-room door. "What's metaphor?"

Harry was counting bullets and would not be interrupted. Molly read on.

I cannot promise payment until the pamphlets are sold, but if you have a suitable satire of about 500 words or a poem of about 350, please bring it to the shop at your earliest convenience.

Yours sincerely,

Jane Carlile, Publisher.

Molly whooped for joy. Her own Thomas Brunt a leading radical and a published poet! That would put Eliza in her place! If only Molly knew where Thistlewood had sent her husband today, she would march straight there, operation or no operation, just for the pleasure of seeing her husband's face when he heard the news. Since Harry was preoccupied, Joe was active in the second unit, and she was not allowed out, there was nobody to tell.

Molly Brunt opened the cage door and invited Boadicea to step on to her finger and hear the good news. All the canary wanted was to fly round the room in wild celebration of her freedom. When at last, she (or he) fell panting on to the kitchen table, Mrs Brunt cradled the bird in her hands and, with great delight, announced that she was married to a leading radical and a published poet. Then Molly popped Boadicea back into her cage and said that a tiny sip of beer would do neither of them no harm while they waited for Mr Brunt's return.

TIDD

Tyburn Turnpike, by Hyde Park, 7.20pm

With the duelling pistols strapped to the belt beneath his overcoat, Richard Tidd could smell victory. Edwards had provided him with the guns, a pocket watch and, should his confidence need a boost, a flask of liquor. His instruction was to count the men who approached him with the correct password (which, at Brunt's suggestion, was "button") and direct them to the Horse and Groom on John Street. Tidd had been waiting since six-thirty. By seven-fifteen, only twenty-two of the expected unit of fifty had arrived; seventeen English and five Irish. It was disappointing, Tidd thought, but manageable, and he could not wait a moment longer. Edwards had instructed him to proceed to the room above the stable in Cato Street for a final committee meeting before the other warriors were summoned from the Horse and Groom.

By the time he set off along the Edgware Road, Tidd had swallowed a third of the liquor against the bitter wind. He wondered whether their Lordships had arrived at Grosvenor Square, and what meal was being prepared in the kitchen. There would be beef no doubt, and batter pudding, with a hundred delicacies besides. Well may the gents enjoy that supper, for it would be their last!

On the corner of John Street, Tidd was surprised to see the conspicuous figure of Will Davidson standing on the corner, chatting to his cowman friend. He greeted them warmly, as if this were any other day, except that his face was more flushed than usual, and his speech a little uneven. Drawing Davidson and Hyden close, Tidd unbuttoned his coat and displayed the pistols.

"The day of glory has come!" he said. "The people will be liberated from the tyrants at last!"

Tom Hyden opened his eyes wide and said that glory must wait for him to deliver some cream. He darted away to furtive cover with the blacksmith on the corner, until his composure returned, when he took a back route to the watch-house on Portman Street.

"I wasn't expecting you here," said Davidson to Tidd.

Tidd guffawed. "It's as clear as daylight," he said, "you've no experience of clandestine operations. Say you had been apprehended with a blunderbuss on your person, and enemy agents had tortured you, you would have told the truth."

"I believe so," said Davidson.

"Exactly," said Tidd. "Nobody would have found a crime in it, and you wouldn't be giving anybody away."

"You mean, Mr Goldworthy's property-speculator friend won't be at the Horse and Groom?"

Tidd considered the question unworthy of reply. Without another word, he led Davidson to the stable on Cato Street. They found Brunt and Ings crouching in candle-light, equally uninformed about the next step. They had discovered, hiding in the straw, guns and a flask of liquor against the cold.

"What the devil's going on, Tiddy?" asked Brunt.

"That's what I want to know!" said Ings. "Where is everybody and what's the plan?"

"You two must stay here," whispered Tidd imperiously.

"We won't miss the main event?" asked Brunt.

"Wait for orders!" commanded Tidd. "You must stand guard, while Davidson describes Harrowby's house for the others. He'll come to you later."

Tidd turned to Ings. "You're certain you can identify Sidmouth and Castlereagh?"

"Their portraits are as fixed in my mind as the hope of glory," replied Ings. "I have the sharpest cutlass in England and a bag for each of their heads!"

Thus assured, Tidd and Davidson lit a candle each and climbed confidently up the ladder into the loft.

SUSAN THISTLEWOOD / ELIZA TIDD

Grosvenor Square, London, 7.30pm

If anyone had asked the gentile woman and her young, male companion why they loitered in the dark in such harsh weather, they would have responded with convincing anxiety that their uncle, Mr Geoffrey Everard, was expected to collect them in his carriage, but seemed to have been delayed by business. They were keeping themselves warm by walking briskly around Grosvenor Square. Not far away, on the corner of South Audley Street, the impoverished silk ribbon-hawker was none other than Eliza Tidd in clothes borrowed from Brunt's landlady, and as alert as a roe deer to activity anywhere on Grosvenor Square.

So far, Susan and Julian Thistlewood had observed no movement at number thirty-nine, apart from the candles that flickered through the curtains of the front room, where, according to Davidson's sketches, the dinner would take place. A man on horse-back had visited briefly, but rode off again a moment later. There had been no evidence of bustle and no last-minute deliveries.

The three conspiring hearts beat a little faster, when a pair of carriages drove up from Upper Brook Street, but the passengers were welcomed into the house next door to thirty-nine. Susan and Julian approached the drivers. No Mr Everard was among the passengers, they said, who were all dinner guests of the Archbishop of York.

Eliza Tidd could contain her patience no longer. Bold as a monkey and without conferring with Mrs Thistlewood, she carried her tray up the steps to Lord Harrowby's house, rapped impertinently at the door, and asked if anyone cared to buy the last of her silk ribbons, and whether a poor widow might warm her frozen hands against the fire a moment. She was taken aback when the young manservant smiled sympathetically at her speech. The butler had business elsewhere, he said, as he beckoned Eliza in. The kindly servant even allowed Eliza to peep inside the downstairs rooms, so long as she didn't touch. Sure enough, the great oak dining table was covered in exquisite lace and laid out with white porcelain, silver cutlery and glistening glass, such as Eliza had never seen in her life. How could a person employ so many items to eat one dinner?

"I 'ope I ain't disturbin' no party, mister," Eliza, intent on imitating the poorest creature in Shoreditch. She was warming her hands by the fire in the butler's kitchen.

"Not at all ma'am," said the servant. "There should have been a dinner, but we had a message, ten minutes ago, that it's happening somewhere else. Didn't half cause a ruckus in the kitchen! Security reasons, but we're well protected."

"Really?"

453

"Don't worry," said the servant, misunderstanding his visitor's alarm. "No harm will come to you."

He indicated a pistol on the sideboard.

"Should you have a trio of villainous cousins, hiding in the gardens, you tell 'em Johnny Baines done his country proud at Waterloo! There's a patrole in the kitchen, an' all."

"Take a look, young man!" replied Eliza, feigning indignation. "If I had willinus relations, would you see me in this extreme state of poverty? Now then, how about a ribbon or two for the missus? Penny a piece?"

It was a performance Eliza would be proud of for the rest of her life, and a story her grandchildren and great grandchildren would recite for ever more.

As soon as the servant had closed the door behind her, she dropped the tray of ribbons into the Archbishop's stairwell, picked up the hem of her skirts and ran in search Susan and Julian Thistlewood.

The dinner, Eliza revealed, was cancelled! They must alert the men at once, if Mrs T would kindly lead the way. That is when they realized that not one of them had the faintest idea where the men might be.

THISTLEWOOD
The Loft, Cato Street, 8.15pm

Twenty-one warriors of Thistlewood's first unit crammed into the small room above the stable. Illuminated by the flickering shadows, they leaned against walls or sat on the floor. The Irish from Gee's Court and Vauxhall, still wary of the English, preferred to perch in the shadows of the beams above. Arthur Thistlewood sat with Edwards, Tidd and Davidson at the table, which was laid out with the armoury; hand grenades and fire-balls developed by Edwards, pike handles made at New Fish Street and the spikes sharpened there, with old bayonets, knives, daggers, fuses, boxes of nails, bullets, belts, pistols and muskets. On the floor was a box of almost a thousand ball cartridges, each one wrapped in flannel and manufactured in Molly Brunt's kitchen.

Arthur Thistlewood, his back as stiff as a board and his trusty French sword at his side, welcomed the unit and disclosed the final details of the operation. Then he allowed the men to relax for a while and release their high spirits. They made gleeful imitations of the Ministers' squeals at Armageddon and speculated about trophies.

"I shall take Sidmouth's gold rings!" called someone.

"I'll cut away Wellington's ears and nose for my wife to pickle!" called a Londoner near the entrance, "since his care-lessness cost us three boys."

"Why not take his privates for your mantel, for I shall have Castlereagh's!" cried an Irishman from above.

"No! I'll be sure and cut off the general's, for he's a Dubliner!" called another.

There was a chorus of lusty whoops, until Thistlewood stood.

"Hush my brothers, hush now," he said. "Even here, there are neighbours and perhaps others, who wish us harm. We must never, for a single moment, forget our purpose! We are not here to exercise personal revenge. Our mission is to remove, quickly and efficiently, the outdated machinery of state and open the gate to a fair and prosperous society for all."

An Irish voice called down

"The King and his Ministers might be machines of iron, Thistlewood," called an Irish voice from above, "but we are men with boiling blood. Our anger, on behalf of the slaughtered innocents of Ireland and Manchester, is righteous and justified! Every time we look at our starving children, our hearts must ache. Who would not be vengeful?"

"Your revenge will be sweeter, Tom Dwyer, when we succeed!" replied Thistlewood. "Success depends on every man acting bravely according to orders, and never submitting to private passions. As long as we proceed with vigour and self-control, success will be ours. Now, come down, Tom Dwyer and all your friends, and let each man shake the hand of his English brothers."

"And Scots!" added Davidson, admitting that he coveted Melville's tartan, in which he might look quite fetching, though he had no private dispute with his Lordship.

A murmur of laughter softened the tension, and the Irishmen slipped to the ground to grasp the hands of their fellow warriors. Thistlewood summoned each man, name by name to issue a few private words of instruction and encouragement. Edwards and Davidson shook their hands too, and wished each man well, as Tidd allocated the weapons according to the list he had memorized.

When every man was armed, Thistlewood spoke again.

"This operation is only the start," he said. "We must proceed as humanely as possible. Be sparing with your weapons, and leave none behind that can be used against us."

Thistlewood asked if the aide de camp had anything further to say. Looking round at the men, Edwards said how proud they made him, because despite every hardship they faced and every obstruction, they had been moulded into a disciplined fighting force.

"As many of you know, every battle depends not on inspiring leadership alone," Edwards continued, "but on the well-being of its army. Now, please feast at your pleasure, and then may the operation commence!"

In a cupboard by the back window, there was enough bread, cheese and gin for company twice the size. Thistlewood, who had no appetite, stood up and spoke of his own pride at sharing the last supper of the old order with so many selfless patriots.

"Thanks to your bravery, my brothers," he said, the sun will rise tomorrow on a new order, and all of this great country shall begin a life of hope!"

"Indeed!" added Davidson, "and our nation will feel again the spirit of the ancient tribes and of the Barons who composed the Magna Carta!"

Then, to a room of silence, candles and tense anticipation, Davidson said that instead of Grace, he would sing an ancient song, snatched from obscurity by Robert Burns, which began -
Should auld acquaintance be forgot,
and never brought to mind?

From his place at Thistlewood's side, Edwards watched Will Davidson, whose sharp, enquiring mind had so concerned him that he had considered another mission at the Monument. But there had been no discovery by Davidson, nor anyone else, no unravelling of his plan, no hint, even, of suspicion, and now his little lambs were on their way to slaughter.

As the men took their supper, Edwards summoned Thistlewood into a side room. Should by any grave misfortune, the operation be abandoned, Edwards said, he had arranged safe lodgings with John Harris, who was leading the second unit. The address was White Street in Little Moorfields, where the front door of number eight would be on the latch all night, and Mrs Harris would expect a lodger.

"Shall I write out the address?" asked Edwards.

"And if it is found in my pocket, implicate an innocent family?" replied Thistlewood. "We must hope it won't be necessary, but I shall remember it and thank Harris tomorrow at Mansion House! For now, thank you, my excellent friend. Without your steadfast support and insights, we would never have arrived at this moment."

Before Edwards could respond, there was a clattering outside the door, at the top of the ladder. Crushing his candle and urging Edwards to stay low, Thistlewood drew his sword. As he pushed the door open, a sneering voice called out,

"Now here's a pretty nest of you, gentlemen!"

"Police!" called a second officer. "Lay down your arms!"

It was too late. Thistlewood's blade had penetrated the torso of the first officer, who toppled to the ground, blocking the exit. The man's face was to the floor, but from his figure, Thistlewood was confident he had finished off John Stafford.

"That's done for you, you weasel!" he cried and tussled with the fellow behind him.

"Kill the bastards" roared Edwards, discharging a musket into the air. "Throw them down the stairs!"

Davidson snuffed out every candle with his hat, snatched a knife and leapt into the hay chute towards the stable below. In his rush to escape, Tidd tripped over the fallen officer, but picked himself up at the top of the stairs and shot his two pistols into the darkness below and gave a high-pitched battle cry.

"Here comes Richard Tidd! Give me liberty or give me Death!!"

Thistlewood snapped instructions to men he could not see and called up to Nott, the long-legged messenger, hiding, like a spider, in the beams, to take heed. It was Nott's signal to report to the second unit. When Thistlewood called out for Edwards, there was no answer. Was his aide mortally hurt, or had he followed Davidson down the chute? More officers were mounting the stairs, with Tidd trying to beat them off. Thistlewood drew his sword, and a third constable fought back until he was struck on the head by the butt of Tidd's pistol.

"He's done-for!" said Tidd.

"Run for it!" cried Thistlewood.

With a storm of bullets, crackling and hurtling from the windows above and all around him, Tidd stayed exactly where he was, Thistlewood escaped, coughing, through the smoky darkness, down the stairs and crept through the yard, past the approaching platoon of Cold Stream Guards and on to the Edgware Road. Neither his racing heart and nor his delirious mind was yet convinced of defeat.

INGS

Cato Street, 8.30pm

Ings was downstairs in the stable, when pandemonium broke out in the loft. The police swarming like hornets, there was smoke everywhere and guns shooting from the window above. Brunt, who had experience of warfare, told him they would meet again at Mansion House, and slipped into the darkness. Ings hesitated. If he ran for it, he would almost certainly be shot or cut through. If he stayed in the stable and was not found, but a fuse was ignited amid the tumult upstairs, he would be burnt alive. Outside, he heard the sharp order of an army captain and more horses, approaching. Was it his death sentence, or the very distraction he needed? Hearing more gunshots from above, Ings decided to crawl away like Brunt, before the soldiers dismounted.

Ings had advanced no more tha three yards, when he was set upon by a constable. He fought like an animal, and in a short time, pressed the office against a wall. As the fellow struggled and grunted like a rutting pig, Ings thought he heard Tidd's voice, shouting at him to stand back. He supposed that it was also Tidd who fired at his opponent, while he fled, ducking and diving between the excited horses.

Just as Ings thought himself free, another constable, this one a giant, with muscles like a steer, grabbed him by the collar. With his jacket little more than an assemblage of rags, Ings slipped away easily. He saw another officer nearby, knocking Tidd into a dung hill. When Ings turned to help his friend, the giant began beating him about the head. Whether driven by instinct or almighty will, Ings was possessed by the strength of Hercules. He tore himself away and ran, for his life, to the Edgware Road. The giant pursued him, with another man behind, and then Ings tripped on what might have been an abandoned well-cover.

"So, you're the butcher who would have the heads of Sidmouth and Castlereagh!" cried the giant.

The trusty apron, worn by his father and his father's father, had given Ings away.

"What if I am?" he asked, boldly.

With a hefty back-hander, the constable's stick hit Ings's right eyebrow. There was a flash of light, which, for all Ings knew at the time, was the merciful Gate of Heaven.

BRUNT

Edgware Road, 8.45 pm

The gunfire on Cato Street continued as he raced down the Edgware Road. Horses reared, whinnying in alarm, while pedestrians, driven by unfathomable curiosity, were running towards the bedlam. Brunt stopped in a doorway to cut a wedge of shrapnel from his leg, which was the left, just above his bad ankle. The wound was bleeding, but he felt no pain. His heart was on fire, and he was determined to get to Grosvenor Square. If none of the other men made it, there were sufficient cartridge balls and fuses in his pocket and knives in his belt to finish the business alone. He was descended from a hero, he thought, and if Thomas Brunt's fate was to die a martyr, then so be it. Molly could marry again, if anyone would have her. If not, their sons could expect an easier life burdened by only one old parent instead of two. Brunt's plans changed sharply at the corner of George Street, when George Edwards emerged from the shadows.

"Brunt!" he said, as casually as if they had met just any day on Fleet Street. "How are you, my brother?"

"Middling, since you ask," replied Brunt.

"A cup of good wine will help," said Edwards.

"I have a commitment." replied Brunt, indicating his pockets.

"That arrangement has been postponed." said Edwards.

"What!?" said Brunt, incredulous. "Are you sure?"

"I'm just back from the location. Nothing doing."

"How are my friends?"

Edwards smiled grimly, but said only that there were further instructions.

"If the job's done-for," said Brunt, I'd rather go home and put vinegar on my leg."

"Here, this kerchief will stop the bleeding" said Edwards. "There's a different job for you."

As Edwards peered into the chaos of the street for a cab, Brunt's battered mind was clear enough to speculate that if George Edwards had been to Grosvenor Square and back, he had done it in mighty quick time.

THISTLEWOOD

White Street, Little Moorfields, 9.30pm

As soon as he pushed it, the front door opened and Thistlewood was met in the kitchen by Mrs Harris.

"Mr Harris is working tonight," she said, by way of greeting, "and the front door's broke."

A tiny woman, nervous as a sparrow, she ladled tater soup into a bowl, and asked why Mr T was so late arriving.

"I know from your looks something's afoot," she said. "I neither know nor care what it is, so long as my husband's employment is safe. Thirty years, Mr Harris has give to Caslon and Catherwood, through thick and thin."

"Don't you worry, Mrs Harris," replied Thistlewood. "There's only John and my deputy knows I'm here."

"John Harris is a good man," she said, "but he's come over all silent lately, and I'd trust the rats in my cellar further than I'd trust George Edwards or his brother, for that matter. I have second sight, Mr T and an instinct for these things."

"I promise, you have nothing to fear, Mrs Harris" said Thistlewood, who had no appetite for soup or conversation.

"You got nothin' to fear neither," said Mrs Harris, as they climbed the stairs to her spare room, "since I shall lock your room as well as my own."

CHAPTER TWENTY-TWO

Wednesday, 23rd February, 1820
(continued)

MARY TIDD BARKER

Hole in the Wall Passage, Holborn

When Mary told the twins that their parents were visiting the
Pimlico aunt, who had become gravely ill, her little sister was
not at all satisfied with the explanation.

"I saw ma walk down the passage with a trayful of ribbons,"
Marjorie had said. "Why would she walk all the way to Pimlico,
when she never goes further than the market? Especially not
with such a burden round her neck. And why should a distant
relative be given silk ribbons, when her daughters and new
granddaughter have none?"

Mary began to wish that she had found another excuse,
because the twin pestered her all evening, even throwing doubts
on the existence of the ancient relative, to whom Marjorie had
never actually been introduced. The questioning, and the boys'
noisy fighting stopped when the children heard the unmistakable sound of pa, outside the door. There was gin in his voice.

"Hush!" said Mary sharply. "Into your bed!"

Quick as a flash, all six little ones sprang beneath the
covers and froze. Mary closed the back-room door and took

the candle to greet her father. He was covered in a mixture of muck and blood, his face a portrait of despair.

"Sit down," said Mary." Let me help."

"Is ma home?" asked Tidd.

"No," replied Mary. "Is it done?"

Tidd hesitated, and then he said, "Mary, I have killed a tyrant, and for that, you must always be proud of your pa!"

For the first time in her life, Mary saw her beloved step-father weeping. She was still hugging him when her mother arrived with no sign of any tray or ribbons.

"Thank God my husband is safe, but I fear we are done for!" said Eliza, closing the door. That message was heard by the children, who ran from their mats. The family clung to-gether, each sobbing, because the others were sobbing, and because nobody had any idea where comfort might be found. The huddle was intact ten minutes later, when the patrole ar-rived and tore it apart.

INGS

Coldbath Fields Goal

They pinned his wrists and dragged him along Cato Street by the hair, but Ings made not a sound. To the interrogation at The Horse and Groom, even when they said that at least one constable was killed, and he might be culpable of murder, Ings responded with a sullen glare. His innards were as mashed as a box of mince, his heart and spirit as chilled as his cold store, as they pushed him into a carriage to sit between haughty officers.

He closed his eyes, and with the steady clip-clop of the horses and the occasional jolt as they crossed a hole in the road, a picture formed itself at the back of the butcher's mind of the last time he rode in such a vehicle. He saw Celia again and the light in her eyes, the confusion of excitement and trepidation that they had experienced in their different ways, when they drove into London on the last day of April. How right his dear wife's judgment had been of the wickedness of the city, and how foolish he was not to have heeded her. From nowhere, sweet Margaret came into his mind, and Ings sensed a new heaviness in his heart. It was sorrowful, but it was not, as it might have been, the descent of impending doom. Instead, crushed between two stern officers, as the carriage climbed slowly up to Cold Bath Fields, James Ings experienced his second or possibly his third epiphany.

He knew, quite suddenly, that although he would always remember her, Margaret had been the fancy of a soul ravaged by loneliness. The politics had provided a kind of purpose to a tradesman robbed of his trade. He had been seduced into co-operation with a gang, whose world had seemed full of adventure, but which, in truth, had nothing in common with his own. What did the other men know or care about Hampshire or butchery or the family life he enjoyed before Croxton intervened? If only old Uncle Silas had written a different will, and they had never set foot in this city of sin! Ings must have yelped because the officer on his left chuckled and asked if the devil had come visiting.

Once he had settled in a cell, Ings found his tongue, his common sense and a good portion of clarity. He told his guard that death would be a pleasure; he would sooner be hanged tonight than turned into the street, for he would not know where to get a bit of bread for his family, who had been forced by poverty to live apart from him, and whose fate haunted his every living moment. The guard must have been moved by the little speech because he granted Ings's request for a pencil and paper to write to Celia, and even promised to have the letter delivered to Portsea in exchange for the butcher's cap, which, for its notoriety, must be an item of value.

> *The House of Correction,*
>
> *Cold Bath Fields,*
>
> *Clerkenwell*

My Dearest Celia,

I love my family more today than ever before, and I promise, no matter what slander you read in the press, that I never killed a man. I advise, if you can, to avoid all newspapers and trust that my only motive was the hope for a better future for our country and ourselves. And yet, dear wife, you must prepare yourselves for the worst, because my punishment will surely be final.

It is my solemn wish and instruction that nobody bearing the name Ings should attempt the journey to London to see me. My family must stay in Portsea and hold fast to our happiest memories. I prefer to remember my wife and children in happy times than to suffer a meeting in sorrow and tears, the memory of which would disturb you all your lives. Lizzie must be given my grand-mother's blue woollen shawl as a token of my gratitude. My heart, my soul, and the rest of my property, should remain always and affectionately with Celia, William, Celia-Ann, Thirza and Emeline Ings.

I remain your most devoted husband,

James Ings

SUSAN THISTLEWOOD

Stanhope Street, Lincoln's Inn Field

By the time they arrived, she had shredded and burnt the most sensitive paperwork. With his blessing, she had given Julian a sleeping draft, so that he would be rested for whatever Thursday might bring. She had succeeded in concentrating on a verse in her latest library book, when there was a loud knock at the door. Four constables demanded to enter. Susan opened the door gently and asked them to stay quiet for the sake of her child and the neighbours and to provide their authority to search her apartment. When the senior officer produced his document, she led the men to the bedroom upstairs, calmly and without a word as they searched for Thistlewood under the bed, where no human could fit and in the corner, where Julian slept like a baby on his mat. She led the way down again, and sat on the yellow settee, watching them with a composure so rare in the senior officer's experience, that it unsettled him. He flipped open her book to examine it for seditious content. Finding the *Tales and Historic Scenes* to be not only poetic, but authored by a female, he raised his eyebrows and let it be.

Wondering how a misfit like Thistlewood had bewitched such a dignified creature, he turned his attention to the desk. When the other constables began throwing the contents into a sack, Susan spoke out, but only to beg them to leave the glass inkstand, which was her son's heirloom from his great-grandfather. The senior officer studied it, as if some mystery might lurk in the ink.

"If this item had a tongue to speak with," he said, "it would tell a merry tale!"

"It would, indeed," replied Susan, "of the climate in Lincolnshire and the progress of crops."

The ink-stand was spared, and the officers found nothing of interest in her kitchen, but removed any item that might be used to inflict harm – poker, knives, toasting fork and her rolling pin. Then they told Mrs Thistlewood to sit at the table, where two constables fired questions, while the others stood by, apparently analysing her movements and changes in expression. Her husband had left home at about midday, she said, and she had noticed nothing strange in his behaviour. She had not seen him since and had no idea why he was late, or where he had been today. Of course, she knew about Mr Thistlewood's political interests and was sympathetic to the causes he represented, namely suffrage, freedom from tyranny and the improvement of the lives of Britain's majority.

"Now, if you please, gentlemen, I should like to sleep," said Susan, rising and moving towards the parlour. "If you return tomorrow, you will find me here, and I shall answer any further questions then. Good night."

"We're not done yet," said the senior officer. "Hold her fast, fellows!"

"What do you want?" asked Susan coolly, as two of his colleagues seized her elbows.

"How do we know what you have hidden about your pretty person?" asked the fourth constable.

"There's no need for force," said Susan. "Do keep your hands away!"

Under the awed gaze of four constables, brusquely and impersonally, Mrs Thistlewood removed her cap and apron, her slippers and stockings, her dress, her stays and her petticoats and offered each item for examination. All that was left to cover her were a simple shift and bloomers. The officers stared, each cowed by the combination of dignity, beauty and his own shame. As they left, they thanked Mrs Thistlewood for her cooperation. They would be sure to visit her again, they said, and her son should expect a few questions, too.

An hour or so later, wearing her night-gown and wrapped in the blanket her mother had knitted, Susan sat on the settee, brushing her hair, when there was another knock at the door. She hurried to respond, bright with hope that her husband had returned without his key, even though logic suggested otherwise, and the patrole was likely to be waiting outside.

INGS / TIDD / DAVIDSON
Cold Bath Fields Gaol

When his letter was gone and his tears had dried, Ings's cell door opened. Blinking at the brightness of the candles, he saw two officers with another prisoner. Dear old Tiddy. There was a wild look about him, which softened when he saw Ings.

Ten minutes later, they were trussed up like a pair of partridges, their legs weighed down by chains. A guard slumped in the corner, with four candles, a pot of ale and a pack of cards, which he shuffled into a game of solo.

"You should see 't size of your phizzog!" said Tidd to Ings. "Black as coal and double what it was before."

"Where was you taken?" asked Ings.

"At home," said Tidd. "Wife and children followed; I could hear 't caterwauling, all 't way up 't Baynes Road."

"I never told 'em where to find you," said Ings.

"I know that, Jim," whispered Tidd. "Reckon Tom Hyden turned traitor."

"The dairy man?" asked Ings, no longer capable of surprise.

"He went off to deliver cream, but there was no cream about him, unless some tiny pot in his pocket, and he didn't come back, neither."

"What a coward," said Ings.

"Weren't no coward's look on his face, when he ran off," said Tidd, and then, with a hint of satisfaction in his voice. "Tiddy shall face a murder charge."

The guard looked up from his card-game.

"What? For the officer who attacked me?" asked Ings.

"Better!" replied Tidd. "Tiddy fired straight into the heart of an army captain! If 't world is rid of a single tyrant, I shall face 't gallows with a proud heart."

"You shall be disappointed, Mr Tidd," snarled the guard.

"Says you," replied Tidd.

"You singed that gentleman's collar, no more. He'll be lying on top of his tart now, which is more than you'll ever do again. When he's finished, I expect he'll have a juicy steak and a brandy, and a good laugh with his cronies about you and all your non-sense!"

"Close your ears up, Tiddy!" advised Ings. "It's their sport to provoke us."

"Wait till you hear which captain you missed by an inch, Richard Tidd," the guard continued. "Frederick Fitzclarence, bastard grandson of the man you failed to kill sixteen years ago; King George the third, God rest his Soul!"

It was crushing news. Tidd growled long and low, and Ings knew when to keep his trap shut. Except for the irregular snoring of the guard, the cell remained quiet for long time, until they heard the full-throated delivery of a Scottish battle song.

Scots wha hae' wi Wallace bled -

When Davidson was led into their cell and saw Ings and Tidd, his eyes lighted up. After that, apart from a glance of sadness, deep as a well, he ignored them, and once pinioned, crouched in the corner, muttering to himself recitations from Burns or the Bible.

Later that night, the three prisoners were allocated separate cells. Ings, who had no previous experience of gaol, said he preferred to stay with his friends.

"Saving for the purposes of justice," scoffed the guard, "as long as you live, James Ings, you shall have no company but the devil and your own bad conscience."

Ings replied that in that case, he intended to write his testament, so that a record of the truth might survive him. He needed a ream of writing paper and a box of pencils. The guard said he could have it all in return for his butcher's apron, which would fetch a pretty penny at auction. Having no further purpose for the apron, and plenty for the paper, Ings agreed.

BRUNT
Chiswell Street, Little Moorfields

The second unit sat on long benches at a table in a wine cellar near the Caslon and Catherwood foundry. A bright fire kept the place warm, and there were baked potatoes and mackerel. Far from mourning the collapse of a magnificent mission, the men were as merry as a wedding party. They seemed not to notice when two members of the committee walked down the stairs.

Among the revellers were faces Brunt knew from meetings, but apart from his apprentice, Hale, unit leader, Harris, who had made all the bullets, and Nott the messenger, he could attach names to none of them. Edwards indicated a smiling fellow with a red scarf, who sat shuffling cards, twisting and stretching them out to amuse his neighbours.

Drawing him to the shadows, Edwards offered Brunt a cup of wine and sipped the medicinal water he had secured for himself.

"What's this job you had in mind?" asked Brunt.

"Take a very good look at the card-player," said Edwards. "Name's Palin, and if he tries to leave the cellar, you must stop him."

"Seems like a decent fellow," said Brunt, "efficient, and he has the respect of his unit."

Brunt found the wine a little sour, but he drank it all the same, while Edwards whispered about Palin.

"After he checked the bonfires were ready for lighting, he went straight to Bow Street to inform the chief clerk, who, as you well know, is the secret eyes and ears of the Home Secretary. I must tell you Tom Brunt, that the man wearing that red scarf, was responsible not only for the failure of the operation, but also for the death of Richard Tidd."

"Tiddy is dead?" asked Brunt.

"As a door-post," replied Edwards.

"I don't believe it."

"Ask Palin!"

Brunt's mind was spinning. Poor Eliza! Not only foolish, but lost, now, and a widow! Six little children, fatherless! As Brunt tried to imagine a world without Tidd, Edwards placed a musket on the table beside him. Still managing his shock, Brunt did not take the hint.

"What of Thistlewood?" he asked. "Ings and Davidson? Are they dead too?"

"In hiding!" replied Edwards. "Tomorrow they sail for America, which you shall too, Brunt, with your family, as soon as we rid London of that traitor and his accomplice!"

Edwards indicated the musket.

"That will do for Palin. His accomplice is a whitesmith in the Borough; Potter of Snow Fields. It was the whitesmith cut Tidd through."

"Tiddy was stabbed?" asked Brunt.

"By Potter of Snow Fields!" repeated Edwards.

"How may I kill him?" asked Brunt.

"Are there no cartridges left in the store?" asked Edwards. "Put them in a basket, cover them with a pretty cloth, just like you did with the herrings, and everyone will think you're taking eggs to the market."

"I'm covered in muck and bruises," said Brunt, "and my bad leg's shot."

"You can say you fell in the hen house," replied Edwards impatiently. "Worry about that tomorrow, Brunt. Palin is in spitting distance!"

"I've escaped one battle today," said Brunt. "Not sure I can stomach another. The unit's jollity is surface, George. The men are happy to be alive, but one gunshot will lead to a blood bath!"

"I don't mean you to do it here," snapped Edwards.

"Another thing," said Brunt, revisiting his unease about the fellow. "Why are Thistlewood, Ings and Davidson off to America, if there's been no arrests and the operation is incomplete?

Brunt was still navigating his confusion, and Edwards still urging him to seize the moment, when they saw William Edwards descending the cellar steps in a state of agitation. He hurried towards them, pulled his brother aside and whispered to him. The expression on Edwards's face barely changed, as he stood up, instructed Brunt to act quickly or regret it forever, and followed his brother to the exit.

Brunt crossed over to study Palin, who sat on the far side of the table. A candle illuminated his features, as he studied his cards. He seemed a gentle fellow, with rosy cheeks to match his scarf. But if he had indeed betrayed them and murdered Richard Tidd, Palin had forfeited his right to life.

Weariness and the new pain in his leg had taken hold of Brunt's passions; he wanted only his home and his family. Edwards must deal with his spy himself, he decided. He put the musket in his sack, so it would not be found or abused, but as he stood up, Brunt felt dizzy. Thinking he would not make it to Holborn without help, he called as brightly as he could to his apprentice.

"Come on Joe; time to head home!"

"As long there's free liquor, I'm going nowhere," retorted Hale, bold from the wine. "And you want to wash your face, Master, before you give the missus a fright!"

A few fellows laughed drunkenly, and Brunt turned and climbed, as best he could, up the steps to the exit. When he opened the latch, the great door resisted, because of the snow, tumbling on to Chiswell Street, thick as goose down. The frozen air blasted his cheeks, and Brunt picked up a clump of snow, squeezed it and pressed it against his injury. He felt in his pocket for a flannel cartridge, tore the knot open, tipped the powder out, shook the cloth and tied it round his leg. Molly had cut that square, he thought, and now he must tell the poor creature that, but for this bandage, she had wasted her time and her sheets, and their best friend was dead.

Brunt's melancholy was distracted by the distinctive smell of fish. He had arrived at the very destination of his first herring adventure with Tidd! Here was the fishmonger's yard, where they left the stinking barrels, and there was the very trough, by the foundry, opposite, where they tethered the pony. With its covering of fresh, white snow, glittering in the lamp-light, how different Chiswell Street looked now from that steaming day in July. How they had laughed together, he and his best friend, as they drove though London, high as kites, pursued by a battalion of flies! How they had laughed on that innocent day in Goodge Street, too, when the pig ran into the road, and they were drenched and desperate, but had no mind to weep. Richard Tidd was the truest friend and partner a man could wish for, and now he was dead! With sudden purpose, Brunt turned back to the vault. He heaved the door open again, stood at the top of the stairs, and with as much executive authority as he could summon, shouted. "Palin! A word, citizen, if you please!"

The man in the red scarf looked up in faint surprise. Recognizing a member of the committee, he abandoned his cards to a neighbour. When he arrived in the street, Brunt stood there, a fierce expression on his face and an unsteady grasp on the musket.

"Are you the traitor who killed Richard Tidd?" asked Brunt.

"Tidd was the lucky one," said Palin, without the due alarm. "He ran clear away."

"Tiddy lives? You saw him?" asked Brunt. "I don't believe it."

"Put the weapon away!" said Palin, "You're not well, Mr Brunt, and you'll do yourself an injury."

"Tell me you saw Richard Tidd alive!" said Brunt.

"How could I see him," asked Palin, "if Tidd was in the first unit, I'm in the second and I've been building bonfires all day? Nott, the messenger saw Tidd escape, and he has no reason to lie. He saw Ings and Davidson, too; arrested, but fighting fit, at Cato Street. Who gave you the idea, I killed Tidd?"

"You're quite sure Tiddy's alive?" asked Brunt, "Ings and Davidson captured?"

"Ask Nott," said Palin. "He was on his way when the cavalry arrived. He hid in the stable so he knew what to tell us when he got here. Lad's lucky to be alive."

"Was Thistlewood taken?"

"Escaped."

Brunt was confused. Palin gave the impression of a man who would no more kill a man than jump over the moon. Perhaps he had borrowed the red scarf from the true culprit, and in the half light of the wine-vault, Edwards had identified the wrong fellow.

"Mr Edwards told me Tidd is dead from a wound, inflicted by you and Mr Potter, the whitesmith," said Brunt. "Perhaps in the turmoil, he was mistaken."

"I was nowhere near any turmoil. Neither was Edwards, or not for long," replied Palin. "You ask the Irishmen! Edwards threw a rope through the back window and ran for it, before the army arrived."

"I met him on the Edgware Road," protested Brunt.

"Mr Brunt," replied Palin. "I tell you most earnestly that you're mistaken about me and Potter. I warn you against Edwards. I confronted him once and I presume your threat is his response. He's trying to trap you, Brunt, get you to commit murder. If there's a traitor in our midst, I'd wager my children's souls, it's George Edwards. Did you never wonder how he could afford to drive round in cabs all day?" asked Palin.

"Prosperous relations in Bavaria," replied Brunt.

"Bah!" scoffed Palin.

Bunt relaxed his musket and allowed Palin's explanation to unravel in his mind.

"I'm going back to my cards," said Palin. "Shall I tell Hale to help you home?"

"No need," said Brunt. "And if anybody asks you, this conversation is about your bonfires and nothing more."

When Palin nodded and turned away, Brunt thought about shooting George Edwards instead, but he had no idea where

William had taken him. He saw a well-cover and tried to open it and drop the musket down, but cover was stuck fast in the ice, and he stuffed the gun back into his rucksack instead, and hoped he would find his way to Holborn without mishap.

He considered visiting the Tidds' apartment on the way home, but decided he was too exhausted to face Eliza in a state of anxiety or – should Palin have lied and Edwards not - inconsolable grief. If Tiddy still lived, they would face the impossible likelihood together, tomorrow, that, of all people, George Edwards had betrayed them.

It was a miracle that Brunt arrived at Fox Court without being attacked by thugs or locked up by a watchman. That Wednesday night, with arctic temperatures and rumours of a battle in the West End, even the most unsavoury Londoners preferred to stay indoors. When, at last he crawled up the icy steps at Fox Court, he was greeted with exceptional effusion by his wife, but even Molly's grand literary news failed to excite a response.

EDWARDS
Banks Court, Cripplegate

It was a five-minute walk from the wine vault to his mother's home, and George Edwards was fuming. He had been pulled out of a meeting before his intentions for Brunt and Palin were complete, leaving a dangerous loop-hole, should the two fellows remain sober enough to communicate. His witless brother had abandoned his post outside the house where Britain's most wanted criminal was confined. His hard-won reward was at stake, all because their mother deemed it urgent and essential that her first born son attend her immediately. There would be a price to pay, Edwards thought, if he lost his bonuses because of another broken window, which William or her gentlemen callers were too lazy to fix.

The house stank of foul eggs and when, with a sharp greeting, he entered the parlour, Mrs G was rocking in her chair. Without responding to the arrival of her first-born, she stood up, dropped a piece of coal on to the fire, wiped the blackened fingers on her apron and sat down again. Behind her, Edwards refused to break the silence.

"After everything I've done for you!" she cried, at last.

Edwards would not be provoked.

"Look at me when I speak!" ordered Mrs G.

Edwards moved forward and rested his steely eyes on his mother.

"Why was I excluded from my son's wedding?" she asked.

"You pursue me late at night, ma, and when I'm extremely busy at work, to ask such a question?" asked Edwards, wondering what role Tilly had played in the situation.

"Tell me why!" repeated Mrs G, her eyes blazing.

"It was a necessary wedding; not one which either I or the bride wished to celebrate," said Edwards.

"I'll say it was necessary!" said Mrs G. "Do you know what humiliation I have faced tonight?"

"I doubt it," replied Edwards.

"Look! Look at this!" cried Mrs G, pulling a square of paper from her apron.

An urchin had delivered the note from a Mrs Harriot Parker, and since Mrs G had no idea where to find George, she had been forced to haul her rheumatic bones and leaky boots out into the snow to ask his brother who by good fortune, had mentioned that he was on duty in a street, which by further good fortune was not very far away.

"You know this Mrs Parker, I suppose?" asked Mrs G, when Edwards declined to look at the message.

"What does she want?" he asked flatly.

"She informs me we shall both be grandmothers again by morning."

"I see."

Edwards had forgotten or did not know that Tilly's confinement was imminent.

"What is this 'again'?" cried Mrs G. "What else have you not told me?"

"Now is not the time, ma!" replied Edwards.

"I hope you'll go to her, this poor, neglected Matilda and help her, where I was never helped?"

"Your false sentiment revolts me," said Edwards and turned towards the door.

"Bring my granddaughter to me," choked Mrs G, "and if it thrives, bring the new child, too. I beg you, George."

Behind her the door slammed, and Mrs G had no comfort, only the crushing memory of her sweet, smiling Hannah, lost in a fire because George was too slow to the rescue.

Out in the yard, Edwards vented his anger on the rainwater barrel, kicking it over and over again. How dare Tilly meddle in his private affairs! By which devious means had the vixen discovered his mother's address? Why, of all the days and nights, had she chosen this one to produce her brat? Edwards kicked and kicked until the last snow had fallen from the barrel, and his foot was sore because it was packed solid with ice.

He stood still for a few moments, remembering his mission and the extra reward he would lose, if he failed to retrieve his temper and act swiftly. Not entirely composed, Edwards set off for White Street to meet his brother, who was standing guard over Harris's house. William was spared a thick ear by confirming that the room where Thistlewood rested was firmly locked, and the front door still on the latch.

Edwards was weary, but he had one further task, and in the absence of night-time cabs, at least an hour of strenuous walking. It was the encounter he had anticipated for ten months. As he marched across hardened snow to Lincoln's Inn Field, the prospect cooled his cross mood and awakened his heart to tremulous pleasure.

CHAPTER TWENTY-THREE

Wednesday, 23rd February
(continued)

EDWARDS / SUSAN THISTLEWOOD

Stanhope Street, Lincoln's Inn Field

"Arthur?"

When Edwards heard his angel's voice, he forgot the bitter cold and the weariness. He imagined that soldiers felt this way, returning to their brides. Susan was anxious, and he would comfort her. She was forsaken, and he would rescue her.

"It's me," he said, "George."

She was wrapped in a blue blanket, and the glorious hair was loose, falling almost to her waist. Her eyes flickered with concern, the Celtic Sea glistening in autumn sunlight.

"Thank Goodness," she said, presuming from Edwards's steady gaze that nothing dreadful had occurred.

"Arthur?" she asked, a little unsteadily.

"Fit as a flea" said Edwards.

"Safe?" She was breathless.

"Of course," said Edwards.

"What happened? We didn't know where you were, and the police would tell me nothing."

"The operation failed at the last moment. Arthur and I escaped."

As she brushed snow from his greatcoat and knelt to loosen his wet boot-laces, her soft hair brushed against his breeches.

"The patrole is outside. How did you get past them?" she asked.

"I'm a physician, Mrs Thistlewood, come to check on Julian."

"What a master of counterfeit you are, George Edwards! There's parkin left, if you're hungry."

Edwards sat on the familiar yellow settee, and as Susan went to fetch his snack, he picked up her book. She had been reading a poem, *The Widow of Crescentius*. How brave and refined she was, how sad the sentiments she was reading.

Then sinks the mind, a blighted flower,
Dead to the sunbeam and the shower;
A broken gem, whose inborn light
Is scatter'd, ne'er to reunite.

"Arthur's sleeping soundly at my mother's house," he ventured, as she returned from the kitchen.

"Where?"

"Moorfields. We went straight there and I stayed with him until he instructed me to come here."

"I must go to him," said Susan. "Would you stay, George, in case Julian wakes?"

It was not the response Edwards anticipated.

"You can't go out now," he said.

"I'm his wife," said Susan, lifting her coat from its hook. "What address in Moorfields?"

She pulled the coat over her nightdress, Edwards leapt up to block her way.

"It's thick with snow," he said, "it's freezing, and the patrole is outside."

"Give me the address," said Susan. "I'm sure you can distract the patrole, George, and then come back here, in case Julian wakes."

"Sit down" said Edwards. "There's something you must know."

"What?" asked Susan, her voice fracturing, as she dropped on to the settee.

"I'm very afraid that we are lost," said Edwards.

"How lost? You said there was no evidence."

"Not yet. You remember the traitor, John Castles?"

"Certainly, I do."

"It appears that Ings and Davidson are also not the men we supposed them to be."

"What!" cried Susan. "Impossible. No gentler creature ever lived than Will Davidson, and Ings is a decent country fellow! Such straightforward, committed men, George, with none of the vulgar duplicity of Castles! Now, tell me where your mother lives."

"Hear me, Susan. We must act quickly. We shall sail to America with Julian."

The scrutiny, combined with Edwards's now drained and anxious face unsettled her.

"Didn't Arthur promise, when this is all over, to take you to Pennsylvania?" he asked.

"Massachusetts," said Susan, "and it's not all over."

"We must leave now. Tomorrow, the police will return and perhaps they will take you away, and Julian. Come, we can fetch Arthur, and go straight to the docks."

"How can that be safe, if there are police everywhere?"

"It is Arthur's wish. He told me so, just an hour ago, and we have the tickets to sail."

"He said nothing to me."

"He did not expect this outcome," said Edwards.

"You are confusing me, George! What else do I not know? Where is Arthur? Are you sure he's alive?"

Edwards was unprepared for an inquisition. After the long, exhausting day, his mind was less lucid than when he rehearsed the scenario at Ranelagh Place.

"Believe me," Edwards continued. "The situation is precarious. Arthur is safe at my mother's house, and he has instructed me to take you and Julian away. He will join us if he can."

"And if he can't?" asked Susan. "If he's arrested again?"

"There would be no hope" said Edwards.

"What then?" asked Susan.

"I shall take care of you," replied Edwards. "Far away from here. No more politics! No more poverty! A new life in Massachusetts, Susan. I shall easily find work. Julian will train to be a great artist, and you can read poetry all day long."

There! He had revealed himself.

"Get out!" said Susan, very quietly.

Edwards's self-control abandoned him. He seized Susan's waist and when she struggled, grabbed her hair and pressed her shoulders on to the settee with his elbows.

"Stop!" she commanded, unwilling to scream for fear of alerting the patrole outside. "Have you gone mad?"

"You know you've always wanted this! Whispering secrets, tempting me with that pretty neck."

He pressed his mouth on to hers. Susan Thistlewood punched and kicked. His hands tugged at her night gown. She remembered her mother's advice and was about to lift her knee, when Edwards cursed and howled and fell away. Yelping like an animal, he scuttled out of the apartment, stopping only to claim his boots and great-coat.

When Susan gathered her breath and opened her eyes, there stood Julian, clutching an old poker from Tupholme Hall, which the officers had failed to see in its nook beside the fireplace.

"I gave him a good whack," he said sleepily. "Three, actually."

They held each other tight.

"Mr Edwards forgot himself, Julian, that's all. He is tired and gravely disappointed. He forgot himself, and you, Julian, are my hero!"

"Will you tell papa?"

"Papa must never know. Nobody must know."

"Mr Edwards is a wicked man," said Julian. "He hurt you and told you lies."

"What lies?" asked Susan.

"Firstly, how did he know that the police have been here and will return tomorrow?"

"It's a fair presumption," said Susan.

"If Mr Edwards escaped the raid with pa and they have been at his mother's house ever since, how can he know that Mr Ings and Mr Davidson betrayed us?"

Susan replied that there was an explanation for everything. She expected they would be reunited with pa tomorrow, and now it was time to sleep.

As Susan considered Julian's observations, another suspicion crept into the back of her mind. Edwards had once mentioned a fire, in which his mother died, trying to rescue her baby. Perhaps there is a step-mother, she thought, but since Edwards had never mentioned such a relative, her home seemed an unlikely refuge in crisis. If his mother lived, why had he lied about the fire? Was Edwards a fantasist? He had demonstrated himself as such with his bestial behaviour, misplaced disappointment, perhaps a consequence of the operation's failure. What if Julian's instincts were right? What if she and Arthur had been diabolically deceived, and George Edwards was a traitor? But if he were a spy and his work was done, why had he risked his life to visit her, instead of seeking the protection of his paymasters?

Confounded by inconsistencies, Susan concluded that the only important truth was that she was unable to comfort her husband in his present distress. Nor did she have any evidence that her husband was still alive.

Edwards slipped into the same murky yard where once he had startled a chimney sweep. He pushed past a courting couple. The woman disentangled herself, and the man lashed out and told him to stop snooping, bugger off and find treats of his own. Edwards heard none of it. The financial reward for the capture of Thistlewood quite forgotten, he sobbed, and he slumped to the cold, hard earth and he wished that it would swallow him.

BRUNT / HALE
Fox Court, Holborn

On Wednesday night, when Joe Hale arrived home about an hour after the master, he found Mrs Brunt at the kitchen table in a state of anxiety noisier than any he had witnessed during the two years of his apprenticeship. Apart from the prophecy that they were all doomed, the mistress's explanation made no sense.

"In an operation this size, Mrs B," he said, "setbacks must be expected."

At this wisdom, which, in his state of mild inebriation, Hale found perfectly reasonable, Mrs Brunt sobbed even louder, told Hale he was monumentally deceived and begged for anything she could blow her nose on.

Thursday, 24th February, 1820

At six thirty in the morning, Hale was dozing with his head on the kitchen table. when Brunt slapped his shoulder and told him to clean the boots because they were off to the Borough to sell eggs.

When the impertinent youth required an explanation after the night he'd just had, the master told him to stop asking cheeky questions and fetch the cloth, the oil and brushes. Hale responded with a grunt and an unnecessary remark about the bruise on the master's forehead.

As he laid the fire, as usual, for his wife and son, Brunt tried to clarify his thoughts. He could not remember everything he ought to remember from the night before. His only fixed memory was Edwards's instruction to carry a basket of cartridges to the Borough and pretend they were eggs. He could not, for the life of him, recall the purpose of the mission. Perhaps, as with the operation, he would be greeted by more information on arrival. It was best, he decided, to prepare the weapons, and hope for insights, when the thunder in his head receded.

"When did Ings get home?" he enquired a moment later.

"He never did," said Joe. The boots had dried in the hearth overnight, but they weren't giving much of a shine.

Brunt crept into the store room, and sure enough, while Harry slept like a baby, Ings was absent from his mat. Unable to solve that particular riddle, as he reached for some cartridges and dropped them into his apron pocket, Brunt encountered a mystery of his own. He remembered the failed operation. He remembered that he had hobbled home across the snow from a vault at Moorfields. Beyond that, Brunt was confused. Had Edwards instructed him to shoot two men: Potter the white-smith in Southwark, who had killed Tidd, and a fellow, with a red scarf who was a spy? Or was it all a dream? Brunt was pretty certain he had not crossed the bridge last night, but had he or had he not shot the spy? One minute, he seemed to imagine the deed precisely, and the next he was equally convinced it had never happened. Either way, a traitor was at large, and his family and apprentice were in danger.

"Is that good enough?" asked Hale, lifting a boot for inspection.

"That toe needs more elbow-grease," grunted Brunt, taking a basket from the cupboard and directing his thoughts to a pretty cover for the eggs that were not eggs. He decided on the apron, which they used as a curtain between the weapon store and the sleeping mats. It was his wife's best, embroidered before their marriage, but it was a sacrifice Molly would have to accept. He reached for the scissors.

Hale was polishing the third boot, and Brunt completing his basket, when someone rapped at the door.

"There you are, Jimmy!" called Brunt. "Come and warm yourself up!"

Instead of James Ings, four constables stared down at him. For a moment, Brunt looked at them, stunned. Then, inexplicably, his mind seemed to clear, and he knew that he was tired of all the action, weary of the desperation, and very slightly relieved.

"Is Ings taken, too?" he asked, as he offered his wrists for binding. "And Tidd?"

The constables seem not to have heard him.

"Take me quietly," he said, "so my wife and son aren't forced to witness my shame. My family and my apprentice are entirely innocent, and I myself have never committed an act of which I am not proud."

Brunt turned to Joe Hale.

"I know I have been strict sometimes, Joe, but it has made you a fine young man, and I'm sorry that your apprenticeship must end like this. Your final instruction from me is to take the cover off that cage and carry the canary through to Molly, to help her, when she wakes."

As Hale stood there, looming and lost for words, two constables led Tom Brunt away, closing the door, as their colleagues began searching the apartment.

At the top of his stairwell, Brunt felt the gently falling snow on his face, and he was surprised to see a small crowd, cheering in the yard below.

The headache had gone, and he felt strangely roused. The officer allowed Brunt to raise his arms, and he wished his neighbours a very good morning and thanked them for leaving their homes to say goodbye.

"Speech!" shouted someone.

The officers were not unsympathetic to a prisoner who showed dignity, and had probably been duped by Thistlewood.

"If we cannot have liberty," Brunt declared, "then I, at least, shall face death. But if I had fifty necks, I would rather have them all broken, one after the other, than see my family starve."

"They'll starve soon enough, Tommy, without you looking on!" shouted Mrs Rogers.

There was not a single note of approval for the landlady's observation.

"Farewell, my friends," said Brunt. "Now, please let the officers pass in peace. They're only doing their work."

"God Save your soul, Tom Brunt!"

And the neighbours chanted, "God Save Brunt! God Save Brunt!" as they followed the little party into Grays Inn Lane, where the offers pushed Brunt into the waiting cab and sat on each side of him.

Twenty minutes later, as Harry played marbles listlessly by the fire, and Boadicea sang to poor, stupefied Molly Brunt, Joe Hale slipped through the door with nothing to show for his apprenticeship, but a heavy heart and a memento in the shape of a ball cartridge, wrapped in flannel and brown paper.

A constable was guarding the stairs. He confiscated the weapon at once, and said he had every reason to arrest Master Hale for conspiracy. But he had been a friend of Joe's late father, Joseph Hale, bootmaker of St Giles, and it would be a crying shame if Joe's ma were reduced to the same wretched condition as Mrs Brunt. Nothing Master Hale did, or did not do, could help his master now. Brunt's life was over, and a man's first responsibility must be to his own flesh and blood. Joe faced a choice; either to break his mother's heart and be deported (or worse) for High Treason or secure a bright future for all his family.

When Hale said he had no money, not a farthing, to pay the officer, the constable replied that it was not money he was after, but for Joe to follow him to Bow Street and tell the truth, whole and unvarnished.

THISTLEWOOD

White Street, Little Moorfields

At nine o'clock on Thursday morning, Mrs Harris was startled by the unannounced appearance in her kitchen of four constables of the Bow Street patrole. She had insufficient schooling to read the search warrant, and she objected stoically to their demand to enter her lodger's room, but eventually submitted the key and ran off tearfully to the Caslon and Catherwood Foundry to find her husband.

Officers Ruthven, Lavender, Bishop and Salmon removed their boots to climb the staircase softly. Thistlewood was still in bed. He seemed neither alarmed nor dismayed, and submitted silently to instructions to empty all his pockets, dress himself quickly and present his wrists to be cuffed.

Thistlewood had met Ruthven before, the senior officer who read, without much fluency, the charges of High Treason and the murder of a police officer.

"I deny Treason," he replied, "but I neither deny, nor regret the murder of John Stafford, though I'm sorry for the suffering widow; her only mistake was to marry a weasel."

"Mrs Stafford ain't got no worries I know of," said Salmon.

"Apart from her bunions," added Lavender, who, even at an historic arrest, considered himself a wag.

"It's a miserable wife, who rejoices in the death of her husband," replied Thistlewood.

"I'm sure there was a resemblance in the dark," said Ruthven, "but it weren't Mr Stafford you done in, Arthur. It were Constable Smithers, died in a stranger's arms at the 'Orse and Groom."

It was a disappointment, and Thistlewood fell silent, until the coach slipped and rumbled along the short, icy route to Bow Street.

"I am sorry for Smithers, as indeed I'm sorry for you all," he said. "My great ambition is to improve the lives of Englishmen, but too few of you will listen. You have no faith in your own strength! Why not take control of your lives instead of demeaning yourselves and earning a few shillings as the tyrants' slaves?"

"Insolent dog!" responded Lavender, and punched Thistlewood's left cheek

"Here's one for Mrs Smithers!" cried Bishop, punching the right.

"And his old ma and the children!" added Salmon, opposite, reaching out to give the prisoner's nose a vicious twist.

Ignoring them all, Thistlewood asked how much Mrs Harris was paid for the betrayal.

"Not a penny," said Ruthven.

"Except the tuppence you paid in rent," added Lavender.

"She knew nothing about it," said Ruthven. "Show 'im, Salmon."

Constable Salmon took a document from his top pocket and opened it for Thistlewood to read. It was an extraordinary proclamation by the *London Gazette*, offering one thousand pounds for information leading to the arrest of Arthur Thistlewood.

"What a fellow could do with one thousand pounds!" said Lavender. "What would you do, Bishop?"

Constable Bishop grunted, the answer beyond his imagination.

Thistlewood's mind raced. If Mrs Harris had not betrayed him, then who? Lavender guessed his thoughts.

"Why do you think Mr Edwards would go to all that trouble to find your lodgings?" he asked.

"I know no man by the name Edwards," said Thistlewood, calmly.

"We know two of them!" said Lavender. "Don't we, lads? Constable William Edwards and his brother George, what ordered William to stand guard, so you couldn't run off before the reward was published."

Thistlewood was accustomed to the provocative banter of constables, whose only entertainment was to compete in the taunting of captives. Pressed between the officers, he leaned forward to look out of the window, but a kind of nausea was rising in his belly.

"Why was your room locked last night?" taunted one of the officers.

"Who was it broke the lock on Harris's front door yesterday?" said another.

"And why did he break it? "

"Coz he knew we was on our way!"

Now, Thistlewood tensed and Constables Bishop and Lavender, who were pressed tight against his sides, knew they had him.

"George Edwards has made a great big figgy dumpling of a fool of you, Arthur Thistlewood!" said Salmon.

"John Stafford –" began Bishop.

"Or his ghost," chortled Lavender.

"- is sure to acquaint you with the facts."

"Mr Stafford knows all there is to know about you!" said Ruthven. "Down to the contents of your pantry and the colour of your wife's bloomers. My Lord Sidmouth does too, because, after you, Arthur, George Edwards is his most eager correspondent."

Submitting to exhaustion and, in his new perplexity, hardly knowing himself, Thistlewood allowed himself to be dragged into Bow Police station, where John Stafford was waiting to welcome him.

"Well, well," he said. "If it's not the Lincolnshire Napoleon again! It's an honour to be hosting you, Arthur, though I fear your return to His Majesty's hostelry is likely to be terminal."

Thistlewood refused to be roused, and he refused to answer questions. Nor, for fear for breaking down, did he ask for confirmation of the traitor's identity. In all Thistlewood's forty-eight years, nothing, not his father's accident, the deaths of his first wife or his parents, nor Robespierre's brutality in France, not Castles, nor even the collapse of the operation, had cut him more deeply than this most personal betrayal.

There was a further humiliation on Thursday afternoon, when Thistlewood was taken to Whitehall to be gloated at and questioned by the Privy Council, which included the very lords and gentlemen, who had failed to attend the dinner party in Grosvenor Square. Thistlewood was made to wait in an ante-room upstairs, while they examined the weapons carried from the loft at Cato Street. The door of the council chamber was open, and Thistlewood's flesh chilled at those flush pink faces, the humanity abandoned to greed, false grandeur and corruption.

When, finally, he was summoned into the chamber, Thistlewood looked again at the grenades and cartridges, knives, pike heads and boxes of nails, that had been so laboriously gathered or constructed by so many for the love of Britain. How pathetic, they seemed, how insignificant, laid out on a blue velvet cloth upon a shining mahogany table.

An unmistakeable note of triumph laced Sidmouth's command that the prisoner perch on a stool at the foot of the table. Thistlewood declined to respond with more than monosyllables, but as they questioned him, he looked into the eyes of each man by turn. With the possible exception of Wellington, he saw that each one of them feared him and everything that he continued to represent. Arthur Thistlewood knew he must die soon, but it would be with the certainty that his cause would not die with him.

Monday, 28ᵗʰ February, 1820

CELIA INGS

The road to London.

It was perfectly clear in Celia's mind that her husband had been coerced into actions that were entirely against his nature. It was her marital duty to ignore Jimmy's decision, which he had made while of unsound mind. She would travel to London to persuade his enemies of their folly in prosecuting a man whose only ambition was to keep his family fed. The nation should be spared the expense of a grand trial, she had concluded. and the money spent on reducing poverty instead. Jack's widow, Lizzie offered at once to accompany Celia and her daughters to London, while Bill minded the shop. On Sunday, a special collection was made at Chapel, while at the Unitarian Church, Lizzie accepted a sizeable donation from Portsmouth's Member of Parliament.

On Monday morning, they set off for London in a coach loaned by the same generous politician. When Lizzie proposed staying at The Saracen's Head, which their benefactor had recommended for its comfort and proximity to the Old Bailey, Celia protested that to book rooms so close to the court-house would weaken her proposal that there was no case to answer. But apart from Cooper's on Bouverie Street, or the Black Lion on Water Lane, both of which contained happy, but painful memories of her husband, Celia could propose no alternative and conceded to Lizzie's choice.

The children tried bravely to improve the mood with songs that Celia had sung to them in better days. After fifteen minutes, the driver begged for peace and handed down some newspapers. Celia was in no mood for reading, but Lizzie was thankful and soon repeated an item about crowds flocking to Cato Street and paying a shilling each to visit the loft where the alleged offences took place. The scheme had been established by an enterprising cowman named Firth, she reported, who had vowed to spend the profit on an agricultural school for the poor children of London.

Lizzie Ings was glad that someone would benefit from the whole fiasco. Celia demanded an apology for the thoughtless sentiment, especially since it was Lizzie's husband - and not her own - who was to blame for the family's misfortune. If Cousin Jack had learnt to ride properly, he would never have fallen off that horse. If he had learnt to swim, he would never have drowned in Portsbridge Creek. Furthermore, Jack had been either foolish or drunk to have purchased such a wayward beast in the first place. Lizzie retorted that next to the Lord Jesus, Jack Ings had been the family's only saviour. It was Celia's inability to keep her husband at home that had brought disgrace on them all. Before Celia could match her indignation with words, Annie protested.

"Ma! Aunt Lizzie! My father is all alone in a dungeon, and probably very frightened. Whatever he has done, he has done it for our sakes, and because he loves us. Must he die believing that we waste our lives in squabbles?"

"My husband will not die!" cried Celia.

"We must be very afraid he will, ma," replied Annie.

"James Ings is innocent!" insisted Celia.

"Yes, ma. Yes, he is!" said Annie. "We know that, and let's hope pa knows it too. But the people who judge him don't live like us, ma, and they don't think like us, neither. They're harsh, city folk, worse than Southampton, who will judge and punish him according to rules that we shan't never understand."

"Then we must persuade them that our ways are fairer and more honest," said Celia.

"Ma! We cannot!"

Annie's voice cracked, and she could say no more. Lizzie bent forward to kiss her little cousin and praised her wisdom and bravery in speaking out. Celia agreed that Annie had a wise little head and proposed they hold each other's hands for the rest of the journey. The family sat quietly until the border with Surrey, where Celia's strength returned sufficiently to recite her twenty third psalm.

Tuesday, 29th February, 1820

Coldbath Fields Prison, Mount Pleasant, Clerkenwell

Apart from the lock-up at Portsmouth barracks, Celia had never seen a prison before, but when she caught sight of the high, forbidding wall, she could not doubt that she had arrived at one. There were no windows, and only the occasional tolling of a bell persuaded her that there was anything on the other side. At last she found a door, big enough for a giant. Into the stone above it were engraved the words "*House of Correction for the County of Middlesex.*" Celia felt her knees weaken and told herself sternly that it was no good going soft now. The date was auspicious, and as long as she remained calm and bright, success would be hers.

The prison governor was pleased to hear that Mrs Ings had travelled all the way from the Hampshire coast and invited her to take tea in his office. The invitation was exactly the opportunity Celia needed. She had not expected a prison governor to be as accommodating as Mr Adkins, nor his rooms to be quite so luxuriously appointed. There was more velvet and more gold trimming than in Mr Pyke's office at Chancery Lane. A servant in prison clothing poured tea into porcelain cups.

"How is my husband doing?" asked Celia.

"He's a lively one!" said the governor.

"I'll say he is!" said Celia proudly, "and innocent as a baby, Mr Adkins."

"They all say that, Mrs Ings. I'm a prison governor, not the judge."

"Mr Ings shall be coming home, shan't he?" asked Celia, with her sweetest smile.

"Place your faith in British justice, dear lady. It's the best in the world!"

Adkins drank his tea with great slurps.

"Mr Ings needs to be in the best possible shape for his trial," he continued. "To keep him mentally and physically fit, I recommend our special regime. Instead of oats and water, he should take beef and porter twice a day, and spend extra time on the tread-wheel. What do you say?"

"Anything that helps my husband is advantageous," replied Celia and sipped her tea.

"The cost will be three pounds a week," said Adkins.

Celia dropped her cup on to her saucer.

"Or, for an advance of twenty pounds," the governor continued, "we can be sure that your husband begins his trial with every possible advantage."

Celia put the cup and the saucer on the table, her appetite for tea gone with the wind.

"Twenty pounds?" she cried. "Where do you suppose a countrywoman with almost no husband will find such a sum?"

"You refuse to help the prisoner, Mrs Ings?"

"I need time to consider," she replied, firmly. "I thank you for your tea, and if you please, I should now like to visit my husband."

"I'm afraid your husband is busy."

"Mr Adkins, I have travelled from the south coast. Mr Ings has not seen his wife for seven months, and I have no doubt that he would choose to be disturbed."

"Come again tomorrow, Mrs Ings, and if you wish the best for your husband, bring twenty pounds."

When Celia left the fortress, she had no strength to visit Mrs Tidd or Mrs Brunt, who allegedly lived close by and whose addresses were in her pocket. Instead, she hurried back to the Saracen's Head to hold her children tight and seek Cousin Lizzie's advice.

Governor Adkins, whose mind and morality had been curdled by ten years at one of the most corrupt institutions in London, sent a messenger to inform Prisoner Ings that his wife had attended an interview, but preferred not to visit him. In the subsequent days, Ings's sobbing could be heard all down the corridor. In a heartrending request that was to become the governor's particular favourite, Ings begged for his body to be conveyed to Windsor Castle, where His Majesty's cooks might chop him up and make turtle soup of him for the King.

Thursday, 2ⁿᵈ March, 1820

DAVIDSON / INGS
Whitehall, London

In his own mind, Will Davidson had been guilty of nothing at Cato Street, except the scratching of an army captain's hand with a cutlass, and that was in self-defence. Not once had he discharged the blunderbuss, neither had he gone to Cato Street with any malicious intent. He had been tricked into going there, and until he arrived, had no knowledge that an operation was imminent, nor of what form it might take. Indeed, there had been no operation, even though, under the terms of the Magna Carta an operation was justified, because ministers of the sovereign (in fact, of two kings) had failed to address wrongs committed upon the people and ignored reasonable requests to do so. Not only that, the Regent had, presumably on the advice of the same ministers, responded to the massacre of his own people in Manchester by thanking the assassins.

Davidson admitted to his interrogators that he had visited the house of his former employer, Lord Harrowby, and had drawn those sketches, found in the loft at Cato Street, consistent with a trained cabinet-maker. The sketches did not make him guilty of a heinous crime. In other words, the accusations should be dropped at once, and he must be set free to perform his duties as a husband and father.

Unfortunately, the members of the Privy Council, chaired in the Home Department by Lord Sidmouth, took a different view. At twelve o'clock on Thursday, William Davidson, along with other members of the Cato Street Conspiracy, were formerly charged with High Treason, and Thistlewood with the additional charge of murdering a constable. Their time in Coldbath Felds was over, and they would be driven from Whitehall to the Tower of London.

It was a particular annoyance to Davidson that he should face the august Privy Council while handcuffed to James Ings, whose clownish behaviour made it impossible to sustain his dignity. When the prisoners were marched out to the street, Davidson was still attached to the butcher, who had entirely abandoned his decorum and hollered that he was being led like a bullock to Smithfield. They were pushed into the Hackney cab, and faced each other, with officers on each side. Thistlewood and Brunt, solemn as owls, rode in the cab ahead and Tidd, with three guards (on account of his bad temper and criminal record) alone, in the vehicle behind.

As they set off along Whitehall, all London seemed to line the streets, waving flags and shouting messages; whether of blame or favour, Davison could not tell. Ings smiled through the window, waved at the people, and remarked that he knew exactly how the king felt on occasions of state. Among the incoherent shouts as they crossed Westminster Bridge, Davidson heard a woman call, "God Save Will Davidson!" Unable to look out, and unwilling to look ahead at the Hampshire butcher, Davidson looked down at his filthy feet and the heavy chains around them, with all the history they might claim, but it was all meaningless against his vision of the contempt on his father's face. The shouts that mocked his ears were not the clamouring crowd outside, but the taunts of his aunts and cousins, scorning him for bringing shame where only pride belonged, and a chorus of furious dead uncles, screaming that he had squandered his liberty, and failed to rescue a single slave, not even his beloved nurse.

They travelled on, through the Borough and over London Bridge, where Will Davidson looked out at the sailing ships heading east towards the wide, open sea. He was reminded of the lush island he had left behind, of sunshine, his mother's broken dreams, and of baby Duncan, who would have a far better life in Jamaica than his siblings in London. As they rode past Billingsgate, up New Fish Street and past the Monument, Davidson was distracted again by Ings's excited declamations, which stopped, as they drove past the warehouses of the East and West India Companies, into Trinity Square and through the Tower Gate.

The Tower of London

Solitude was bliss, when, at last, Davidson was allotted a cell in the Tower water-works. Thistlewood was sent, where Sir Walter Raleigh and two wives of Henry VIII were sent, to the Bloody Tower, while Tidd was allotted the Seven Battery and Brunt went to a cell above the kitchens. When the Hampshire butcher was also assigned to the water-works, and begged not to be left alone, Davidson feared that they might be forced to share, but the butcher was given a neighbouring cell. Even through those ancient walls, Ings could be heard moaning and wailing endlessly about turtle soup. Davidson tried to smother the racket with song, but his spirit could not raise a strong enough voice. After a sleepless night, he protested to a gaoler, who told him to shut his black mouth. On the fourth such night, Davidson demanded to see the Tower physician and complained about the fierce cold of the waterworks. If he died of pneumonia, he would be denied the process of clearing his name.

On the fifth day, Davidson was visited by the fort-major, Dr Elrington, who apologised, led the interesting prisoner personally to the Bull Tower, where they shared a meal of beefsteak and porter, and Davidson heard that Walter Scott was to be made a baronet for his part in returning the Scottish Crown Jewels. Davidson accepted the food and drink, but informed the fort-major that Oliver Cromwell had buried those jewels for good reason. A trained lawyer like Walter Scott must know that, he protested, and the King had no more right to the jewels than a Spanish fisherman. Elrington had stationery delivered to the cell, but when Davidson tried to formulate his complaint, he concluded that it would be more pertinent to congratulate his compatriot on the baronetcy, invite him to visit the maligned son of a Scottish lawyer and consider supporting his case.

On Davidson's sixth day at the Tower, his wife held him tightly at last. She vowed always to love him and that the children would always honour him. Will kissed her and said there was no need for sorrow. He was the victim of a monumental deception, help was on its way and he would be released soon, and they would live together in Scotland or Jamaica, or wherever the children could best grow strong and proud.

Sarah begged him to stop deluding himself. She believed in her husband, but the government had no interest in Will Davidson's point of view. The Home Department was probably unaware of the complexity of Edwards's deceits; nor did it care about them, as long as there was a well-publicized trial and the tavern radicals were seen to be punished. Sarah's wisdom and the taste of truth shook the core of Will Davidson. He surrendered to tears, silent and unashamed.

"I am unmanned," he said, "by the failure to meet my responsibilities to you and the children"

"Hush," said Sarah. "Will Davidson; your work has not been in vain. I bring encouraging news."

With all the committee wives' support, Mrs Thistlewood had visited Alderman Wood, who was a personal friend of the new Queen and shared Her Majesty's sympathy for the radical cause. As a Member of Parliament, Mr Wood was at liberty to make enquiries that could lead to the arrest of George Edwards.

Davidson thought it good news indeed and asked his wife to congratulate Mrs Thistlewood on her boldness. Then he took a deep breath, and he said, "Sarah this is my last request; my mother must know that her son served the cause of liberty until the end."

"I shall write to her, with care," she replied, "and I also have a request for you, Will Davidson; if die you must, let it be in peace."

He would only vanquish the devil, Sarah continued, if he confessed his sins in prayer, forgave his enemies, endured his trial and any punishment with grace, and prepared to face the final judgment in humility, acknowledging the love of God. Will Davidson replied that indeed, he forgave all his trespassers, he loved his children, and would be faithful to his wife's wishes until the last breath.

After five minutes, the gaolers prized the couple apart. When the last key turned in the last lock, and he was alone, Davidson fell against the cold stone wall and slid to the ground, convulsed by the loss of Sarah. He prayed to his God, and when no comfort came, he wept for Tulloch, which was the ancient home of the Davidson clan, and the name given to his gentle African nurse, who had always kissed away his tears with song.

CHAPTER TWENTY-FOUR

25th March, 1820

HIS MAJESTY, THE KING
Carlton House, St James, London

It would be the first formal meeting with a Minister since his accession. His Majesty had hoped to attend the fittings for Lisbet's new gowns. His new mistress had sizzled all the way from Brighton, and he had no heart to suggest a postponement. Even if he disposed of his Home Secretary and the damned Recorder quickly, which seemed unlikely, a regiment of artists and designers was waiting to discuss the refurbishment of Carlton House and all its fittings, in accordance with His Majesty's elevated status.

Lady Elizabeth Conyngham had lately replaced their mutual friend, Lady Hertford as the King's favourite. The sea air and Lisbet's enthusiastic attentions had combined to rejuvenate His Majesty to half his fifty-eight years. Finding himself in a state of almost constant arousal, he did not feel like being King just yet. Especially, he did not anticipate the imminent meetings with anything but distaste.

The subject, his Private Secretary had informed him, was the large number of condemned prisoners at Newgate Gaol, who were anxious for certainty. The king must either authorize their executions, or, in a few cases, exercise the clemency that was the prerogative of a new monarch. Having lost one brother and a father already this year and suffered his own close encounter with mortality, His Majesty would have preferred to discuss shipping, India or even the grain supplies.

It was unfair to suggest that the king disliked Henry Addington, who had made, at best, an uninspiring Prime Minister, but as the ennobled Home Secretary Sidmouth, had become dogmatic and obsessed with intrigue. Wherever he suspected dissent, Henry scattered spies. To the King's mind, the policy was vulgar; it sent trouble underground and had, at the very least, contributed to the catastrophe in Manchester. It continued to irritate His Majesty that, as Regent, he had been persuaded to write to the damn fool city magistrates, condoning their actions, when the truth was that he did not know the truth and had probably been manipulated into protecting the reputations - and the salaries - of a few measly-minded friends of the Privy Council. Now that he was King, His Majesty was determined not to be coerced into accepting every one of his Ministers' recommendations. But today, he was in no mood for a fight.

"Good morning, Lord!" he said, as Henry approached. "Take a seat! How are you, dear boy? Cherry brandy?"

His Majesty was surprised to learn that evidence was still being gathered against the Cato Street gang, for whom he had developed a secret fondness. He knew each man by name and occupation and understood that they loved their country but despised the system that controlled it. If Thistlewood's sword had penetrated the constable's arm instead of his liver, His Majesty might have argued for clemency.

During his darkest days, after the old King's death, Lady Conyngham had snatched the new King from Satan's claws with her carefree frivolity and entertaining understanding of current affairs. How he laughed when she boasted that her first lover was strung up during the Reign of Terror and rescued at the very last moment by two peasant-women who wanted

505

him between their legs! Whenever Lisbet was occupied with matters concerning her beauty, instead of to his secretary or to his Ministers' concerns, His new Majesty had turned to Schiller and read again, during his convalescence, in German, the clandestine favourites of his youth, *William Tell* and *The Robbers*. He found himself furtively admiring the revolutionaries and certainly envied their freedom to live as they chose, indulging their boldest dreams and inventing a better future. If only he could be free of his chains and build the Britain he desired!

"Better you keep your head!" Lisbet had said, and the Hertfords agreed.

He could never, of course, confess his private inclinations to his Ministers nor to any of his brothers or sisters, particularly as the Brunswick duchess (as he called his wife) made such a commotion with her political proclivities, and it might be rumoured that he agreed with her. Aware that his Home Secretary's eyes were burning on him, the King took a sip of brandy.

"If not the Cato Street boys, who are we stringing up next?" he asked.

"The Recorder will provide details, Your Majesty," replied Sidmouth.

"Can't we just let them off? Tell them their King is sorry to have kept them waiting, and as an act of royal grace on his accession, or in memory of King George 111, or some such reason, they may go free?

"You jest, sire."

"No, Henry" said the King. "I am weary of death."

"We would need to involve the Justices," said the Home Secretary, with undisguised irritation.

"What will the Justices say?" asked the king.

"I would expect them to mention precedence."

"In other words?"

"If we release or even transport a man from Newgate for an offence that is normally capital, then a judge here or in Yorkshire or anywhere else will struggle to issue the death penalty for a similar offence at a later date. The country would be amuck with murderers and horse thieves in no time. Is that Your Majesty's wish?"

"I see," said His Majesty, disappointed. "You may send the Recorder in five minutes. Good bye Henry."

"Until tonight," said Sidmouth.

"Really?" asked the King, who remembered no detail beyond five o'clock.

"The Duke of Devonshire is submitting his new orchid, Sire."

"So he is."

"And Signor Belzoni, fresh from Africa, is eager to present Your Majesty with Nubian antiquities."

"I suppose so. Send in your man, Henry," said the King and commanded a page to bring his silver casket.

As Sidmouth hurried away to brief the Recorder on the king's mood, His Majesty ordered his page and the footmen to turn their faces to the wall while he administered his laudanum.

April, 1820

MUCH ADO
The City of London

The spy who had engineered it all was forgotten in the public circus of the trials at the Old Bailey. While His Majesty the King was represented by the cream of the British judiciary, led by the Attorney General and supported by weeks of preparation, the defendants discovered the names of their representatives just hours before the trial began. With a jury of over two hundred, there was little room in the Session House for the public, hungry for sensation. As clerks prepared to get rich quick with sometimes dubious accounts of proceedings, swarms of enthusiasts arrived by foot, horse, cart, cab and carriage from all corners of London and further afield. Fences were erected on Newgate and Ludgate Hill, with fees collected from every passing vehicle. As clamour filled the streets, tension mounted amongst the enforcers of peace. Precautionary posters were stored in secret places; the Riot Act had been read, screamed the lettering, and the people must disperse quietly.

In the courtroom, gallery seats could be purchased by the rich and famous. Elsewhere, the most punctual and persuasive were allotted seats according to their dress and social class. At Arthur Thistlewood's first appearance, a shabby stranger approached with a plate of five oranges, which he placed humbly before the prisoner. The intruder and his gift were removed for fear of sabotage.

Alongside the testimonies of Thomas Hyden and Joseph Hale, one hundred and sixty minor witnesses were called for the Crown versus Thistlewood, Brunt, Ings, Tidd and Davidson. Alongside the police officers and gaolers, there were tavern keepers from The Black Lion on Water Lane, The Crown and Anchor and The Scotch Arms on the Strand, The Old Bell, The Boar's Head and The Mitre on Fleet Street, The White Lion on Wych Street, The Black Dog on St Clement's Lane, the Black Dog on Grays Inn Lane, The White Hart by Brooke's Market, The Pontefract Castle on Wigmore Street, The Ram at Smithfield and The Dolphin at Spitalfields. Mr Aldous, pawnbroker of Berwick Street, confirmed that William Davidson had removed a blunderbuss on the day of the attempted assassination and John Baker, the butler, reported his visit to Grosvenor Square. Hector Morrison, cutler of Drury Lane, testified that both Ings and Thistlewood had sharpened various swords, blades and cutlasses in the days prior to the alleged attacks, while Brunt's landlady,

Mrs Rogers, and the ironmonger from Brooke's Market spoke volumes about the comings and goings at Fox Court, and Davidson's neighbours mentioned hushed political meetings and domestic turmoil at number 12, Elliott's Row, St Marylebone.

Although many were privately sympathetic, witnesses feared reprisals if they refused to comply, and most argued that whatever he or she gave or failed to give in evidence, the prisoners were bound to die. Some enjoyed brief celebrity, others lost customers and life-long friends.

The defence lawyer, John Adolphus, a long-time associate of Sidmouth, argued with passion that the conspirators' efforts and their resources had been too pathetic to engender any kind of Revolution. Until the end, Thistlewood remained confident of a not guilty verdict.

George Edwards was often mentioned in court, but never called. He had disappeared, it seemed, into thin air. The government was alarmed by a groundswell of anger against him, which Alderman Wood continued to ventilate by preparing a charge of High Treason and encouraging emotive petitions to support the prisoners' families.

Meanwhile, after the relative luxury of the Tower, the men were housed in Newgate Gaol behind the Old Bailey, fed on bread and water and provided with writing materials. Thistlewood devoted himself to composing and revising a speech, which he would read out, should the sentence be negative, and by which posterity would remember him. Echoing Homer and Robespierre, he condemned the futility of the present trial and its perpetrators and vilified a system that created monsters like Sidmouth and Edwards. Thistlewood longed "only for the silent grave," he wrote, "where the earth would protect me from the harshness of the wind, as it whistled over the wide fields of my native Lincolnshire, which I abandoned only to perform my duty to a suffering populace, and to which my bones must now return for burial in my ancestral home."

Brunt was distracted from his fate by a heady wave of inspiration, and wrote a series of poems for his family, posterity, and the attention of Mrs Carlile, who might profit from his notoriety and send a donation to Molly.

Tidd refused the freely offered pencils and paper.

"The entire process," he told his gaoler, "is a farce, and a waste of good time and money. I should rather end my days, serving some useful purpose."

"What possible use can be served by a villain like you?" asked his gaoler.

"In exchange for a small donation to my family," replied Tidd, "I would repair and clean 't boots of every man in Newgate."

"Aye, and use your knives and hammers to murder us all in the dark!"

"If I must be idle" said Tidd, "I will swap all my Tower privileges for a pipe and an ounce of good baccy."

But Tidd was left with nothing but his rage and the contemplation of the fate he had expected since 1803.

Ings continued to rave about turtle soup, while in more lucid moments, he composed sweet letters to be shown, post-mortem, to his wife, son and three daughters. Otherwise, the Hampshire butcher spent his time recalling his wife's pies or the games he played in Portsea with Jack in their childhood. Sometimes he compared his own pain to the poor old King's, who must be pitied for the loss of America and several cherished children.

Will Davidson received a pleasant reply from Sir Walter Scott, who feared he lacked expertise in English law to offer advice of any consequence. Nevertheless, the new baronet was observed more than once at the trials, taking notes, up in the guinea seats. Davidson hoped for a private visit, and when it failed to materialize, dismissed Sir Walter as a turncoat and immersed himself in the works of Alexander Pope, which Sarah had delivered, in the hope of helping her husband to a higher understanding of man's place in a fractured world, and which he now applied to the preparation of his defence. Drawing strength from warrior forebears of both the Davidson and the Yoruba clans, he found the strength to sing once or twice a day, accepting particular requests from the gaolers, whose lives he pitied.

In Lord Sidmouth's and Lord Castlereagh's daily post, the death threats multiplied. Written almost exclusively by men and women of tangible passion and integrity, but lacking the advantage of schooling, the letters were ridiculed by civil servants, and destroyed before their Lordships could see them. Sidmouth's temper at this time was intolerable, even without reading his post, while Castlereagh (who, in two years' time, would cut his own throat) again pronounced himself misunderstood and wallowed in melancholy.

With censorship widespread and effective, newspapers and pamphlets were unable to reflect public opinion and dispensed the government's emphasis on the degeneracy of the conspirators and the wickedness of their intentions towards a benevolent state. As many more editors were to discover, truth was dispensable, but there was profit in circulating righteous disgust, dismay and indignation.

Saturday, 29ᵗʰ April, 1820

HIS MAJESTY, THE KING
Carlton House, St James, London

On Friday morning, Sir Charles Abbott, Lord Chief Justice of the King's Bench was driven to the Old Bailey to deliver his verdict to the Cato Street Conspirators. The five principal defendants would hang on Monday, and six other members of their gang would be transported to the colonies. The Recorder being indisposed, the Commons Serjeant went on Saturday to Carlton House to enlighten the King and members of his Privy Council, which included the same eminent judge. The Serjeant was pleased to report that there had been no irregular behaviour either within or without the court, not even the customary jubilation. By contrast, many in the crowd were seen weeping, far more than could reasonably have been related by blood or marriage to the condemned men.

Lord Sidmouth had received an urgent plea from a Mrs Mary Barker of Holborn and enquired whether the Serjeant had any information about such a person.

"Indeed, My Lord," said the Serjeant. "Mrs Barker is the daughter, precisely, step-daughter of the condemned bootmaker, Richard Tidd. She gave evidence at each trial on behalf of the accused and was commended for her clear speaking and bravery in circumstances that would have undone most women."

"I like a spirited girl," said the King, turning to his Home Secretary.

"Tell me, Henry; what does Mrs Barker ask, and is she pretty? I'm inclined to please her."

"Sire," replied Sidmouth, "the lady writes that she has not seen her father since his arrest, while other family members have been permitted visits. I understand that Mr Tidd was involved with Despard's plot against George the Third."

"Was he, by Jove? replied the King. "What mischief we'd have been spared, Henry, if he'd succeeded!"

"Perhaps, Sire," replied Sidmouth. "Mr Tidd has a previous conviction for violence and a blasted mean temper. I do not advise rewarding him with a visit by his daughter, no matter how spirited she is."

It was a mild contradiction, but it wiped out His Majesty's good humour and reminded him of his status.

"May I point out, Lord," he said, "that it was not the prisoner, but Mrs Barker, who made the request. A daughter cannot be blamed for her father's actions, any more than I can be for the strategies of George lll or Henry VIII. I dare say, Mrs Barker was refused access in case her testimony was prejudiced. Charles?"

"Indeed, Sire, that is the case," replied Lord Chief Justice.

"In that case, what, tell Mrs Barker that her King personally grants his permission. And another thing -"

"Sire?" asked the Home Secretary.

"These wretched men are patriots, whose striving for a better life is to be commended, even though their methods were foul. It is my most private conviction that they've been led astray. If they must be killed by the state, and I wish I had the power to prevent it, then let the occasion be civilized. Let them be hanged, and if he must, have the surgeon remove the heads. Leave it at that. Doubt not that the nation will mourn these men! There must be no provocation, no spilling of guts in the French style, no parading of body parts through our capital. What say you, Charles?"

"Your Majesty speaks, as ever, with admirable wisdom," replied the Lord Chief Justice. "It is my advice, with your approval, on the delicate matter of disposal, that the corpses may not be available as relics, for the purposes of morbid sentiment or publicity. Is His Majesty in agreement that they be presented to the hospitals for dissection?"

"Indeed no, Charles, he is not. They will be buried inside the prison, in a manner that prevents the possibility of sabotage."

The King cast around for the most knowledgeable respondent, and his eyes met the steely smile of Lord Wellington.

"Arthur – what's your suggestion?

"Quicklime, Your Majesty," replied the great General.

"Quicklime it is! said the King, "and may those be my last words on the matter."

CHAPTER TWENTY-FIVE

Monday, 5th June, 1820

EDWARDS

The Isle of Guernsey

On the day when the new King's wife returned to England to face charges of treasonable adultery, George Edwards sat on a rock on the coast of Guernsey, sketching a farmer's daughter. Aged about fifteen, the girl had curled her sweet body into the shape of a mermaid, her long black locks blown to confusion by the breeze. She shivered, her flesh taut and sinewy beneath a thin, royal blue shift, as she struggled to keep the pose. Officially, "Mr Parker" paid for his keep with ink portraits of his host's family. Unofficially, he had discovered that the dairy farmer, an upright member of the island community, enjoyed illicit relations with several of his labourers. These occupations distracted Edwards, who was bored to the bone by the island and loathed the odour of fish and the infinite monotony of the sea.

At least he had sufficient stationery to write frequently to Whitehall. Henry Hobhouse responded with infuriating nonchalance, but Edwards kept himself informed by careful analysis of whatever newspapers he could find. Since the election, in which the government was returned with an increased majority, confidence at Whitehall was soaring, while the widows' eloquent ally, Alderman Wood was distracted by a new cause célèbre, the forthcoming trial of his dear friend, the would-be queen consort. The press was similarly distracted, and public sympathy had shifted to poor, neglected Caroline of Brunswick. Since Edwards could no longer damage the Establishment, Lord Sidmouth, it seemed, was content to neglect him.

Naturally, Edwards had not informed the Home Department of his well-being. They had bled him dry, driven him to all manner of deceits, and now abandoned him to this windswept, desolate place with no company but the damn-fool farmer and a few fishermen, who could not even speak English. Edwards's hard-earned bonuses had vanished in the mountain of debts he had been obliged to honour before being removed to safety. There was nothing aboard the Weymouth pacquet, the latest vessel to arrive from England.

"You can rage all you like," the crewman had said. "There'd still be no post addressed to Mr Parker on my boat, no cash nor gold, no crates of fine furniture neither, nor medicines for your blessed stomach and certainly no family!"

Charm proved less effective than bribery in persuading the same sailor to carry Edwards's new letters back to England, of which two attempted to pacify his wife and mother, and the third had a coded destination.

Mr H.H

I thank you for your attention and the ticket, which Capt. Rose of the Cutter Starling attempted to provide, when he docked at Guernsey last week. I remain firm in my resolve to go nowhere without the furniture from my house in Pimlico, for which the lease remains valid. Nor will I travel without my dear wife, her children and her mother, who live, also under the name of Parker, in St John's Street, Clerkenwell. In addition, I should be obliged to receive the overdue instalment, as I am now almost without food and need medicine urgently for my stomach, which has always been poorly, and, since crossing the channel, plagues me beyond endurance. I do not much care which colony shall be my new home, so long as I do not have to live on fish and am not obliged to travel in a vessel as feeble as the Starling.

I remain, sir,

your humble and obedient servant,

HW

"Can I move now?" asked the farmer's daughter, when she caught the artist gazing out to sea.

The sketch had been ruined by salty spray. Edwards tore it up and walked away.

Friday, 8ᵗʰ September, 1820 –
Thursday, 15ᵗʰ March, 1821

Albany, Cape Colony.

On the day when John Baird and Andrew Hardie, weavers and commanders of the Scottish radicals, were hanged and beheaded in Stirling – the last punishment of its kind in Britain – George Edwards and his family sailed into Algoa Bay, about five hundred miles east of Cape Town. After twelve weeks in a state of near oblivion, Edwards endured a fortnight's quarantine, before he and the other new settlers were allowed to disembark. While everyone else camped on a crowded beach for weeks, awaiting transport, the Parker family, on direct instruction from Acting

Governor Donkin, was immediately allocated its one hundred acres with a loan for cattle and seed and invited to depart.

Major General Sir Rufane Shawe Donkin was a fellow of contrasting political colours to his predecessor, Lord Charles Somerset, who was away in England, in part to support his friend, the uncrowned king in these challenging times. Appalled by his predecessor's stringent, elitist policies, Donkin had set about overturning whatever he could of a system that forced missionaries to work as spies, and – whether deliberately or not – set British against Dutch, rich against poor and white against black. Under Somerset, the eastern frontier, though nominated no-man's land, was occupied by a scattered population of Xhosa, Khoi Khoi and tough Dutch farmers. Each community claimed rights to the disputed territory, and all competed for survival in a largely untamed landscape. Murderous raids were not un-common, while wild beasts and precipitous geography made travel exceptionally hazardous.

Into this desperate situation, the Parker family of three adults and four children, was dispatched by the Landrost at Grahamstown, Captain Henry Somerset. Son of the absent Governor, Sir Charles Somerset, the young man enjoyed ig-noring instructions from his father's temporary replacement, Acting Governor Donkin, but he could see no benefit in op-posing this one. The removal was not motivated entirely by the desire to keep the unsavoury Edwards at a distance from the Administration. Donkin's plan for the frontier was to create peace by fostering trade, of which the first stage was to install properly equipped settlers, who could provide employment, rear cattle and grow crops for the colony.

Captain Somerset had been told nothing of the new ar-rivals' history, only that they were sensitive personnel. He was charmed, of course, by young Mrs Parker, who attended his office, when Mr Parker was indisposed, to negotiate the arrangements. If she and her mother could survive on farm in Ireland, Tilly informed him, they would do very well in Africa, where the climate was so much more convenient. Unlike his father, Henry Somerset had an impulsive, flighty nature. He found Mrs Parker – privately, of course - mildly entertaining and enjoyed the idea of this feisty soul floundering in the wilderness beyond. Even when he offered to lend the family, who had an enormous quantity of luggage, two extra waggons and twenty-four oxen, with a crew of Africans and Boers, armed with spears, pistols and elephant guns, Tilly's optimism remained hearty. Nevertheless, it was agreed to engage an experienced Dutch farmer, Hubert Joubert and his servant, Black Piet to guide and support them in their first year.

On the first day of the trek, the children howled incessantly. Their bodies were sore and nauseous from the vigorous bouncing and swaying of the waggon, while dust attacked their little eyes and noses. Harriot Parker shrieked at every turn that they would be thrown to their deaths on rocky roads or tipped into a ravine to be slaughtered by leopards, hyenas or inquisitive baboons. Hubert Joubert, a rough fellow of fifty with a very long beard, closed his ears to better concentrate on driving. His co-driver, Piet, who was not quite twenty, with ebony skin and a perpetual smile, considered the journey the greatest entertainment.

When they reached a wide, green plain, and the driving was steadier, Hubert shouted to the Khoi Khoi youth, who was guiding the oxen, to halt so that the passengers could perform their ablutions, the animals and crew might rest a while, and he could sit under the acacia tree with his tobacco pipe. When he returned to the waggon, Tilly was holding his reins. She said she had driven a cart all the way to Dublin once, and she had been watching him carefully. Hubert shrugged, relit his enormous pipe and climbed up beside her. Occasionally, and for no reason Tilly could fathom – on her other side, Piet was concentrating very hard on the road ahead – Hubert took out his pipe and cackled with apparent contentment. The Dutchman caught her glancing at him, and said something in his own language that she could not understand, but she laughed too, and then the journey seemed to Tilly more tolerable, despite his beard. (Didn't one of her admirals have a beard? And wasn't George remarkably cold since they sailed?)

Every afternoon at five, the Africans would go off with their spears in pursuit of bush meat and generally return carrying an antelope or a few plump birds. Piet would tend to the oxen and build a fire. Harriot, who had explained that to avoid confusion among the staff. she preferred the name Mrs P, shook her old limbs about, picked up her skirts and chased the children from their explorations. The landscape was not so different, she often said, from the wild coast of Ireland.

While Edwards sat listlessly beside an empty sketch book, Tilly took lessons from Hubert on cleaning pistols and harnessing oxen. At night, the family drew up the canvas and huddled inside their waggon, accustoming themselves to the howling jackals or the sinister sound of faraway drums. The crew slumbered easily outside, with Piet dreaming, perhaps, of another time and another place, and Hubert leaning on his pistol, sipping his Kaap Smaak brandy and grinning at Tilly's attempts to soothe the children to sleep with song.

One night, the family was awoken by such a ferocious cacophony of snarling and yelping that Mrs P feared her blood would curdle. A single gun-shot was followed by silence. No human was hurt, but one of the dogs had been torn apart and an ox mauled. The shot had finished off the ox and frightened a pair of lions away. The anticipation of a rich ox stew did nothing to calm Mrs P, even when Tilly reminded her of their good fortune to have such strong protectors as Black Piet and Hubert Joubert.

When at last they arrived at the allotted location, they found it pleasantly situated by a river, with mountains on two sides. The crew helped to cut down willow and reeds, and as soon as a temporary homestead had been constructed, they all set off with the spare waggons and most of the oxen to collect another party of settlers. The impact of transport, heat and aggressive insects on his furniture distressed Edwards more than Tilly and Mrs P found sensible. He complained bitterly of stomach pain and did little to help on the farm. He enjoyed the company of his daughters, four-year-old Hattie and little Hannah, who would totter after him, whenever he went to gather clay from the riverbank. As he moulded it, Edwards tried in vain to recall the features of Arthur Thistlewood or any of the gang he had sketched so meticulously for the Bow Street patrole. They had dissolved in his memory, just as his cruel father and Cornelius Thwaite made ever greater claims on his state of mind.

The cheap labour they had been promised was nowhere to be found, and their only neighbour within two miles was a half-wild Dutch woman who said her family was dead, and sold them three good horses. Despite the terrible blight and the drought and against all expectation, both Mrs Parkers thrived and boasted regularly that compared to any winter in Kerry, the farming was easy. While Mrs P found Black Piet biddable and competent in all she asked of him, she refused to accept advice from no bearded Dutchman. Her own recommendations therefore excluded pre-cautions against the herd of elephants that would march across their first miserable field of wheat, or against the yellow tulps which, for lack of an adequate fence, killed most of the cattle.

It was the first week of March, about the time baby Elizabeth of Clarence and St Andrews died at St James's Palace and her infant cousin, Alexandrine Victoria became the King's heir apparent. Harriot Parker had stopped to rub away a stain in the laundry she was pulling from the line, when she heard a rumbling sound. The clouds had been welcome, she thought, but surely never dark enough for thunder. She looked up and saw a line of approaching horses, ridden by men, black as coal, with painted faces and alarming spears. Dropping the laundry, she ran to the barn and announced that they had visitors and that Piet must go to welcome them.

Piet understood, just as Hubert did, that the land occupied by the Parker party was not only more fertile than the territory allotted to the Xhosa nation, but probably rich in cultural significance, too. When they opened the barn door to investigate, it seemed clear, as they had half-anticipated, that warriors had been sent to reclaim it. Black Piet said nothing of this to Harriot, only that he had no common language with the men, but would try his best. Hubert hung lanterns outside to frighten the superstitious Xhosa away and gathered the family quickly to hide in the barn with the animals.

Edwards preferred to stay in his house and negotiate. Unfortunately, the warriors were not interested in trading his life for the Swiss clock or the elegant chairs from Pimlico. When they pulled out their daggers and charged at his yellow settee, Edwards flew into a rage and ended the night in a pool of blood, his skull cracked and his working arm severed at the elbow.

The rain that fell the following day came too late to salvage anything of their home and outbuildings, which were burnt to the ground. Their waggon, oxen, horses, tools and every last hen had been taken by the Xhosa. The family and the Dutchman were spared, but when Black Piet was nowhere to be found, Hubert turned on Harriot, screaming that the fate of his loyal friend must forever stain her conscience. If Piet had survived the ordeal, he would be enslaved to a vengeful chief for the rest of his days.

The rain continued to fall as Hubert Joubert walked ten miles to the mission-station to beg for transport and medicine. While Edwards was treated for his injuries, Tilly asked to take the waggon to Grahamstown and plead with the Landrost. Hubert insisted that it was too dangerous to travel alone, and he would drive her. During the journey, Tilly said how sorry she was that he had lost his dear friend, Piet.

"Ag, he'll be just fine," said Hubert. "I was angry at your ma, that's all, and her superior airs."

"You think he's alive and free?"

"Life and liberty is all that matters, Tilly," he said. "The Xhosa would never carry a corpse away. We found nothing, there were no vultures. Most likely Piet's already in some better employment. We might run across him in Grahamstown."

Perhaps Hubert Joubert went looking for his friend, or perhaps for a new supply of tobacco and Kaap Smaak, while Tilly brushed herself down, put on her best smile and daintiest walk and went to meet Captain Henry Somerset.

Although he agreed that fresh air and the African sun had done wonders for her, the young Landrost was less accommodating than on Tilly's first visit. The administration was irritated by the stream of written complaints from Mr Parker, and had ordered him to keep the wretched man far away from government offices. Nevertheless, under the grievous circumstances described by Mrs Parker, Captain Somerset offered to help the family one last time and suggested they drive to Port Elizabeth and prepare to sail west to Simons Bay. The news was only partially welcome.

"My husband's state of health is such" said Tilly, "that despite the grave hardships, we would prefer an overland journey, with Mr Joubert to guide us, of course."

The Landrost agreed to provide one more waggon and two pair of oxen, which the family need not return, when they arrived in the west. The original loan would be dissolved, but no extra financial help was available. Finally, Captain Somerset explained that if further correspondence from any member of the Parker family were to reach him or Government House in Cape Town or any other authority in the colony, they would all be escorted, regardless of their state of health, to the first available vessel to London.

Tuesday, 1st May, 1821

Green Point, Cape Colony

While Harry Brunt marked his fifteenth birthday by climbing on to the roof of St. Sepulchre's and swearing an oath to the memory of his father, the waggon carrying George Edwards and his family rumbled into Cape Town. As the oxen hauled them through streets of white-washed houses beneath the majestic Table Mountain, the children's spirits were revived by the breeze and the sparkling ocean ahead. At Green Point, they begged to stop a while and watch the men, rowing out to work at athe new lighthouse. The sand whipped at the children's bare legs, and they laughed as the cool water teased and cleaned their hot, grubby little feet. Inquisitive toddler, Hannah was scooped by Hubert Joubert from the edge of a giant jellyfish that squatted in the sand. Tilly bought fresh bread and fried fish from a stall, and the adults, all except Edwards, pulled off their boots and ran into the water. When Hubert proposed, on condition it also served Kaap Smaak, opening a gin palace right here in Green Point, Tilly danced for joy and sang her old song about the lark, the words of the Bard lost in the ocean spray. Harriot clapped and whooped and called Hubert Joubert a genius worthy of the island of Ireland.

Edwards, who loathed the sea, who had sacrificed body and soul to live a more glorious life, had no appetite for bread and certainly none for fish. Dropping the items into the sand, he turned and began to run back to the waggon. Before the others saw him, he would take the reins and drive off to a new, solitary life in the mountains to the north, where he would become a famous for his figurines of local wild-life. For a moment, the ache in his skull diminished. Then he remembered his lost working arm. George Edwards stopped still, and as he watched his family, frolicking in the sand with Hubert Joubert, he knew, with miserable certainty, that he would descend, on this remote, windswept shore, into deep obscurity.

Thursday, 19ᵗʰ July, 1821

A CORONATION
Hyde Park, London

Marjorie Tidd, the red-haired twin, ten years old and thin as a pin, wove and twisted her way through the pressing crowd, pausing only to study one of the lanterns that hung from branches all over the park. It was scarlet with gold and black markings, and it flapped and danced in the breeze, tantalizing her with its declaration of an exotic, faraway world. She hurried on, impatient to reach her goal. Today, the King might get his crown at last, but Marjorie Tidd would see her first elephant.

Ma had tried to stop her from attending the celebration at all.

"It would defile your father's memory!" Eliza had said, and, for once, clever Harry Brunt took Aunt Tidd's side.

"The tyrants must have no reason to think we have forgotten," he said.

"What does the King care," pleaded Marjorie, "if a few harmless children admire his elephants?"

"It's not a matter of offending or not offending the King," explained Mary Barker, "but of remaining true to our convictions and loyal to one another."

"You mean if ma wants us to stay away from elephants and the golden cart and turn our eyes away from the Chinese decorations, then we must?" asked Francis, Marjorie's twin.

"At least, it would be respectful to pa and Uncle Brunt," replied Mary.

"The elephants got nothing to do with the King!" insisted Marjorie. "Pa would have cursed him for enslaving them and done his best to set them free!"

"Bravo!" cried little Horace Barker.

Mary Barker proposed a show of hands, and it was agreed that Marjorie should exercise her right to curiosity and return with an educational description of the elephant.

Eventually, Aunt Tidd and Mary were persuaded to attend the fête with all the children, but only because the longevity of the old King suggested that no other such grand occasion might occur in her life-time. Aunt Brunt said she preferred to come along than to spend the day all alone in Fulham.

In perpetual memory of Mr Tidd and Mr Brunt, and in response to the nationwide petition for support, the two families lived as one in a spacious house in Fulham. There was a shared kitchen and parlour, with duties divided equally. Aunt Brunt, Harry and the canary (renamed Hope) occupied private rooms on the ground floor, while the Tidds and the Barkers had exclusive access to the rest of the property. The young ones benefitted from extra schooling, and despite differences of opinion in other matters. Aunt Brunt, Aunt Tidd and Mary were unanimous in their determination that the children of heroes should face the world with pride, engaging their hearts, their brains and all their talents in the construction of a better future for all.

As His Majesty proceeded unsteadily down the nave of Westminster Abbey, Marjorie Tidd in Hyde Park caught her breath, and her heart filled with wonder. She marvelled at the great ears, the tusks and the trunk, then gazed at the elephant's tiny little eyes and the longest, sweetest eyelashes she had ever seen. She looked up at the driver, a bright-eyed black man with a mauve turban embellished with precious stones. He shot her a pearly smile, and Marjorie Tidd felt a surge of joy. The world was full of glories, and if she could be as brave as her pa (but not spend all her money on ale and baccy), she would not waste her days scrubbing taters and cleaning floors but lead a life full of meaning. Although she knew she oughtn't, Marjorie sent a silent message of thanks to His Majesty for the elephants and for giving her this moment.

Horncastle, Lincolnshire

On the day when the Brunswick duchess hammered in vain at the doors of Westminster Abbey, and the King was crowned alone, Susan Thistlewood was weighing out chops and sausages at her father's shop on Horncastle High Street. Wilkinson Butchers were not officially open, but Susan had no interest in the celebrations on the market square and preferred to prepare Friday's orders. Julian had bowed to pressure to take his late mother's surname, and being apprenticed to a stone mason at the Cathedral, spent the day working in Lincoln. The Wilkinsons had loaned him a horse, so that on Sundays, he could ride out to Horncastle to visit his step-mother and to Gautby to see Aunt Mary Innett, whose spirit was alive, but fading fast. The famous free dispensary was still operating well, but Dr Chislett had died peacefully in his sleep, and Dr Harrison had moved just recently to London to promote his cures nationwide.

Susan had been promised, by her father, to his friend and neighbour, Mr Henry Turner. She had agreed to the arrangement because, above all else, Mrs Thistlewood was a practical woman, and she knew that there would never be a love to match Arthur's. Mr Turner was a successful coal merchant with a fine house on South Street, and he might yet provide her with children of her own. That Mr Turner was dull and a little didactic, did not trouble Susan, since he appeared not to object to her philanthropic ambitions, which included founding a society for the thinking women of eastern England.

Kingston, Jamaica

As the jewelled crown settled for the first time on His Majesty's head, little Duncan Davidson was woken by a new back tooth. The healthy screaming woke his mother, and she hurried to relieve the nurse, who was elderly and needed a good night's sleep.

As the new King in London repeated his vows of alle-giance to his country and all her colonies, Sarah Lane Davidson Mennie held her smallest boy close and comforted him in his toothache with a Scottish song she had heard his father sing a hundred times or more.

She had been married to the kindly Dr Mennie since Christmas, and was too busy to give much thought to her old life in England. She had opened a school for plantation workers, and her sons had resettled well. Phoebe Davidson had stopped blaming her for Will's political activities and his lack of commercial success, while Dr Mennie's skills at diplomacy had achieved an accord with his old friend, the retired Attorney General. John Davidson had softened in retirement and encouraged the boys to accompany him on social outings on his horse or his boat. His namesake, little John Davidson was growing into a cheeky, inquisitive child; perfect qualifications, his grandfather told himself, for a lawyer.

Mid-Atlantic

At about the same time, Celia Ings, half-way across the Atlantic, woke in her hammock and checked, as she did frequently, that her children still breathed. They had sailed with HMS Europe in late June from Portsmouth and would disembark at Quebec next week and travel onward to Nova Scotia where her late husband's brother, Frederick settled five years earlier. Her son, Bill had been unwilling to leave their relatives and the shop behind, but accepted that the family needed a man, which must be his role, at least until his sisters were married. The cost of resettlement and a small pension had been arranged, by public donation and with the help of Portsmouth's Member of Parliament. The support had almost been lost, when Celia refused to abandon her husband's name, which, she insisted, tied them to his memory and to the beautiful county of Hampshire. She and her children would forever be proud to be called Ings, she had declared, and nobody in the Maritime Provinces would know the shame that had been attached to that name in Great Britain.

The ocean heaved this morning. and when, a little later than usual, Celia collected her family's breakfast of biscuits and goat's milk, she carried the tray carefully to avoid spillage.

Westminster

King George IV meanwhile, sat upon another throne among three hundred men at Westminster Hall, awaiting the coronation banquet. (Wives were permitted to watch from the gallery). To His Majesty's right, at a table with the Bishops, sat Lord Charles Somerset, his thoughts floating inevitably, during prayers, to the colony to which he would return soon with a new wife and a whole regiment to overturn the chaos imposed in his absence by the damned Whig, Donkin.

A young aristocrat, waiting on The King, offered the three delectable soups, which would be followed by a dozen main courses, hundreds of side dishes, sauces and desserts. His Majesty pulled back his robes, lifted his spoon and commanded;

"If it's not over-salted, Denbigh, let us start with the turtle."

At seven thirty, the King abandoned his courtiers to their romps. The journey to Carlton House was blocked by two upturned vehicles, and there was no alternative for the royal party than the route through the poorest quarters of Westminster.

Despite his occasional philosophical fancies, His Majesty found the proximity of dire poverty more life-threatening even than Napoleon, and he called for the guard to ride close to his windows. The carriage was obliged to drive over a bridge, which had been condemned, and almost collapsed under the weight of the vehicle and its passengers, the most senior of whom was enormously fat.

In a mischievous turn of history, on the day of his Coronation, King George IV almost drowned in a canal, and when Molly Brunt returned from Hyde Park, her son was not at home. Nobody discovered how the vehicles had blocked that particular road in Westminster, and although his mother questioned him several times, Harold Moreton Brunt's whereabouts on that particular day were never clarified.

Final Letters of James Ings

From George Theodore Wilkinson's account of the plot, the trial and the execution, 1820

WRITTEN IN NEWGATE JAIL. 30 APRIL 1820

To my wife

My dear Celia

I hardly know how to begin, or what to say for the laws of tyrants have parted us forever. My dear, this is the last time you will ever hear from me. I hope you will perform your duty without delay, which is for the benefit of yourself and children, which I have explained to you before. My dear, of the anxiety and regard I have for you and the children, I know not how to explain myself, and I must die according to law, and leave you in a land full of corruption, where justice and liberty have taken their flight from, to other shores. My dear, I have heard men remark how they would not marry a widow, not without her husband was hanged. Now my dear, I hope that you will bear in mind that the cause of my being consigned to the scaffold was a pure motive.

I thought I should have rendered my starving fellow-men, women and children service; and my wish is, when you make another choice, that this question you will put, before you tie the fatal knot. My dear, it is if no use for me to make remarks to you respecting my children. I am convinced you will do your duty as far as lies in your power. My dear, your leaving me but a few lines before I wrote these few lines, I have nothing more to say. Farewell! Farewell, my dear wife and children forever. Give my love to our mother and Elizabeth. I conclude a constant lover you and your children and all friends. I die the same, but an enemy to all tyrants.

JAMES INGS

PS My dear wife, give my love to my father and mother, brother and sisters and aunt Mary, and beg them to think nothing of my unfortunate fate; for I am gone out of a very troublesome world, and I hope you will let it pass like a summer cloud over the earth.

4 o'clock, Sunday afternoon.

To my dear daughters –

My dear little girls, receive my kind love and affection, once more, forever; and adhere to my sincere wishes, and recollect though in a short time you will hear nothing more of your father, let me entreat you to be kind and obedient to your poor mother, and strive all in your powers to comfort her, and assist her while you exist in this transitory world, and let your conduct throughout life be that of virtue, honesty and industry.; and endeavour to avoid all temptation, and at the same time put your trust in God. I hope unity, peace and concord will remain amongst you all. Farewell! Farewell my dear children, Your unfortunate father,

JAMES INGS

To my son

My dear little boy, Wm Stone Ings, I hope you will have time to read these few lines when the remains of yr. poor father is mouldered to dust. My dr. boy, I hope you will bear in mind the unfortunate end of your father, and not place any confidence in any person or persons whatever for the deception, the corruption and the ingenuity in man I am at a loss to comprehend, it is beyond all calculation. My dear boy, I hope you will make a bright man in society, and it appears to me the road you ought to pursue is to be honest, sober, industrious, and upright in all your dealings; and do unto all men as you would they should do unto you. My dear boy, put your trust in one God, and be cautious of every shrewd, designing, flattering tongue. My dear boy be a good, kind and obedient child to your poor mother, and comfort herm, and be a loving brother to your sisters. My dear boy, I sincerely hope and trust you will regard these my last instructions. Yr loving and unfortunate father.

JAMES INGS

Sunday night, 8 o'clock.

John Thomas Brunt's Final Poem

Tho' in a cell I'm close confin'd
No fears alarm the noble mind;
Tho' death itself appears in view,
Daunts not the soul sincerely true!
Let Sidmouth and his base colleagues
Cajole and plot their dark intrigues;
Still each Briton's last words shall be,
Oh! Give me death or liberty!

JT Brunt, Newgate, April 30, 1820

APPENDIX

Fact and Fiction

Turtle Soup for the King draws extensively on archive material and is further informed by the author's experience of troubled communities in Northern Ireland, South Africa and elsewhere.

In an attempt to record complex events in a faithful, but fictional account, there are, inevitably, considered omissions and imaginative leaps, which may offend some historians, but which are intended to clarify the conspirators' stories.

While the novel is as close as possible to available historical facts, there are occasional deviations. By focusing on the main perpetrators of the Conspiracy, I have neglected many other known participants with the sole purpose of coherence. Other considered changes were made for the benefit of the story. For instance, William Davidson first met the other conspirators in London, not at his workplace in Staffordshire. No-one can be certain that either Davidson, Tidd or Ings travelled to Manchester in August 1816, though Davidson was politically active in north-west England. While Carlile certainly visited Smedley Cottage near Manchester, he did not lodge there with Johnson and Hunt. For these and other inaccuracies, I take full responsibility. For expert factual accounts, please refer to

Peterloo, The English Uprising by Robert Poole (Oxford University Press, 2019)

Peterloo, The Manchester Massacre by Jacqueline Riding, with a foreword by Mike Leigh (Apollo / Head of Zeus, 1818)

Peterloo, Witnesses to a Massacre, Graphic Novel by Poole, Schlunke and Polyp (New Internationalist / Myriad Press, 1819)

A series of academic essays, which at the time of writing, I have been unable to access: *The Cato Street Conspiracy, Plotting Intelligence and the Revolutionary Tradition in Britain and Ireland,* ed, McElligott and Conboy (Manchester University Press, 2020)

CHARACTERS – LOCATIONS – TAVERNS, INNS and HOTELS

While some historical names and dates are lost, those available are shown. A character's given status refers usually to the time-span in which she or he appears in the novel.

Entirely fictional characters or places are marked **F**. Semi-fictional characters or places, i.e. those with some factual basis, are marked **SF**

Italics represent an estimated date or an assumed name or profession, also where a common forename, e.g. Ann or William, has been changed to avoid confusion.

CHARACTERS

Abbott, Sir Charles, Lord Chief Justice, Canterbury and London 1762-1832

Adkins, Harry, Governor, House of Correction, Cold Bath Fields in London *1757*-1822

Alcock, John, property developer, publisher of The New Times in London

Aldous, James, pawn-broker, Berwick Street, Soho in London

Archbishop of York, Hon Edward Venables Vernon (neighbour of Lord Harrowby) 1757-1847

Atkins, John ("Smoke Jack"), Lord Mayor of London, shipping merchant, London 1754-1838

Alexandrine Victoria, child of Duke of Kent, future Queen, Kensington, Windsor 1819-1901

Amelia, Princess, youngest daughter of George III Windsor, Kawin London 1783-1810

Bacon, Josiah, pseudonym used by Cornelius Thwaite to trick Tilly **F**

Baines, John, Waterloo veteran, servant of Lord Harrowby **F**

Baird, John, weaver, condemned commander of Scottish radicals d 1820

Banks, Sir Joseph, President of the Royal Society, Lord of Horncastle Manor 1743-1820

Baker, John, butler to Lord Harrowby, Grosvenor Square in London

Barker, small children adopted by Tidds, *Ellen* and *Horace*

Barker, Gerald, clerk, Mary Tidd's husband, father of two children from an earlier marriage

Barker, Mary Tidd, *Eliza* Tidd's daughter, later, wife and stepmother b.*1793*

Beard, William, weaver at Peterloo, Heaton Norris in Stockport

Belzoni, Giovanni Battista, explorer and archaeologist in Egypt. Padua, Venice 1788-1823

Bench, Master, assistant to Miss North at a riverside factory in Lambeth **F**

Bentham, Jeremy, philosopher, social reformer in London 1748-1832

Birch, William, Deputy Constable, Stockport police b.1792

Bishop, Daniel, Constable at Bow Street working with Lavender, Ruthven and Salmon

Bonaparte, Napoleon (Boney), French General of Italian / Corsican descent 1769-1821

Boulton, John, shoemaker at Peterloo, Stockport

Brodie, Deacon William, cabinet-maker, city councillor, "Robin Hood", Edinburgh 1741-88

Brooke, Mr and Mrs, shoemakers, Union St, off Oxford St in London, Brunt's Master.

Brown, Mr, landlord, Scotch Arms, off the Strand in London

Brunt, John Thomas (*Tom*), boot-closer, radical in London 1781-1820,

Brunt, *Harry Moreton*, son of John Thomas, Fox Court, Holborn in London b.1805

Brunt, *Walter*, tailor, Tom's father, Union Street, off Oxford St in London

Brunt, Mrs Moreton, Tom's mother. Union Street, off Oxford St in London

Brunt Mary (*Molly*) Welch, Tom's wife, mother of Harry and John. Derby, Holborn, b.*1783*

Buck, Tilly (also known as Mrs Edwards / Parker) entertainer. London, The Cape **SF**

Bunyan, John, English author of The Pilgrim's Progress, Bedfordshire in London 1628-1688

Burnett, Mr and Mrs, shopkeepers, AT's maternal grandparents, Horsington in Lincolnshire

Burns, Robert / Rabbie, Scottish poet, Alloway, Edinburgh, Dumfries 1759-1796

Byng, Sir John, Major-General. Commander of the British army, northern district 1772-1860

Cante, *Geoffrey*, bootmaker, Tidd's Master. Guild member, Grantham in Lincolnshire

Cante, Mrs, *Geoffrey*'s wife, Grantham, Lincolnshire

Carlile, Jane, publisher, Richard's first wife, mother of 3 small children, Plymouth, London

Carlile, Mary, publisher, Richard's unmarried sister, Ashburton in Devon, London

Carlile, Richard, tinsmith, radical journalist, editor and publisher, Devon, London 1790-1843

Caroline, Queen, Princess of Brunswick, uncrowned wife of George IV 1768-1821

Castles John, whitesmith, radical, spy, Yorkshire, London, emigrant to *Ontario* b1785

Castlereagh, Lord, Robert Stewart, Irish born Foreign Secretary 1769-1822

Charlotte, Princess, child of George IV and Caroline of Brunswick 1796-1817

Charlotte, Queen, German princess, wife of George III, mother of George IV 1744-1818

Chislett, Mr or Dr John, apothecary and surgeon, Horncastle

Collier, Sir George, Commodore, West Africa Squadron, enforcing abolition 1773-1851

Conyngham, Lady Elizabeth (*Lisbet*) mistress of George IV London, Brighton 1769-1861

Cookson, Hercules, night-watchman, Portsea **F**

Cooper, Robert, landlord, Cooper's, Bouverie St and Black Lion, Water Lane in London

Croxton, Thomas, land and building developer, Portsea in Hampshire

Cumberland, Duke of (see Prince Ernest) later also King of Hanover, warrior, 1771-1851

Dart, Mr and Mrs, wherryman and his wife, Portsea to Gosport, by Portsmouth Harbour **F**

Davidson, children of Sarah and Mr Lane, Abraham b.1805, Thomas, Joseph and William.

Davidson, children of Sarah and William, London, John b 1815, Duncan b1819

Davidson, *John,* Anglo-Scottish, reputed Attorney-General of Jamaica, Davidson's father

Davidson, *Phoebe,* Davidson's mother, a wealthy Jamaican

Davidson, Sarah Lane, Sunday-school teacher, wife of William, mother of 6 boys

Davidson, William, cabinetmaker, radical. Jamaica, Edinburgh, London, Staffs. 1781/6-1820

Denbigh, 7th Earl of, William Feilding, the King's Carver, Shropshire, London 1796-1865

Despard, Colonel, soldier, Anglo-Irish radical, convicted of plot to kill George III 1751-1803

Devonshire, Duke William George Spencer Cavendish, Whig, horticulturalist 1790-1858

Dolan, Paddy, roof-tiler, radical, Ireland, Gees Court, off Oxford Street in London **F**

Donkin, Sir Rufane Shaw, Whig, Acting Governor, Cape Colony 1772-1841

Dwyer, Tom, bricklayer, radical, traitor, Ireland, London 1772-1841

Edwards, children by Tilly: Hattie b1816, Hannah, b1819 in London, The Cape **SF**

Edwards, George, model-maker, spy, agent provocateur, London, The Cape 1781-1843

Edwards, Hannah, George's late baby sister, London **F**

Edwards, Mr. George's runaway father, English west country

Edwards, William, George's younger brother, undercover policeman, London b. *1786*

Elizabeth, Princess, heir to throne, daughter of Duke and Duchess of Clarence 1820-21

Elrington, Dr. John Henry, Fort-Major, Tower of London 1771-1857

Ernest, Prince, 5th son of George III. From 1799, Duke of Cumberland, warrior,1771-1851

Ethelston, Reverend Charles Wickstead, magistrate, Manchester 1767-1830

Fairlea, John, bookseller, Johnsons Court off Fleet Street in London **SF**

Firth, Elias, Cow-man, tenant at the stable and loft in Cato Street in London

Fitzclarence Fred., Cold Stream Guard, son of Duke of Clarence / Dora Jordan 1799-1854

Fox, Charles James, Prominent British statesman, Whig, considered radical 1749-1806

Frederick, Duke of York, soldier and third son of King George III 1763-1827

Fullwell, James, anchor-smith, Southwark **F**

G. Mrs, business-woman, mother of George, William and *Hannah,* London b*1765*

Gast, John, shipwright, activist, early trade unionist. Deptford, London 1772-1837

George III, King since his grandfather, George II's death 1760. Windsor, London 1738-1820

George IV, King from 29th Jan.,1820. Former Regent. Brighton, Windsor, London 1762-1830

Godbold family, French cutlers of Spitalfields **F**

Godfrey, Henry Hunt's manservant, seen in Salford and Manchester **SF**

Goldworthy, Cabinet maker, Davidson's former employer, Liverpool, London

Grant, Isabella, mother of Thistlewood's son, Bardney, Lincolnshire d.1808 **F**

Hale, Joseph (Joe), Brunt's apprentice, St Giles and Holborn in London b*1803*

Hale, Mrs, Joe's widowed mother, St Giles in London

Hardie, Andrew, weaver and condemned 2nd commander of Scottish radicals 1793- 1820

Harding, Mr and Mrs, landlords The Old Bell Inn, St Bride's, off Fleet Street in London

Harris, Elizabeth, landlady, Little Moorfields in London

Harris, John, her husband, type setter and radical, Little Moorfields in London

Harrison, Dr Edward, experimental physician, Edinburgh, Horncastle, London 1766-1838

Harrison, Margaret, Edward's wife, *piano teacher*, Horncastle d.1817

Harrison, Parson / Rev. Joseph, Baptist preacher, radical activist, Essex, Stockport 1779-1848

Harrowby, Lord, Dudley Ryder, Lord reside of the Council, Cabinet member1762-1847

Hay, Reverend William, lawyer, vicar, magistrate, Manchester 1786-1861

Jackson, Ned, apprentice cabinet maker at Lord Harrowby's Staffordshire estate **F**

Jackson, Ned's parents, workers at Lord Harrowby's Staffordshire estate **F**

Jefferson, Thomas, Founding Father, 3rd U.S President, reformer Virginia, Europe 1743-1826

Johnson, Joseph, entrepreneur, radical, journalist, co-founder, The Observer 1791-1872

Johnson, Mrs (Margaret), Joseph's pregnant wife, Cheetham, near Manchester (d.1821)

Jordan, Dora, Anglo Irish actor, mother of Duke of Clarence's surviving children 1761-1816

Joubert, Hubert. Dutchman / Boer, driver, bodyguard, Eastern Cape Province **F**

Lavender, Stephen, Constable at Bow Street, working with Bishop, Salmon and Ruthven

Liverpool, Lord, Robert Banks Jenkinson, British Prime Minister, London 1770-1828

Luther, Martin, (see Saxon monk) Religious reformer, Eisleben, Wittenberg 1483-1646

Margaret, spinner at Peterloo (and weaver brothers) Chadderton by Manchester d1819 **SF**

Marie-Antoinette, Queen of France, wife of Louis XVI Vienna, Paris 1755-1793

Mennie, Dr Duncan, Aberdeen, London and Jamaica **F**

Moreton, *Harold*, deceased veteran, Tom, Brunt's maternal grandfather, London **SF**

Morrison, John Hector, journeyman at Underwood cutlers, Drury Lane in London

Murphy, Father John, Catholic Priest, central to 1798 Irish Rebellion, Wexford 1753-1789

Murray, John, ginger-bread-baker and police spy, Withy Grove off Shude Hill, Manchester

Nadin, Joseph, thief-taker, Deputy Constable, Manchester 1765-1848

Napoleon (see Bonaparte), French General, former Emperor 1769-1821

Nelson, Admiral Horatio, war hero, Norfolk, London 1758-1805

North, Miss Eleanora, factory owner, Lambeth **F**

Orator, The, (See Henry Hunt) 1773-1835

Paine, Thomas, Anglo American activist, theorist and writer, Norfolk, New York 1737-1809

Palin (or Peeling) John, sailor, child's chairmaker, radical

Parker, Harriot, Mrs P, Irish-born mother of Tilly, Kerry, London, The Cape **SF**

Pelham, Charles Anderson, Whig M.P, Founder, Royal Yacht Squadron. Cowes 1781-1846

Philbin, Patrick, Irish veteran, invalid, street sweeper, Wexford, London **F**

Piet, Black, Cape Malay servant and friend of Hubert Joubert, Eastern Cape Province **F**

Pike, Mr, lawyer, Chancery Lane in London **F**

Pimlico Aunt, an invention of Tidd as excuse for his political outings **F**

Pitt, William (Pitt the Younger: Tory Prime Minister, 1783-180 / 1804-1806) 1759-1806

Alexander Pope, English discursive poet and translator of Homer, London 1688-1744

Potter, whitesmith, radical, Snow Fields, Southwark near London

Prinny, nickname of the Regent (see Regent and George IV)

Quirke, Danny, soldier, drummer boy, Union St, London, Waterloo, d1815 **F**

Quirke family, run a wash-house on Union St, near Oxford St in London

Regent (see George IV) represents his father, George III from 1811 to January, 1820

Robespierre, Maximilien, French lawyer, radical, Arras, Paris 1758-1794

Rogers, Mrs, The Brunts' landlady, Fox Court, Holborn in London

Rose, Capt. Cutter Starling, English Channel **SF**

Ruthven, George, Snr Constable at Bow Street, working with Salmon, Lavender and Bishop

Sally, daughter of the Horncastle wheelwright, sweetheart of young Arthur Thistlewood **F**

Salmon, William, Constable at Bow Street, working with Ruthven, Lavender and Bishop

Salt, Mr, rich industrialist, Lichfield in Staffordshire

Salt, Miss, Salt's 16-year-old daughter, briefly Davidson's fiancée, Lichfield in Staffordshire

Saxon monk, rescued a group of nuns by hiding them in herring barrels (see Luther)

Schiller, Friedrich, German poet and dramatist, Marbach, Weimar 1759-1805

Scott, Sir Walter, Scottish advocate, historical novelist, Edinburgh, Abbotsford 1771-1832

Sidmouth, Lord, Henry Addington, Home Secretary, London, Devon, Richmond 1757-1844

Smithers, Richard, Police Constable at Bow Street in London, d1820

Somerset, Sir Charles, absent Governor of The Cape Colony, Tory 1767-1831

Somerset, Henry, Capt., son of Charles, Landrost, Grahamstown, Eastern Cape 1794-1862

Spence, Ann (*Grace*) Thomas's 2nd wife, herbalist, shopkeeper, Little Turnstile in London

Spence, Thomas, radical philanthropist, Newcastle on Tyne 1750-1814

Spence, William, (*Willie*) Thomas's son by first wife, Radical

Stafford, John, chief clerk, Bow Street, recruiter of spies, London 1776-1837

Stoddart, John, ex-editor, The Times, editor, The New Times, Salisbury, London 1773-1856

Stone, Silas, butcher, Whitechapel, Celia Ings's uncle d1819 **SF**

Tannahill, Robert, Scottish weaver poet, Paisley 1774-1810

Taylor, Sir Herbert, Maj. General, Private Secretary to George III and IV Windsor 1775-1839

Thorpe, Gideon, spinner, Stockport, d1819 **F**

Thistlewood, Annie Burnett, AT's mother, Horsington and Tupholme in Lincs 1752-1791

Thistlewood, Ann (*Jane*) Farmer John's second wife, AT's step-grandmother, Tupholme

Thistlewood, Ann, AT's sister, later wife of the Vicar of Bardney, Tupholme 1777-1800

Thistlewood, Arthur (AT) apothecary, soldier, swordsman, radical, Lincs, London *1773*-1820

Thistlewood John, AT's uncle, died, probably killed in Jamaica, Tupholme 1740-1765

Thistlewood, John, AT's younger brother, Tupholme and Louth in Lincs 1781-1857

Thistlewood, Julian, son of AT and an unknown Lincolnshire woman, b*1808*

Thistlewood, Lydia Dance, AT's paternal grandmother, Tupholme in Lincs d1783

Thistlewood, Susan Wilkinson, AT's wife, Horncastle, London b*1790*

Thistlewood, Tom, AT's great uncle, slave-driver and weather-forecaster, Jamaica 1720-1786

Thistlewood, Wm John (*Farmer John*) AT's grandfather, land-agent, Tupholme, 1716-1793

Thistlewood, William, AT's father (invalidity deduced) 1743-
1794

Thwaite, Cornelius, (Uncle Con) **F**, sculptor, paedophile, Stoke
on Trent, London

Tidd, Charlie, Richard's uncle, manager of a Grantham coaching
inn. **F** (one of the Tidds' children is also called Charlie. **SF**)

Tidd, Mary *(Eliza) Parry*, seamstress, Richard's wife, mother
of five, London b*1775*

Tidd, Mary, *Eliza* Tidd's daughter, marries Gerald Barker.
b*1793*

Tidd, Richard (*Tiddy*) shoemaker, deserter, radical, father, step-
father of Mary 1773-1820

Tidd, children of Richard and Eliza, *twins, Jeremy & Charlie
(b.1808)*

Tidd, children of Richard and Eliza; *twins, Marjorie and Francis
(b. 1811)*

Tulloch, Davidson's childhood nurse, Jamaica **F**

Turner, Henry, coal merchant, Horncastle, betrothed to the
widowed Susan Thistlewood

Valline *Gabriel,* weaver, Spitalfields (fictional great-nephew of
historical weavers' hero)

Vertue, former sea captain, long-boat captain, Trent and Mersey
Canal, Staffordshire **F**

Vyner, Robert Snr, Whig M.P, wealthy land-owner Gautby in
Lincs, London 1717-1799

Vyner, Robert Jnr, his son, Sheriff and Whig M.P, Gautby in
Lincs, London 1762-1810

Vyner, Henry, his son, heir to the Vyner lands and fortune,
Yorkshire, Gautby 1805 - 1861

Ward / Wards, George / Henry, pseudonyms used by the historical George Edwards

Ward, Walter's Human Pyramid **SF** at Astley's Amphitheatre

Watson, General, John Tadwell, owner of Cato Street premises in London, Calais 1748-1826

Watson, Dr James, "Old Watson" surgeon, radical, prisoner, Scotland, London 1766-1838

Watson, James, "Young Watson" Dr Watson's son, radical, London, emigrant to America

Wedderburn, Robert, Jamaican-born abolitionist, unitarian, radical, London 1762-1835

Wedgwood, Josiah, potter, entrepreneur (master, **F** of Thwaite) Stoke on Trent, 1730-1795

Welch, Sam and wife, Molly Brunt's cousins, tanners, Southwark by London **F**

Wellington, Lord, Anglo-Irish warrior, Master Gen. of the Ordnance, Cabinet 1769-1852

Wilkinson, Mr and Mrs, Susan Thistlewood's parents, prosperous butchers, Horncastle

Williamson, associate of Davidson /Goldworthy, sailed to The Cape on the Belle Alliance

Wolseley, Charles, chair, Sandy Brow rally in Stockport. Birmingham reformer 1769-1846

Wood, Alderman Matthew, Whig, friend of Queen Caroline, Devon, London 1768-1843

Wren, Sir Christopher, architect of St Paul's, St Bride's, St Magnus Martyr etc. 1632-1723

ALSO:

Ringo and Lottie/Boadicea/ Hope – the Brunts' canaries **F**

Gulliver (Portsea) and Jupiter (London) – the Ings's horses **F**

Mr Pitt - the Johnsons' donkey. (Named, ironically after William Pitt the Younger, late Tory

Prime Minister, opponent of Fox, friend and one-time rival of Sidmouth) **F**

LOCATIONS

Artillery Ground, Bunhill Row / City Rd, London. Since 1638 (and still) of the Honourable Artillery Company, from which the Royal Marines and the Grenadier Guards were formed.

Astley's Amphitheatre, a famous circus, often burnt and re-constructed, Lambeth 1773-1863

Baker's Row, Whitechapel, London Site of the Ings's first London home. Now demolished, Bakers Row was known to Jack the Ripper and part of a road renamed in 1896 as Vallance Road, where the notorious Kray Twins lived at no.178

Banks Court, Cripplegate, London Mrs. G's home was one of many cramped alleys near the Bunhill Burial Ground, which were demolished for the Victorian Peabody Estate

Brooke's (or Brook's) Market, Holborn in London survives as a smaller public space near Leather Lane with its still vibrant market

Bullocksmithy, Cheshire. A village renamed in 1835 as Hazel Grove, now part of Stockport

Bunhill Burial Ground still exists, with remains of Bunyan, Defoe and William Blake

The Cape of Good Hope. The Cape Colony was ceded to Britain by the Dutch Government in 1814. In 1910, The Cape combined with Natal, Transvaal and Orange Free State to become the self-governing South Africa, gaining full independence from Britain in 1961.

Algoa Bay landing place of the 1820-21 settlers in the Eastern Cape Province. Renamed Port Elizabeth by Acting Governor Donkin in memory of his late wife

Cape Town administrative capital of the colony, with HQ at Government House

Grahamstown (now **Makhanda**) Garrison town of the Eastern Cape Province, it was attacked in April 1819 by 10,000 Xhosa, led by Maqana, who was jailed (as later, Mandela) on Robben Island. Now a handsome town containing Rhodes University

Green Point. George Edwards settled here (fact and fiction) On the Atlantic coast, it is now a vibrant district of Cape Town, containing a world cup football stadium

Simons Town. Naval base south of Cape Town and landing place for the Western Cape. Now a historic town with marine and navy activities, famous also for penguins

Cato Street, mews road, off Edgware Road, where the conspirators met for the last time. After the scandal, it was renamed Horace Street until about 1943. It's now Cato Street again.

Chiswell Street, Moorfields/ Cripplegate was the site of a livery, the Caslon and Catherwood iron foundry and (until recently) a brewery. There was also wine vault

Cock Lane ran (and still runs) from Smithfield Square to Snow Hill

Conduit St in Mayfair in London now connects Bond Street to Regent St. Some old houses remain, including No 9, built for the Thistlewoods' employer and landlord, Robert Vyner MP in 1779.

Cold Bath Field House of Correction, Clerkenwell in London, 1794-1855, It held the Cato Street men, and also Col Despard and Robert Wedderburn. The site now contains the Mount Pleasant Sorting Office in Farringdon

Elliott's Row, Old Lords Cricket Ground. Last London home of Will Davidson and family. Demolished about 1820 to build Dorset Square

Fleet Market in London opened in 1737 after the culverting of the filthy River Fleet. It was cleared in 1829 for the construction of Farringdon Road, approximately on the same site

55-55½, Fleet Street in London. The site of Richard Carlile's print shop and coffee shop, also the temporary home and workplace of James Ings. The building remains directly opposite the entrance to Johnson's Court, and is still in use as business premises

Fox Court, Brooke's Market, Holborn in London. Home of the Brunts and their apprentice Joe Hale. A cramped alley between Brooke's Market and Grays Inn Lane, Fox Court has been replaced by an office block of the same name at 14, Grays Inn Road

Gautby Hall and estate in Lincolnshire, 5 miles from Tupholme. The historic home of the Vyner family was built in 1756 and demolished in 1872. Stable and gardens with lake remain, as does the medieval All Saints Church, Gautby, rebuilt for Robert Vyner in 1754

Golden Lane, off Old St in London, site of Thwaite's **F** studio, the street still exists. In life, young George Edwards was arrested on Golden Lane for theft

Grosvenor Square Lord Harrowby's house, site of the planned, was at no 39. Since renumbered 44, now the Millennium hotel. Alexander Litvinenko was poisoned there in 2006

Hole in the Wall Passage, Brooke's Market Holborn in London. Home of Richard Tidd and family, an alley between Baldwin Gardens and Dorrington /Torrington) St. at one side of

Brooke's Market. Bombed in WW2. Today's Leigh Place is either the same or very close

Horncastle, Lincolnshire market town, 22m east of Lincoln, 5m west of Tupholme

> **Dispensary**, St Mary's Churchyard. Opened 3rd December 1789. Building still exists
>
> **Dog Kennel Yard** small area still near the centre of town, once noted for prostitution
>
> **High Street** John Chislett, apothecary's premises unknown, assumed to be here
>
> **No. 5,** Wilkinson's butchery, now a reputedly haunted greengrocer. A butcher's hook is still there, either from Wilkinsons or the Victorian butcher, Uriah Spratt
>
> **Grammar School,** near St Marys Church, attended by Thistlewood. Building still exists but the school was relocated and renamed the Queen Elizabeth School.
>
> **South Street** home of Henry Turner, coal and corn merchant and land-agent, future husband of Susan Thistlewood
>
> **West Street,** Dr Harrison's home and the small asylum still stand at No 30

Horsham County Gaol 1779-1845, recorded by Thistlewood as the worst gaol he ever saw

Horsington, Lincolnshire village 4 miles east of Tupholme. The cottage where Thistlewood was born is in private hands, renamed Thistlewood Cottage

Johnson's Court still exists, its entrance opposite 55 Fleet St., Edwards lived there

Little Turnstile, by Lincolns Inn Field in London. Tidd, as a bachelor, had lodgings here opposite Thomas Spence's radical bookshop, The Hive of Liberty. One side of the old alley remains, the other contains modern buildings

St Luke's Asylum, Old Street, between Bath St and the now City Rd roundabout. 1786-1916. Mary Brunt stayed there. Used for printing bank notes, then demolished 1963

St Magnus Martyr Church, by London Bridge, exists, rebuilt by Wren after the Great Fire

Manchester Exchange, where 400 shopkeeper and property-owners were sworn in as special constables prior to Peterloo. Built 1809, it was on the junction of Market St and Exchange St

Manchester Mews in London. Tom Hyden's family lived at No 2. The mews remans partly as it was, but the Spanish Chapel was replaced by St Joseph's R.C Church

Marshalsea Goal, Southwark, 1373-1842, historic prison where Tom Hyden was held. Last building demolished in 1870, but part of a wall remains on Angel Place. The prison was on the current Borough High St, north of the junction with Tabard St, now John Harvard library

Military Academy, Grays Inn Lane. Lost, presumed amalgamated with Sandhurst

Mount Street in Manchester, by St Peters Field, site of the house used by the Magistrates to oversee the 1819 rally / massacre of Peterloo. Street still exists, rebuilt by Victorians

New Bayley / Salford House of Correction, built in 1754 and visited by Henry Hunt in August,1819. Replaced in 1868 by Strangeways, now known as Manchester Prison

New Fish Street in London. The riverside dwellings have all burnt or been demolished. New Fish St. was developed by Victorians and renamed Fish St. Hill. Edwards's **F** connection is drawn from the records of a Mary Edwards who lived by the river in 1788.

Newgate Gaol was at the junction of Giltspur St, Newgate and Old Bailey. Operated 1188-1902. Destroyed in the Gordon riots of 1780, rebuilt 1785, connected to the Criminal Court

Old Bailey in London Central Criminal Court, named after street, rebuilt 1785 (again 1902)

St Peter's Field. The site of the 1819 Manchester Massacre or Battle of Peterloo) was approximately on the site of St Peter's Square by the Renaissance Hotel

Pickford's Timber Yard, Portland St. Manchester Gathering place of the Salford and Manchester Yeoman before Peterloo. Pickford was a local family, but the haulage company had been taken over in 1816. Portland Street was developed by Victorians

Portsea, Hampshire is an island close to Portsmouth and was almost entirely rebuilt after bombing in WW2. The extended Ings family lived there as butchers and landlords.

Ranelagh Place, Pimlico in London, Edwards's hideaway, number lost. The street still exists, partially rebuilt and re-named Grosvenor Gdns Mews North, off Ebury St, Belgravia

Sandon Hall, Staffordshire remains the ancestral home of Lord Harrowby's family. Rebuilt 1852 after a fire, parts of the house and lush grounds are now used for exclusive weddings.

St Sepulchre Church, City of London. Medieval church, destroyed by the Great Fire of 1666 and rebuilt. Referenced in the song *Oranges and Lemons* as The Bells of Old Bailey

Shude Hill, Manchester. Just north of the city centre, it held Johnson's brush factory and is now the centre of Shudehill transport hub.

Smedley's Cottage. On the corner of Smedley Lane and what was, for a time, Johnson's Lane. Urban Smedley is 2.3 miles north of Manchester, east of Cheetham Hill, on the banks of the River Irk. The cottage, which no longer exists had a large garden with fruit trees

Smithfield Market in east London was rebuilt by the Victorians and remains a successful meat market for the wholesale trade. No livestock has been sold there since 1852

Smithfield Square in east London, site of historic rallies, including two with Thistlewood. Now dominated by a car park near the market and St Bartholomew's Hospital

Spa Field, Islington still exists as a much smaller public space, on a site beside the present London Metropolitan Archive, between Exmouth Market and Northampton Road

Stanhope St, Clare Market, Lincoln Inn Field. The street where the Thistlewoods lived has been demolished. Clare Market is now dominated by the London School of Economics

Stockport, Cheshire, town, now part of Greater Manchester

John Street, home of shoemaker, John Boulton. Lost except street name

Lamb's Fold, Heaton Norris, home of weaver, Wm. Beard. Lost except street name

Heaton Lane passed by marcher to Peterloo. This section is now Heaton Road

Sandy Brow, site of a rally attended by Davidson at which Rev Harrison made a controversial speech. Between St Petersgate and Wellington Street in Stockport.

Windmill Rooms Community centre beside Parson Harrison's Sunday School.

Swallow Street. near Oxford St in London, mostly absorbed into the new Regent St in 1820

Tin Street fictional street in a district of old Portsea, where streets were named after metals.

Tupholme in Lincolnshire. A hamlet, dominated by arable farmland, 9m east of Horncastle, 22 miles east of Lincoln. District of East Lindsey.

Tupholme Hall Tudor mansion, rebuilt by the Vyner Family c1700. Home of their tenants / land-agents, the Thistlewoods after the Vyners moved to Gautby in 1756. Demolished c1980.

Union Street, north of Oxford St in London. Brunt's childhood home, it ran from Upper Newman St (Now Cleveland St) to Gt Titchfield St. Lost, area now part of Riding House St

Wandiwash Anglicised Vandivasi in Tamil Nadu, where a decisive battle in 1760 against the French cemented British supremacy in India. Brunt's grandfather was (fictionally) there

White Cross Gaol, White Cross St, Cripplegate, held Thistlewood's early close associate, Old Dr Watson. Built 1813 to ease overcrowding at Newgate. Demolished 1870

White Moss Field, Chadderton, 6 miles north of Manchester, a centre for cotton spinning. Once open wetland, White Moss is heavily industrialised and crossed by the M60 motorway

White Street, Moorfields in London ran parallel with Chiswell St (now c. Moorgate Station)

Windmill Street, Manchester. The Manchester Exhibition and Conference Centre is on the present Windmill Street. The site of a specific atrocity in 1819 is at its rear carpark.

Withy Grove, a continuation of Shude Hill in north central Manchester, it contained the spy, John Murray's gingerbread bakery.

TAVERNS, INNS and HOTELS

Unless specified otherwise, all premises were (and some still are) in London

Bag O'Nails was on Arabella Row / Kings Row in Pimlico (now Grosvenor Place /Buckingham Palace Road.) Used by Edwards. Demolished

Black Dog, Grays Inn Lane (now Grays Inn Road) used by Thistlewood and Edwards

Black Dog, St Clements Lane, used by Thistlewood and Edwards (at least by Ings)

Black Lion, Water Lane, off Fleet Street. Until August 1819, the principal meeting place of Thistlewood's Group. Water Lane with its arch, was replaced by Whitefriars Street

Boar's Head, 66, Fleet Street. Historic Irish tavern, stone-built in 1605, it survived the Great Fire of 1666. Refitted by Victorians and again in the 1960s. Now called The Tipperary

Brown's coffee house, Mitre Court, Fleet Street, used by Edwards

Bull Inn, Horncastle, popular tavern and ballroom, used by the Thistlewoods. Still exists

Bullocksmithy coaching inn, 15 miles south of Manchester, used by Henry Hunt and Richard Carlile, whose encounter there with Joseph Johnson is imagined in the novel. It was rebuilt but remains a popular public house on a corner of the A6 London to Manchester road

Cooper's, Bouverie St, off Fleet St in London. Family hotel connected to Back Lion Tavern. The Street exists, the hotel is lost.

Crown and Anchor (south side of Strand/ St Clements/ Arundel Street) Historic tavern, used by Thistlewood prior to the Smithfield meeting and by Davidson. Destroyed by fire, 1854.

Crown and Sceptre, Little Arthur Street, off Golden Lane, Cripplegate, Mrs G's regular. The area was partially developed by Victorians and bombed in WW2

Dolphin Ale House historic tavern between Spitalfields and Bethnal Green, used by Thistlewood, Edwards and Brunt. Lost to Victorian development and WW2 bombs

Grays Inn Lane, Now Grays Inn Road, ancient route between London and Hampstead

Horse and Groom, 42, John Street, near Cato Street, off Edgware Road. Gathering place for the conspirators before the operation. PC Smithers was carried to the first floor, where he died. John Street was later renamed Crawford Place and redeveloped by Victorians

Mitre, Mitre Court, Fleet Street. Tavern since at least 1610, it burnt down in 1829. Rebuilt nearby and renamed c1987 The Clachan and in 2005 Serjeants. Closed 2007

Old Bell (via Bride Lane, off Fleet Street) Still exists, with another entrance at 95 Fleet Street

Pontefract Castle, Wigmore Street. In use until 2015. Façade remains

The Ram Tavern 78, West Smithfield, used before and after the Smithfield Rally. Lost

Roundabout Tavern in Shadwell, used by Edwards, normally by coal heavers and marine community. Shadwell and the docks were largely destroyed in WW2, then redeveloped

Saracens Head, Snow Hill, Holborn - between Newgate and Smithfield) Celia Ings stayed here when Ings was held at Coldbath Fields. Demolished 1868, now Snow Hill Police station

Scotch Arms (New Round Court, western end of the Strand) used by Ings **F** and by Davidson and the New Shoemakers' Guild. Within a network of alleys, since demolished

Ship Tavern, Little Turnstile, by Lincolns Inn Fields, used by Tidd **F**. Still exists

Star Inn, Deansgate in Manchester, gathering place of the Magistrates before the rally. Lost

Talbot Inn, Lichfield used by Davidson. Named after a 16th Century family, the Georgian coaching inn on Beacon St, near the Cathedral, renamed The Angel Croft, is now residential

White Hart, Brooke's Market, Holborn. Lost

White Horse, Fetter Lane, coaching inn for Oxford and Portsmouth, used by Celia Ings in fiction and quite possibly fact. Demolished 1989

White Lion, Wych Street, off Drury Lane. Demolished by Victorians to make way for the loop road known as Aldwych, running from Covent Garden to The Royal Courts of Justice.

About the Author

The child of a police trainer and a comptometer operator in London, Judy Meewezen has created stories since before she could hold a pencil. She knew for certain that one day, she would write, when her teacher at primary school announced to the class that she ought to. As a student of German, Judy told stories in the children's home in southern Austria, where she worked during vacations. As a schools radio producer and broadcaster in the Solomon Islands, West Pacific, she adapted local stories as radio plays. After writing a thesis on the Austrian writer, Peter Handke, she worked part-time, teaching text analysis at Manchester University Drama Department and assisting in the literary department of The Royal Exchange

Theatre. There followed a twenty career in radio arts journalism and in television documentary and drama, mostly at the BBC, and which she eventually abandoned to write full time. Often hunched over a computer in libraries and other odd corners of the world, Judy also enjoys retreating to her home in a diverse district of north London, where her garden lives in hope.